BURN THE KINGDOM DOWN

PRAISE FOR AN AFFAIR OF POISONS

★ "This debut novelist manages to set the tone, introduce the characters, and kill the king of France all in the first chapter... [A] fast-paced and refreshing page-turner."
—*School Library Journal*, Starred Review

"*An Affair of Poisons* is beautifully written; like one of Mirabelle's potions, it's the perfect blend of history and dark fantasy, with a tasteful splash of blood, a simmering romance, and an ending that leaves you wanting more."
—Mary Taranta, author of *Shimmer and Burn*

"A rich immersion into a dangerous, alternative world of seventeenth century France... Thrilling, romantic, and addictive."
—Rosalyn Eves, author of the Blood Rose Rebellion trilogy

"An indulgent and exhilarating adventure, Thorley takes an extravagant historical setting and infuses it with a lusciously dark dose of magic and alchemy. *An Affair of Poisons* takes hold of the reader immediately and refuses to let go. The only cure is to finish it."
—Lyndsay Ely, author of *Gunslinger Girl*

"A stunning, immersive adventure, filled with magic, self-discovery, and sumptuous period detail. I fell in love with *An Affair of Poisons*!"

—Lee Kelly, author of *A Criminal Magic*

PRAISE FOR
NIGHT SPINNER

"[A] tightly wound, laser-focused epic…satisfies as a stand-alone and leaves fans of fantasy, mystery, and thrillers clamoring for more."

—*Kirkus Reviews*

"Enebish's prowess as an eagle trainer, however, is a high point, and readers will applaud her journey toward empowerment. The combination of tangible spirituality, battle magic, and steppe-inspired setting may appeal to readers who enjoyed [Emily A.] Duncan's *Wicked Saints*."

—*Bulletin Center for Children's Books*

"Thorley thoroughly utilizes descriptive language throughout the text, bolstering the imagery. Readers will enjoy this fast-paced adventure, enticed by all of the narrative's twists and turns… A thrilling retelling that will circulate well among fans of young adult fantasies."

—*School Library Journal*

BURN THE KINGDOM DOWN

ADDIE THORLEY

Copyright © 2026 by Addie Thorley
Cover and internal design © 2026 by Sourcebooks
Cover art © Jessica Cruickshank
Cover design by Erin Fitzsimmons/Sourcebooks
Chapter header images © Chorna Olena/Getty Images

Sourcebooks and the colophon are registered trademarks of Sourcebooks.

All rights reserved. No part of this book may be reproduced in any form or by any electronic or mechanical means, including information storage and retrieval systems—except in the case of brief quotations embodied in critical articles or reviews—without permission in writing from its publisher, Sourcebooks.

No part of this book may be used or reproduced in any manner for the purpose of training artificial intelligence technologies or systems.

The characters and events portrayed in this book are fictitious or are used fictitiously. Any similarity to real persons, living or dead, is purely coincidental and not intended by the author.

Published by Sourcebooks Fire, an imprint of Sourcebooks
1935 Brookdale RD, Naperville, IL 60563-2773
(630) 961-3900
sourcebooks.com

Cataloging-in-Publication Data is on file with the Library of Congress.

The authorized representative in the EEA is Dorling Kindersley
Verlag GmbH. Arnulfstr. 124, 80636 Munich, Germany

Manufactured in the UK by Clays and distributed by
Dorling Kindersley Limited, London
UID 001-358226-Apr/26
10 9 8 7 6 5 4 3 2 1

FOR AMARA, THE
FIERCE LITTLE SISTER
OF OUR FAMILY.

THE AX FORGETS, BUT
THE TREE REMEMBERS...

—AFRICAN PROVERB

PROLOGUE

M Y SISTER WORE CHAINS ON HER WEDDING DAY. They jangled from her wrists like bracelets and squeezed her neck like a collar. They cascaded from her waist in a waterfall of silver, cutting deep furrows into the earth—long straight planting rows that trailed her as she emerged from the hillock palace and paraded down High Street.

When Father saw her, his cheeks flamed red as a beet and he covered his eyes, afraid of what the Vanzadorians would think. What sort of bride *chooses* to wear chains instead of silk?

A stronger king would have been proud of Rowenna's defiance. A stronger *father* would have been charging into battle, refusing to let our enemies take her. But there Father stood, as useless as a rock, retreating into the blackness of his mind.

Beside him, Mother shook her head with disapproval, though I swore the tiniest of grins teased her lips.

On the opposite side of the road, the Vanzadorians stood in their too-straight lines and too-little clothing, whispering and pointing as if Rowenna's chains were more shocking and inappropriate than the bejeweled jackets that revealed their *bare* chests.

Ro didn't so much as blink at our parents or her future husband. She was playing to the throng of Tashiri planters crowding the streets behind us like an overgrown flower bed. Every man, woman, and child in our kingdom had come out to see her wed, and they roared their approval of her styling. She blew them kisses and waved in long arching strokes—clinging and clanking the chains to their full advantage.

Rowenna had always had a flair for the dramatic, but this was extravagant, even by her standards. Instead of wearing the traditional wedding wrap of Tashir—a gorgeous gown that Mother's seamstresses had spent months hand-beading with tiny purple bagrava buds—this gown was made entirely of chain mail. It poured down her arms in big, belled sleeves, then cut close to her figure like a bodice. And the skirt—*the skirt!*—must have weighed nine stone. Nearly as much as Rowenna herself. Yet, somehow, her steps were smooth, her face serene, as she rattled like a prison wagon toward her future husband.

The poor Vanzadorian prince couldn't keep the horror from spreading across his face like a blight.

I slapped a hand over my smile.

Where, in all the green hills of Tashir, had she found so many tiny rings of steel? It would have taken months to collect so many. *Years*. Our sentries wore wooden armor, not chain mail. And who had constructed the gown in secret?

Actually, I knew the answer to that.

Haddesh, the blacksmith's apprentice, had been in love with Rowenna for as long as I could remember. He would have gladly forged each ring himself, heedless of the burns and backbreaking work, if it helped Rowenna make this final statement as the crown princess of Tashir. So everyone would know this was no ordinary wedding—not even by royal standards, which often necessitate political unions—because there was no *unity* between Vanzador and Tashir. Rowenna was a captive bride, and she wanted her new "family," and our people, to always remember that.

Ro winked at me as she passed—her eyelids painted gold, her brown hair plaited with zinnias. "Do you think they're ready for me?" she whispered conspiratorially.

She wanted me to laugh and clap and play into her bravado. My reaction mattered, more than all the rest. But my smile withered like a weed-choked flower, and my hands instinctively shot out, grasping for the chain mail rings. Praying they were strong enough to hold her back.

Even if *she* was ready to go to Vanzador, *I* would never be ready to let her go. To be left here.

Alone.

"*Indira*," Father scolded.

I snatched my hands back and dropped my gaze to my boots, drowning in shame. I would be in Tashir, with our parents, surrounded by our people. *Rowenna* was the one being sacrificed to Vanzador. Yet I was the one sputtering, stumbling.

Falling apart.

"Chin up, little sister. Their cold, craggy mountains can't crush a girl made of steel." She chucked me under the chin and gestured proudly to her gown. Then she sauntered up to the altar.

But Rowenna was never a girl made of steel. Beneath that gleaming armor, she was as green as any sapling. A tiny bud, just beginning to reach toward the sky. Full of such potential, but still incredibly delicate—like everything that comes from the earth.

Like all of us from Tashir.

ONE

ONE YEAR LATER

'M IN THE ROYAL GARDEN, SWEATING LIKE A SALTED eggplant, when I hear the scream. A long jagged cry that rattles the cornstalks and shakes the heart-shaped leaves of the newly sprouted bagrava.

I immediately think of Rowenna.

Not because she'd scream like that—my sister would rather die than look so weak—but because it reminds me of the screams that filled my head the day she left.

They day the Vanzadorians *took* her.

The trowel I'm holding slides through my fingers... which is when I realize they're shaking.

"What was that?" Lewis sits back on his heels and squints across the rows of purple bagrava to the colorful patchwork of fields beyond.

There are squares of corn, beans, soy, and wheat as

far as the eye can see, but Lewis and I, like the two other master gardeners Earth Mother blessed with the ability to cultivate bagrava, are always here—meticulously tending our most precious crop. If we fail to harvest the fleshy purple fruit and return it to the earth to enrich the fallow soil, nothing else will grow. Our beautiful farmlands will once again become as desolate as the surrounding Tomb Flats and our people will starve.

No pressure.

"I'm sure it was nothing," I say, waving my trowel in the direction of the noise.

But Lewis continues biting his lip and peering into the distance. "That didn't sound like nothing, Indira. And who would be so careless this close to harvest?"

He has a point. Even Tashiri toddlers know how finicky the bagrava seedlings are. They must be constantly coaxed with Earth Mother's sacred incantations until the stalks are mature enough to form leaves. Then the fruit must be left to grow in relative silence until harvest. Any disturbance will cause it to wither to half its size—and half its strength.

"I'm sure it was just a baby or an animal," I say. "Have you considered all your worrying is just as loud?" I toss a clot of soil at Lewis's chest, but he doesn't even crack a smile.

"It sounded...*distressed*."

I give him a blistering look. The one Rowenna insists

is to blame for my lack of friends. But I don't have time for friends—other than her—and "the look" is good for productivity.

"I didn't spend the last two weeks slathered in turkey dung, singing until my voice ran out, for the fruit to wither now—over nothing," I scold. "This field needs to be sown with peas by the week's end, but that can't happen unless it's conditioned first—which means we need to do more harvesting and less blustering."

Lewis shakes his head and mutters, "I thought this crop of bagrava was headed to Vanzador?"

"Half of it is," I say bitterly. "Which is precisely why we don't have time to sit here and fret. Harvest is going to be tight."

"Harvest is always tight, thanks to those rock pushers," Lewis grumbles as he gets back to work.

I do the same, spreading my arms over the bagrava like a mother hen, enjoying the comforting rhythm of scraping trowels and our murmured incantations. The beat is so steady, the smell of freshly churned soil so soothing, I almost forget the scream. Almost convince myself we imagined it.

But then it comes again—more of a wail this time.

The hairs on my arms lift one by one. Lewis and I lock eyes, and this time, I don't bother trying to invent an excuse. The shrill, mournful voice is too drawn out to be a child. Too early in the evening to be the shrieking bats that wreak havoc on our mango trees. And too familiar to be anyone other than my mother—the unflinching queen of Tashir—screaming.

I shoot to my feet, heart pounding like a fist in my chest, trying to make sense of what I'm hearing.

What I *can't* be hearing.

Mother's like Ro. She isn't the sort to scream about a mouse in the pantry or an impudent servant. In fact, she alone remained calm when floods swept through the hillock palace the summer I turned seven. And during the blight-filled year I turned ten. Yet her earsplitting cry is unmistakable, carrying across the fields even louder than the noisy crows that always perch on the fence. Even they have fallen disconcertingly quiet, heads cocked toward the palace.

Go, my pounding heart urges. *Make sure everyone is safe*.

But an old, infected splinter of a thought keeps my boots rooted to the soil.

Would Mother come running if *I* were the one screaming? Would she even hear me? She and Father have hardly glanced in my direction since Rowenna left. Growing up, I always—*naïvely*—assumed they loved us equally. Isn't that what all parents say? *I could never choose between you!* But there's no denying the discontinued family dinners, the forgotten banquets and birthdays...

Stop this, Indira, Rowenna's voice snaps like a twig in

my ear, as clear as if she were standing beside me. *This is no time to get caught up in silly comparisons.*

It isn't the first time my sister has spoken to me. I've been hearing her for a year now. Since the day she left for Vanzador. It's the only way I've been able to cope with having half of my heart ripped out and dragged across the Tomb Flats.

Mother screams again, and now the Rowenna in my head is screaming to.

If you're so eager to be like me, move! *I would be home already.*

Swallowing the bitter lump clogging my throat, I take off running, careful not to trample the bagrava Lewis and I have nursed more lovingly than a newborn babe.

"Indira, wait!" he calls after me. "We're not finished! And it might not be safe. At least let me escort you!" He gives chase—as if he truly cares—but his big clumsy feet can't navigate the planting rows as quickly as mine. And everyone knows it's Rowenna he loves. He only glommed on to me after she left because I look like her—same curly brown hair and freckle-dusted cheeks. He's accidentally called me by her name more times than I can count. I'd have weeded him out ages ago if I didn't require a planting partner and if he wasn't the second-best master gardener in Tashir.

Lewis continues shouting, but I quicken my pace, my haversack thumping wildly against my back. It's probably hanging open and spilling seeds, since I didn't stop to buckle it. The thought of daisies pushing up through the carefully-manicured stone pathway and lemon balm sneaking into the lettuce beds would normally make me twitch. But another cry blasts across the fields, and I run faster. Trowels and spades swing wildly from my hip belt. The vials of plant food strapped across my chest rattle and clank.

In the surrounding bagrava fields, the two other master gardeners sit still as scarecrows, their eyes wide and their faces turned toward the green knoll of the hillock palace. Instead of murmuring to the bagrava, they speak to each other, uttering words we were never supposed to hear after Father signed the treaty with King Soren of Vanzador:

"Invasion. Marauders."

My eyes instinctively go to the jagged mountain range standing sentinel over our fields. Three years ago, King Soren used his power to erect the rocky barrier along the length of Tashir's border in exchange for monthly tributes of bagrava and my sister, when she came of age at eighteen. He promised it would seal the Marauders out, and so far, it has. The robbers haven't stepped foot in Tashir to loot our bagrava in so long, memories of the relentless raids of my childhood have finally begun to soften.

But one scream from Mother, and they rise again, like phantoms from the shadows. I can hear the Marauders' horrible whoops as they raze and pillage the fields, see their ferocious, giddy faces as they inhale the purple smoke and spiral into mad euphoria, feel Rowenna's clammy hand in mine as we huddle in the underground keep for hours, praying they don't take the entire crop.

Focus, Indira, Ro commands. *You can't help if you're unraveling.*

"Of course I'm unraveling!" I fire back, as if she's really here. Seeds and soil, I wish she were. I've never faced the Marauders without her.

We've upheld our end of the treaty. Tashir is safe, Rowenna maintains with steely resolve.

But what if this has nothing to do with the treaty? What if the Marauders found a way to circumvent the mountains?

I leap over a stone wall that separates the growing fields from the royal residences and scan the myriad of colorful doors and windows nestled into the hillside. Nothing seems out of place, but there also isn't a soul in sight. No trace of the servants and courtiers who are always streaming in and out like ants from a hill.

"Birdie!" I cry as I bang into the smokehouse. The sudden dark of under the hill washes over me, and my boots knock into the buckets of grease beside the ovens. "Birdie, what's happening?" I cry again. But our flour-cheeked cook isn't at the ovens or the stove, no matter that supper should be served in half an hour.

Panic sprouts anew in my belly and propels me into the pantry. Empty. Cold cellar. Also empty.

"Jareth! Despina!" I call for Father's valet, for Mother's attendant. But silence echoes back through the tunnel halls. There isn't even a guard making methodical rounds.

I duck down the nearest servants' tunnel and sprint toward the receiving courtyard, my breath ragged, my mind conjuring every worst-case scenario.

There's no need to panic, Rowenna insists. *The Marauders would start with the fields, not the palace. The bagrava is of greater value than anything in the kingdom. Don't let—*

"I'm not as brave as you!" I shout, feeling like a fool for ever thinking I could be.

"Mama?" I call as I burst into the dying scarlet light of the courtyard—still stabbingly bright compared to under the hill. My terrified voice echoes in the eerie quiet. Why is it so quiet? Hundreds of people are packed into the plaza— practically every courtier and servant from the palace— but none of them are speaking. Or even whispering.

I stumble over a stable boy and ram into a cluster of chambermaids, all with their hands to their mouths.

"What's wrong? What is it?" I ask, but they just stare at me with eyes as wet as river rock. The knot of terror in my stomach slides up into my throat. "Someone answer me!" I beg as I shove past the maids, searching for a familiar face.

At last, I catch sight of Birdie near the front and call her name, desperate for her hearty, comforting smile. But tears flood her cheeks as soon as our eyes meet. The courtiers in front of her sob into leaf-embroidered handkerchiefs. Beside them, Despina wails on Jareth's shoulder.

"Where's Father? What's happened to Mother? Is it the Marauders?" I babble to no one in particular.

Mother's scream rises again, as if in answer. The shrill ring of it echoes off the windows and porticos like the slash of a reaping scythe. I batter through another cluster of onlookers and at last they come into view—Father, standing as still as an ancient oak tree, and Mother, splayed across the cobbles near his feet. Her ornate silver gown is filthy and rumpled, and I'm so focused on finding a horrifying splash of red in the fabric, it takes me an entire minute to notice that she's draped over a box. A long wooden box, held shut with a padlock and chains.

Behind the box stands a line of black boots with spiked soles. The kind worn on slippery mountain slopes, not a garden bed. My gaze continues upward, taking in the fitted breeches, the vibrant jewel-toned jackets, and the smooth bare chests, before stopping finally at the stone-cut faces of the Vanzadorians. They truly look more granite than flesh, crowned with dark hair and cool indifference.

Most of the entourage has the decency to keep their eyes on the ground, but the two tallest men in the center boldly meet my stare: Rowenna's husband, Alaric Alaverdi, the crown prince of Vanzador. And his father, King Soren Alaverdi.

But where's my sister?

I spin around, searching the crowd again. "Where's Ro?" I demand. "What's going on?"

She sent no word of a visit. I've written her nearly every day, begging for this very thing. Even a short visit. *They can't hold you hostage on the mountain for the rest of your life*, I argued, to which she assured me they could.

But now they're here. Without her.

She'd never allow it.

Choking on unease, I dodge around Mother, and the corner of the box bashes my shins. But I don't feel pain. Only icy panic, seeping through my core. "Where is she?" I whisper.

No one answers. And the weight of every eye in the courtyard drills into me.

When a soft hand comes down on my shoulder, I shriek as I whirl around. Then I want to shriek again because my father has never looked more weathered and blighted—his skin gray, his eyes hollow.

After a long pause he quietly says, "There was an accident in Vanzador… Rowenna is gone."

The words chop my legs out from under me, and I fall, narrowly missing the box.

The *body*-sized box.

I glare at the rough-hewn wood, willing it to disappear. When it doesn't, I curl into myself, shaking and shivering. Feverishly wishing the Marauders were invading Tashir. Wishing the bagrava fields were burning. Even wishing it was Mother who lay dying, as I initially feared—as wicked as that sounds. But Mother continues wailing. And the Vanzadorians continue staring with thinly veiled contempt. And the long wooden box, with its thick padlock, looms larger than ever behind me.

I pray there's room inside for me as well.

Rowenna has finally returned from Vanzador—just as I wished.

Wearing very different sorts of chains.

TWO

I sit there, staring, as Father's terrible declaration pounds into my chest like a stake. The pain is so sharp and splintering, I can't breathe. Can't possibly survive this.

I grip my forehead and try to imagine a world without my sister, but it's impossible. Unfathomable. Memories pummel me like a midsummer downpour. Rowenna, crawling into my bed every time I had a nightmare and whispering stories that featured *me* as the fearless heroine; Rowenna, insisting I be included when Haddesh and the other boys played cabbage ball; Rowenna, splashing pomegranate wine down her finest breeches the first time my monthly courses came so no one would mock me.

Even though she was across the Tomb Flats in Vanzador, at least I knew she was out there, living and breathing, waking to the same golden sun and dreaming beneath the same blazing stars. I can't accept that we'll never share another joke, just by locking eyes. Or run barefoot through the dewy grass beneath a harvest moon.

I reach out and run a shaky finger along the box, refusing to believe Ro lies within. She's too vibrant and clever and *alive* to fit in such a sad, cramped space. And I would have known. I would have *felt* her passing. I would have charged across the Tomb Flats to stop it.

I push up to my elbows and look to Father. "Tell me you're lying," I beg. But he chokes back a sob and stares down at his feet. I drag myself closer to Mother, fisting her skirt. "Tell me it isn't true." But fresh tears spill down her cheeks, and she gently rests her head against the box.

Coffin, I correct myself. That crude pinewood abomination is Rowenna's final resting place. The Vanzadorians couldn't even be bothered to make her comfortable or show her proper respect.

King Soren and Prince Alaric regard us with cruel impatience, drumming their gloved fingers and shifting from foot to foot—as if they can't wait to leave. As if my sister's death, on *their* watch, is an irksome inconvenience.

Rowenna would be mortified. Not to mention furious.

Do something, Indira, she says.

Her voice in my head is as loud and commanding as ever, which shouldn't be possible if she's dead. And what does she expect me to do, other than lie here like a gutted pig and beg her to take me with her? I have no desire to spend another day on this earth without her, and I haven't a seeds-forsaken clue how to fix any of this.

We are shackled to the Vanzadorians. If King Soren stops feeding his magic into the ground, the mountain range protecting our border will crumble, leaving us exposed to the Marauders. Which means I can't be hurling accusations. We can't even demand answers or accountability. We just have to accept this blow like all the rest and swallow yet another bitter pill every time the price of Soren's protection grows steeper. And it's always getting steeper. First, he demanded twenty percent of our bagrava. Then thirty. Then my sister's freedom. Now her death.

It will never end.

The Vanzadorians have us trapped, like a rabbit in a snare, and the more I think about it, the more I feel like I'm wriggling and spinning. Waiting for a blade to plunge into my side. I almost wish they'd hurry up and put us out of our misery, but they just stand there, looking down with false pity.

The gawking servants and courtiers are hardly better, buzzing about like hungry flies, transfixed by our pain.

I want them all gone.

I have never been one to shout commands. I've never even raised my voice to the staff or publicly argued with our parents. Rowenna is the one who strode around the palace, going toe to toe with Father's ministers and navigating courtly politics. But I can't stand this torture for another second, so I force myself to my knees and take a deep breath.

"Leave us to grieve in peace," I cry, hating how my voice cracks and catches. It was supposed to roar and rumble—as loud as the storm raging in my heart—but no one even looks my way. They've all turned toward a different frantic shout, rising from the rear of the courtyard.

"Let me through! Where is she?" Haddesh's hysterical voice blasts above the commotion—the way mine should have—and he cuts through the crowd like the swords he's learning to forge.

He must have come directly straight from the blacksmith's shop the moment he heard the news, because he's still wearing his leather apron and streaks of soot darken his cheeks, making the whites of his eyes look even wider. Wilder. He clutches a poker in one hand, the tip still smoldering red, and after he takes in the scene—Mother and me on the ground beside the coffin, and Father bent over like a wilted flower—he levels the molten steel at King Soren and Prince Alaric.

"What did you do to Rowenna?" Haddesh roars.

Five Vanzadorian guards leap between him and King Soren, even though Soren is more than capable of defending himself. With a snap of his fingers, he could snatch the ground out from under Haddesh. Or carve a section of earth from the hillock palace and drop it on our heads.

Instead, Soren watches Haddesh from behind his guards, a smile in his eyes. "Who are you, boy? And what business do you have approaching me?"

"What business did you have taking Rowenna if you couldn't keep her safe?" Haddesh retorts, waving a muscled arm at the coffin. "How dare you bring her back like this?"

"How dare you address the king of an allied nation with such disrespect?" King Soren volleys back.

Father stumbles forward, grabs the younger, but much larger, boy by the elbow, and tugs him back. "Forgive Haddesh," Father says to Soren. "He means no disrespect. He's simply in shock. He and Rowenna were friends—"

"Why are *you* apologizing when *they* failed to keep Ro safe?" Haddesh wrenches free from Father's grip. "And we weren't just friends. I was in *love* with her." His voice breaks on the word *love*, and he looks defiantly at Soren. "I would have married her if you hadn't taken her captive."

Father darts a glance at Soren and laughs nervously. "The Vanzadorians didn't take anyone captive. Both nations agreed to the terms of the treaty. This was a tragic accident. If anything, Soren deserves our gratitude for returning Rowenna's body. They were under no obligation to do so."

Droplets of sweat fly from Haddesh's wet hair as he furiously shakes his head. "Do you hear yourself? The treaty mentioned nothing about Ro's body because her safety was guaranteed, so long as the bagrava shipments arrived on schedule. Which they have! We've done nothing wrong! *She* did nothing wrong. Act like a true king for once, and defend your own daughter!"

Father flinches, but Haddesh doesn't apologize, and none of the courtiers or ministers come to Father's defense. Mother and me included.

Father has always been soft-spoken and unassuming, humble and hardworking. His kind heart and gentle demeanor are the reason our people adore him, and up until he sent Rowenna to Vanzador, I prided myself on being more like him. We were the calm waters to Mother and Rowenna's raging fire. But now I see these attributes for the weaknesses they are. Father's blind trust and endless compassion are the reason the Marauders and Vanzadorians take advantage of Tashir. He's the reason Ro felt the need to push herself so hard, to learn everything about politics and ruling the kingdom, so she could better serve our people someday.

And now, she'll never get to.

Because Soren knew how formidable she was. He knew he would never be able to bully Ro into submission the way he has Father. That's why he took her captive—to ensure she'd never become queen of Tashir. And Father didn't even try to protect her.

He *still* isn't trying.

"Look at them!" Haddesh explodes, swinging his poker erratically. The nearest courtiers shriek and scatter, but his steely eyes remain focused on Soren and Alaric, who have been exchanging bemused glances. "They're clearly *enjoying* this. Rowenna's death was no accident. They murdered her in cold blood!"

"I would be *very* careful with your baseless accusations," Soren warns.

Alaric steps up beside his father. "We provided Rowenna with the finest care and hospitality—a wardrobe fit for a queen, the most delectable food and drink Vanzador has to offer, maids who tended to her every need, and guards appointed solely for her protection. There's nothing more we could have done."

He says all the right things in his honey-smooth voice and flashes a smoldering smile that undoubtedly bends most people to his will, but it doesn't fool Haddesh.

Or me.

Not anymore.

I'm ashamed to admit I once found the Vanzadorian prince attractive. Beyond horrified I let myself be taken in by his sharp cheekbones and even sharper wit when he visited Tashir with his father when we were young. Back then, I couldn't fathom how Rowenna could possibly prefer Haddesh, with his black fingernails and rough manners, to Alaric's glittering eyes and cut-marble chest. But Rowenna was always more perceptive than me. She saw through to the core of each boy—brave, passionate, and loyal Haddesh. Cruel, arrogant, and conniving Alaric.

"We often reminded Rowenna the mountains were treacherous for someone unused to the steep terrain," Alaric continues with a theatrically somber expression, "especially for someone so clumsy. But she refused to heed our warnings and tumbled over a cliff edge."

Mother gasps into the back of her hand, and Father's face drains of blood. The courtiers shake their heads and murmur things like "How horrible," and "Can you imagine?"

But I barely hear any of it over the high-pitched ringing in my ears. My pulse beats against my temples as my heart thrashes around my rib cage.

Alaric is lying.

I know it bone-deep—the way I know when a new shoot emerges from a bagrava seed, no matter that it happens a foot belowground.

No one who's met Rowenna would ever describe her as clumsy. She has always been as nimble as a barn cat, slipping out of our bedroom windows and navigating the mossy slope of the hillock palace with ease. Or running full tilt across the top of the narrow stone walls surrounding the bagrava beds. *I* was the one who ended up with bloody scrapes and unsightly bruises when I tried to follow her. The only way Ro would have *tumbled* over a cliff is if someone pushed her.

Haddesh's nostrils flare, and the terrifying glint in his eyes tells me he's arrived at the same conclusion. "I think *you* pushed her off that cliff," he says, taking a bold step closer to Alaric.

The Vanzadorian prince brings a dramatic hand to his chest. "Are you accusing me of murdering my own wife?"

"That's exactly what I'm saying."

There's a moment of stillness, like a storm holding its breath before lightning forks across the sky, and Rowenna's voice crackles through the charged silence.

Stop him, Indira!

But it's too late.

Haddesh lunges at Alaric, slashing his poker like a sword. "Murderer!"

The Vanzadorian guards dart forward again with their swords raised, but this time, King Soren steps past them and slashes his hand toward the ground. With a grinding *pop*, the blue-gray cobblestones scrape into motion, cresting into a wave that hurtles toward Haddesh. He grits his teeth and widens his stance, but even his broad stature can't contend with the power of the earth. The roiling ground tosses him the length of an entire planting row, as if his muscled body is as flimsy as the straw dolls Ro and I played with as children. It's only when he smashes against a marble column and a bone-chilling *crack* fills the courtyard that I remind myself straw could never sound so solid and wet.

All around me, servants and courtiers scream and scatter darting for the safety of the palace walls. But I can't move. Can't look away from the pool of blood spreading from the back of Haddesh's head. How can his neck be bent at such a grotesque angle? He must be in agony, yet he doesn't wail. I don't even see his chest rising and falling. Mine, on the other hand, heaves and sputters. I can't seem to catch my breath, no matter how quickly I inhale.

"Haddesh!" I finally croak out, but his dark eyes stare blankly at the sky above. His bulging arms lie limp and useless at his sides.

He's gone, just like that.

Just like Rowenna.

"At least they're together now, in the Great Fields Beyond," one of the remaining courtiers blubbers. But instead of comfort, this makes my shock and sadness boil over into outrage. Haddesh had so much heart, so much love and ferocity, and Soren wiped it out with a flick of his wrist. And the thought of Haddesh and my sister running hand in hand through endless fields of silver-dusted wheat makes me want to scream.

Why am I always the one left behind?

Because you did nothing, my guilty conscience murmurs. *You sat back and watched the Vanzadorians take her, and whimpered uselessly now, when they returned her lifeless body. At least Haddesh tried to defend her.*

We shouldn't have to defend ourselves against our

allies. How is Tashir ever supposed to prevail against power like Soren's? It's like asking a weed to go to battle against the ground itself.

As if reading my mind, Soren glowers down at Mother, Father, and me from beneath his caterpillar brows. Then his gaze sweeps across the remaining horrified onlookers. "Would anyone else care to lob groundless accusations?" After a moment of silence, Soren says with a vicious chuckle, "I didn't think so."

His arrogant laughter stirs something in the depths of my belly. Something slick, black, and baring its fangs. Part of me knows I should crush it with the heel of my boot. Nothing good can come from this hissing, thrashing rage. But another part of me likes the way it feels as it surges through my chest and pours down my arms. How it guides my hand to the trowel on my belt and curls my fingers around the handle like a dagger.

"Indira, stop!" Father says, gaping down at my makeshift weapon with horror. "Fighting helps nothing. *Clearly.*" He nods gravely at Haddesh's unseeing eyes and twisted mouth. "This isn't what your sister would want."

I want to tell him he's wrong. Rowenna was always the first to charge into battle and stand up to every injustice. I can't even begin to count all the times she stood up for *me*—helping me navigate courtly politics and barking at anyone who tried to take advantage of my ability to grow bagrava. But she never lobbed the first insult. Never threw the first punch. And that's what finally makes me drop my trowel with a sob. Rowenna didn't start fights; she finished them. She fought only to defend the people she loved, and I failed to return the favor. Lashing out now would only make things worse for my family.

And for Tashir.

I wilt back to the cobbles, feeling even smaller and emptier than before.

Father turns to Soren. "We won't burden you with our grief any longer. The journey is long. I'm sure you want to be on your way." He even musters a friendly smile, as if this man didn't kill his eldest daughter. As if we're somehow the trespassers on our own land.

"Actually, we won't be returning to Vanzador until *after* the burial," King Soren announces. "We traveled all this way... We'd like to see the task properly finished. *And* enjoy the bounty of Tashir, of course." He adjusts his belt over the swell of his hairy stomach and flashes a self-satisfied smile.

Of course.

The Vanzadorians return my sister's body in a box, kill anyone who questions them, and still expect us to lay a banquet for them.

THREE

THE ROYAL GUARDS USHER THE LAST OF THE GAWK-ing onlookers into the palace while Jareth and Despina somberly escort the Vanzadorians to the guest suites. Leaving Mother, Father, and me in the empty, echoing courtyard. Staring at Haddesh's body and Rowenna's coffin.

Without all the cries and commotion, I realize Mother's doing more than just sobbing. She's whispering a stream of feverish words. I only catch bits and pieces, but it's more than enough to parse out the theme.

Stronger. Promised. Failed.

It's painful enough that Rowenna is gone, but if I'm forced to watch our formidable mother crumble to pieces and blame herself, I don't know how I'll recover. And worse, I don't know how *Tashir* will recover.

Mother has always been the steely spine of our kingdom.

The justice to Father's mercy. It's why my grandparents selected her—a gritty field-worker—to be his bride. They knew Father needed an assertive, carnivorous cobra lily to grow beside him. Someone shrewd and aggressive enough to devour any threat, because their son was no better than a tulip—all pretty petals with a merry bobbing head. But instead of snapping to action like Mother always has in the past, she remains draped over the coffin like a funeral spray.

Eventually, Father clears his throat and smooths his tunic with trembling hands. "I-I suppose we should call the guards and have them move the bodies to the chapel, so Father Alonzo can prepare them for burial."

The bodies.

He can't even say Rowenna's name. He plans to lump her in with Haddesh and leave her burial preparations to a virtual stranger, rather than pull on gloves and wade into the mire himself.

Ro deserves so much better. She's suffered so much indignation already. Her final moments should be spent with someone who knew her. Someone who loved her.

"No!" I blurt with surprising ferocity.

Father gapes at me as if leaves are growing out of my head, and I automatically lower my voice.

"I would like to prepare Rowenna for burial myself. Please," I add.

"You couldn't possibly," Father sputters. "You don't know the first thing about preparing a body."

"I'll learn," I insist, wedging my fingers beneath the coffin. "Let me do this. *Help* me do this. It's what Ro would want."

Father chews his lower lip before shaking his head. "It wouldn't be proper. According to tradition—"

"What about any of this is proper or traditional?" I demand, feeling it again—the twist of vicious claws and teeth, stirring deep inside me. "*You* sent Ro to live with those cold, heartless stone people, so it's only fair *you* should deal with the consequences."

Father blinks at me for an entire minute, as if realizing, for the first time, that I might have thorns too. That his quiet, dutiful daughter who happily tends the bagrava might be capable of drawing blood, just like Rowenna— our kingdom's prized rose.

With a slow nod, he takes up the other end of the coffin, and we lug Rowenna's body across the courtyard. When we reach the latticework door of the chapel, I shoulder through without hesitation, but Father stops at the threshold and sets down his end of the coffin. He peers warily into the dank, shadowed space, down the mossy aisle, past the cobwebbed benches, to the hewn-stump altar. "I-I'm sorry, Indira. I can't. It's too much," he says without meeting my eyes. Then he retreats back across the courtyard to Mother's side, where he can wallow in misery and pretend this isn't all his fault.

I grit my teeth and drag Rowenna's coffin through the

loamy soil myself, step by excruciating step. When I reach the altar, Tashir's lone hedge-priest, Father Alonzo, shuffles out from the shadows.

"Have you come to pray, my child?" he starts, but his milky eyes pop wide as he takes in the scene. "What's all this?"

"Go and collect the other body from the courtyard," I order without glancing up.

"There's *another* body? Whose? What happened?" His wrinkled hands flutter to his chest in the sign of the sacred harvest.

"It's too late to ward off evil, Father. The Vanzadorians murdered Rowenna and brought her back in this box. And they just killed Haddesh, the blacksmith's apprentice."

The old man clutches his bagrava seed rosary and reverently murmurs, "May Earth Mother accept their souls." Then he totters out into the courtyard, leaving my sister and me alone in the sage-scented candlelight.

I kneel beside the coffin and watch the light from the swinging braziers dart across the wood, licking the silver chains with fire. An old key dangles on a ring beside a heavy padlock, and my breath quickens as I take the key in my hand and fit it into the keyhole.

I have never seen a dead body—not before it's been prepared for burial. When Chancellor Orrin died three years ago, his casket was laid open in the center of High Street, and all of Tashir came to place a shiny apple in his coffin and a fresh-cut flower on the surrounding banquet tables. He looked precisely as he had in life—heavy-browed and jowl-cheeked, despite being cut down by sickness, and dressed in an impeccable wrap embroidered with daisies, the heritage flower of his family.

Before Orrin's death, during the dark days of the relentless Marauder raids, the dead had been too numerous to hold individual burials. Their bodies were lowered into a pit in the fallow fields beyond the cabbage beds, and Mother forbade us from visiting.

A warning I heeded.

Rowenna did not.

Now part of me wishes I'd been brave enough to follow her and Haddesh the night they snuck out to see the pits. At least then I'd know what to expect. Though I doubt those bodies held any similarities to hers.

How does it look when someone "falls" off a cliff? When bone and muscle and sinew meet unyielding stone?

I shiver and nearly drop the key.

I don't want to look.

I have to look.

As much as I'd like to only remember Ro's fierce smile and laughing eyes, I need to bear witness to her suffering. I need to be the one to care for her. She'd have done the same for me. She'd have already opened the casket by now.

I wouldn't have allowed you to go to Vanzador at all,

Rowenna whispers. Not in an accusatory way. Just a matter of fact.

A sob breaks loose in my chest, and with a breath that feels both too shallow and too deep, I turn my wrist until I hear a click.

The chains slide to the floor with a jarring *clank*, and I throw back the lid before I lose my nerve.

Then I scream.

And scream.

And scream.

I thought I was prepared to see my sister's lifeless face, but maybe that's the problem...

Rowenna has no face.

She's almost unrecognizable, with black bruises mottling her cheeks, one of which has collapsed entirely. And the skin from her slender neck all the way down her shoulders looks nauseatingly similar to the ground beef Birdie puts in her pies.

My stomach expels every bite of food I've eaten today. I doubt I'll ever be able to eat again. But I force my gaze to continue downward, taking in Ro's long brown curls, dark with blood and matted to her back. Her collarbone is broken, as are both her legs. The bones stab angrily through her skin and the torn remnants of her gown—if you can even call it that.

She's dressed in the sheer Vanzadorian fashion: black-mesh sleeves, a neckline that plunges clear to her navel, and an equally revealing skirt that cuts away to expose the legs. It's garish, impractical, and *wrong*. So wrong that she was wearing this when she died.

Before I realize what I'm doing, my fingers sink into the hideous fabric—like they did a year ago, when I grabbed for her chain mail rings—except now I close my fist. With a howl of fury, I tear, wrench, and rip with wild desperation. Convinced that if I remove all evidence of Vanzador, it will somehow bring Rowenna back. But even once the gauze and glitter are stripped away, she lies there, shattered and bloodied, her freckles painting a dark constellation across her too-pale torso.

I trail a finger over her freezing skin, remembering how she'd steal Father's expensive ink pens when we were little, and we'd take turns drawing pictures of blooming flowers and crawling ivy by connecting the freckles on each other's arms. Then, when she was eighteen and I was sixteen, right before she left for Vanzador, we had identical clovers inked onto the underside of our wrists. Permanently connecting our souls by connecting our freckles. Three leaves, not four.

We don't need the universe's luck—we'll make our own, she said.

And Ro *was* lucky. Cunning and nimble and observant too.

Which is how I know she didn't *fall* to her death.

I reach for her arm and gently turn her wrist, practically

sobbing with relief when the clover shines up at me, untouched by scrapes and scratches. It looks so crisp and green, so inexplicably *alive*, compared to the cold, gray skin surrounding it.

Tears blur my vision as I press my clover against Rowenna's, and I find myself murmuring the incantations I sing to the bagrava. Wishing it could imbue her with life. Wishing I could do something—*anything*—to bring her back.

I don't know how long I sit there. Time serves little purpose other than to mock me—reminding me, with every excruciating tick, of the endless hours and days and years I must live without her.

When I finally run out of strength and tears, I lay my head on the edge of the coffin and try to recall everything about my sister, desperate to preserve all the tiny details time will attempt to steal from me. Like the feel of her hands braiding my hair. Or how her laughter whistled through her nose when she thought something was truly funny. And the look in her eyes when she watched me tend the bagrava—as if I were the most extraordinary person she'd ever met. Even though we both knew I'd never be half as accomplished as she was.

I don't have a single memory without her. Ro was my constant from the very beginning—standing on tiptoe and leaning over Mother's bed to watch me draw my first breath. And I fully intended to be hunched old crones together, holding hands as we wheezed our last. Maybe that's why my lungs feel so unbearably tight.

I don't know how to breathe without her; don't know how to do any of this without her.

You shouldn't have to, she murmurs, and despite the chill of Rowenna's skin, a spark of heat flares where our wrists meet. A flicker of fury and resolve that rushes through my body, feeding the newfound darkness in my stomach. It feels dangerous to give it any ground, but it's the only thing strong enough to rival the pain. The only thing keeping me moving. So I let it surge and simmer as I roll up my sleeves and get to work.

With careful hands, I remove the last of Ro's dress and pull off her shoes—the same muddy gardening boots she wore the day she left for Vanzador, I note with a sad smile. Then I rummage through the annex for Father Alonzo's oils and scrolls, and whisper a final vow to my sister as I knead the myrrh and cassia into her hardening skin.

I will live for us both. I will honor Rowenna the only way I know how—the only way she would want.

By making the Vanzadorians pay.

FOUR

All of Tashir gathers for Rowenna's burial two days later. Instead of fruit stands and vegetable carts, High Street teems with white-clad mourners from the farthest planting fields all the way to the courtyard of the hillock palace. The grieving faces of our people are painted a myriad of colors—beet red, saffron yellow, and deepest blackberry—as is customary when there's a death in the royal family. Each gardener makes a pulp of their finest produce and streaks their face with color, which runs off their chin and drips onto their spotless garments throughout the funeral. Tears made of the earth, returning to the earth.

Most faces are painted orange with barberry, because it is widely known as Ro's favorite color. Lewis even had the nerve to show up outside my bedroom window this morning clutching a bowl of thick orange paste.

"I-I think Rowenna would want us to paint each other," he said through sniffles. As if he'd meant anything to her. "Rowenna always looked so lovely in orange..." he continued, gazing into the bowl as if he could see her reflection in the dye.

Without a word, I rotated the circular window and slammed it shut. Then I crossed my chamber to the vanity and dipped my fingers into the mortar bowl of crushed bagrava I'd illegally harvested before sunrise. The juice is a deep purple-red, like blood. *Actual* blood, not the garish red of beetroot like the stories would have you believe. The bagrava pulp was even warm like blood as I painted thin vertical stripes down my face.

Everyone would be wearing orange in Ro's honor, which is why it would mean nothing. No one else would be bold enough, or reckless enough, to wear bagrava purple. Every tiny seed, and even the rind of the fruit, was allocated either for the Vanzadorians' tribute or our fields, and still there was never close to enough—let alone extra to use as face paint.

Which was precisely why I chose it.

Bagrava may have been the most precious commodity to the rest of them, but Rowenna would always be the most precious to me. That's why I let the lifeblood of Soren's power drip down my face—to show him how little I respected them, how easily I saw through their lies. And to show Rowenna I was good on my word. I would do everything in my power to ruin them and avenge her.

"I-Indira! Is th-that—" Father stammers when I join him and Mother in the courtyard for the funeral procession.

"Don't ask questions you don't wish to know the answer to," I breezily reply, which sends him into an even louder fit of dithering.

"What's come over you? You've always been..."

Passive. Biddable. Weak.

No more.

Not now that I'm living for Rowenna too.

I channel her brash confidence as we march down High Street, holding my chin high and waving my bagrava-stained hands. During Father Alonzo's bland graveside liturgy, I shake my head so the dark juice flies from my cheeks and speckles the ground around King Soren and his son. They haven't taken their beady eyes off of me since I joined the procession. My painted face is a relatively small defiance. But there's no denying it's that: defiance. A needling reminder they're not fully in control, because they don't have a clue what I might do next.

Obviously, I know better than to attack them outright like Haddesh, but there are other ways to unsettle and agitate them. Slow, calculated ways to poke them and retreat.

Prince Alaric stands opposite the grave from me, wearing the flashiest jacket I've seen yet—red velvet held together with pewter chains that crisscross his bare chest. It would be inappropriate for any occasion, let alone his wife's funeral. As Father Alonzo speaks, Alaric jabs his knuckles into his eyes to produce the appearance of tears, but they refuse to come because he isn't sorry my sister is dead. I'd wager our entire crop of bagrava he pushed Ro off that cliff.

It's always the husband.

Alaric glances up, as if he can feel my gaze drilling into his skull. His eyes are stone gray, and his dark hair hangs in loose waves across his forehead, reminding me of the twisted innards of the voles that nibble on our crops. The ones that meet their end on the sharp edge of my shovel.

I narrow my eyes at him. *I know what you did.*

He stares back, not with defensiveness or outrage, but boredom. He's so assured in his superiority—in *Vanzador's* superiority—he doesn't fear retaliation. He knows there's nothing we can do.

I have the sudden urge to throw myself across the open grave and claw the demeaning expression off his face, but Mother grabs my wrist, sinking her fingernails into my skin. Proof she's still in there somewhere, fighting the crushing winds of grief.

Father looks immediately to King Soren, more worried about egos and appearances than his own family's pain.

Soren, for his part, notices none of it. He drums his fingers against his crossed arms and glares at the sun, as if willing it to hurry its arc across the sky.

Father Alonzo closes the services and invites us all to return to the hillock palace for the mourning feast. For the first time all day, Soren looks attentive. He even licks his lips.

"I hope he chokes on the honey-roasted squash," I grumble as we trudge back to the palace behind the Vanzadorians, who are practically sprinting to reach the banquet.

Father holds out a stiff arm and stops me. "You cannot say such things. I know you're grieving, but—"

"Didn't you teach me to always tell the truth?" I fire back.

"I also taught you to use your head. Just cooperate and get through today."

"Then what?" I snap. "We continue being the Vanzadorians' slaves and pretend they didn't murder Rowenna?"

"What other choice do we have? You know my hands are tied."

Father looks to Mother for support, but she's floated away again, back into her cocoon of grief. She stares blankly as we shuffle into the atrium under the hill, oblivious to the breathtaking decorations the servants arranged while we were at the burial.

Fairy lights weave through the flowering shrubberies, and vibrant blue wisteria dangles overhead like a canopy, filling the air with its heady perfume. The irrigation troughs have even been rerouted from the fields to create tinkling waterfalls and still reflecting pools.

It's all so right...and so horrifically wrong. Rowenna deserves a celebration like this, but it should have been for her coronation. Or her wedding—to anyone other than Alaric Alaverdi. Not her funeral.

There's also the glaring fact that we can't afford any of this. The panels of chiffon draped between each pillar were supposed to be saved for *my* wedding wrap someday. And our people have only been permitted to bathe once a week for the better part of this year—the crops must always come first. But now a month's worth of wash water is dribbling into a puddle for nothing but the Vanzadorians' enjoyment.

Luxury is what Soren expects, so that's what Father gives him. No matter the cost to the rest of us.

I snatch the nearest panel of chiffon and tear it down. "I don't think your hands are truly tied, Father. I think they're just trembling too hard to do anything useful."

Father gapes at me and then the shred of fabric. "Stop this, Indira! I do not appreciate this...this...*side of you*."

"Unfortunately, it's all that's left. The best parts of me are in the ground—with Rowenna."

I toss the fabric in his face, turn on my heel, and march to the nearest banquet table. It's heaped high with fried squash blossoms, fresh pomegranate wine, and basil-encrusted cheese, all of it artfully arranged with flowers, herbs, and berries, creating a feast for the eyes that rivals the feast for the belly. I scowl at it all, even as my mouth waters, because, once again, these are luxuries we can't afford

The line of Tashiri mourners knows this, and they respectfully fill their plates, admiring the exquisiteness of the meal and remarking on the freshness of the beans and the sweetness of the tomatoes. The Vanzadorians, on the other hand, dig into the spread like the wild boars that tromp through the woods and flatten our mushrooms. They take one bite of the sweet, speckled corn before tossing it to the ground and pour mead down their chins instead of into their mouths. They chomp, slurp, and toast amongst themselves, as if this isn't a somber occasion. As if the rest of us aren't present and deserve no acknowledgment for the feast.

Fury wavers at the edges of my vision like heat rising from a pot.

Rowenna told me all about the Vanzadorians' disgusting food, and even more disgusting manners, in her letters. She said their water tastes foul due to minerals and sediment, and they gnaw on massive slabs of overcooked, unseasoned meat that's as bland and gray as their mountains. But they clearly aren't struggling to enjoy themselves now. One of the prince's attendants lets out a juicy belch, garnering raucous cheers from his comrades.

"Couldn't you have poisoned their dishes?" I mutter as Birdie bustles by with a tray of cheese-stuffed dates.

She snorts indignantly. "And lose my reputation as the finest cook in Tashir, not to mention my head?"

"You could have done it discreetly."

"And then what? Watch the mountains crumble?" Birdie blows a lock of hair out of her sweaty face. "Be patient, love. The rockheads'll be gone soon enough. I *did* cut the cantaloupe slightly larger than usual—due to running out of time—but if we have any manner of luck, one of them will choke."

She bustles away with a dark chuckle, and I move among the tables, filling my plate with all of Ro's favorites. Then I look for a place to sit.

But Rowenna isn't here. Neither is Haddesh. And sitting with my parents is out of the question. There are at least a dozen of Father's advisors and their families in attendance, but none have bothered to save a space for me, and I can't blame them. I never bothered making friends with anyone other than my sister. It wasn't intentional; there's nothing wrong with any of the courtiers. Rowenna and I just preferred when it was the two of us. And after she was gone, it was too awkward to try and fit in. You can't ignore people for sixteen years, then expect to be welcomed into their circle, even if you're royalty.

Which leaves only Lewis.

He waves a forkful of mashed potatoes a little too eagerly from the corner, but I pretend not to see him and plunk down at the children's table, next to ribbon-haired girls and bespectacled boys, all from Tashir's highest-ranking families. I should probably know their names and what their parents grow. Rowenna would. She would have regaled them with tales of her adventures, loving how they hung on her every word and stared at her with enormous button-mushroom eyes. But I don't have a clue where to start, and I don't have the will to try, so I tuck into my food and pretend not to notice their raised brows and lolling mouths.

I eat until I'm stuffed to bursting, mostly to avoid conversation, but also because Birdie has truly outdone herself. By the time Father stands to close the banquet, I'm slumped over in my chair like a frothing slug, dreaming of my bed and the sweet escape of sleep. Hoping against hope I'll wake up and this will all have been a bad dream.

"In honor of my daughter, Rowenna Ilissium Harrak, I wish health to your bodies and bounty to your fields!" Father says. His voice is so weak and wispy, there's no way it carries to the farthest tables. He can't even manage to lead a toast, yet somehow he's supposed to lead this country. But everyone raises a glass and echoes the appropriate refrain anyway—probably because they feel sorry for him.

"Bounty to our fields!"

The room breaks into applause, but before anyone can drink, King Soren clears his throat and rises from his seat at the Vanzadorians' table.

Father fumbles his wine glass, spilling a bit down his robe. "I didn't realize you wished to speak. My deepest apologies, Soren. I should have offered—"

Soren silences Father with a flip of his hand. As if Father's a dithering valet, not an allied king. "I have nothing to say of dear Rowenna that these services haven't already said far better and more eloquently."

The five glasses of pomegranate wine I downed in quick succession churn in my stomach, and hateful words bubble up my throat. "You have nothing to say about *'Dear Rowenna'* because you didn't actually know her. Or care about her. Take your false pity back to your loathsome mountains."

The children surrounding me giggle, their noble parents frown and murmur, and Father looks like he swallowed a watermelon whole, but King Soren smiles even wider.

"I will happily return home just as soon as we discuss how this tragedy affects the treaty between our nations..."

A hush descends on the hall like late spring frost. Somewhere down the banquet table, a spoon clatters into an empty bowl. Several ladies gasp.

This isn't the first time Soren has wanted to *discuss* our treaty, and every time the terms get worse for Tashir.

I clench my fists, trying to uproot the panic twining through my chest. He's toying with us, trying to intimidate Father. Soren would never rescind his protection. Not when he and Alaric need the bagrava just as desperately as we do. They don't use our precious plant to improve farming conditions in Vanzador or to induce euphoria like the

Marauders, but to amplify their ability to move the earth—which might be even more unforgivable. Somehow, they've found a way to twist Earth Mother's gift, taking the miracle that saved our ancestors from starving to death on the Tomb Flats, and using it to crumble and carve out the land rather than fortifying it. And the worst part is, we don't have a clue how they do it.

Over the years, Father has arrested scores of heretics who were caught experimenting with bagrava, trying to imbue themselves with power like Soren's, but none have ever come close to replicating his abilities. All we know is Soren and his son continue to grow stronger, while we're forced to watch our planting fields go fallow due to insufficient bagrava to condition the soil. Just this fall, three more fields were reclaimed by the Tomb Flats. Even if we have a hearty yield this harvest, there's a good chance we'll run out of grain before the winter's through.

Father forces a cough—his best attempt at sternness. "Let's retire to my office, Soren. This isn't the place to discuss such matters—"

"The treaty states that Tashir will send a monthly shipment of bagrava along with a princess for my son to wed in exchange for our protection," Soren forges on.

"Which we did." Father gestures wildly in the direction of High Street—to the burial grounds at the road's end, where Rowenna lies.

"Unfortunately, Rowenna is no longer with us." Soren

holds out his hands, as if he's blameless in all of this. "And without proper motivation, I'm concerned you'll no longer feel obligated to send the quantities of bagrava we require."

"This is absurd!" Father shoots to his feet. "Unconscionable!"

Mother clutches Father's robe and rises too, her eyes clearer than I've seen in days. "What exactly are you saying, Soren?"

"I'm saying," Soren speaks slowly, taunting us with each measured syllable, "our treaty once again demands fulfillment. If you wish to continue receiving our protection, you must pay the negotiated price." He turns to me, not even trying to suppress his smirk. "Which means Miss Indira will be returning with us to Vanzador."

FIVE

Soren's words tumble through my head like pebbles in a raging river, refusing to make sense.

They're taking *me* to Vanzador?

The notion is so ridiculous, I let out a shrill laugh. The Vanzadorian king has never glanced in my direction before today. Rowenna was the oldest, the heir, the obvious choice. I'm a terrible replacement. I pose no political threat. I will never be half the queen she would have been.

"We'd have chosen Indira from the outset, had we been privy to her *gift*," Soren continues, plunging me back beneath the surface before I've had a chance to catch my breath. "It's quite disappointing you didn't tell us sooner…" He tuts at Father, then appraises me again from the top of my head to the tips of my toes.

The hunger in his eyes makes me shudder, but it's that word—*gift*—that bites into me with the force of an ax. We have never, *never* revealed who among us are master gardeners. The Vanzadorians must protect us all in exchange for their shipments of bagrava.

But Soren knows.

I stumble backward, gaping at my parents. They're the only ones in Tashir who correspond with the Vanzadorian king, and they've been so consumed with the absence of their beloved oldest daughter, they must have slipped and said something.

Or maybe it wasn't an accident at all.

Mother blinks at me with wide, guilty eyes, and Father can't meet my gaze at all. I suppose their shock might be genuine, but I'm willing to bet all the grain in the storehouse their distress stems from being caught.

You know that isn't true, Rowenna is quick to counter. But the only thing I *know* is I'm not fierce, bold, and brave like Ro. I'm not strong enough to be the queen Tashir needs. My parents may not have consciously come to this conclusion, but their actions reveal their true feelings.

I am expendable.

"How could you?" I shout at them.

To my surprise, Father is already yelling, even louder—twice as loud as I thought possible. "Get out!" He points a trembling finger at King Soren and his entourage. "Out of my palace! Out of my country!"

When no one moves, Father roars like a landslide and overturns his banquet table.

Screams fill the atrium as the heavy table slams onto the ground. Jam spatters the columns like blood. Peach scones fly like severed body parts, and under any other circumstance, I would have burst into applause. For once, Father isn't dithering, bumbling, or apologizing. He's shouting and overturning tables.

For you, Rowenna whispers.

But it's too little too late.

King Soren kicks his spiked boots up on his table and looks from me to my parents, smiling as if he hasn't had this much fun in ages. "You can't dismiss us yet, Bastian. We haven't even had dessert."

Mother's entire frame trembles as she elbows past Father and slams her palms on the table in front of Soren. "You've had more than enough!"

Despite how livid I am with them both, I immediately feel calmer. Safer. My odds of remaining in Tashir are much higher if Mother has awoken from her grief-stricken stupor.

Something in her eyes must frighten Soren, at least a little, because the Vanzadorian king takes his feet down and perches on the edge of his seat. "We'll leave, if that's truly your wish, Ianthe. I'm just surprised you've already forgotten the dark days of the Marauders' raids. Memories of you on your knees, begging for my protection, remain crystal clear."

Mother's laughter could freeze every plant in the greenhouse. "You 'protect' us as a cat protects a mouse—only to toy with us and devour us."

Instead of responding, Soren defers to Alaric, who's been waiting at the ready, practically stamping his foot like a restless horse. "We wouldn't need to *toy* with you, as you put it, if you simply honored our requests."

"Your requests keep going up!" Mother snaps back. "We can't survive on only sixty percent of our yield."

"You could if you worked harder," Soren says as if he knows anything about farming. Rowenna's letters detailed how useless and slothful he is, always sitting on his granite throne, drinking mead like a slimy toad.

"Our people are working themselves to death." Father pants and pulls at his hair. Even Mother is unraveling like the frayed hem of her finest gown.

Have we always looked this shabby and weak? Or is it just especially glaring beside the Vanzadorians' gleaming attire and ruthless ambition?

"There are only so many hours of sunlight in the day," Father continues, "and we have only a few master gardeners to prepare the fields, which is why you can't take Indira. It would drastically decrease the size of your tribute."

Technically, Father's defending me, but I stare down at the spilled wine trickling through the cobblestones, so no one can see the tears brimming along my lashes. It's just as I suspected. His outburst had nothing to do with loving or protecting me and everything to do with the harvest. It always comes back to the bloody harvest.

Even to my own parents, I'm a master gardener first and a daughter second.

"A captive bride is unnecessary," Father continues, imploring. "We both need Indira here, cultivating the bagrava. We're clearly in no position to rebel…"

"You're in no position to *negotiate*." King Soren brushes past Father and approaches me, taking my chin in his hands. His soft leather gloves are jarring compared to the tightness of his grip, and I shiver as he appraises me with vulture eyes. "I suspect we won't need Tashir at all once I'm able to cultivate bagrava on the mountain…"

I lurch back, shaking my head. "I won't—" *go with you. Help you grow bagrava.*

But Soren snaps his fingers in front of my nose before I can finish. "Gather your things, Indira. We leave at once— with a full load of bagrava." He gives this last instruction to no one in particular. As if all Tashiri are capable of harvesting and preparing the tribute. As if we all live just to serve him.

"But another shipment isn't due for half a moon cycle," Domynic, Father's foremost advisor, cries.

"Consider it a bereavement gift for my son. Or recompense for withholding essential information about Indira and sending us the lesser princess."

Hysterical laughter punches from my lungs. Only a fool would deem *Rowenna* the lesser princess.

"The tribute takes days to prepare," another advisor cries. "It isn't possible."

Soren waves a dismissive hand. "I'm certain you'll find a way. If you don't, we'll take every last bundle of bagrava and level the mountains as we go."

The crowd of mourners watch in stunned silence as he strides out of the atrium, followed by Alaric and their entourage. No one moves because there's nothing to do. No way to stop this. Supposedly, we're allies with Vanzador, which means we should be equals. But Tashir never seems to have the upper hand. Or even a comparable hand.

Without warning, Father takes up a chair and smashes it against the ground, after which he crumples into the splinters and weeps into his hands. The guests whisper and dart nervous glances at each other, growing more and more unnerved the longer the moment stretches and the louder Father wails. We need a confident, commanding ruler now more than ever, so, naturally, he has melted into a puddle.

One of the noble children at my table dashes to her parents and tearfully cries, "We're all going to die, aren't we?"

That's all it takes.

Shouts and sobs fill the atrium as the mourners rush to flee, trampling the decorations and wasted food. The only benefit of the stampede is it forces Mother to spring back into motion. With a look of grim resolve, she wrenches Father up by his livery collar, sinks her ice-cold fingers into my wrist, and drags us back inside the palace.

I assume she'll take us to the keep, where we've always taken shelter during storms or invasions, but instead of following the spiral staircase downward, Mother charges through the tunnels toward the royal residences.

"Where are we going?" I ask as bile licks the back of my throat. The keep is the safest place in the hillock palace. The only place the Vanzadorians won't be able to reach us.

Instead of answering, Mother rounds another corner and herds us into *my* chambers. She deposits Father, who's still hysterical, onto the armchair where I study and shoos me toward the wardrobe with her hands. "Don't just stand there like a scarecrow, Indira. Change into traveling clothes and gather your things."

A warbling cry escapes my lips as the true direness of my situation dawns.

Father only wishes to keep me here because of my gardening abilities, and Mother doesn't plan to keep me here at all. She's going to hand me over to my sister's murderers without a semblance of a fight.

"Don't pack anything, Indira!" Father suddenly catapults out of the armchair and strides toward us, shrinking only slightly beneath Mother's withering scowl. "We cannot let them take her, Ianthe! We can't give in to these outrageous demands. You're the one who's always telling me I must be stronger and bolder and make a stand for Tashir. Well, now I've done it, and you're not going to stand with me?"

"It's too late." She brushes him aside and flaps her hands at me. "Pack, Indira! They'll be here any second."

Father wedges himself between us again. "Soren won't actually level the mountains. It's time to call their bluff and assert ourselves."

"The time to assert ourselves has long since passed." Mother jabs Father's chest with a shaking finger. "*You* missed that opportunity, and once again, our daughter must put her life in peril to correct your mistakes."

This time, when she shoves past Father, he averts his eyes and lets her go.

With sharp efficiency, Mother unfastens the collar of my mourning dress and guides my arms and legs back into the clothes I wear every day: lightweight pants with a myriad of pockets and a loose linen shirt, over which she straps my shoulder holsters and bottles. Then she buckles my hip satchel and uses it to drag me closer.

"I'm sorry we can't do more to protect you, but perhaps Rowenna can. When you reach Vanzador, locate her things—assuming the Vanzadorians haven't destroyed them already. Look for her gowns, her books, her stationery, anything and everything she might have left behind, and scour them for clues. Knowing your sister, she would have been plotting and planning—"

Frantic fists pound the chamber door, cutting Mother off.

"Your Majesties!" Jareth's voice sounds wild and unraveling.

"Are we not allowed a single moment to bid our daughter farewell?" Mother shouts over her shoulder. "Dismiss your valet," she says to Father, who obediently shuffles over to the door and opens it a crack.

"Please, Jareth. Surely you can manage things for a few minutes?"

"The people have set fire to the fields!" Jareth interjects.

It feels like all the air has been sucked from the room. Jareth must be mistaken. The people would never...

"*Please*, your Majesties!" Jareth begs again. "Tashir is burning. You must come at once."

Mother and Father exchange a tense glance. We've been so consumed with our own outrage and grief, we didn't think of the people. *Our people*, who are bereft about Rowenna and terrified of the Vanzadorians' threats. They're panicking, and who can blame them? The soil of the life they've always known is washing away beneath their feet.

Mother takes my hand in a crushing grip and leads me through the door. Father drops his chin and follows.

"It's madness! I don't know what's come over them," Jareth sputters the moment we join him in the hall.

"I do." Mother mutters darkly. "A trapped weasel will

do anything to escape the gardener's trowel—even if it means gnawing off its own foot. Our people would rather watch Tashir burn than allow the Vanzadorians to take it."

SIX

THE MOMENT WE OPEN THE DOOR, OVEN-LIKE heat slaps us across the face. I raise my arms, but it does little to block the snapping yellow flames and plumes of purple smoke devouring our precious crops.

"Not even the Marauders destroyed so much," Father cries as he doubles over, coughing.

The smoke is as thick as a wool blanket, and I sputter and gag as it stings my eyes and clogs my throat.

When growing in the ground, and even after it's been cut and dried, bagrava flowers and fruit produce a scent similar to a lily, only more potent. When heated in any way, however—be it burned, boiled, or smoked—it reeks of charred flesh. It's a smell you can never forget—Earth Mother's natural attempt to ensure we feed the fruit to the land, not our bellies—and one foul whiff makes my stomach heave the way it did three years ago. The last time the Marauders raided Tashir.

I can still see the robbers hauling barrows full of bagrava from the storehouse and setting them ablaze. My ears still ring with ululating cries as they danced in the smoke, reveling in an immediate fix before carrying the rest of the crop back to the Tomb Flats.

Ingesting the raw fruit produces the strongest, longest-lasting high, but inhaling the purple smoke is the quickest means of delivery. And it was more than enough to turn the robbers into manic, snarling brutes who lashed out at anything that came between them and their prize.

If we're not careful now, the smoke will poison us too. Render us wild, erratic, and useless.

I stuff my nose inside my tunic and motion for the others to do the same.

"This will be the end of Tashir, the end of everything," Father wails through the fabric.

"Only if we do nothing," Mother snaps. She looks like she wants to strangle him, but she turns her attention to Jareth. "Redirect the irrigation pumps to flood the burning fields. Indira will try to stabilize the bagrava." She looks to me, and I nod. "Salvage everything you can, and alert the other master gardeners to do the same. The king and I"—Mother casts another irritated glance at Father—"will attempt to quell the people."

We all nod, even though quelling this madness feels as impossible as raising Rowenna from the dead.

For a terrible moment, we stand there, staring into the rippling blaze. It's like something out of a nightmare. Dark, streaking shadows and waving torches. Terrified screams and roaring flames. Our kind, hardworking people are hurling shovels and pitchforks, destroying their own land and homes.

For you, Rowenna murmurs for the second time today. *To keep you from going to Vanzador. See how they adore you?*

My heart wrenches painfully, and I shake my head. As much as I've always secretly craved the devotion our people had to Ro, I know none of this is for me. The same way Father's outburst wasn't for me. Real love inspires people to be kinder and braver, to stand taller and work harder. This is explosive. Desperate. They don't love *me*. They simply can't bear the thought of losing anything more. Like a feral dog defending its last shard of bone.

I glance over at Mother and Father—at the exhaustion etched in their wrinkles and the fear in their grim expressions. They look every bit as broken and petrified as I feel, and it makes me want to reach out to them.

"Be careful—" I start to say.

I love you.

That's what I wish I could say. What I wish *they* would say to *me*. But after divulging my secrets to Soren and allowing him to take me, it would be nothing but a blatant lie.

Thankfully, I don't need my parents' love or encouragement. I haven't needed it for a year now—not ever, if I'm honest. Rowenna and the bagrava have always been my roots, and I choose to focus on that—on *her*—as I sprint into the billowing smoke.

With every step, the air grows hotter. I can't see more than a few lengths ahead, but I clumsily hurdle three stone walls and land in the largest bagrava field. Flames hungrily consume the rows. Deep indigo smoke tries to curl up my nostrils, tickling and tantalizing, promising unimaginable pleasure if I stand a little taller, inhale a little deeper.

I spit out a cough and drop to my knees, taking short, shallow breaths. I would never break our promise to Earth Mother—never choose my own selfish pleasure over the well-being of my people and the land.

Slowly, I drag myself forward on my elbows, belting the sacred incantations to the bagrava. My words are weak and choppy and scrape my ash-clogged throat. But a few leaves still unfurl in response. Energy ripples down their stalks and into the earth, and my body welcomes the invigorating thrum.

If the other master gardeners are anywhere near the fields, they'll feel it too. They'll hear the bagravas' cry for help. If we all work together, and if Jareth can beat back the worst of the blaze with irrigation water, we might be able to salvage enough fruit to condition the scorched ground and replant a few fields of grain.

As I sing, I harvest any fruit remotely close to ripe and stuff it into my satchel, but most of it's still green and shrinking by the second. And there's still no sign of Jareth with the water.

That child at the banquet was probably right.

We're all going to die.

Don't think like that, Rowenna commands. *Keep singing. Keep moving.*

Her words are a steady heartbeat in my ears. Her ghost hands wrap around my wrists and drag me down the next row of bagrava. Then the next. But all the soothing incantations in the world can't strengthen plants that have burned to a crisp.

When the fire is close enough to snap at my fingers, I shrug out of my satchel and swing it at the blaze. I know it's too high and hot to smother, but I keep swinging anyway, because I have to do something. Have to keep fighting.

I strike the blaze again and again, spinning so wildly, lashing out so desperately, I assume I must have lost my balance when my knees hit the rocks. But then the earth heaves again, lurching as it would during an earthquake, and I spot them. Six dark figures streak through the ash and rubble, riding horses much faster and sleeker than our plow animals.

The Vanzadorians.

Their velvet waistcoats flap like enemy banners. Their golden buttons and chains flash like swords as they gallop toward our storehouse.

They're really going to do it—take all of our bagrava and leave us to perish.

"*No!*"

The force of my voice startles me, carrying over the crackle and whoosh of the flames. It sounds like hundreds of Tashiri planters are screaming with me.

A moment later, I realize it's because they are.

At least two hundred gardeners pour from the storehouse, armed with shovels, hoes, and rakes, prepared to defend our home and our bagrava to the death. The sight should comfort me—a mob that size should easily be able to cut down six invaders—but with a flick of King Soren's wrist, the ground opens like a hungry mouth, gnashing my people in its jagged-rock teeth before spitting their bloody carcasses into a sinkhole.

This time when I scream, Rowenna screams with me. And that's what breaks me—the hopelessness of it all. Even if every soul in Tashir rises up in rebellion, it won't be enough. The Vanzadorians will never stop.

Not unless someone stops them

Not unless you *stop them*, Rowenna whispers. And it could be a hallucination born of the noxious bagrava fumes, but I swear I see her face in the curls of smoke—her eyes brimming with love, pride, and conviction. Urging me to be brave. To do this—for her and for Tashir.

This is how you keep your promise. This is how you avenge me.

"What can I possibly do?" I cry.

Go with them to Vanzador and find their weaknesses. Punish my murderers and burn their kingdom down.

There are a million things wrong with her plan—or lack thereof—but I trust Ro, so I press a kiss to the clover on my wrist and sprint forward, toward the storehouse. If we don't stop the Vanzadorians from taking the remaining bagrava, there will be nothing left of Tashir to save.

The earth continues to buckle and tilt as I run, dumping me perilously close to the gash Soren ripped in the world. The wounded hands of my people grasp at my clothes and reach for my ankles, begging me to pull them up. And I want to. I want to save them all. But Ro won't let me stop.

Faster! she shouts in my ear. *You'll save more people by saving the storehouse.*

The Vanzadorians are nearly there. A dwindling line of brave gardeners are all that stands between Soren and our stores of harvested bagrava.

Faster! Ro cries again.

But we both know I won't make it. And I could hardly stop their charging cavalry single-handedly.

But I know something that can.

I grapple for the vial of neem-oil strapped across my chest—a potent blend that rids the bagrava of aphids and mites. Then I pinch a handful of fertilizer from the pouch at my hip and add it to the vial. Dropping to my knees,

I hold my breath and thrust my hand into the flames devouring the nearby grass.

Pain scorches my fingers, and my body begs me to drop the vial, but I grit my teeth and make sure the oil catches. Then I hurl the burning glass into the space between the storehouse and the charging Vanzadorians.

Ringing fills my ears. Blood dribbles from my bitten lips. And my burning hand throbs as I watch the makeshift bomb arc across the yellow sky.

The Vanzadorians are less than five lengths from the storehouse when it explodes. A searing white blaze plumes into the air like a geyser, slamming the storehouse doors inward and beating the Vanzadorians back. Creating a trough between the enemy and our precious supply of bagrava.

"Traitors!" King Soren booms as his horse rears. "How dare you attempt to assassinate your allies!"

Bitter laughter rumbles in my throat. We have *never* been allies. Even if we were, I threw one tiny vial—well in front of them—while they're sweeping our people into an abyss by the droves.

"Enough!" I shout, trying to channel Ro's swaggering gait as I dodge through the wreckage and position myself in the gap created by the explosion. I'm thankful for the strangling smoke and the excuse it provides for my shaking voice. "I'll go with you if you leave the bagrava—and my people—in peace."

King Soren motions for his men to halt and squints down at me.

"Indira?" he says with a gruff chuckle. "I assumed you weren't coming when you raced off into the palace with Mommy and Daddy. Do they know you're out here, endangering yourself against their wishes? And after they've already sacrificed so much to protect you?" He gestures to our burning fields.

I want to tell him he knows nothing about my parents' wishes. If they shared a wish, I'm certain it's that *I* had been the one to perish instead of Rowenna.

Focus, sister. Ro's fingers slide beneath my chin, strong but gentle. Helping me stare brazenly up at her killers.

"I'm here now," I say. "Let's go."

King Soren smirks and turns to his son. "It looks like you're getting married today after all."

It's hard to see through the smoke, but I swear Alaric flinches—just the slightest—before flashing me a leering smile and joining in with his snickering guards.

"Now, all we need is our tribute, and we'll be on our way. Leave your parents to clean up this little mess. Look, I'll even help." King Soren wags his gloved fingers, and giant swathes of dirt rise up and fall across the blaze, smothering it in less than a minute.

Bloodred fury clouds my vision. He could have extinguished the fires immediately. He could have saved my people so much suffering, so much destruction.

But he didn't.

Because we're easier to control when we're broken.

I want to fly at King Soren and plunge my spade into his exposed stomach, but my hand is too slow and stinging from the burns, and Rowenna's voice is too adamant.

Be patient. Bide your time.

It nearly kills me, but I watch silently as two of Soren's guards move toward the storehouse. Several brave Tashiri rebels step forward to block the way, but I call them off. "Let the Vanzadorians pass."

My people look like they want to stab me with their pitchforks, like I'm some sort of traitor to our country, but they have to see this is the only way.

"Better to let them take their share early than steal the entire supply," I say through gritted teeth.

Grudgingly, they stand aside, and several minutes later, the Vanzadorian guards reemerge with two full bags of bagrava. Two more fields we won't be able to condition.

After strapping the bagrava to their horses and mounting, one of the guards nudges their horse toward me and offers me a thick vambraced arm.

Before I take it, I steal a final glance over my shoulder—at my people's anguished faces and the smoldering fields, trying to memorize their precise shape and color through the smoke. Truly appreciating, for perhaps the first and last time, this beautiful place Rowenna and I grew up in together. A place she died for.

A place *I* might die for.

Before I lose my nerve, I reach up and allow the guard to hoist me across his saddle.

And then we ride.

SEVEN

We gallop across the Tomb Flats, chased by a shroud of purple-gray smoke. My haversack thumps painfully against my side, heavy with the underripe bagrava I harvested from the burning fields, and I cry out in agony every time it brushes my blistered hand.

To my shock, my riding companion offers to take my pack, but I refuse with a suspicious scowl. I'm not about to hand over my possessions to a strange Vanzadorian. Despite my blatant hostility, he still gives me ample space in the saddle, routinely asks how I'm faring, and even offers his spare gloves to cover my burns.

With every offer, my frown deepens and my hackles rise. Rowenna's letters outlined, in great detail, the horrors of her own journey to Vanzador—how they bound and gagged her as soon as the hillock palace was out of sight.

How they mocked and ridiculed her, and refused to stop so she could relieve herself. I'm not about to fall for this overly chivalrous act.

After what feels like an eternity, the horses finally slow to a walk. The wind, however, continues howling past, more violently than I've ever felt. The Tomb Flats are completely barren. No flowering knolls or groves of trees. Not even a lone crooked shrub to impede the gusts. Just slickrock and sand.

And Marauders.

My skin crawls as I peer into the dark of the desert. I have no doubt they're out there, watching us, waiting for the perfect moment to strike. It's how the robbers have always survived on these inhospitable plains. They raid every caravan that attempts to cross. I've read dozens of accounts from my ancestors, detailing how the Marauders stole their animals, supplies, and even their children. Then once they had a taste of our bagrava, they became even more bloodthirsty and insatiable.

Soren has to know they will come. Every month, they attempt to steal the tribute of bagrava we send to the mountains, injuring, and sometimes even killing, the Tashiri planters and Vanzadorian guards responsible for the transport. And while I'd rather not die today, it would be poetic, in a way, to watch the ravenous thieves steal the bagrava Soren and his son stole from us.

You forget Soren can bury the Marauders beneath a

mountain of rubble before they get within one hundred lengths, Rowenna reminds me.

"Do you need help getting down?" My riding companion dismounts and offers me a hand, which I pointedly refuse.

"I grew up in a farming community. I know how to ride," I say with a haughty tilt of my chin.

He gives an amiable shrug. "Suit yourself, but even my legs are sore after such a long time in the saddle."

I roll my eyes and swing out of the stirrups, but either the horse has grown taller or the slickrock is harder than I realized, because pain jolts through my legs and I crumple to the shale. A sharp rock slices through the blisters on my palm, and while I hiss and clutch my hand, the guard rushes to my side, trying to inspect the wound.

"You should have let me help you. Or at least taken my gloves."

"Why are you being so nice?" I snap.

The guard has the audacity to look offended. "Because we promised to keep you safe."

"The way you kept *Rowenna* safe?"

"Oh no, I plan to keep a *much* closer eye on you," King Soren interjects as he dismounts. "You're of far greater value than Alaric's previous bride."

"I'll never cultivate bagrava for you," I spit, to which Soren waves a dismissive hand.

"You'll do as I say."

Or you'll end up dead. Like your sister.

Soren doesn't actually utter these words, but we all hear them, echoing across the Tomb Flats.

"Are you finally admitting you murdered Rowenna?" I demand.

He gives a nonchalant shrug and passes his horse off to a guard. "Would it matter if I was? Your sister was nothing but a useless annoyance. I can't even remember her name."

I know better than to rise to his bait, but my vision goes red, and I pounce at the Vanzadorian king like the jackals that prowl the Tomb Flats.

"You will not speak ill of the dead!" I shout. Except my voice comes out in a smoky cough, and my legs are too sore and wobbly to support my weight. As I crumple to the ground, Soren chuckles, unlatches a water horn from his belt, and tosses it at me.

"Clean yourself up. I won't make my son go to bed with a hog on his wedding night."

The word *bed* makes the hairs on my arms prickle, and I wrap them tightly across my chest. Of course I know the treaty calls for a captive bride, but I assumed the union was more about joining Vanzador to the bagrava than man to wife. Soren can't actually expect me to perform *wifely* duties, can he?

Was Ro required to perform them?

The thought makes my heart stutter and break. Ro and I shared most things in life, but I have no desire to share this—to share *Alaric*—with her.

I whirl around to gauge the prince's reaction, praying he'll protest. He must be just as averse to this as I am. But he's laughing as the guards playfully elbow him, and when he catches me staring, he winks.

My cheeks burn, which only makes Alaric's entourage laugh harder.

"Something tells me the princess hasn't got much experience in the bedroom..." one of the guards jeers.

"Not to worry, sweet pea," another calls. "Alaric has enough experience for you both."

"I'm sure she'll be a quick study," the first guard says to Alaric in a mock whisper, "what with all of her time spent handling zucchinis..."

"And cucumbers!" another guffaws.

I can't stand to be near them a second longer.

With a withering glare, I grab the water horn and stomp away from where they begin making camp. No one follows me. They know I won't run. I can't if I want to protect my people and avenge Rowenna.

My only choice is to plow ahead to Vanzador and find a fracture in the bedrock of their mountain. No one is invincible. Not even Soren and Alaric Alaverdi. So while they wink and mock and threaten me, I'll whittle away at the foundation of their fortress. I'll find a weakness in Soren's power—or in the people or the land itself—and I'll use it to destroy them.

I uncork the water horn and pour it over my face, scrubbing at the streaks of soot and dried blood. *Not* for Alaric. I don't give a fig if he finds me repulsive. I'm washing for myself—to remove the terrible stench of burned bagrava and to clear my head, figure out my first move.

It's as I'm untangling my hair from its disheveled topknot that inspiration comes. Instead of returning my hair to a tight bun as I planned, I weave the top portion into an intricate seven-stranded braid. The very same braid Rowenna wore on the day she married this very same prince. I even manage to find some poppy cuttings in my haversack that aren't too wilted, and I add them to the plait. They aren't the vibrant zinnias that crowned Ro's head like fire, and my hands aren't nearly as nimble, but all in all, it's a good likeness. Most important, it makes me feel stronger. More like my sister.

People have always remarked on our striking similarities: dark hair and eyes, golden skin sprinkled with freckles. I take a handful of mustard seeds from my pack, crush them into powder, and dab it across my eyelids—to imitate the shimmering gold she wore on her wedding day. Now, if only I had chain mail...

I want to be Ro's perfect likeness. I want Alaric and his

father to see the ghost of his murdered bride rising from the grave for vengeance, as I utter my marriage vows.

When I'm satisfied with my appearance, I return to camp to test my handiwork.

The guards are perched on rocks around a fire, cooking lumps of unidentifiable meat on sticks.

"Want one?" The man I rode with holds out a greasy blob, but I shake my head and twist my face with disgust.

"That doesn't look fit for a dog," I purposely goad them. So they'll look up and see Rowenna's face in mine. So they'll realize I'm not going to let them kill her and carry on as if nothing happened.

But there's no pulse of recognition. No inkling of guilt. Instead of dropping their skewers and blinking with shock, the guards simply exchange exaggerated eye rolls.

As if my sister never even existed.

Their blatant disregard for her life makes me want to dive at them like the hunting crows we raise in Tashir—tenacious predators that keep the locusts from destroying our crops—but I save my energy. If these fools don't remember Ro, it's a reflection on *them*. They probably weren't even in attendance at the wedding.

Soren and Alaric, however, won't be able to ignore the similarities between my sister and me. And they're the ones I need to frighten.

They're the ones who must pay for her death.

I stomp past the fire toward a tent the guards must

have erected while I washed. Lanterns burn within, projecting Soren and Alaric's silhouettes on the fabric. They're pouring drinks and lounging on cushions, as if they haven't a care in the world. As if they didn't just leave my entire life and kingdom in ashes.

Put them in their place, Rowenna whispers.

Yesterday, I wouldn't have dared to speak to the Vanzadorian king, let alone confront him, but yesterday I wasn't living for myself *and* my sister. I wasn't carrying the weight of an entire country on my shoulders.

I clench my fists, march up to the tent, and duck through the flap. "You've kept me waiting long enough. Let's get this wedding over with."

Both men fly to their feet, and Soren bellows an unintelligible threat, but I hold my ground and let them take in my appearance, hoping they see Ro's bent and bloody limbs, her bruised and sunken face. After a long beat, filled with more blinks of confusion than recognition, however, King Soren chuckles and claps his son on the back.

"Look how eager she is to marry you!"

Alaric laughs along, but the grin doesn't quite reach his eyes. And I catch him squinting sideways at me when he thinks I'm not looking.

"Like what you see?" I flip my hair over my shoulder precisely how Rowenna used to, making sure to display the clover on my wrist.

For a second, two deep valleys form between Alaric's

brows, but with a shake of his head, they vanish, replaced by a cold, cutting smile. "I do," he says, prowling toward me. "Very much."

The shift is so abrupt and unnatural, the vacant look in his eyes so eerie and unsettling, I inadvertently step back. It's the precise sort of cold-blooded callousness I imagine it would take to shove your own wife off a cliff.

"What's the matter, Indira?" Alaric purrs. "I thought you wanted me to look. To cherish this moment. You're the picture of bridal beauty…"

"I wish I could say the same for you," I spit, gesturing at his filthy clothes and grimy hands, which clearly haven't been washed. "Apparently, you can't be expected to go to bed with a hog but have no problem smelling like one yourself."

Soren steps forward and grabs my arm. "Watch your tongue, girl. You will not disrespect your husband in such a manner."

"He's not my husband yet," I retort.

"Clearly, it's time to rectify that." Soren hauls me from the tent and toward the fire. "Donovan and Eska will serve as witnesses." He points at two scraggly-bearded men and motions for them to stand. "The rest of you will repeat the vow of the binding."

I don't know what "the vow of the binding" is, but it brings to mind images of Alaric and me side by side in the stocks, a clapper locked tight around our necks.

"You, over there." Soren directs me to the smoky side of the fire and positions Alaric across from me.

In the flickering light, Alaric's disheveled hair shines blue-black as a raven's wing, and his eyes are the gray of wet granite. He's disgustingly handsome, blinding me with the smoldering grin he wears like armor. I have no doubt it renders most women into beet pulp, but all I see when I look at him is an aristolochia flower—a carnivorous plant that has dark masklike petals and luminous "eyes," which it uses to attract and devour insects. The aristolochia also happens to smell of rotting flesh, which seems appropriate, given my sister's blood is still practically dripping from his fingers.

"Take her hand," King Soren orders Alaric, "and hold it tight."

I may not be wearing chains like Rowenna did during her ceremony, but I'm just as much a prisoner.

The Vanzadorians at least pretended it was a "joining of our nations" when Rowenna and Alaric were wed. They let us perform the ceremony in Tashir, beneath the watchful eyes of Earth Mother, and allowed every planter in the kingdom to gather in the grove of maple trees, beneath a trellis woven with bagrava. Mother sprinkled the sacred oils over their hands, and Father intoned the Tashiri words of unification.

"Alive as flowers that spring toward the sun
Join these two hearts, as vines, into one.

Grow up together, create, bloom, and flower

Then return at life's end for the earth to devour."

Neither Rowenna nor Alaric looked pleased, but there was still something beautiful about the service, about the words themselves, uttered in such a picturesque location, with bees humming and honeysuckle tossing in the breeze.

There's nothing beautiful about the Vanzadorian wedding ceremony.

King Soren stumbles through the rite, either making it up as he goes or forgetting half the words. Something about the "strength of a sure foundation" and "standing together as tall as the sky." Things I will never do or be with his son, so I don't bother listening.

When he finally finishes, he collects a skull-sized rock and raises it overhead. While his guards chant indecipherable words, he brings the rock crashing down on the boulders encircling the fire. It shatters like blown glass. Something a person without Vanzadorian power could never manage.

Soren scrapes up the fragments and sprinkles them, first over Alaric's head, and then over mine. As I cough, he has the audacity to say, "Congratulations, you may kiss your bride."

The guards hoot and whistle, but thankfully, Alaric doesn't lean in. I yank my hands free and turn, eager to flee into the darkness beyond the fire, but Soren blocks my path.

"Ah, ah, ah. Your marriage bed is *that* way." He gestures grandly to the tent, and the whistles and jeers grow louder. As if this day hasn't been horrifying and humiliating enough.

I want to spit in Soren's face and take off running, but Rowenna seizes my wrist and tugs me forward.

Stay calm. Use this time to question Alaric. Catch him off guard and get under his skin.

Manic laughter bubbles up my throat, because this is *not* how most women would get "under the skin" of their husband on their wedding night.

Alaric stiffens and his smirk falters, which gives me an inordinate amount of pleasure.

"What's wrong with you?" he mutters. "What about any of this could possibly be funny?"

"Unlace your breeches and I'll show you," I whisper, laughing even harder when his cheeks flush a mortifying shade of pink.

"Go on! Enjoy your wedding night!" Soren booms, encouraging the guards to resume whistling.

Alaric curses under his breath, snatches my hand, and tugs me toward the tent.

I force myself to continue laughing, hoping it conceals the terror I feel about spending the night as husband and wife.

EIGHT

ALARIC SHOVES ME THROUGH THE TENT FLAP AND into the shadowed space, which feels much smaller than it did when I confronted him and Soren before the ceremony.

As Alaric crowds in behind me, I'm surrounded by his wind and leather scent, acutely aware of his formidable bulk. Everything inside me wants to flee to the opposite corner of the tent, but that's not what Rowenna would do. Not what a leader who's going to save her kingdom would do. So I stand my ground and glare at him over my shoulder.

"Must you stand so close?"

Alaric sighs and steps back. "What am I supposed to do when you stop so suddenly?"

"I wouldn't have stopped so suddenly if our

accommodations weren't so repulsive." I gesture to the lone blanket spread across the tent floor. It stinks of sweat and mildew and was, almost certainly, draped across the back of a horse less than an hour ago. "Not exactly how I pictured my marriage bed…"

"I thought you dirt pushers loved to be covered in grime and animal hair…" Alaric mutters.

"At least we're covered in *something*."

A devious expression flits across Alaric's features, and he looks me dead in the eyes as he slowly unfastens the decorative chains across his chest. "Is *this* closer to what you imagined on your wedding night?" He opens the front of his long navy jacket and raises his arms toward the ceiling in an exaggerated stretch, exposing the lean muscles leading down toward his breeches.

I don't mean to look, but it's unavoidable in such close quarters, and my cheeks burn with mortification when he catches me.

"What's the matter, gardener? No more witty jabs?" he drawls as he stoops to unlace his boots.

"Is it that difficult to put on a shirt?" I blurt. "Or are your tailors too unskilled to make them?"

"Of course our tailors can sew a shirt."

"Then I suppose the problem lies with *you*. You're too daft to figure out which holes are for the head and which are for the arms."

Alaric snorts and looks up, just enough to lock eyes with me from beneath his disheveled hair. "I've got your stems all in a tangle, haven't I? You don't want to admit you like what you see..."

"The only thing I'd *like* to see is my sharpest spade buried in your throat."

"Who knew you were so provocative? I've never engaged in *that* sort of fun, but I'm willing to try anything once..." He gives me another slow, seductive wink, and I lurch back, tripping on that seeds-forsaken horse blanket and landing hard on my backside.

Alaric's eyes sparkle with laughter. "Don't play games you can't win, princess. It makes you look ridiculous."

"No more ridiculous than *you*!" I wave my hands at his open jacket again. I don't know what else to say or do. I'm so far out of my depth, if I were a plant, my roots would be growing up and out of the soil.

Alaric plunks down on the ground, leans over his knees, and considers me. "You're clearly not going to drop this, but perhaps you'll be less uncomfortable with our manner of dress if I educate you. In Vanzador, our clothing is a mark of our strength and status. The Fortress is high in the mountains, where the air is cold and thin. It takes years to adapt to the frigid temperatures. The highest discipline and self-mastery are required to forgo undershirts."

I don't even try to withhold my snort of laughter. "Why wear anything at all then? Why not run up and down the mountainside naked? Wouldn't that prove you're the strongest of all?"

With a heavy sigh, Alaric removes a flask from his breeches and takes a long sip. "I don't know why I bothered. You gardeners can't understand anything more complex than dirt." He lies down and folds his hands behind his head. "Now, if you're finished mocking my culture, I'd like to sleep. Your presence is exhausting."

He closes his eyes, as if he really thinks I'm going to let him have the last word.

"This is just the beginning of your exhaustion, *dearest husband*," I snap. "You get to enjoy the pleasure of my company *for as long as we both shall live*."

"At least it will be more tolerable once we reach Vanzador," he mumbles.

"Why is that? Because you plan to push me off a cliff, like my sister?"

Alaric's eyes slit open. "I had nothing to do with Rowenna's death."

"Then why haven't you mentioned her, even once?"

"Why would I?"

"Because you were married to her! Because she was my sister and I look just like her!" I gesture to myself. "Any semiobservant person with half a conscience would have noticed I'm the spitting image of her on the day you wed. It should have dredged up memories. Comparisons. *Something*. But you didn't even notice."

Alaric leans up on one elbow and looks me over briefly. "I suppose you do look like her," he says with an offhanded shrug.

"That's really all you have to say?"

He groans and takes another long pull from his flask. "Make it stop."

"Oh, I'm just getting started." I lean forward, finally on the offensive. "I know you didn't choose to marry Rowenna, but she was a person. *My* person. With hopes, dreams, and plans for the future. You were wed for nearly a year, and all you have to say is that you *suppose I look like her*?"

"What more do you want me to say? That you're prettier? Because you are."

"Unbelievable!" I laugh bitterly. "And insulting! I couldn't care less who *you* deem prettier."

Not to mention it isn't true. There's a reason every eye was drawn to Ro whenever we entered a room. I am pleasing to look at, but *she* was impossible to look away from. And if Alaric can't see that, there's little point arguing with him.

How did Ro endure being married to him for an entire year? I want to strangle him after less than five minutes. Was she forced to suffer and endure *other* things too?

"Did you share my sister's bed?" I suddenly blurt before he can lie back down.

I don't actually want to know the answer, but I *have* to know. *I need* to know just how much she was subjected to.

"Gods, no." Alaric's face contorts with horror. "At least...I hope not."

"What do you mean you *hope not*? Do you bed so many girls, you can't tell one from the next? Is that what your guards were referring to when they spoke of your *experience*?"

"Is that jealousy I detect?" Alaric arches a taunting brow while taking another swig from his flask.

"Or perhaps the problem is you drink too much to remember anything. Give me that." I snatch the flask.

He flops back down without trying to reclaim it. "You'd drink this much, too, if you were me."

"Yes, it must be *so* difficult, being the beloved heir to a prosperous kingdom," I snap. "Never needing to worry about attacks or invasion, since you can literally crush your enemies with power you amplify by stealing from another kingdom."

Alaric says nothing. Because he has no defense. But I have plenty more to say.

"You wouldn't be half as strong without our bagrava. You wouldn't be able to throw a stone across this tent."

"I honestly don't know what you're talking about," he mumbles wearily, "but whatever it is, I'm sure you're right." He sounds like an exhausted parent reasoning with a toddler. He even pinches the bridge of his nose. "I'm going to sleep now. I have a massive headache."

Before I think about what I'm doing, I lean over and

pry his hand away from his face, momentarily forgetting my burns. "No one is sleeping until you tell me what really happened to my sister," I growl through the pain."

Alaric jolts free and clutches his arm against his chest as if my touch somehow burned him through his sleeve. "Don't ever put your hands on me."

"Then don't ignore me!"

"Enough! You're wasting your time with all of your conspiracy theories and vengeful bravado."

"Why? Because you plan to sabotage my efforts?"

"There's no need. You won't find anything that connects me, or anyone else in my country, to Rowenna's death."

I fold my arms. "How can you be so sure?"

"Let's just say Vanzadorians aren't the most..." He looks up and swirls a hand through the air, searching for the right word. "Forthcoming," he finally says. "Investigate your sister's death all you want. It will lead nowhere."

"Sounds exactly like what someone guilty of murder who doesn't want me poking around would say," I retort.

"Tell me, what did I stand to gain by killing Rowenna? Am I free to live as I please?" He gestures to me and the tent with a cruel laugh. "Your sister's death got me another sham of a marriage—and to the more obnoxious sister. At least Rowenna was smart enough to shut her mouth and keep to herself."

I shake my head, because there's no way my sister

went quietly to Vanzador. She would have argued and meddled and made Alaric's life a living hell—just as I am.

"Rowenna was far bolder and more outspoken than I'll ever be," I say.

Alaric shrugs. "If you say so."

I toss my hands with frustration. "How can you sit there and act as if you hardly knew her?"

"Because I didn't know her at all!" he explodes, eyes flashing. "Do you think I had time to dine with her each night? Or accompany her to social calls and luncheons and however else she filled her days? We were strangers, with separate chambers and beds. Most nights I slept in my study."

"Did that make it easier?" I ask softly, sounding much calmer than I feel.

"Make what easier?"

"To push her."

Alaric buries his hands in his hair, and his voice leaks out in a growl. "For the millionth time, I didn't push her."

"Then why are you so angry, if you have nothing to hide?"

"Because you're infuriating!" He rolls to face the wall and adds in a menacing whisper, "I'm far more tempted to shove *you* off a cliff than I ever was your sister."

"How romantic," I coo. "Just what I hoped my husband would whisper on our wedding night."

"*Don't* call me that."

"Then what should I call you?"

"Nothing. You have no reason to speak to me. Pretend I don't exist."

I'm quiet for several minutes. Long enough to let Alaric think he won. Then I crawl across the tent and position myself directly behind him. So he can feel my breath on the back of his neck when I whisper, "Hopefully I won't have to *pretend* you don't exist much longer."

Alaric jolts, arms pinwheeling as he yells, "What are you doing? Get away from me!"

But I'm already gone, curled up on the opposite side of the tent, laughing as Rowenna's boisterous applause lulls me to sleep—the most enchanting lullaby.

NINE

WAKE TO WATERY YELLOW LIGHT STREAMING THROUGH the tent walls and a growling stomach. Not a single robin or sparrow chatters to welcome the day, like they do in Tashir. Even the birds know better than to nest on the Tomb Flats.

I roll onto my back and peek across the tent, secretly hoping to find the Vanzadorian prince with his mouth hanging open and drool dribbling off his chin. It would be so satisfying to learn he's an ugly sleeper. Though it's far more likely he'll be the one perched on his side, sneering at my snarled hair and sleep-lined face.

To my surprise, Alaric is doing neither.

He sits cross-legged and straight-backed, with one hand pressed to the ground beside him and the other covering his eyes like a blindfold. He appears to be quietly muttering something. Probably a curse on our marriage and me.

Except he and Soren need you, Ro reminds me. *Never forget that.*

I sit up and watch Alaric for another minute before I slam my hand against the ground and shout, "What in all the green hills of Tashir are you doing?"

Alaric jerks from his pose, and his features immediately crumple into a frown. "I *was* praying, until you rudely interrupted."

"*Praying?*" I scoff. The thought of our oppressors engaging in something that requires humility seems more unnatural than a fern sprouting from slickrock.

"Yeah, you know, where you kneel and offer thanks and beg forgiveness? Maybe you're unfamiliar with the practice, since you Tashiri have never done anything wrong. Always the bloody victims…"

I leap to my feet, every trace of tiredness gone. "We *are* the victims! *You* terrorize *us*!"

Alaric grabs his coat and heads for the door, grumbling as he goes.

I bolt after him. "Where are you going in such a hurry? Didn't you enjoy our conversation last night? I thought we could continue bonding today."

"I enjoyed it so much, I've already forgotten most of it," he snaps before striding off toward the firepit.

I stand there, panting and smiling, relishing this small victory.

The guards come to take down the tent, and we're

back in our saddles before the sun is fully up. I assumed I would ride with Alaric, now that we're wed, but he makes excuses about needing to help Soren clear the trail and orders me to ride with the same guard as the day before. Which is fine by me. Preferable, even. I won't have to be on my toes, ready to spar at a moment's notice. And I won't have to cling to Alaric's muscled torso and inhale the annoying wind and leather scent of him.

Hour after hour, we gallop across the endless Tomb Flats. It's all so uniform, I could almost believe we're running in place if not for the dark triangular shadows that appear on the horizon, growing steadily taller. And King Soren and Alaric's occasional manipulation of the land.

On our second day of travel, they raise a rock wall to shield us from a pelting sandstorm. And when a guard claims to spot something trailing us across the dunes on the fourth day, the Vanzadorian rulers carve a tunnel into the earth, and we ride belowground for the rest of the day.

Alaric never returns to our marriage tent. I tell myself it's due to my sharp tongue and intimidating presence, but if the yammering guards are to be believed, it's because he's keeping watch through the night with Soren, guarding us—and, more importantly, the bagrava—from the Marauders.

Sometimes I think I see the wild-eyed thieves darting in my periphery. Other times, I swear I hear their battle cries in the yapping howl of the jackals. But on the seventh day of travel, we arrive at the base of the mountains unscathed.

The towering slabs of stone hardly make me feel safer, though.

I always thought the mountains protecting Tashir were high, but I was wrong. The slopes Soren erected along our border are an anthill compared to the soaring peaks of Vanzador. Proving, yet again, that King Soren's "protection" and "allyship" are a shadow of what he truly has to offer. A mockery more than anything.

I crane my neck to survey the craggy bluffs, jutting from the earth like the world's tallest forest. Each stony branch rises higher than the next, creating a canopy of cliffs that swallows us in its shadow. The air is at least ten degrees colder than it was on the Tomb Flats, and a whistling breeze tears through my linen shirt as if it's made of cobwebs.

I have never felt more insignificant and exposed.

The guards dismount and unbuckle their saddlebags, which they convert into satchels they sling across their shoulders. Hiking poles unfold from tent support beams, spurs become hand picks, and lead ropes are knotted into longer climbing ropes. Everything, it seems, has a double purpose. Everything is adaptable to the mountain.

Except for me.

A low rumble brings my gaze back to the base of the peak, where Soren stands with his hands raised. As the rumbling intensifies, a channel opens in the earth, roughly the size of an irrigation ditch, and a steel contraption lurches down tracks embedded in the hillside.

It comes to a stop with a hiss, and Soren climbs into the compartment, motioning for Alaric to follow. "Ride with me—and bring your bride. The bagrava too. The people will be eager to see the fruits of our conquest."

I stagger back, furiously shaking my head. This is precisely what they did to Rowenna. She told me all about this strange contraption and the crowd of ravenous Vanzadorians waiting at the top. They mocked and ridiculed her, picking her apart like hungry vultures.

"I'd rather walk," I say.

To my surprise, Alaric mutters something at the exact same moment. Something that sounds an awful lot like, *Don't you ever tire of the production?*

I gape over at him, certain I must have misheard.

King Soren turns slowly back around. "What was that, my boy?" His tone is perfectly pleasant, the lines of his body relaxed, but something about it lifts the hairs on my neck.

"I said, 'Don't you think she needs instruction?'" Alaric lies smoothly. "As much as I'd prefer to ride with you, Father, I think it would be wise to teach my new wife to climb. Sure-footedness clearly isn't a family trait, and Indira has expressed *so* many concerns about falling to her death."

"How dare you act as if my worries are unfounded!" I bark at him, but Alaric continues talking over me.

"We can't risk losing *this* sister. It would be a much greater waste."

While I sputter with outrage, Soren considers me and nods. "You're right. She's of no use to us dead. Ensure she makes it to the top."

He raps on the ceiling of the contraption, and it starts its steep and puffing ascent up the rock face. I watch it go, marveling at how effortlessly it climbs, like a spider on a windowpane.

"Well, aren't you going to thank me?" Alaric asks once Soren is out of sight.

"For what, exactly?"

Alaric holds my gaze for a long tenuous moment. "For not making you ride to the top."

I glare back without blinking. "Don't pretend that was for me. You were covering your own backside. I heard what you actually said."

"I don't have a clue what you're talking about. The altitude must be affecting you. It's known to addle the weak."

"I know what I heard. And I'm not weak," I say through my teeth.

"Then you should have no trouble keeping up."

Alaric turns on his heel and starts up the trail. His guards fall in behind him, and I have to jog to keep up, even though they're burdened with gear and I'm carrying nothing but my haversack. As the hours pass, the trail grows steadily steeper, and the cold air burns my lungs. My tired muscles ache before we're even a third of the way up this endless trail. Alaric never looks back to check on me, but the guard I rode with does, giving me silent, encouraging smiles that feel like a mockery.

Just when I think I might keel over from exhaustion, a great walled city appears through the clouds, crowning the summit of the mountain with tall needlelike spires.

I grind to a halt, head tilted back and eyes blinking with terror and awe.

It isn't any wonder the Vanzadorians call their city the Fortress. If someone asked me to picture the most imposing and impenetrable stronghold I could imagine, this would be it. Even from a distance, I count dozens of pointed towers, a maze of stone walls topped with wicked crenellations, and a massive black gate that looks like a gaping mouth. Rows of enormous steel spikes protrude outward like fangs, and the trail we're on is the serpent's long winding tongue.

Now do you see why I couldn't visit on a whim? Rowenna grumbles.

"Seeds and soil," I mutter aloud.

It looks like a prison.

It's worse than a prison, Ro affirms.

"Impressed?" Alaric throws his arms wide and pulls

the chilly air deep into his lungs, clearly invigorated by the sight of his home—and my horror.

"The only thing that *impresses* me is the depth of your greed and lies," I say, averting my gaze from the Fortress.

Alaric snorts. "How, pray tell, can a mountain be a symbol of greed? And what exactly are we lying about?"

Don't take his bait, Rowenna warns, but I'm too wrung out and exhausted to censor myself.

"You led my people to believe the power required to maintain the mountain range surrounding Tashir is equal to the sacrifices we make to produce your bagrava tributes. Or that *we* are somehow deficient, since you're constantly demanding more and more bagrava. Then you took my sister and *killed* her, all under the guise of fair trade, but you've clearly given us a fraction of the power you're truly capable of!" I stab a finger at the imposing city that looks to be resting in the clouds. "Our protection is a rickety old fence in comparison."

"Has your mountain kept the Marauders from invading?" Alaric asks with infuriating calm.

"Yes, but—"

"Then we've done our part."

"Why should we be required to sacrifice so much when it clearly requires very little from you?" My roaring voice echoes off the stone edifices.

I expect Alaric to shrug or goad me with one of his infuriating grins, but he removes the flask from his breeches, takes a long swallow, and resumes walking. "You know nothing about the cost of our power."

I charge after him, steam practically pouring from my ears despite the cold. "I know *everything* about the cost of your power! Namely that it's of little cost to you since it's enhanced by *our* bagrava. And I know it isn't divinely appointed from Earth Mother. Your ancestors forcibly *took* power from the earth, just as you take bagrava from Tashir. You've earned none of it."

"Are you done ranting?" Alaric takes a sharp left at a fork in the trail, and the pitch grows even steeper.

"I'll never be done until you treat us as equals," I retort following so close behind the prince I *accidentally* clip the heel of his boot. He stumbles but, unfortunately, doesn't fall.

He shoots me a seething look. "Must you walk so close?"

"You're teaching me to climb, remember?" I do my best imitation of his voice.

Rather than snipe back at me, Alaric picks up his pace and orders the guards to do the same. Thanks to their spike-soled boots, they easily vault from stone to stone like mountain goats. My worn, muddy gardening boots, on the other hand, might as well be slathered with butter. For every step I take forward, I slide at least two back, causing pebbles to cascade down the slope.

Soon, I'm so far behind, the prince and his entourage

look like a line of marching ants. My muscles tremble and scream, and the thin mountain air refuses to fill my lungs. My vision goes dark and fuzzy around the edges.

How did Ro ever manage this climb in her heavy chain mail gown?

I didn't. Her voice swirls around me on a gust of wind.

"But you took nothing else when you left," I say.

I decided to embrace Vanzadorian tradition. I wanted to display my willingness to adapt to their customs...

"What, exactly, does that mean?" I ask, though I have a terrible feeling I know where this is headed.

I climbed naked, Ro announces with wicked glee.

I laugh so hard I trip over a root on the trail. "You didn't! You wouldn't!"

I would. And I did.

"I wish I could have seen our husband's reaction to *that*."

I hear Ro's laughter in the cry of a hawk, feel her wink in the blaze of sunshine burning my nose. *Why do you think Alaric was so keen to climb with you instead of riding with his father?*

Now I'm laughing even harder. So hard, I'm making little gasping noises. "The only way I'd allow Alaric to see me naked is if he was dead and I was dancing around his corpse the way our ancestors used to."

When did you become so vicious? Rowenna asks, a hint of pride in her voice.

"When they took you," I say without hesitation.

That's the moment that ripped me in two—a distinct before and after. But Rowenna doesn't agree right away, and I wonder if she's trying to tell me something.

Some lemon trees never give fruit. Not because they don't have the ability or potential, but because the tree has never been given the proper amount of water and sunlight. Perhaps seedlings of her rage and tenacity have always lain dormant with in me, but I never had occasion to cultivate them because she produced enough for us both.

But maybe I'm like her in that way. Maybe that part of her lives on in me.

The thought makes me clap with delight.

"What's she doing?" a faraway voice asks.

I turn to look for the speaker, but all I see are smears of gray.

"And why is she flopping around like that?" another disembodied voice says. "And cackling?"

I don't realize they're talking about me or that I've crumpled to the ground, until fingers close around my bicep and yank me upright.

"She's suffering from altitude sickness."

This voice, I recognize. Apparently, my darling husband has come to save me.

"Leave me alone. I don't want your help," I mumble and swat at the air.

"And I don't want to help you, but neither of us are in a position to get what we want." Alaric picks me up and holds me in his arms like an infant—or like an actual bride being carried into the marriage chamber.

"Under no circumstance will I allow this!" I cry. But when I try to wriggle free, my body jiggles uselessly. It's humiliating and beyond infuriating, and even though I want to scream, I find myself giggling because Rowenna is giggling. I can practically feel her shaking with laughter.

Bravo, baby sister. He looks absolutely miserable. This is almost better than my naked climb.

"Imagine if I was naked too," I say between gasps.

Alaric's hands falter, and for a terrifying moment, I think he might drop me. "Why, in the name of the kings, would I imagine that?" he demands.

"I wasn't talking to *you*," I try to say, but a wave of nausea squeezes my stomach, and I vomit all down the front of his shirt.

Except he isn't wearing a shirt—because he's never wearing a shirt—so my vomit spatters Prince Alaric's fancy velvet jacket and clings to his bare chest like lumpy porridge.

"You are, without a doubt, the most vile and irritating person I've ever met," he grumbles.

"Thank you," I say as I wipe my mouth on his shoulder.

"Don't thank me—it wasn't a compliment."

"Coming from you, it most certainly was."

TEN

ALARIC MUTTERS CURSES FOR THE DURATION OF our trek up the mountain. As if I'm not equally appalled at the feel of his sweat seeping through my tunic and his wiry hair invading my mouth.

Unfortunately for both of us, his assistance is undeniably helpful. My lungs are slowly remembering how to fill, and the haze shimmering across my vision has finally dissipated.

"You can put me down now," I say when we reach the outer wall of the Fortress and the gargantuan black gate lowers like a drawbridge. "I want to walk."

I *need* to walk. The Vanzadorians will never respect me if I'm carried into their city like a simpering maiden. But Alaric strides across the gate before it has even stopped shuddering.

I pound my fists against his chest—and immediately regret it when my singed hand throbs painfully. "Put me down *now*," I command.

"And let you stagger about like a madwoman? You'll scare the children. Or trip and fall, and I'd *hate* for you to tumble over a cliff or scrape up that pretty face."

"Don't antagonize me." I thump him even harder—with my good hand this time.

"Can't I give my wife a compliment?"

"No," I say, wriggling like a worm.

Stop. Rowenna's command is so sharp and unexpected, I freeze. *Maybe it isn't a bad thing if they underestimate you*, she explains.

But I cut her off with a shake of my head. *Is this the first impression* you *would choose to make? We both know you wouldn't be caught dead being carried into the Fortress.*

Exactly. Her voice is soft, somber. *My methods clearly weren't the best.*

We're both quiet then, contemplating what she could have done differently. What *I* can possibly do to survive my time in Vanzador and make our oppressors pay.

While Rowenna and I have our quiet discourse, Alaric lugs me through another granite door. Once inside, I expect to find the sprawl of cold, labyrinthine streets and crude stone houses Ro described in her letters, but we must have come through a different entrance, because we emerge not into a filthy, unkempt slum but a spacious plaza that rivals the receiving courtyard in Tashir in size and beauty.

The air in here is still and warm, unlike the punishing wind outside the walls, and the orange glow of the setting sun dances across a mosaic floor made of swirling black onyx and white quartz. A gurgling fountain occupies the center of the square, and tidy rings of vendor carts ripple outward, offering breads and cheeses, as well as glittering stone necklaces and earrings.

Droves of people dressed in the scandalous Vanzadorian fashion—sheer lace dresses with plunging necklines and waistcoats corded in silver and gold—meander about with baskets in hand, giggling and gossiping, while groups of men and women wearing more practical tunics and trousers make their way toward gemstone mines indicated on wooden placards. Around the fountain, children play a game of tag while loose dogs bound through the chaos, gobbling up crumbs.

It's all so ordinary. So *normal*. If not for the ridiculous clothing, it could almost be the marketplace in Tashir.

Which is wrong.

Vanzador is *nothing* like Tashir.

As Alaric carries me across the square, the people slowly become aware of our presence. No one says or does anything overtly hostile, but each pointed finger makes me flinch. I'm surprised to feel Alaric flinching too, since the stares and whispers clearly aren't aimed at him. The people bow as he passes. Some eagerly wave and call his name. But he ignores them all, tightens his grip, and walks faster.

"Ah, there they are!" King Soren's voice booms from across the square, where he sits on a throne of chiseled quartz beneath a gaudy canopy. A valet holds a near-empty board of sliced meats at Soren's elbow, giving the impression he's been lounging there a very long while, awaiting our entrance.

A small contingent of men and women wearing stone-blue robes with tasseled caps surround their king, surveying the comings and goings of the square with a critical eye. Beyond them, groups of courtiers in elegant coats and dresses chat amiably with miners clad in dirt-streaked tunics. Despite the obvious disparity in rank, they all seem to be united by a common goal: winning King Soren's favor.

They gaze at their king as if he's as bright and life-giving as the sun itself, and jostle to get nearer to his warmth.

For his part, Soren smiles and laughs freely, and it's so contrary to the cruel tyrant who returned Rowenna in a coffin and left Tashir in ashes, I find myself wondering if it's the same man. Could he truly be such a skilled actor? Or are his people just that blind and naïve?

Soren stands and waves to his son. "Come, present your new bride!" he shouts for all to hear. "I'm glad to see you're attending to your husbandly duties—just as I taught you." He gestures to me in Alaric's arms and gives a theatrical wink that makes his audience titter. "But you had her all to yourself during your romantic stroll up the mountain. Let the rest of us bask in the splendor and charms of Miss Indira Harrak."

Soren smiles delightedly, and there are so many things wrong with this moment.

"I've also just heard the reports from the mines," Soren continues, nodding to the workers. "Your suggestion to widen the Pyrea Trench, rather than drilling deeper, proved most fruitful, my son. Come rub it in my face and bask in your accomplishment."

The miners stomp their feet and whoop loudly, and the courtiers join in with eager applause, but King Soren is more effusive than them all. He beams proudly and beckons for Alaric the way you would a puppy—not a nearly full-grown man. It's excessive, and more than a little embarrassing, but I also find it secretly endearing. I'd give anything for my parents to acknowledge my efforts with half as much enthusiasm.

I fully expect Alaric to bound over and accept his praise and head scratches, but one of the blue-robed spectators steps forward—an elderly man with long steel-gray hair.

Unlike the rest of the audience, he and his comrades aren't smiling. Or clapping. They stand with their heads tilted together and exchange furtive whispers that make

Alaric stiffen. His fingers curl into my skin with painful pressure as the old man lays a gentle hand on Soren's shoulder.

"Alaric's bride is clearly unwell from the climb, Your Majesty," he says to Soren, though his gaze is fixed doggedly on Alaric. "Go care for her, my prince. She needs you more than we do."

Tension crackles through Alaric's limbs, and his weight shifts slightly forward, reminding me of a cornered fox in the moment it must decide whether to attack or retreat to the safety of its den. For my sake, I sincerely hope it's the latter. I'd rather not be literally carried into battle.

Alaric's eyes dart between his father and the old man, and even though Soren is still smiling and the majority of the crowd is cheering, Alaric steps back with a deferential nod. "He's right, Father. I must attend to my wife. I'll meet you in your study to go over the mining reports once she's settled." Alaric turns and sets off across the square at an even brisker clip, ignoring his Father's calls to reconsider and the disappointed hum of the crowd.

I don't know what just passed between Alaric and the old man, and I don't believe for a second it had anything to do with my needs or comfort, but I happily let him carry me out of the sparkling square that's nothing like the Vanzador Rowenna described in her letters. Eager to get away from the merry, laughing king, who's somehow tricked his people into loving him.

Once we enter the castle proper, I'm certain I'll find the dark, loathsome underbelly of this place. The true Vanzador, where everything will make more sense.

Alaric steps quickly past the vendor stalls, under an enormous archway, and down an open-air corridor lined with statues of bobcats and mountain lions. As soon as we're out of view, he finally sets me down. "Keep up, or I'll be forced to carry you again," he warns.

I nod and follow him through a pebble garden and past smaller courtyards partitioned by fluttering sheer curtains. Every time we enter a new space, I expect the luxury to fall away—for decrepit tunnels and sewage-filled streets to reveal themselves, and for people to start hurling rocks and insults at me—but every interconnecting plaza is as grand as the next, and the people we pass watch with respectful interest—*if* they watch at all.

Servants, artisans, and errand boys go about their business with placid smiles, while courtiers sit cross-legged on cushions with one palm pressed into the earth and the other draped across their eyes. It's the same position Alaric assumed when praying on the Tomb Flats, and even though they look perfectly peaceful, unease scuttles down my neck like a spider.

My anxiety only grows when we enter the castle itself, because it doesn't feel like a dungeon either. The ceilings are high and vaulted, like an old forest letting in dappled sunlight through the leafy canopy. I find myself wondering if we could recreate something similar under the hill until Rowenna clucks her tongue.

Don't fall prey to their deception. You're better than this.

I glare at every vibrant tapestry and gleaming candelabra we pass, my guilt and disquiet steadily growing. I don't want to doubt Rowenna, but I can't deny what I'm seeing. There must be another explanation. Perhaps they blindfolded her and tossed her directly into a prison cell because they knew she was a threat, and they have no such fears about me?

I don't realize I've stopped walking until Alaric turns and glances back. It could be the shadows, but I'd swear he's suppressing a smirk. "What's the matter? Isn't our palace to your liking?"

"I've seen more than enough of the splendors of your kingdom. Just take me to the dungeon already."

"*Dungeon?*" He has the gall to sound confused—and amused.

"We both know that's where you intend to keep me. Rowenna sent letters detailing everything about her time here."

Alaric raises one dark brow. "I don't know what your sister told you, but she never set foot inside a prison cell. We treated her with the utmost care and hospitality, as promised by the treaty."

"I don't believe you."

"See for yourself." He leads me up a twisting flight

of stairs to a white-painted door. "Your sister occupied these very same rooms. Her belongings might still be in the drawers for all I know. We treated her exactly as we're treating you."

With a dubious scowl, I brush past him and prowl the perimeter of the room, blatantly checking for bars on the windows and padlocks on the doors. I find neither, but that doesn't mean there aren't other ways of locking someone in and holding them captive.

The space is twice as big as my chambers under the hill, and every corner is filled with exquisite stone furniture—a pink quartz vanity, a set of upholstered jade chairs, and a sleigh-style bed made of carved onyx. All of this pales in comparison to the walls themselves, though, which are made of gemstones from floor to ceiling. Amythest protrusions bloom like violets to my left. Emerald crenellations sprout like maple leaves to my right. There's turquoise, topaz, and opal, set ablaze by intense mountain sunlight that filters through the glass ceiling, filling the room with ever-changing rainbows.

It's breathtaking and, at the same time, makes me want to vomit, dredging up old memories of King Soren's first visit to Tashir—back when he still pretended to be our valiant rescuer. I'll never forget how he galloped through our fields on the shiniest horse I'd ever seen and vowed to save us from the Marauders. He even brought gifts for Rowenna and me—round stones that looked like nothing special from the outside, but when he split them in two, the centers revealed a world of spectacular color, just like this room.

He called them geodes. I called it magic. Now I know it was an omen. Soren has me trapped in the center of a geode—threating to cleave me in two.

My haversack slides from my shoulders and lands with a thump on the carpet.

"Well, what do you think?" Alaric asks, even though my horrified expression makes my feelings perfectly clear. "You have an opinion about everything. Don't hold back now."

I glare and hold my tongue, just to spite him.

"I'll leave you to settle in. My chamber is just around the corner, if you need anything," he says. But his sharp tone and acidic smile make it clear I'd better *not* need anything.

Before he vanishes, I call out, "How can you live with yourself?"

Alaric pauses and scrubs a hand over his face—as if I'm the one who's exhausting and unreasonable. "What are you talking about? We're treating you like a queen." He gestures around my glittering chamber, then widens the arc of his arm to encompass the entire walled city beyond.

"This is the room Rowenna occupied when she *died*. Don't you find that a bit insensitive? Not to mention *foreboding*?" I give him a critical look. "Or have you already forgotten you were married to my sister first?"

"I do my best to forget irritating people. Now, believe it or not, I have work to do that doesn't involve babysitting."

"Yes, I'm sure you're busy planning the raid of another vulnerable kingdom," I shout at his back. "Or perhaps the murder of your second wife!"

"The latter sounds more appealing every second," he says, slamming the door in my face.

I continue standing there, heaving for breath, my thoughts as erratic as the rainbow light refracting off the gemstone walls. I didn't expect a smooth transition to life on the mountain, but I didn't expect everything to feel so horribly *wrong* either.

Nothing is what I expected—or how Rowenna described in her letters. I'd blame the discrepancy on my poor reading comprehension or failing memory, but her descriptions were too vivid and visceral to forget. She described these rooms like a prison cell: cold thick walls without a single window, and a reeking chamber pot beside the bed.

Technically, none of it is a lie. She said the room was *like* a prison cell, not that it was one. And the part about the windows and chamber pot are true too. But it's hardly the whole truth. The entire ceiling is made of glass, so the room isn't dark and dreary, despite its lack of windows. And, in addition to the chamber pot, there's an en suite bathing room almost as large as this room.

"Was this truly your chamber?" I ask the echoing

room. "If so, why paint such a grim picture? Why lead me to believe you were imprisoned here when this castle is finer than the hillock palace in every way?"

Ro remains silent for so long, I think she's not going to answer. But then she says with a steely edge to her voice, *A gilded cage is still a cage, little sister.*

ELEVEN

SPEND ALL NIGHT INSPECTING MY ROOMS THE WAY I would a toxic plant. The gigantic feathered bed with a poker to see if it snaps shut like a Venus flytrap. Then I slowly pull down the gauzy bed curtains the way I'd pluck petals from the center of a poisonous flower.

There's a reason the Vanzadorians put me—and Rowenna, if Alaric is telling the truth—in this chamber. A reason she felt compelled to paint a distorted picture of this place in her letters, and I won't rest until I've uncovered them.

Hour after hour, I tear through the wardrobe, chests, and drawers, looking for letters or notes or baubles. Something personal, to prove my sister was actually here. But all I find are delicate lace gowns, silky bloomers, bejeweled gloves and stockings, and too many frilly shoes to count. All of which I toss to the floor.

Ro might have worn these things, but they didn't *belong* to her.

I kick through the mess of finery, despising each piece more. Then, as dawn peeks through the skylights, I stomp into the adjoining washroom, which of course, is as lavish as the rest of the palace. The bathtub is white marble swirled with soft coral pink, and bottles of every shape and size line the shelves. Towels as fluffy as freshly washed wool hang from bejeweled hooks, and tall crystal vases filled with scrub oak are artfully arranged across the countertop. It makes me want to scream, because it's all so different from the quarters Rowenna described in her letters. I know she would never lie to me, so if she insisted her time here was torturous, I believe her. Which means there's a reason for these discrepancies. Something she was trying to tell me.

I make my way past the vanity to a small door nestled in the corner of the washroom. I expect to find a linen closet or laundry chute, but the door swings into a much larger, darker space. While I grapple about for a lantern or torch, my legs slam into something hard, and I pitch forward with a scream. I close my eyes and brace myself to hit the unforgiving stone floor, but I land on something soft and lumpy instead.

Something that groans and *moves* beneath me.

I scream again and stumble back into the washroom, crashing into the tub so hard I nearly fall in. "Who are you? And what are you doing in my rooms?" I demand as I fumble for something to use as a weapon. When my hands close around a long-handled scrubbing brush, I laugh bitterly. I'm certain no one has ever *washed* an assailant to death, but I raise it like a sword anyway.

"Come out!" I command, cursing the tremor in my voice.

After a long second, there's a soft creak, followed by a shamble of feet. A thin oval face appears in the doorway, and I don't know what I was expecting—perhaps the mysterious hooded assassin who murdered Rowenna, not a girl who looks to be my age. She has thick golden hair that hangs in a rumpled braid, and she's wearing a plain black shift. A ratty blanket falls around her shoulders and her eyes blink furiously, still heavy with sleep.

"I-I live here," she stammers. "In case you need anything. B-but I don't have to, if it's not to your liking." Frantic, like a bird whose nest has been discovered by a fox, she retreats into the dark and begins dragging something that makes a horrid metallic screech.

"You *live* in here?" I ask, venturing back toward the door. "Like a maid?"

We don't keep maids in Tashir. Not personal ones. Every hand is far more useful tending to the hillock palace as a whole, and most especially, in the fields.

The girl nervously blathers as she attempts to angle a cot through the door. "I'll take my things to the hall. Or back to the balcony, like Miss Rowenna preferred. Though the wind is bitter cold at night."

"Wait... Did you say Rowenna?"

The girl gives a little nod but refuses to meet my eyes.

"You worked for my sister?" I rush toward her—a bee drawn to nectar—but when I'm still several lengths away, she drops the cot with a shriek and holds her arms above her head.

I freeze and raise my hands to show her I'm not a threat. "It's okay—" I start to say, but she gives another shriveled cry and dodges past me. Swifter than a jackrabbit, she bolts into the bedchamber, and by the time I turn and follow, the door to the hallway hangs open, and her blanket is all that remains of her, strewn across the ground like a rumpled rug.

I pick it up, rubbing the worn fabric between my fingers. Why did the girl act as if *I* was the terrifying stranger hiding in the dark? And flinch as if she expected me to strike her? If I didn't know better, I'd think she was scared of Rowenna—and me by extension—but my sister rarely yelled at the servants in Tashir and certainly never struck one. Obviously, she wasn't pleased to go to Vanzador as Alaric's captive bride, but she wouldn't have taken out her anger and frustration on a maid—not even a Vanzadorian one. Perhaps the girl just assumed Ro would be as cruel as Soren and Alaric because that's all she's ever known. Or maybe she was part of the plot to kill Rowenna, and now she's frightened that I've come for vengeance.

That would explain why Rowenna banished the girl to the balcony. She could sense her duplicity.

My gaze flits back to the toppled cot and the shadowed maid's quarters beyond. The girl might not look dangerous, but appearances can be deceiving. She knows something. There's a reason she's so scared.

I retrieve a honeysuckle candle from the vanity and carefully approach the cupboard door. The space is even smaller than I realized—musty and cold, with a low ceiling and walls of dark-stained wood. It would probably feel suffocating to most, but the space wallops me with a heap of homesickness because it feels like Tashir. The peaceful, embracing dark of under the hill.

The serving girl doesn't have much. There's a small trunk in the corner, a pillow that must have fallen from the cot, and several black uniform dresses scattered haphazardly across the floor. Nothing personal or sentimental. I raise the candle higher and move toward the walls, looking for pictures or trinkets. Anything that will give me information about this strange, suspicious girl.

Instead, I find carvings.

Crude, angry hash marks have been viciously cut into the boards, clearly counting something. Days? Or weeks? And around the hash marks, the same three words are scrawled over and over again:

BLOOD, FLESH, BONE.
BLOOD, FLESH, BONE.

Sometimes the letters are small and neat. Other times, they're slashing and unwieldy, sideways and upside-down.

I back away with a terrified yelp and crash into the opposite wall. But that only makes me scream louder, because these boards are covered with the same haunting words. Along with a name, cut clear and deep into the wood.

Rowenna's name.

The letters are jagged and uneven, as if carved in a hurry—or with extreme force.

I tell myself to breathe, but it feels like my head is trapped underwater. Like I'm tumbling end over end down a flooded irrigation ditch. No matter how innocent and frightened the serving girl seemed, she clearly had a grudge against my sister. And she's clearly not of a sound mind. I can't have someone like that living in my rooms. Or roaming freely about the Fortress. Not if I want to survive long enough to avenge Rowenna.

I let out a garbled cry, wishing I could curl up in a ball and sleep for days. Pretend this is a bad dream, and when I wake up, Ro will be alive, and we'll be back in Tashir. But I couldn't have imagined this terrible, eerie room, not even in my worst nightmares. And sitting here, in the chamber Ro occupied when she died, is more likely to result in *my* murder than answers. So despite the terror taking root in my chest and the humiliating prospect of admitting I need Alaric's help after *one* night, I clench my fists and march into the hall.

"Take me to Prince Alaric's rooms," I order the guards I expect to find outside my chamber. But only silence echoes back. The hall is empty and eerily quiet in either direction. No guards. Not a single servant.

Where is everyone? The hillock palace is always teeming like a beehive, especially near the royal residences. The wrongness of it all makes me stumble over my feet.

"Hello?" I call out again.

Rowenna's voice is the only one that answers: *Who needs guards on top of a mountain no enemy can reach?*

Tingling with unease, I hurry around the corner and knock on the first door I come to. It also happens to be the only door I come to.

"Alaric?"

No answer.

I pound harder. "I demand an audience!" I yell, refusing to utter the word *help*. "I found disturbing carvings in my chambermaid's room. Threatening things about blood, flesh, and bone, along with my sister's name."

It isn't until the words are out that I realize *he* could be responsible. He could have carved the threats himself. Or ordered my maid to do it. It could be a ploy to keep me fumbling and reeling. To bring me running for help.

"Was it you?" I slam my fist against the wood with all my strength. "Is this your idea of a *welcoming gift*?"

At last, I hear movement—the shuffle of feet and a sharp intake of breath—but it comes from behind me, not within Alaric's chamber.

I'm not alone in this hall.

TWELVE

WHIRL AROUND, WISHING FOR THE THOUSANDTH time I had a weapon, but the fight goes out of me as I take in the stranger. A girl, dressed in a lacy skirt and plunging amethyst bodice, is pressed against the opposite wall of the corridor. She's flouncing and feminine in every way, with deep brown skin that glows in the candlelight, long braids that are twisted into intricate loops, and soft brown eyes that blink at me with horror—as if *I* snuck up on *her*.

Just like my infuriating maid.

Apparently, I have this effect on everyone in this blooming country.

"Who are you? And what do you want?" I demand.

"Forgive the intrusion," she says tentatively, "but I heard you yelling and thought I should inform you His Royal

Highness is in the king's council chamber. The meet each morning and won't be finished until suppertime."

She smiles, as if she's simply being helpful, but my frown deepens. The only way she could have heard me yelling is if she was already in this private wing of the castle. And if she knew Alaric would be gone, it means she came here looking specifically for *me*.

I cross my arms and blatantly look her up and down. She doesn't look dangerous, but then, neither does pretty, purple bagrava fruit.

"Who are you? And what are you doing here?" I demand again.

"I'm Elodie Tomasko, daughter of Councilwoman Tomasko," the girl says with an outlandish curtsy. "And I came to introduce myself, of course. I wanted to be the first to meet the new Tashiri princess."

She smooths her dress and ventures a hopeful smile, but I'm far too tired and on edge to deal with social climbers already. I turn on my heel and march back toward my chamber, muttering, "I'd hardly call myself *new*. I've been a princess all my life."

The girl follows, giggling into her gloved hand as if I just said the most amusing thing she's ever heard. "You're quite the comedian. Her Majesty, Queen Tessa, is going to adore you."

"I sincerely hope not."

"Just as she adored Rowenna," Elodie continues prattling. "We *all* adored Ro."

My sister's nickname freezes me in place.

I slowly spin back around. "*You* knew Rowenna?"

The noble girl laughs and taps my shoulder with the lacy fan dangling from her wrist. "Of course. I knew her even better than I know myself."

"You're lying."

She has to be. Rowenna would have never befriended a member of King Soren's court. She rarely interacted with our own courtiers in Tashir. She was always too busy running the kingdom. And when she did have downtime, she preferred to spend it with me and sometimes Haddesh. She adored our people, of course, but she was happiest when it was just the two of us. We both were.

Elodie blinks at me with big watery eyes. "I assure you, Rowenna and I are the dearest of friends. Or we *were* the dearest of friends," she softly amends. "I still cry every night when I think of her. Ro was like the sister I never had. She, of course, had you," she adds meekly, "but I like to think I was a second sister to her—her Vanzadorian sister. She must have mentioned me in her letters?"

Rowenna would never *consider a Vanzadorian her sister*, I want to snap. But when Elodie's brown eyes lift cautiously to mine, they look so lost, so genuinely sad, I bite back my cutting remarks. Whether or not it's true, if she fancies herself Ro's best friend, it would be unwise to dismiss her before I mine her for information.

"Elodie Tomasko..." I tap my chin. "Why, *yes*. Yes, of course! Rowenna mentioned you at length."

The girl beams and takes both of my hands in hers. "Oh, it's such a relief to finally meet you, Indira. You're the only person who understands the depth of my grief. I still can't fathom a world without Rowenna, but at least we're together now. You and I shall carry each other through these dark days and fill the void in the other's heart. We will never forget or replace Rowenna, of course," she says solemnly. "But she'd want us to carry on in her memory, don't you think?"

My mind flashes back to Lewis saying this very thing outside my chamber window the morning of Ro's funeral, and I decide he and Elodie would make a fine, brainless pair.

She sniffles loudly and stares with tearful intensity, which is when I realize her question isn't rhetorical. She actually expects me to validate her declaration and seal our bond of friendship.

"Um, yes. I suppose that *is* what Rowenna would want," I say cautiously. "Perhaps she even led you to me now, in this moment. I'm having a bit of trouble with my maid, you see, and I need someone to help me find—"

"It looks like you're having a *lot* of trouble with your maid," Elodie interrupts, crinkling her nose as she looks me up and down.

Despite the wardrobe full of luxurious gowns in my chamber, I'm still wearing the same disgusting trousers and tunic I wore across the Tomb Flats. They're stiff with dried sweat and blood, and I know I smell worse than a group of ten-year-old boys picking strawberries in high summer, but I refuse to don the Vanzadorians' finery.

"Do you know the serving girl?" I press. "Did Ro have trouble with her too?"

But Elodie isn't listening. "I can't believe she let you leave your chamber in such a state. Not to worry. I'll fix you up before anyone sees."

"But—"

Elodie links her arm through mine and tugs me down the corridor, in the opposite direction of my room and the carvings. We bustle through another, more crowded wing of the palace and into a room with shockingly green marble pillars. No fewer than ten mirrored vanities stand along the back wall, and I choke on a cloud of cloying oleander perfume as Elodie positions me in front of one. With her fingers tapping her chin, she circles me three times, her frown deepening with each revolution.

Then, without a word of warning, she yanks on my belt buckle so hard, my pants nearly come off with it.

"What are you doing?" I grapple for the waistband.

Elodie gives me a wry look in the mirror, then firmly shakes her braids. "You can't wear this to the queen's salon."

"The *queen's salon*?" I repeat, unable to keep the horror from my voice. "Why would I go there?"

"Because that's where *everyone* passes the day."

"Not me."

"Rowenna never missed a salon," Elodie says with hushed reverence. "She said they reminded her of the many lavish teas and soirees she hosted in Tashir."

While I stutter with surprise, Elodie deftly tugs my arms out of my tunic and forces me into a tub full of fragrant, soapy water.

The closest thing we've ever had to a soiree was Rowenna's funeral. Our celebrations are always about the harvest and the land itself. About coming together and sharing Earth Mother's bounty with all, not a select few nobles in a gilded parlor. Ro would have hated being stuffed into a flashy gown and made to chat with pompous courtiers. She hardly interacted with our own nobility, aside from accepting their thanks. They would praise her beauty and admire her cunning and strength, and she would share her plans to bring even more prosperity to Tashir, but they were hardly *friendly*. Which is further proof Elodie is lying. She didn't know my sister at all.

"What else did Ro tell you about Tashir?" I ask as Elodie scrubs my skin raw.

"Oh, not much. She rarely mentioned your country. She was eager to leave the dull, dirty fields behind. She said she felt like she could finally breathe up here in the dazzling mountain air, surrounded by finer people and amenities."

Even though I know it isn't true, the words still land like a gut punch.

When I suck in a painful breath, Elodie's hand flies to her mouth, and she looks down sheepishly. "Oh, I didn't mean—I'm sorry if that's difficult to hear. Ro missed *you* terribly, of course. You were the bright spot amidst the doldrums of such a *simple* life."

I nod my head and dredge up a small smile, but inside, my mind is spinning. Rowenna loved Tashir. I know it as surely as I know she loved me. She must have used these false declarations to ingratiate herself with the Vanzadorians. She needed to gain their trust in order to uncover their weaknesses.

Exactly, Ro whispers with approval. *It was all a part of my plan*.

"Tell me more about Ro's time in the Fortress," I say as Elodie towels me off and tugs a shift over my head.

"Oh, Rowenna was an absolute delight! She was so good at matching the perfect skirt with the perfect bodice. And she could make anyone's eyes look twice as large with that pot of sandalwood ash she brought from Tashir. What's it called? Kohl?"

Once again, I can't breathe, and it has nothing to do with Elodie cinching the stays of my dress. "Rowenna did your *makeup*? And consulted on your dresses?"

Not once in my entire life did my sister apply kohl to her own eyes. She would hardly sit still for Mother's maids to paint her face on her wedding day. And she didn't even *own* a proper gown in Tashir, yet I'm supposed to believe she willingly played dress-up with girls like Elodie?

"And she was *such* a splendid dancer," Elodie prattles on, oblivious. "And a magnificent hostess. Her luncheons were second to none. Never have you seen such darling finger sandwiches!"

Every painfully wrong word jabs my flesh like a beesting. Rowenna could be charming when she needed to be, but she was never a social butterfly by nature. She preferred to earn the admiration and respect of our people through her work not her parties. Could she really have carried out such an elaborate act the entire time she was in Vanzador?

Elodie clears her throat. "Prince Alaric will be at the salon too," she says with a mischievous grin.

"All the more reason not to go," I say firmly.

"But don't you need to speak with him? I found you banging on his chamber door. It sounded urgent." She gazes at me with exaggerated concern, clearly waiting for me to divulge my secrets. When I don't, she lowers her voice, even though we're alone in this room. "Are you having a lovers' quarrel already?"

A sharp laugh escapes me. "That would require being in love in the first place."

Elodie joins in laughing and smacks my shoulder again with her fan. "There's no need to be bashful. Every eligible girl on this mountain is in love with Prince Alaric. It's impossible *not* to be smitten by that handsome face. Plus have you caught a glimpse when his jacket falls open?" Elodie mimes fanning herself. "You should have seen how Rowenna giggled and swooned over him. She and I would often stay up late dissecting their every interaction."

"*No*," I blurt.

Just one word, but it echoes around us like thunder.

Ro may have pranced about the castle in these hideous dresses and gossiped with silly courtiers like Elodie, but she *never* would have fawned over Alaric Alaverdi. It's too much. Too degrading and contrary to the core of who she was and what she wanted. The more Elodie says about Rowenna's time in Vanzador, the more I'm convinced she was never here. She was body snatched crossing the Tomb Flats, and a changeling was sent in her place.

I strain to hear Ro's voice through the silence, certain she must have a reasonable explanation, but for once my sister is oddly quiet.

"Forgive me," Elodie says gently. "I've clearly said too much. It must be strange to be married to the same man as your sister. To worry and compare your relationship to theirs. But I have no doubt you'll win Alaric's affection in no time. Look at you—you're stunning in your own right. Our fashion suits you so splendidly!"

She takes me by the shoulders and turns me to face the mirrors, each of them reflecting from a slightly different angle.

It's all I can do not to scream.

My sister's blue-tinged, white-lipped corpse looks back at me from each pane of glass. It's all I will ever be able to see when I look at these lacy Vanzadorian gowns.

Elodie mistakes my gasp of horror for delight. "You're quite welcome," she says as she links her arm through mine and pulls me back into the hall. Apparently, we're required to hold hands everywhere we go.

Elodie escorts me through parlor after endless parlor, nattering on about which courtiers I should befriend, who is feuding with whom, and how I mustn't, under any circumstance, mention Lady Hawthorne's recently deceased child. I want to point out that I didn't even know of the child's existence, let alone death, but Elodie is already on to the next subject. And I'm too gobsmacked by each opulent ballroom and ostentatious parlor we pass to dwell on it.

Soren's castle is luxury, purely for the sake of luxury. Greed for the sake of greed.

At last, we stop before a mint green door trimmed in gold, and Elodie takes both of my hands. "Are you ready to make your debut?" When I don't answer, she leans closer, squeezes my fingers, and says, "Don't worry. I'll be stitched to your side the entire time."

As if this should be a comfort.

She thrusts her shoulder against the double doors, and we parade into a world of a thousand dancing colors. It's so bright, I don't know where to look first. The room is packed with whipping fans and swishing gowns in every shade of blush and chartreuse. Men stride by in velvety vermilion coats and boots with diamond-studded buckles. And glittering above it all, casting everything in its rich, vibrant glow, is a stained-glass window made of deep indigo and sunrise yellow panes that perfectly capture the contrast of night and day.

Before I have time to fully take in the beauty—though I would never admit to doing such a thing—the chatter of the room falls away and every head turns to look at us.

When you spend as much time in the fields as I do, you see a fair amount of wildlife. Some of it's harmless, though annoying—like the rabbits and squirrels that nibble our produce. I'd put Elodie firmly in this category. But there are predators out there too. Pumas hide in the tall grass at the edge of the growing fields. Bears lumber through the stone walls. I've come face-to-face with a wolf, nose-to-nose with a fox. All of which were less terrifying than this room full of Vanzadorian nobles.

Beads of sweat stipple my hairline, and my throat feels as thick and itchy as it does each spring when the pollen swirls. The urge to wrench free from Elodie's hold and sprint back through the doors is overwhelming, but I keep my feet rooted to the spot. I need answers. Which means I need to experience Ro's life here. See what she saw. Meet who she met. Act how she acted.

Drawing a deep breath through my nose, I raise my chin and summon my best imitation of her enigmatic smile as Elodie tugs me forward, presenting me with a dramatic sweep of her arm. "Look who I found!"

But none of the fifty or so courtiers in attendance utters a word of greeting. They simply stare at me with bored eyes and bland smiles.

"This is Rowenna's sister, Indira." Elodie tries again.

Still, no reaction.

"Rowenna was Prince Alaric's former Tashiri bride," she says with a hint of irritation. "And now Indira is his new bride." She gestures to me again.

Finally, a few heads nod, though most continue staring. I swear someone even whispers they didn't know the first bride was gone—which shouldn't be possible if Rowenna truly spent *every day* in this salon.

After what feels like a lifetime, a middle-aged woman in the center of the throng speaks, her voice as crisp and devastating as late spring frost.

"Indira Harrak... *Come*. Let me look at you."

THIRTEEN

I KNOW THIS WOMAN IS MY MOTHER-IN-LAW, QUEEN Tessa, even though no one introduces her as such and the courtiers surrounding her are just as finely dressed. It's the way she carries herself—the haughty tilt of her chin, the exquisite line of her jaw, and the raven black hair, tumbling over her shoulders in shining waves.

She bears a striking resemblance to her son, which makes me instantly dislike her. Her icy appraisal doesn't help.

"Turn," Queen Tessa commands with a little twirl of her finger.

The men and women surrounding her titter, and my cheeks flame.

Did they subject Ro to such humiliation? I can't imagine her standing here, taking this.

I shouldn't stand for it either. This is the precise sort of cowardice that allowed the Vanzadorians to take my sister in the first place. A character flaw I no doubt inherited from Father. But, unlike him, I can choose to act. Fight.

I take a deep breath and tighten my fists, but Rowenna interjects before I can speak.

Let them laugh now, little sister. We'll be laughing in the end.

Why would I back down now when I've finally summoned the courage to stand up for myself and for you? I silently argue.

Patience, Ro says soothingly. *It will all be worth the wait.*

I don't want to wait. Waiting feels like the exact opposite of what Rowenna would do, but I trust her instincts more than my own, so I grit my teeth and begin a slow, humiliating rotation.

"Stop, Indira! *Stop!*" Queen Tessa lets out a great whinny of laughter before I complete the turn, and the rest of the room joins in. "I was only teasing. I never dreamed you'd actually comply. Do you truly think us so monstrous?"

Yes, I want to say. *You killed my sister.*

But I can practically *feel* Rowenna's cold dead hand plastered across my lips.

Queen Tessa pats the striped divan beside her and smiles. "Please, join me. There's no need to be shy. We're family now."

That word, and her sudden shift in demeanor, is so jarring, I stand there like a pumpkin rotting on the vine. How can she go from inspecting me like livestock to proclaiming me *family* in a matter of seconds?

"Go on." Elodie ushers me forward. "Her Majesty simply likes to have a little fun. She's quite fond of pranks—it's one of the reasons she and Rowenna got along so well."

"*What?*" Every time I think I've gotten my bearings here on the mountain, the soil shifts and the ground slides out from under me again.

Rowenna *did* love pranks. When we were young, she'd do little things like swap the sugar for the salt and laugh hysterically as Birdie chased her around the ovens. And she loved nothing more than to pester Father's irritating advisors. We'd plop frogs in their porridge or exchange official scrolls with scandalous love letters we penned ourselves, then listen at the door of their meetings as they babbled with embarrassment.

But why would Ro reveal that side of herself *here*? When none of this was supposed to be real?

"Forgive me for playing that little trick on you," Queen Tessa says as I thump down hard on the divan beside her. "It was clearly too soon. I can't imagine how difficult losing your sister must have been. Not to mention growing up in such a *grueling* environment. But that's all behind you now. I have no doubt you'll adjust to life in Vanzador as splendidly as Rowenna did."

She smiles kindly and pats my arm, and it's too much.

Rowenna is dead! I want to scream. *Last I checked, there's nothing* splendid *about that.*

But the words won't come—probably because Rowenna's still holding my voice box in her death grip.

You'll never learn anything useful if you're hostile.

"Now, tell us all about yourself, Indira," Queen Tessa says with a delighted clap. "What's the single most memorable thing about you?"

I narrow my eyes and hold my tongue because they already *know* the "most memorable" thing about me. It's the reason Soren brought me here.

"Go on," Elodie prods, "don't be shy."

Instead of answering, I ask, "What did Rowenna consider to be the most memorable thing about herself?"

Queen Tessa looks up at the intricate ceiling tiles with a thoughtful expression. Then she says on a breathy sigh, "Rowenna was such a delight. So witty and charming. She truly embraced our way of life. I often forget she wasn't one of us by birth."

Her musings receive a bevy of appreciative nods, even though she didn't answer my question. I don't care what the queen of Vanzador thought of my sister. I want to know what Rowenna said about herself.

"And she hosted the loveliest luncheons," an elderly woman with a pouf of purple-gray hair says, corroborating Elodie's claims.

"Let's not forget the time she asked if she could try her hand at stone throwing," a muscular man with a thick black mustache adds. "I'm certain she would have excelled at it, too, had it been fitting for our future queen to engage in such antics."

This elicits even more smiles and laughs, and I almost find myself smiling too. I'm not surprised they have so many fond memories of her. Ro was gregarious and impressive and thrived in the spotlight. Even though they didn't know the *real* version of her, they clearly admired the version she let them see.

Though, if that were true, how did she end up dead at the bottom of a cliff?

"Her tenacity," a young man standing near the door interjects, pulling me back from my thoughts. He's dressed the same as the people who were gathered around Soren when Alaric carried me into the Fortress—his smooth copper skin gleaming against stone-blue robes and the tassel on his cap a perfect complement to his deep auburn hair. He holds my gaze with startling intensity as he repeats himself. "Rowenna said the most memorable thing about her was her tenacity."

The attention of the entire room shifts from me to this boy, who seems to grow taller as he confidently continues. "Rowenna told us a story about a surprise party you threw for your mother. It was flower-fairy themed, and the two of you made everyone wings of chicken wire and tulle, and decorated the gardens with jars of fireflies and flower garlands. But it rained the night of the celebration, and everything was ruined. The rest of you lamented the unfortunate timing and were ready to move on, but Rowenna refused to accept defeat. She didn't eat, do her lessons, or leave your chambers until the entire kingdom agreed to recreate the party—down to the smallest detail—and pretend the first had never happened."

The courtiers shoot the young man quizzical looks. Several shake their heads and whisper. Elodie insists Rowenna never told such a tale and whisks me off into other conversations. But I can't stop glancing back at the copper-haired boy, whose eyes remain fixed on me as the hours pass. Insistent and unabashed.

More than once, I try to slip away and corner him. I need to know who he is and how he knew my sister. But Elodie and the queen's ladies are harder to escape than a briar patch. Every time I try to get away, I become more entangled. I'm almost relieved when the door bangs open and King Soren saunters into the room, signaling the end of the salon. Alaric and at least a dozen blue-robed men and women follow.

"Ah, excellent. Just the Tashiri daughter-in-law I was hoping to find!" Soren booms in the same jovial voice he used in the square. "What do you say to a little predinner show?" he asks the gathered crowd.

The courtiers erupt with applause, and dread curls

through my chest like a thorny vine. The only reason they'd be excited for a "show" from me is if they're already aware of my ability to grow bagrava.

Does the entire seeds-forsaken mountain know my secret?

King Soren rummages around in his waistcoat and makes a production of kneeling before me, holding out a tiny purple seed in the center of his palm. "Would you regale us with your talents, darling Indira?"

My eyes dart from Soren's wide ugly face to the perfect, delicate bagrava seed. They couldn't be more opposite. They have no business being this close.

I lurch to my feet and stumble past Soren, feeling like I'm going to vomit. I don't know where I'm going, but I have to get out of here. Away from the Vanzadorian king and the treason he expects me to commit against Tashir.

I knew he'd demand I grow bagrava, of course. He made his expectations clear. I just didn't expect to be ambushed so soon—in front of an audience. I don't want to show these people this most sacred inner part of me. It's bad enough they take the harvested bagrava; they can't have my connection with Earth Mother too.

Unfortunately, I only make it two steps before I slam into a rock-hard chest.

Alaric's chest.

Our eyes meet, but he quickly averts his gaze.

"Bring your blushing bride back over here," Soren

commands his son. "There's no need to be shy, Indira," he adds, flashing me a sickly sweet smile. "We're all great admirers of your work. Won't you honor us with a short demonstration?"

"No." The word comes out in a humiliating squeak, but it's something. A few short days ago, I wouldn't have had the courage to disagree with Soren at all, especially in front of a crowd.

King Soren's smile falters a fraction. "Perhaps my new daughter just needs some encouragement?" He looks to the courtiers, who clap even louder.

The sound is thunderous. Maddening. I press my hands over my ears.

Soren motions again to Alaric, who grits his teeth and moves forward, hands outstretched to drive me back.

"Enough!" Queen Tessa's voice rings out over the clamor, and the salon instantly falls quiet. The next thing I know, she's at my side, draping her arm around my shoulders and ushering me away from her son and husband. "That's quite enough. You're going to give the poor girl a heart attack. Indira only just arrived. She's clearly terrified and exhausted. I won't tolerate such cruelty in my salon."

Soren's grin remains intact, but now it's brittle at the edges. "I'd hardly call this cruelty, my dear. We're simply helping Indira feel comfortable and welcome. This is what she'd be doing in Tashir, after all."

"It's too much." Queen Tessa firmly shakes her head.

"In fact, all of this is too much. Too many people, too much commotion. Why don't you all head to dinner?" She points to Soren, Alaric, and their robed followers, as well as the majority of the courtiers. "Indira, my ladies, and I will join you shortly—once she's had a chance to catch her breath."

To my shock, Alaric is the first to head for the door, without a word of complaint. The courtiers follow with only a few whispers and backward glances. Soren lets out a laborious sigh but eventually nods.

"Your heart is too big, my love," he says as he kisses the back of Queen Tessa's hand. But his tone makes it sound more like a criticism than a compliment. "Don't tarry too long—I'd hate for your food to get cold."

"We shan't be but a minute," Tessa says as she plucks her hand free.

Still, Soren doesn't move, and they stare silently at each other, having an entire conversation with their eyes. Finally, he turns and strides out of the salon, leaving me alone with the queen and her ladies—and Elodie, of course.

Queen Tessa leads me back to the divan and pulls me down beside her. "Forgive my husband. He means well, but his enthusiasm can be overwhelming."

I remain silent because I *don't* forgive her husband, nor do I think he means well.

Queen Tessa gives my hand a squeeze, prompting me to look at her. "Now, where were we before Soren so rudely interrupted?"

"Indira was going to tell us more about herself," Elodie chimes in, flashing me an encouraging look. But I'm too shaken to play along. Too exhausted to lie and scheme, or attempt to learn anything useful from these women. I just want to retreat to my chamber.

Flee back to Tashir, if I'm honest.

Slowly, and with perfect gentility, the queen runs the back of her fingers down my cheek, smiling when a full-bodied shiver overtakes me. "Rowenna was happy here. In time, you will be too. We'll give you everything you could ever want. All you have to do is truly ingratiate yourself with our kingdom. Give yourself—and your gifts—over to Vanzador, as she did."

On the surface, Queen Tessa's words are kind, her tone honey-sweet, which is what makes it even worse than Soren's direct approach. She didn't swoop in and rescue me from her husband out of concern for my comfort or well-being. She's simply attacking from a different angle, ambushing me with kindness so I'll let down my guard and agree to grow bagrava.

I lean away from her and, in a quiet but firm voice, say, "You can ask a thousand different ways, but my answer won't change. I refuse to grow bagrava. Your husband has more than enough power."

To my surprise, Queen Tessa laughs, and her ladies join in—all except Elodie, who is inordinately focused on a small string trailing from her gloves.

"Who said anything about my husband or his power?" Queen Tessa asks, still chuckling. She and her ladies exchange a wicked look; then she motions to servants waiting in the wings. A moment later, they emerge carrying trays laden with steaming pots and pretty painted cups. I gag as they begin to pour because the liquid streaming into my teacup is purple—a rich, velvety purple that burns my nostrils with its foul odor.

Only one plant on the continent is this particular color. Only one plant emits this gag-inducing stench.

Queen Tessa brings a cup to her lips, closes her eyes, and inhales the steam with a blissful sigh. "We've always had to ration our bagrava tea so carefully, but now *you* can grant us this small favor in exchange for our hospitality. It seems a fair trade, don't you think?"

I want to knock the cup out of Queen Tessa's hands, but my own hands are shaking too hard. "*Ration* it?" I finally sputter. "You're not supposed to consume bagrava at all! You've seen the Marauders!"

"Do I look unhinged?" Queen Tessa takes a long slow sip, then gestures to her ladies. "Do any of us?"

The women regard me over the tops of their steaming cups, clear-eyed and perfectly poised.

It's unsettling. Not to mention impossible.

"Unlike the Marauders, we've conducted trials to find a dosage that can be consumed without adverse effects," Queen Tessa explains.

"I don't believe you," I argue.

Many Tashiri rebels have gone against Earth Mother's counsel and have experimented like this—hoping to discover a way to feed the blessed plant to themselves rather than the ground. But every attempt resulted in disaster: addiction and tremors, aggression and madness. None of the benefits could ever outweigh the cost. And if my own people couldn't find a way to manipulate the bagrava for safe consumption, I refuse to believe the Vanzadorians have somehow managed it.

"We're in no danger of losing ourselves," Queen Tessa insists, "only enjoying ourselves. In fact, I think we'd all agree we're most content while sipping our daily libation."

"Your *daily* libation?" I repeat, as they jovially clink their glasses. "You drink our bagrava *every day*?"

"Once it's given in tribute, is it not ours to do with as we please?" Queen Tessa counters.

Don't engage, Rowenna begs. *It will change nothing.*

But the bagrava has never been, and will never be, *theirs*.

I shoot to my feet, outrage spewing from my lips, "My people aren't breaking their backs so you can sit in this gilded room and drink our life source for pleasure!"

I can't believe Soren would allow this, that he'd sacrifice even a portion of his fuel for such frivolity.

Queen Tessa patiently waits for me to finish before saying offhandedly, "I'm surprised you're so upset.

Rowenna didn't seem to have a problem with our tea. In fact, she often partook herself." She grins, knowing the revelation will fracture the bedrock of my soul.

You *partook*? I silently accuse gasp at Rowenna. *How could you?*

What other choice did I have? If I had exploded with outrage, they'd have instantly mistrusted and dismissed me. It would have ruined my chances to worm my way into their confidence. Sometimes sacrifices must be made, lines must be crossed. I thought you of all people would understand this. Understand me.

Her accusation lands like a slap across the face, and I stagger backward.

"Are you okay? You look a bit unwell, Indira," Elodie says.

"I fear this dreadful conversation has made us all a bit unwell," Queen Tessa laments as she sets aside her empty teacup. "Thankfully, that can be remedied. Come, let's pray and recenter ourselves. Begin again, and forget these little foibles."

I'm about to point out these are hardly "little foibles," but the queen and her ladies are already settling down onto the plush carpeting. Queen Tessa claps twice, and the young man in the blue tasseled hat, the one who recounted Rowenna's memory of Mother's surprise party, enters the room. He circles us slowly, watching as the queen and her ladies press one hand into the ground and drape the other over their eyes—just like Alaric in our marriage tent and the people in the square when we entered the Fortress.

Elodie shoots me an encouraging glance before she covers her eyes, but I remain where I am, standing rigidly above them—until the young man in the tasseled hat approaches. Without a word of warning, he places his hands on my shoulders and presses me toward the ground.

"What are you doing?" I cry.

I try to knock his hands away, but he easily subdues me, forcing my hands into the same position as the others. Then he leans in close and whispers, "They need to believe I've forced your obedience. When I release you, remain in this position and follow their actions, but don't close your eyes."

I nod, even though I have every intention of bolting the moment he releases me. But when the boy eases back, his hazel eyes are soft and earnest, gazing at me with the same quiet reverence as when he recounted Ro's memory.

Holding a finger to his lips, he stomps his foot once, and Queen Tessa and the other women begin to rock and mutter. He motions for me to do the same as he slowly circles us three times. Then, after another stomp, Queen Tessa and her ladies pick themselves up off the ground. They pat their cheeks and smooth their hair, all of them remarking on how refreshed and recentered they feel. Almost as if awaking from a collective dream.

The boy coughs and spears me with a glare until I

awkwardly mimic the others—blinking, yawning, and fluffing my dress.

Without another word to any of us, he marches out of the room, leaving me to wonder why he would help me. And *how*, exactly, he helped.

Queen Tessa drifts back to the sofa, and her ladies follow, curiously watching me and whispering behind their fans. Elodie rolls her eyes at them and mumbles things like, "*Rowenna's sister*" and "*just arrived*," just like she did when I first entered the salon. As if we haven't spent the past few hours together.

Queen Tessa sinks into the sofa with a contented sigh and pats the cushion beside her. "Indira Harrak, my son's new bride. Come, let me look at you."

At first, I think she's calling back to the prank she played earlier—literally "returning" to the beginning of our acquaintance to start again. But she doesn't laugh or even crack a smile. Neither do her ladies. And when I fail to obey, she thumps the cushion harder.

With a growing sense of unease, I shuffle back to the divan and perch awkwardly beside the Vanzadorian queen. She takes my face in her hands and studies my features intently, as if she's never laid eyes on me before. "Tell me," she says, her voice lilting and mischievous, "what's the single most memorable thing about you?"

FOURTEEN

DINNER PASSES IN A BLUR.

Queen Tessa ushers me into the banquet hall, where Soren, Alaric, and the others have tucked into a feast that looks nothing like the tasteless mush Rowenna described in her letters. There's roasted meat and potatoes, some sort of crusty pie, and even carrots and peas. It doesn't look so different from the food we eat in Tashir. I can't comment on the taste though. It's impossible to enjoy any of it with the vile scent of Queen Tessa's bagrava tea still lingering in my nose. And I can't follow the conversation because I'm too busy dodging King Soren's unrelenting stare, spearing me from across the table, and too consumed with questions about the young man in the blue tasseled hat, who is glaringly absent from the banquet.

I spend the entire meal watching the doors, hoping he'll

reappear, whisk me into the hall, and explain what happened in the queen's salon—and how he knew my sister.

But he never comes.

"Everyone simply adored you! Just look at all those invitations!" Elodie gestures proudly to the pile of calling cards in my hands as she escorts me back to my chambers.

I don't remember receiving any of them, but I suppose I must have choked down my food and nodded along, because my arms are almost as full as my stomach.

"Your calendar will be filled for months," she prattles on, as if I have any intention of accepting these invitations. "I do hope Prince Alaric will join you on occasion. I'm so eager to see the two of you together."

I roll my eyes and grumble, "I'm glad someone is."

Elodie covers her chuckle with a dainty hand. "Indira! You mustn't say such things!"

"Not even if it's the truth? Alaric Alaverdi is infuriating, condescending, and—"

A murderer, that's what I start to say, but Elodie cuts me off with surprising vehemence.

"Do you have any idea how many girls would love to be in your shoes?"

"A captive bride, trapped in an enemy kingdom?" I deadpan, which earns me an elbow to the side.

"I'm being serious. Prince Alaric isn't the most sociable, I'll give you that. And his obsession with the mines is rather intense. *But* there's no arguing he's the best-looking man on the mountain and heir to the throne. At least half the girls at court probably want to kill you for swooping in and stealing him away."

My step falters.

Why didn't I consider this before? Especially when the guards made those crude jokes about Alaric's "experience in the bedroom" while crossing the Tomb Flats. If droves of slighted women want to kill *me* for marrying Alaric, they would have wanted to kill Rowenna too.

I think of all the noble ladies I just met. None of them seemed particularly jealous. Certainly not outright hostile. And I can't picture any of them outsmarting or overpowering Rowenna. But perhaps if they surprised her? If she never saw it coming?

A seemingly innocent invitation to stroll along the cliffs.

One quick shove.

"I know Prince Alaric had many lovers before marrying my sister—*and me*," I tack on grudgingly. "Who were they? Do you think any of them truly thought they would marry him?"

"Oh, I wouldn't call them *lovers*, since Alaric didn't *love* any of them. He supposedly doesn't even remember half of their names, which is why his paramours will never admit to the affairs. Who wants to be known as forgettable? Especially in *that* way?"

Elodie giggles before continuing, "According to my

mother, the parade of girls in Alaric's bed is nothing but a distraction. Something to take his mind off the pressure of filling his father's shoes. And to forget the horrible accident, of course."

I shiver from an unseen draft. "What horrible accident? Do you mean Rowenna's death?"

"Oh, no. Long before that." Elodie waves her hand. "When his older brother, Prince Besnik, died."

Elodie doesn't elaborate, as if dead princes are of little concern or interest. But it's definitely of interest to me. Soren has never mentioned having another son, which seems an odd thing to keep from your allies. And how did the boy die? How must this tragedy have affected Alaric? Did it shatter him the way Ro's death shattered me? Has it changed the very fabric of his being, driving him to do things he never thought he could—or would?

Reckless things.

Violent things.

Like attempting to bring down an entire kingdom.

If Alaric is anything like me, he could be even more dangerous and unpredictable than I feared.

We stop outside my chamber door, and Elodie beams at me like a proud parent. "I'm so glad you're here. I promise you'll love it in time. Now, I'll leave you to rest, but I'll be back to collect you for the stone-throwing contests tomorrow morning."

My disinterest in watching Vanzadorian courtiers

throw rocks must show on my face, because Elodie gives me another playful tap with her fan. "Don't scrunch your nose like that. It's a most amusing pastime. You'll see."

In a whirl of perfume and skirts, Elodie kisses my cheek and flounces down the hall. She's nearly around the corner when I realize I forgot to ask about the young man in the blue robes.

"Wait!" I call after her. "Who was that man in the tasseled hat? The one who watched over our prayers in Queen Tessa's salon?"

"Councilor Garitt Von Nevus?" Elodie turns, her face crinkled with distaste. "What do you want with *him*?"

It's not the reaction I expected from a social climber like Elodie, especially considering the boy's prominent position and good looks.

"I'm just curious about your prayers and customs," I lie. "That was an interesting ritual, and he seemed to be in charge of it."

"He *wishes* he were in charge," Elodie scoffs. "According to my mother, Von Nevus is always attempting to weasel his way through the ranks by any means necessary—many of which are *unsavory*. I make a point to keep my distance from him. You should too. It's unfortunate he oversaw your first prayer. I hope it didn't ruin the experience entirely."

I don't give a fig about their prayers, but I look down at my lap thoughtfully because I need time to unpick all of these tangled threads. Every time I think I've found the end of one problem, it loops back around and I'm ensnared in another.

If Von Nevus is as horrible as Elodie claims, why did Rowenna confide in him?

And why would he help me?

"Was my sister close with Councilor Von Nevus?" I ask.

Elodie raises a perfectly manicured eyebrow. "Why would you think he and Rowenna were close?"

"Because he knew about the flower-fairy party Ro and I planned for our mother when we were young."

Elodie slowly shakes her head. "What are you talking about? I don't recall anything about a fairy party...."

"Von Nevus mentioned it just before dinner, in the queen's salon," I say, trying not to lose my patience. "When I asked about Rowenna's most memorable quality."

Elodie shrugs, clearly just to appease me. "I must have missed it."

You didn't. You were right there!

I want to shake her. Shake all of them. The Vanzadorian nobles are so caught up in their frilly fashions and mindless gossip, there isn't room in their heads for anything else.

Or maybe this is a side effect of their not-so-innocuous bagrava tea.

I think back to the blithe, vacant look in Queen Tessa's eyes when she asked about my most memorable quality a second time—as if the first had never happened—and disquiet crawls across my skin.

I thank Elodie again and retreat into my rooms, where I collapse on the bed and scream into the pillows. How am I ever supposed to avenge my sister and liberate my country when I'm surrounded by murderers, liars, and bumbling fools on every side?

Be patient, play their games, Ro says, but I am *not* in the mood for her advice.

"What about *your* games?" I fire back. "How much longer do I have to play those before you tell me what you were doing? And why nothing is as you described in your letters? I don't even recognize you here."

I stare into the glittering shadows, seething with hurt and frustration while I wait for Rowenna to speak.

But she doesn't answer.

Because *I* don't have the answers.

I'm just a brokenhearted girl, talking to a ghost.

I must have finally succumbed to exhaustion, because I wake face down on the bed with drool dribbling from my lips and my hair plastered against my face. For a single disorienting second, I think I'm back in my bedchamber under the hill, but then blinding light from the geode wall stabs me in the eyes, reminding me exactly where I am.

I roll over with a groan and cover my face with my hands. And that's when I hear it—the sound that must have woken me: the rattle of dishes and the gentle squeak of wheels.

Someone is leaving food outside my chamber door.

Most likely my maid, who I haven't seen since I discovered her horrid little room.

I scramble off the bed and fly across my chamber. "Wait!" I call as I fling the door wide. "I just want to speak with you." But a flash of her skirt and a whip of her golden braid are all I see as she careens around the corner, the cart rattling like a runaway wagon.

I leap over the plate of food she left and take off after her, quickly closing the distance. My legs may be sore from the climb up the mountain, but she's burdened with that cart—which is probably why she abandons it in the middle of the hall.

As soon as I round the corner, I slam into the metal contraption. It crashes onto its side. I fall with it, landing amid shattering plates and clanking forks. It feels like a perfect depiction of my time in Vanzador—painful, frustrating, and beyond embarrassing.

"*Please*," I say before the girl escapes down a winding flight of stairs. "I'm not going to punish you for the carvings. I just want to know what they mean—why you'd carve such awful words?"

My maid doesn't slow.

"My sister was my best friend," I choke out. "But the more I learn about her time here, the more confused and helpless I feel. I just...*miss her*."

My voice is so soft and shattered, there's no way the girl heard. She's probably already several floors below. But when I glance up, she's still standing there, considering me as she heaves for breath.

"If I tell you what happened, will you leave me alone?" she finally asks.

I nod as I wipe my nose on the sleeve of my dress.

After another long silence, she says, "I didn't *want* to carve those things. Your sister *literally* forced me. She curled my fingers around a knife, jabbed another against my throat, and shouted threats until I was willing to do anything to get away from her. But in all the ways that matter, my hands are clean."

She holds up her hands, but I'm already shaking my head. "You're lying!"

The girl laughs bitterly. "I knew you wouldn't believe me." Then she flies down the staircase, disappearing into the shadows of the palace.

I thump down hard on the landing to catch my breath, but the longer I stare down the empty stairwell, the more I wonder if *I'm* the one lying to myself.

I've heard several unbelievable stories about Rowenna's time here, and the others turned out to be true. What if this is another?

Are you really going to believe a random servant over me? Rowenna demands. *Why would I carve threats against myself? It doesn't make sense.*

That's the problem. *Nothing* about her time on the mountain makes sense. Why would she drink bagrava tea and reveal her precious memories to one of Soren's councilors? Why would she send me letters full of falsehoods about Vanzador and act completely out of character?

You shouldn't have to betray the core of who you are in order to uncover your enemy's weaknesses.

Rowenna's laughter feels like an ice-cold draft against my cheek. *It's sweet that you believe that. A testament to how well I sheltered you. Perhaps a little* too *well.*

"I never asked to be sheltered," I snap at the empty stairwell. "I could have handled the truth. In fact, I would have been far more prepared to navigate all of this if you hadn't kept me in the dark."

If I hadn't kept you in the dark, you wouldn't have come at all.

It feels like I've been punched in the gut, because she's right. I would have been too terrified to come here and avenge her if I had known what I would be up against. I would have counted myself out before I even tried. I would have done nothing—like Father.

The realization makes me lurch to my feet, and I storm back to my bedchamber, unsure who I'm more frustrated with: my sister, for always being right, or myself, for being so pathetic and incompetent. The opposite of what Tashir needs.

The moment the door slams behind me, I begin rooting around my chamber like a wild boar. Yesterday, when I first combed the space, I did so slowly and methodically, fearful of potential traps and dangers. This time, *I* am on the attack. I don't know what I'm looking for exactly, but I dart around the room, overturning tables and pulling out drawers, searching for something, *anything*, that proves the *real* Rowenna was here. Some sort of confirmation that I'm on the right path, despite how useless and inadequate I feel.

But I don't find a trace of my sister or the truth.

It's like Rowenna was a ghost before she even died.

With a growl of frustration, I pluck one of the gold-lidded pots off the dressing table and hurl it at the nearest wall. It shatters against a protrusion of blue topaz, and I scream even louder as the glass tinkles into the carpet. "Why am I here? What do you expect me to do?"

When Rowenna doesn't answer, I throw another pot against a fiery-hearted opal. Followed by a jar of perfume that explodes against a cluster of purple amethyst. I hurl every trinket within reach while tears stream down my cheeks, making the room swirl like a watercolor painting.

I attack my haversack next. My fist closes around one of the unripe bagrava fruit I harvested during the fire, and I let it fly. It smashes against a vein of white quartz and turns into a satisfying spray of pulp—all except a small clump of purple flesh that appears to be hovering in midair.

Frowning, I pad over to the gemstone wall and poke around.

Everything inside me goes cold when I find the chunk of bagrava resting on a small doorknob, nestled seamlessly in the quartz. It's so well camouflaged, I could have easily missed it for months. *Years*.

I try the knob, and a hairline fracture appears, forming the shape of a small door. A *hidden* door with direct access to my rooms.

Rooms that also belonged to Rowenna.

I tell myself it's most likely a cupboard. Or another linen closet. But that's of little comfort, because a *person* was living in my washroom closet. And if this door leads somewhere as innocuous as maid's quarters, why bother concealing it so thoroughly?

Everything about this knob feels sinister. Orchestrated

A shudder grips me as I imagine Ro lying fast asleep on the feather bed, serenely floating through dreams of Tashir. Completely unaware of the click and scrape of the door. Oblivious to the shadowy presence creeping across the room. Waking to the cold bite of steel against her throat as an intruder forced her out of bed and marched her to the cliffs.

That scenario is far more believable than Rowenna holding anyone at knifepoint. It would have been easy for the serving girl to swap roles with my sister and paint herself as the victim when she relayed the tale. I have no doubt she knows about this hidden door; she cleans this room every day. And she clearly hated my sister. The only trouble is, it's equally difficult to imagine someone so timid and flighty threatening someone as strong and clever as Ro.

Soren and Alaric, on the other hand...

They must know about this hidden door too. They could have conveniently "forgotten" to secure it. Perhaps they even *encouraged* an assassin to slip in and murder my sister. It would have been the perfect way to keep their royal hands clean and facilitate the exchange. Me for Rowenna.

Do Mother and Father realize they condemned both their daughters when they revealed my abilities as a master gardener? Soren would have never wanted me otherwise. And Ro would have never been killed.

Devastation and fury slosh around my stomach like ice water. I want to scream and cry. Fight and flee. All of it at once.

If I were back in Tashir, I'd sprint to the fields and channel these feelings into my work. Earth Mother and the plants have always been my solace. But that isn't an option here. I won't grow so much as a blade of grass for Soren. Unfortunately, burying my head in the dirt and hoping Tashir will magically be freed isn't an option either.

I tighten my grip on the doorknob and take a breath for courage. I must keep moving, keep pressing, until I discover the truth.

FIFTEEN

SHOULDER THROUGH THE DOOR AND STAGGER NOT into the darkness of a secret tunnel but into a room even brighter than my chambers. It's like emerging from the hillock palace after spending a week belowground. I shield my eyes and steady myself against the door, but I can't stop blinking, even as the details come into focus.

The room is made entirely of glass. So open and exposed. The last place anyone would come to plot or spy.

Cautiously, I move to the nearest wall and raise my fingers to the glass, marveling at the endless blue sky and intense mountain sunshine. Ancient pine trees fill each window, and birds with red-tipped wings nest in the crags of the tallest cliffs. Far down below, a meandering stone wall encloses the bustling fortress city, full of shops and houses no bigger than seed packets, with scores of tiny people who march along like ants.

I don't want to admire anything about Vanzador, but like my glittering bedchamber and the breathtaking courtyards, I'm left without a choice. Everything about the kingdom is stunning. Mesmerizing. The opposite of the cold gray dungeon Rowenna described in her letters.

Technically, I suppose there are walls separating me from the outside world, but they're so clear, I feel like I could step through the glass and bound into the clouds. It's like flying but without the punishing wind and biting cold.

The thought makes my toes tingle inside my boots. I feel suddenly compelled to tilt my head back and raise my arms like wings, pretending to be one of those enormous birds, wheeling between the snowcapped peaks.

"Careful, or someone might catch you enjoying Vanzador...."

I shriek and whip around.

Prince Alaric leans casually against the wall in the opposite corner. Watching me.

"What are you doing here? *How* did you get in here?" I glance back the way I came. I didn't see or hear him follow me in, but I wasn't exactly paying attention.

Stupid! Careless! This is how you end up dead at the bottom of a cliff!

I don't know if Rowenna is scolding me or if I'm

scolding myself this time. Either way, I have to be better than this. Smarter than this.

"Are you spying on me?" I demand, suddenly plagued by images of Alaric hiding in my rooms. He could have been watching me for hours. He could have ambushed me at any moment.

Alaric rolls his eyes. "I have a country to run. I don't have time to waste spying on you."

"But—"

"If I was spying with the intent to kill you, why would I wait for you to find this hidden room? Which you may not have discovered for ages? If ever?"

While I bumble over these inconvenient facts, Alaric pushes away from the wall and crosses the room. The sunlight streaming through the windows makes his curls shine like wet ink, and his freshly shaved jaw looks carved from granite. His midnight blue waistcoat fits him like a second skin and paints the perfect contrast to his pale skin and storm-gray eyes.

Elodie wasn't wrong about his looks—he's as impressive and intimidating as this room—but no amount of outward beauty can hide his rotten, maggot-eaten core.

"If you're not spying on me, what are you doing here?" I finally demand.

"This is *our* solarium." Alaric nods over his shoulder, where the outline of a second door is barely visible in the glass. Beside the door, there's a desk cluttered with quills, inkpots, and a low bookshelf. I was so taken with the view, I didn't notice any of it before. "My chambers are just through there. I often work in here," he says as he slides behind the desk.

"We have adjoining rooms?" I sputter.

"Most married couples do. Is that a problem?"

"It was clearly a problem for Rowenna," I snap.

"How so?"

"How do you think? She turns up dead, and you *just so happen* to have private access to her chambers?"

"Ah, back to accusing me of murder." Alaric picks up a stack of papers and begins to read. "I knew it wouldn't take long."

"Because it's the truth—I'd bet my life on it!"

"You shouldn't be so flippant with your life."

"Why? Because you plan on ending mine?" I challenge.

Alaric flips the page without looking up. "I don't need to plan anything. I'm confident you'll take care of that on your own—just like your sister."

"We both know Ro didn't *fall* off that cliff," I say, glaring at his forehead with the burning intensity of the sun. But he doesn't glance up, and after several excruciating minutes, it feels like a furious swarm of bees are buzzing around my head. "You can't be serious! We're really supposed to just sit in here *together*? Did you do this with Rowenna?"

Alaric finally regards me with a beleaguered sigh. "As

I've told you several times, I rarely saw your sister. She never even discovered this adjoining room."

"You're lying," I automatically argue, even though Rowenna never once mentioned this glass room in her letters. There could be a thousand reasons for that, though. Maybe she rarely came because the view of Vanzador's prosperity made her sick, or maybe she never crossed paths with Alaric here, so it wasn't worth mentioning. Or she could have been worried the Vanzadorians were reading her letters before sending them. Maybe that's why she excluded so many details—she was writing in a sort of code.

"How could you possibly know how Rowenna spent her time here?" Alaric presses.

"Ro was the shrewdest, most observant person I've ever met," I retort. "If you thought she didn't know about this solarium, it was due to her brilliant subterfuge and your lack of awareness. *Or* because you used this secret room to access her chambers and kill her before she could discover it." I shoot him a pointed look.

"Isn't it exhausting to invent so many gruesome and outlandish tales?"

"No. But do you know what *is* exhausting? Having to constantly fight for my family, people, and land. But I'll never stop. I'll never—'"

"Plot and scheme all you'd like," Alaric cuts me off. "But I strongly suggest you get busy growing bagrava while you're at it. Otherwise, my father will stop asking nicely."

Alaric points over my shoulder to a collection of gardening supplies arranged beside my own door. I must have stumbled right past them before my eyes adjusted to the brightness.

There are pots of soil, watering cans, hand shovels, rakes, and a few small bagrava fruit to harvest for seeds.

Under any other circumstance, I would have leaped headlong into the freshly churned soil and palmed every glistening trowel and spade. Even now, my entire body fizzes, desperate to feel a bit of Tashir in this horrible place. But I turn my back on the supplies and face my husband, arms tightly crossed.

"Expecting me to perform on command isn't nice," I retort. "There's nothing *nice* about your father. His merry laughing-ruler act is even more transparent than these glass walls. He showed his true nature when he smirked through Rowenna's funeral and allowed Tashir to burn."

Alaric raises a brow. "How do you know that cruel, blustering tyrant isn't the act? Maybe *this* is his true nature, and he only has ruthless moments."

I bark out a laugh. "Of course you'd make excuses for *dear doting Daddy*. But your opinion doesn't count. You know Soren Alaverdi the father, not the ruler. I doubt you've ever even heard him raise his voice."

"You'd be surprised," Alaric says, averting his eyes. "But that still doesn't explain why our people love him. They wouldn't adore a merciless tyrant."

"They would if they knew the cost of displeasing him. People will do shocking things when they fear for their lives."

The papers crinkle in Alaric's hands, and his voice takes on a steely edge. "No one in Vanzador fears for their lives. Our people are safe, happy, and prosperous. My father is far from perfect—believe me, I'm aware—but he's a good king. Sometimes we must overlook minor flaws and failings for the greater good. It's called compromise."

"In Tashir, we call that denial. And last I checked, enslaving an entire nation and killing their crown princess are hardly *minor failings*. Your father is a monster—and you're just like him."

Alaric slams his papers down on his desk. "What have I done that's so monstrous?"

"Where to begin?" I muse, my confidence growing the more his unravels. I expect a list to pour from my mouth like summer rain, but as I actually think back on our interactions, Alaric's crimes are irritatingly few. Other than a handful of winks and verbal jabs, he's been rather civil.

Accommodating, even.

He convinced Soren to let me walk up the mountain instead of riding in that contraption. Then he carried me a good portion of the way when I got altitude sickness. As soon as we entered the Fortress, he took me to my rooms instead of forcing me to comply with Soren's demands for a bagrava demonstration. And he didn't argue, like his father did, when Queen Tessa excused me from growing bagrava in her salon yesterday.

"That's what I thought," Alaric says, leaning back smugly in his chair. "I'm not the monster here."

"You might not be a monster, but I'm not foolish enough to think you're a friend. This is just another tactic, another coordinated effort by you and your parents to bombard me from every angle and convince me to grow bagrava. But no amount of flattery or coercion will make me forget how you killed my sister and enslaved my people. I won't be tricked. I'll die before I grow bagrava for you."

I expect Alaric to make a snappy comment about how he'd be happy to help me along with dying, but instead he asks, "Who said the bagrava is for me?"

"For your father, then. Same difference," I grind out.

"Interesting…" Alaric cocks his head and studies me. "Is that what you've been told?"

I bristle with cold despite the sunshine blaring through the windows. His reaction is so similar to what Queen Tessa said in her salon—about the bagrava having nothing to do with her husband.

"You really don't know?" Alaric continues.

His words tunnel beneath my skin like termites. Everything inside me wants to shout, *Don't know what?* But I hold my tongue. I won't be lured into his trap.

After a few interminable minutes, Alaric shoves to his feet with a dramatic sigh. "If we're done here, I'll leave you to hunt for killers that don't exist. Or whatever it is you plan to do while the rest of us work." He tucks his papers beneath his arm and strides toward his door.

"You can't honestly consider bedding half the ladies in the kingdom *work*," I call after him.

Alaric chokes on a pop of laughter. "Is that jealousy I detect?"

"Don't flatter yourself."

"Then how I spend my time is none of your concern," he says as he opens the door.

I'm so exhausted and irritated, I'm tempted to let him go. Let him win this one small battle. But that's not what Rowenna would do, and despite how confused and exasperated I am with her, I know there's a reason she led me to this hidden solarium.

I dart past Alaric and wedge myself in his doorframe.

He glares down at me. "Stand aside, Indira."

I brace my arms against the glass and try to ignore the fact that his bare chest is just inches from my face. "How you spend your time, and who with, is definitely my concern, *dearest husband*, since one of the brokenhearted maidens you callously tossed aside could have killed my sister in a jealous rage."

"Except we've established that no one killed Rowenna."

"Or maybe you and your secret lover plotted

Rowenna's death together," I continue spinning. "To ensure she didn't keep you apart."

"I swear, in the name of the kings, I had nothing to do with your sister's death. My hands are clean." Alaric holds both palms out, just like my maid in the stairwell, and another thought occurs. One so obvious, I don't know how I didn't think of it before.

"You weren't working with a former lover. You were working with my maid!"

Alaric touches his fingers to his temple with a grimace. "Your theories are getting more and more outlandish."

"It seems pretty straightforward to me," I argue. "You hired the serving girl to kill Ro—to technically keep your hands clean—and now you've ordered her to do the same to me."

"Do you honestly think my father would let me kill you?"

Once again, I scowl at his bothersome logic. "To frighten and unnerve me, then. Make me more cooperative."

Alaric scoffs. "Nothing on this continent could make *you* more cooperative. And I couldn't distinguish your maid from any other employee in the palace, so I don't know how I could possibly be in league with her." He shoulders past me but then pauses before he vanishes into his rooms. "I *am* curious, though, what she did to frighten and unnerve you so much? Just in case I want to follow her lead," he adds with an acidic smile.

It goes against all of my instincts, but I decide to tell him. Sometimes the body says more than the tongue ever will.

"I found her sleeping in a closet in my washroom, which was disturbing enough. But then I discovered menacing inscriptions covering the walls from floor to ceiling. Grisly things about blood, flesh, and bone along with my sister's name."

"'Blood, flesh, bone'?" Alaric says with a roll of his eyes, but I swear a bit of color leaches from his cheeks, and he abruptly turns to go.

I jam my boot into the door before it closes, wincing as the heavy glass smashes my toes. "Those words clearly mean something to you. Tell me what you know."

Groaning, Alaric attempts to nudge my boot out of the way. "I don't have the time or the energy to do this again."

I catch him by the wrist and dig my nails into his velvet sleeve. "Make time."

His eyes flare, even though my bitten nails are too short to inflict any real damage. "Unhand me," he snaps.

I squeeze tighter. "Maybe you didn't physically carve those words or shove Ro off the cliff, but it's obvious you had something to do with it. An innocent person is dead because of *you*. Doesn't that bother you?"

Alaric reels back as if I slapped him. "You know nothing about the blood on my hands or how it haunts me," he says in a low, shaky whisper. Then he slams the door so hard, the panes of glass rattle behind him.

In the sudden quiet, my nerves rattle too.

SIXTEEN

SIXTEEN

I SPEND THE REST OF THE DAY PACING MY CHAMBER, stewing over my encounter with Alaric.

He was as irritating and condescending and secretive as ever, and he obviously knows more than he's letting on. Part of me wants to storm through the palace and track him down. If I refuse to let him catch his breath or give him time to spin more lies, he just might break and finally tell the truth.

Unless he is *telling the truth*, the other part of me whispers. *Unless he's broken already*

Rowenna scoffs. *Does he look broken to you?*

Not physically, but there was something undeniably vulnerable in the way he stumbled back. A familiar heaviness, hidden in the depths of his silvery eyes.

It isn't until I stop pacing and stand in front of the

floor-length mirror, that I realize what it is. Alaric wears the same haunted expression I see every time I look at my reflection. A face carved out by grief and guilt, not malice.

You're better than this, Indira, Rowenna cuts in. *Don't let sultry eyes cloud your judgment.*

But Alaric's smoldering stare isn't what's causing me to second-guess myself. It's everything else. The things I saw when he finally stopped acting.

For the first time, I allow myself to consider that he really might be innocent.

If he didn't kill Rowenna, though, who did?

I resume pacing, even faster than before. King Soren is the most obvious choice, but I'm certain he would have proudly claimed Rowenna's murder when they returned her body to Tashir—treaty be damned. It would have been the perfect way to intimidate Father even further. To punish him for withholding the truth about my abilities. Soren would be holding it over my head now too—using my sister's death as a warning, a promise of what's to come if I refuse to cooperate and grow bagrava.

That leaves only my erratic maid, who's too timid to come within ten paces of me, or one of the vapid courtiers from the queen's salon. I eye the stack of frilly calling cards on my nightstand. Perhaps they're more threat than invitation. Maybe Elodie and the others aren't as silly and shallow as they seem.

I could attend their luncheons and soirees and try to

charm my way into their confidences. Except that's what Rowenna did, and if she wasn't shrewd enough to navigate that world without being killed, I don't have a prayer. I'll be dead before the week is out.

Which is why I already pointed you in the direction of someone who can help, Rowenna says with a dramatic sigh.

"No one in this seeds-forsaken kingdom is helpful," I grumble. But even as I say it, I think of the courtier in the blue-tasseled hat.

Garitt Von Nevus.

Elodie clearly doesn't care for him, but how much of that is warranted, and how much is the opinion of her mother—another advisor who's also vying for power? Rowenna must have trusted him to some degree—well enough to share her memories with him and realize he could serve a purpose. And he was useful in the queen's salon: helping me pretend to pray and relaying information about my sister that was actually true.

I pause and peer around my twilit room. In the waning light, it's impossible to tell if danger lurks in the inky corners, or if it's just the light, shifting as the sun sets behind the snowcapped peaks. Just as it's impossible to know if Garitt Von Nevus is the answer to my questions or if I'm falling into the same trap that killed my sister.

"If this is what I'm meant to do, send me a sign," I whisper to Rowenna. "Knock over a candlestick. Or chase me with a ghostly draft," I add with a somber chuckle.

At that precise moment, someone raps on my chamber door.

The hairs on my arms prickle, and I trip over my feet as I race for the door. "Ro?" I whisper. "Is it really you?"

But of course, it isn't.

"It's Elodie," the courtier says through the door. She laughs uncomfortably, like she's been standing there, listening to my one-sided conversation with my dead sister. "I came to collect you for the stone-throwing contests, as promised."

I inwardly groan, praying she'll leave if I ignore her.

But she clears her throat and pounds again. "Don't make me knock down this door, Indira!" Elodie punctuates her threat with a lighthearted chuckle, but suddenly, nothing about her appearance feels funny—or happenstance. How is her timing so impeccable? How is she always *there*, waiting for me, at the perfect moment?

I initially chalked her hovering up to boredom. Or desperation for friendship. Or even the universe mocking me. The one person who's always readily available doesn't have a scrap of useful information about Rowenna. But the more I think about it, the more her "friendship" borders on obsession.

Rowenna wouldn't have liked being smothered like this, and she was far less patient than me. What if she snapped and said something to offend Elodie—who turned out to be far more dangerous than she appeared?

I wrench the door open, and there she is with her batting eyelashes and glittering skirts. The picture of innocence. But I'm not buying her little act. Not anymore. No one on this mountain is beyond suspicion.

"Are you ready to go?" she chirps.

I shake my head. "I'm afraid I can't join you for the contests."

"Why not?" Elodie's smile falters, and her voice actually wobbles—like I've broken her heart. It makes me want to scream, because I can't for the life of me tell if its genuine, and if I can't see through someone as seemingly simple as Elodie, what hope do I have of ever catching Ro's killer?

"I have other business to attend to," I say as I brush past her.

Despite my rudeness, Elodie latches onto my sleeve like a burr and trails me down the hall. "What business? With whom?"

"I need to speak with Councilor Garitt Von Nevus. Do you know where his rooms are?"

Elodie stops abruptly. Her surprisingly strong grip on my elbow stops me too. "What do you want with *him*? I told you—"

"If you don't know the way, I can find someone who does," I interrupt. "I just assumed you'd be able to point me in the right direction, but if it's beyond you..."

"Of course I know the way to Von Nevus's rooms." Elodie resumes leading me through the labyrinthine halls.

"You don't need anyone but me," she adds, quiet but firm. Possessive almost. Or am I imagining it?

A few minutes later, we stop outside an ornate mahogany door. "Here we are." Elodie motions with a flourish. "What business do you have with Von Nevus? Shall I accompany you inside to ensure he doesn't give you trouble? Perhaps you don't remember, but my mother—"

I cut her off with a shake of my head. "I need to do this on my own."

"Very well," she says, but her grip on me reflexively tightens, and I don't know how I'm supposed to tell if her concern is valid or if she's just another person trying to manipulate me. She could be even more dangerous than Von Nevus.

I glance between Elodie and the door, mentally reviewing everything I know. Rowenna wouldn't lead me to Von Nevus if he were dangerous. But she also wouldn't have tolerated Elodie's clingy, irritating presence without reason.

Which leaves only one option.

I must play both sides—as I'm sure Rowenna did.

I gratefully pat Elodie's hand. "Thank you for your concern—and help. I don't know what I'd do without you. How about I find you at the stone-throwing contests as soon as I'm finished here? It shouldn't take long." Then I offer a conspiratorial grin that *could* be construed as a promise to tell her everything later.

That does the trick.

Elodie's painted lips break into a wide smile, and she sets me free, promising to save me a seat near the front of the courts before flouncing away.

As soon as she's out of sight, I roll my shoulders back and pound my fist against Von Nevus's door.

"Coming!" calls a low voice within. It's deeper and huskier than I remember, and for some reason, it makes my skin crawl. What if I made the wrong decision? Maybe I should have listened to Elodie. Or at least planned what to say.

The door creaks open, and Councilor Garitt Von Nevus is there in all of his auburn-haired, blue-robed glory. The velvet fabric perfectly complements his gleaming copper skin, and the way his hair curls around the bottom of the tasseled cap makes him look boyish and innocent. His eyes, though, are wise and wary, calculated in the way of someone far older.

"Little Rowenna," he says, leaning against the doorframe. "To what do I owe this honor?" His words and smile are perfectly pleasant, but the crawling sensation intensifies as he looks me up and down with appreciation.

I touch the clover on my wrist and raise my chin to meet his brazen stare. "Why did you help me yesterday in the queen's salon?"

"Are we not even going to pretend to bother with pleasantries?" he asks with wounded amusement.

"I see no reason to."

His laughter is soft, his smile wistful. "Gods of the mountain, you're exactly like her."

I cross my arms and ignore this comment. Garitt Von Nevus couldn't possibly know if I'm *exactly like Rowenna* because he didn't actually know her; no one on this mountain did. Lately, I'm wondering if *I* knew her completely.

"You even get that same little crinkle between your eyebrows when you're annoyed." He points excitedly.

My fingers involuntarily drift toward my forehead. How does a councilor of King Soren know something so personal and intimate about my sister?

Garitt's smile widens.

I drop my hand with a scowl. "I'm not leaving until you answer my questions. Why did you help me? How did you know Rowenna?"

"You're demanding like her too," he says with fond exasperation. Then he glances down the hall in either direction and says quietly, "I'll happily explain—in here." He waves me into his chambers.

Even though this is precisely what I wanted, my gut twists with unease as I peer into Von Nevus's rooms. I glance back down the empty corridor, suddenly wishing I cornered him somewhere more public. Or allowed Elodie to accompany me after all.

It's perfectly fine. Don't you trust me? Rowenna asks, her voice small and laced with hurt.

In the past, I would have instantly fallen to my knees to beg her forgiveness and offered reassurances, but now I stand there for a long uncomfortable moment, waiting for the fingers of anxiety to loosen from around my chest.

Of course I trust my sister. And if Rowenna trusted this boy, I should too.

I proceed into Von Nevus's rooms with a tight smile. Unlike my geode chamber and the adjoining glass solarium, Von Nevus's rooms look precisely how I imagined a mountain fortress would: bleak and ominous, with carpet the color of moss and bronze sconces that provide half enough light for the space. It doesn't help that every window is shuttered, making it feel as claustrophobic as a cave. It's even drafty like a cave.

I wrap my arms around myself as I turn back to face Von Nevus, who has perched on the arm of a wingback chair.

"Sit." He gestures to the chair opposite. "You look like you're going to faint or vomit, just like you did in Queen Tessa's salon. That's why I helped you. I've seen chickens on the chopping block look calmer than you among the courtiers."

He offers a warm smile, but still I deflate with a huff. I tried so hard to be poised and calm among the Vanzadorian nobles—like Rowenna had been.

Clearly, I failed.

"I also have a soft spot for pretty damsels in distress," Von Nevus adds with a playful wag of his eyebrows.

I know he's just trying to lighten the mood, but it has the opposite effect. I'm done being manipulated by charming men.

"Then I'm afraid you'll be disappointed," I snap, "because I'm *not* in distress."

"Of course not. I'm glad we both agree you're pretty, though." He winks, and I sigh loudly.

"Believe it or not, I didn't come here for idle flirtation."

"You don't say," he says dryly. "Rowenna was clearly the fun sister."

I narrow my eyes at him and channel my mother's steady, imposing presence, trying to replicate the way she'd silently take charge of council meetings that slipped from Father's grip. "What business did you have with my sister?" I ask again. "Why do you remember things about her that Queen Tessa and other courtiers don't?"

Garitt slides languidly into his chair, legs draped over one armrest, and shakes his head at me. "So serious and unrelenting. Perhaps you and Alaric *are* a match made in heaven."

Yesterday, this comment would have sent me through the roof. And I still don't like or agree with it. But after my confrontation with Alaric in our solarium, Von Nevus's insult feels more like a prodding finger than a gut punch.

"I won't apologize for being incensed in the wake of my sister's death," I say. "And if you were truly Ro's friend or ally or whatever you were to her, you wouldn't be so cheery either."

This makes Von Nevus bristle. Slowly, he swings to the front of his chair and leans his elbows on his knees. "People grieve in different ways, Little Ro. And maybe I'm not answering your questions because you haven't asked nicely."

I heave to my feet. "Forget it."

"Fine, fine." He waves me back down. "I'll tell you what you want to know."

I sit, arms crossed, glaring until he begins.

"As a member of King Soren's council, I'm familiar with everyone in the royal household, of course, but your sister and I had a special relationship."

It could be my imagination, but the way his lips curl around the word *special* makes my insides tighten.

"Special *how*?"

"I was her mentor, of sorts. Rowenna had such a keen interest in politics and government. She was curious about everything to do with Vanzador. She wanted to learn and contribute, so she could be an adept ruler alongside Alaric someday.

"On several occasions she asked to attend our council meetings, but King Soren wouldn't hear of it. To him, Rowenna was Tashiri and not to be trusted. He said she was a silly girl who belonged in the queen's salon, not his council chambers. You can imagine how well that went over with Rowenna."

Garitt's eyes meet mine and I nod. Because

finally—*finally*—this *does* sound like my sister: learning as much as possible about the inner workings of the Vanzadorian government, raising her voice, secretly scheming and fighting for Tashir.

"So you took her under your wing against the king's wishes?" I raise a brow at Von Nevus. "Doesn't that make you a traitor?"

He waves away the implication. "I knew Soren would have to accept Rowenna eventually. It's not like she could escape back to Tashir—not if she valued the mountains protecting your fields—and someone needed to prepare her to be queen one day. While Soren may have blind faith and pride in his second son, the rest of us know Alaric was never born to rule like his older brother, Besnik. Luckily, Rowenna was just the sort of partner he needed. I simply came to this realization sooner than my colleagues and decided a little risk was worth the reward of being on the right side of Rowenna's cunning mind."

I study King Soren's "trusted advisor" for a long minute, stunned by his audacity. He's admitting to outright treason.

Von Nevus rolls his eyes dramatically. "I can see you're just as narrow-minded as the rest of the council. I'm no traitor. I hardly divulged Vanzador's most guarded secrets. I simply encouraged Ro to do some light reading in the library."

"The library?" I deadpan.

I can count on one hand the number of times my sister visited the library in Tashir. She didn't have time to read. She was action and resolve, instinct and confidence. The thought of her being here, in Vanzador, so close to Soren and Alaric's power and secrets, and choosing to confine herself in the library feels as unnatural as a fox eating cabbage beside a chicken coop.

"You could visit the library too," Von Nevus says offhandedly. "It's free and open to all..."

Something about his offer, or maybe it's the way he says it, feels threatening. Or am I just being paranoid? Seeing menace everywhere because I don't have a clue who to trust?

"Don't you want answers?" he presses. "Or are you afraid of what you might find?"

"I'm more afraid this is some sort of trap," I admit.

He snorts. "If I wanted to hurt you, wouldn't I do so now—while you're alone in my chambers, where no one will hear you scream?"

My eyes instinctively dart to the door, and Garitt laughs. "Relax, Little Ro. You're much more useful to me alive."

"You sound just like Soren and Alaric," I say bitterly.

"Except I don't care about your silly plant. And unlike them, I want you to be informed. I want you to collect all of the available information before you decide who to trust and how to proceed."

"Nothing in your library is going to make me turn against my own country."

"Who says you have to choose between my country and yours?"

"Oh, I don't know, maybe years of oppression," I retort.

Garitt shrugs, saunters back to the door, and opens it for me. "If you want to remain in the dark, go back to your gemstone rooms and spend your days flitting about the queen's salon. Accept your fate as a helpless captive, and rot in this palace. I'm sure Rowenna would understand." He flashes an acidic smile. "*But* if you want to shift the paradigm, there are other opportunities available to you. You just have to be bold enough to pursue them."

"Rowenna was bold. She followed your advice. And look where it got her," I point out.

Garitt's face crumples. "Rowenna's death was a terrible tragedy, but I swear I had nothing to do with it. Not everyone on the mountain is out to get you."

"Just most of you."

"You have to trust someone, you know. You'll never be able to navigate the Fortress on your own."

"Fine," I say as I step back into the hall. "I'll consider your advice."

"That's all I ask," Von Nevus says with a gracious bow. But I feel his eyes on my back, watching intently until I vanish around the corner.

SEVENTEEN

WANT TO GO STRAIGHT TO THE LIBRARY, BUT I DON'T. Just in case it's a trap.

The way Garitt Von Nevus spoke about my sister—the way his eyes lit up with fondness—felt genuine. But so did Soren's interest in Tashir when he first rode across our fields. I must proceed with caution and keep all of my options open, which is why I wind down the endless spiral staircases until I reach the stone-throwing courts in the castle yard.

There are at least a dozen fields of carefully raked sand, each filled with grunting men wearing even less clothing than usual. Scores of spectators in glittering finery sit on the surrounding benches, cheering with as much gusto as my people during the harvest games, but for some reason, it feels more subdued. Curated, almost. After a moment, I realize it's because there aren't any children in attendance. None of their rowdy shouting or tussling. No sticky faces or muddy hands. The noble children must be too busy learning to be proper and refined for fun. They're probably up in their high towers, wearing flowing silks, already being taught to look down on the rest of us.

Elodie spots me and makes a production of waving me over to her courtside seats. Before I can even sit down, she hooks her arm through mine, publicly laying claim to me.

Everything inside me wants to swat her away like a mosquito, but I force myself to flash an excited smile instead.

We watch match after match, and I shout and cheer alongside Elodie, as enthusiastic as any Vanzadorian, even though the contests are as tedious as their name implies. Men hurl rocks across a sand pit to see whose travels farthest. Most of my gasps are based not on the game itself, but on the fact that the Vanzadorians waste their precious energy on a game while my people are literally breaking their backs in the fields.

When the games are finally finished, I beg exhaustion from the "excitement" and allow Elodie to escort me to my rooms. But the moment she's gone, I slip out of my chamber and slink down the winding halls, avoiding courtier and servant alike until I find the library in a forgotten nook on a lower level of the palace.

It's nothing like the rest of the castle. The ceilings here

are low, the shelves are overstuffed and disorganized, and the chairs are drooping and care worn. But my entire body hums with delight as soon as I slip through the creaking door, because it *feels* like the hillock palace. It even smells a bit like dust, moss, and wood.

I inhale deeply and smile for the first time since arriving in Vanzador. This feels right. This is where Ro would have chosen to spend her time—with or without Von Nevus's urging.

I venture down a dusty row of books and into the center of the room, where a shriveled old man sits behind a desk large enough to swallow him. Otherwise, the library appears to be empty.

"Hello," I say with a tentative wave.

The man glances up and scowls at me over the rim of his spectacles. At least I think he's scowling. He has more wrinkles than the bark of a white oak tree.

"We haven't had the pleasure of meeting yet," I continue when it becomes clear he isn't going to speak. I'm—"

"Oh, I know who *you* are. You look just like *her*. Sound like her too." He wiggles a long crooked finger inside his ear. "And just when I'd finally purged her needling voice from my head. She was in here every day, poking around and asking questions. Driving me mad."

I open my mouth, but I don't know what to say. I still don't know how Rowenna managed to make such wildly varied impressions. When I walk into a room, I never know if I'm going to be adored or condemned by association.

"I assume you're here to follow in her meddlesome footsteps," the old man grumbles and hops out of his chair. "Thankfully, I had a feeling I shouldn't reshelve her research quite yet. I knew she'd find a way to pester me from beyond the grave. And look—here you are. Now, are you going to follow me, or are you going to stand there and piddle in your pants? I haven't got all day."

I'm tempted to ask what else could possibly be on his agenda, since the thick coat of dust on the floors and shelves makes it clear the Vanzadorians use this library about as often as my people visit Father Alonzo in his earthen chapel. But I bite my tongue.

At the back of the room, the librarian upends a basket of books onto a round table. "That's all of it, so you have no reason to bother me again."

"All of what?" I ask, which earns me an impatient huff and another disdainful scowl.

"All the books *Her Royal Highness Rowenna* demanded I pull for her—every Vanzadorian history, journal, and discourse on politics. So she could pretend to take an interest in our kingdom. But she didn't fool me. The only interest that girl had in Vanzador was figuring out how to ruin us. I presume you're here to do the same. Well, go ahead and try. Read until your face is more wrinkled than mine— you won't find anything useful in these books because

Vanzador has no cracks. No weaknesses you weed pullers can exploit."

He bangs his fist against the table like it's a judge's gavel and stalks off.

I slide onto a chair and reach for the toppled books. There are about fifteen in total, all thick and leather bound, and they appear to be crammed with text even drier than the ancient sheaves of paper they're written on.

"This can't be what Ro came here for," I mumble as I skim through a book about the Vanzadorian monetary system. The next tome is all about the origin of each of the gemstone mines, along with time stamps from decades' worth of workers. The thickest book is dedicated to Vanzadorian etiquette and customs—, complete with full-color drawings of their questionable fashion—of which I've unfortunately gained plenty of firsthand experience. I've never worn so much sheer lace, or been quite so cold—in all my life.

I toss the book aside. None of this could be the reason Von Nevus sent me here. Unless it was all a ruse. He's probably laughing in his chamber right now, knowing I'm searching for something that doesn't exist.

No. He remembered Rowenna's story. He knew about the lines on her face, for seed's sake. There's something here. Something I need.

I grit my teeth and pick up the next book, clearly the oldest in the stack. It's titled *A History of Kings* and appears to be akin to the ledger we keep in Tashir detailing births, deaths, coronations, and weddings. Long lists of names and dates, and not much else.

I let the cover fall shut with a groan.

"It would be really nice if you'd tell me where to look. Or what I'm looking for," I say to the empty chair across from me, wishing more than ever that Ro was actually here.

I try to picture how she'd lean across the table, brows furrowed with concentration, but I can't remember the exact placement of the freckles dotting her nose or conjure the precise shade of her tawny eyes. With every passing day, her memory gets a little bit fuzzier, and for the first time, I allow myself to wonder if it's because I've truly forgotten, or if it's because the deeper I dig for answers, the more the Rowenna who lived here feels like a stranger.

What if I'm trying to avenge a person who no longer existed? Maybe Rowenna really did leave her former self behind in Tashir and embrace her new life in Vanzador—as Alaric and the courtiers claim.

Or worse.

What if she grew so hopeless and despondent, the cliffs looked more tolerable than life on the mountain?

I shake my head resolutely. Ro would never surrender. She'd never stop fighting, no matter how bleak the circumstance. That's why I still hear her voice in my head. She's encouraging me, guiding me.

Toward what, though?

I've been going in circles since the moment I arrived on

the mountain, and now I've reached yet another dead end.

Maybe the voice has never been Rowenna's, my doubt and frustration murmur. *Maybe you've been talking to yourself. That's why you feel so lost.*

NO.

I shove the useless book across the table. It tumbles over the edge and lands with a *thump* on the floor.

"What the devil are you doing?" the librarian shouts from the opposite end of the room.

"I, um, accidentally fell asleep and a book slid off of my lap," I call back, trying to sound breezy. "Nothing to worry about."

But the old man's footsteps continue echoing through the room—coming closer. "I'll judge whether everything is *fine*."

Quickly, I slide from my seat, toss the book back onto the table, and turn to make my escape, but as the tome lands, a few pages slide loose from the ancient binding. I flinch and look over my shoulder, terrified to imagine how the old man will punish me for this desecration. Frantically, I try to shove the pages back into the book, but there's no place for them, because it's a separate book entirely. A small handwritten journal.

The old man is close now—just on the other side of the nearest shelf—but something compels me to thumb through a few pages. It appears to be nothing more than minutes from council meetings, but then, on the second to the last page, something catches my eye.

A small, dried zinnia.

The flower that adorned Rowenna's hair on her wedding day. A flower that doesn't grow on the mountain.

It's been carefully pressed near the back of the book, still fiery orange and emitting the slightest hint of perfume, and the sight of it makes me choke back a sob. It feels like my sister is wrapping me in a fierce embrace. Like she's proving she hasn't left me.

"What in the name of the kings are you doing back here?" The old man emerges from behind the shelf and frowns at the pile of books, even though they're no messier than when he dumped them unceremoniously from the basket an hour ago.

I take advantage of his blustering and stuff the journal under my skirt. Who would have thought the scandalous thigh-high slits would actually prove useful?

I summon an innocent smile when the librarian looks back to me, but that only makes his frown deepen.

"I don't know what you're really up to, but you're finished for the day," he says, bringing his arm around me like a shepherd's hook.

I allow him to drag me back across the library and out into the hall, where it takes all my restraint not to sprint back to my chambers with my stolen book.

Thanks to Rowenna and her zinnia, my day is far from finished.

EIGHTEEN

As soon as I'm nestled in the gemstone walls of my chamber, I carefully remove the pressed zinnia, set it on the desk beside me, and begin to read.

I pore over the journal long into the night. Until sunlight bleeds through the skylights and sets the gemstone walls ablaze.

The words set my fury ablaze too.

My people have always speculated about how the Vanzadorians acquired their power. There are dozens of stories, songs, and scripture that range from slightly improbable to wholly ridiculous. But none of them comes close to the truth.

At least not the Vanzadorians' version of the truth.

I bark out a laugh and flip back to the beginning of the journal, which belonged to Alaric's great-grandfather, King

Callahan Alaverdi—the man supposedly responsible for awakening their unnatural power.

"His audacity is astounding!" I say for what must be the tenth time. I've been pacing for hours, talking to the zinnia as if it's actually my sister. Voicing the same thoughts I'm certain she had while reading Callahan's account.

"*Mustering the last of our courage, I led the remnant of our army to meet the Marauders at the pass,*" I read, in a theatrical voice. "*We knew we were marching to our deaths. The canyon walls are low and offer little cover, and my people are cave-dwelling miners, not soldiers. Simple men and women with shovels and picks, outnumbered three to one against these insatiable raiders. But we couldn't stand by and watch them steal every scrap of ore and nugget of gold and leave us with nothing to transport across the sea. No way to provide for our families.*"

"Doesn't *that* sound familiar!" I laugh bitterly. "You'd think the Vanzadorians would have a little more empathy for us."

I resume reading. "*The thieves attacked with the vicious strength of wolverines. By sundown, only a handful of men and I remained, and we fought with even more fervor than before. But it wasn't enough. My brother, Gershon, fell first, speared through the gut like a boar. Then my uncle was brutally beheaded beside me, his blood coating my face like mist.*

"*I didn't know what to do, didn't know how to defend my people, and I'm ashamed to admit, I didn't want to go on.*

Blubbering like a coward, I fell to my knees, dug my fingers into the rocky soil, and thought of my family. I pictured the good hardworking people of Vanzador and begged their forgiveness as I called for the Marauders to finish me.

"*But then the strangest thing happened.*

"*I've always heard that your life flashes before your eyes when you die, but the opposite was true for me. The images I'd been clinging to—the faces and memories of the people I loved most—dissolved into a swirl of colors that fell from my eyes in a mudslide of tears. One precious moment after the next coursed down my face and spattered the rocks, sinking into the thirsty ground, until my mind held nothing but blackness.*

"*I was utterly alone, screaming into the quiet dark. I didn't want to die like this, but I also couldn't press on through the emptiness. My soul cried out in agony, and that's when I felt a shuddering, deep within the earth.*

"*All at once, a staggering surge of energy rose through the soil and into my fingers. My ears roared with the rumble of falling rocks. My tongue fizzed with the taste of silt and sediment. And I felt taller, stronger, and more unbreakable than the canyon walls themselves.*

"*I gripped the ground harder, hoping to steady myself against these delusions—for that's what they had to be. But as my fingers closed into fists, the rocks surrounding us gave an ancient, deep-bellied groan. Then they* moved.

"*I shook my head, certain I'd imagined it, but the harder I squeezed, the louder the groaning became. Before I understood what was happening, enormous slabs of stone broke free from the canyon walls and tumbled into the pass, crushing the Marauders and, with them, the remnant of my army.*

"*When the landslide finally ceased, I alone stood in the dust and debris. I fell to my knees and wept prayers of sorrow and thanks, but secretly, I was terrified. Too terrified to touch anything. Or to think too hard about what had happened. Because, impossible though it seemed—as much as I hoped it was all a hallucination induced by terror—I knew I had somehow caused the rockslide. And when I looked down at my shaking hands, there was no denying that the earth had changed me. I could feel it there, in my blood, flesh, and bone.*"

I shiver, even though my room is stifling, and wring my hand around the clover at my wrist until it burns. Rowenna left a zinnia in this book. She clearly wanted me to find Callahan's account and those three cryptic words. The same words that just so happen to be carved into the walls of my maid's quarters. Words, I'm beginning to suspect, that were never a threat against my sister, but a clue. Something *she* orchestrated. Which means my maid was telling the truth. Ro held her at knifepoint and forced her to etch those disturbing words.

But why?

Callahan's account can't be true. *We* are Earth Mother's chosen people. She cast her lot with Tashir when she blessed us with bagrava. She wanted *us* to survive and thrive on this hostile continent, so she never would have blessed the Vanzadorians with even greater power. She would have foreseen how they'd misuse it against us. Which means Callahan must have somehow *stolen* his strength from Earth Mother and invented this tale to absolve himself. But if that's the case, why was Rowenna so fixated on *blood, flesh, bone*?

Even if Callahan's account *is* somehow true, it's hardly a revelation that the power to move the earth is a part of his body the same way the ability to grow bagrava is part of mine. And it doesn't explain Rowenna's obsession. If anything, learning Soren's power is a bodily part of him should have put an end to it. Their power couldn't be stolen, and killing them wasn't an option either, since our protection from the Marauders would perish with them.

So what was her plan?

"What am I missing?" I shout at the little dried zinnia.

When Ro fails to answer, I snatch the flower and journal off the table and march back to Garitt Von Nevus's rooms. He knew the Rowenna who lived on this mountain, and he led me to this account. Which means there's clearly something more he wants me to know.

Probably the very thing that got Rowenna killed, my good sense warns. But I choose to ignore it. Just as I choose to ignore the sense of the prickling unease I felt in Von Nevus's presence. If he wanted to hurt me, he could have easily done so during my first visit.

"I took your advice and did some reading!" I call out

as I pound on his chamber door. A passing guard gives me a curious look, but I wave him off as I've seen Soren and Alaric do a dozen times.

As soon as Von Nevus's face appears, I shoulder through the door, nearly knocking him over in my excitement to wave the leather journal in his face. "Is this what you sent me to find?"

After a few rapid blinks, Garitt closes the door, and by the time he turns to face me, his startled expression has morphed into an amused smirk. "Well done, Little Ro. That didn't take long. Did you learn anything interesting?"

"Rowenna seemed to think so." I open Callahan's journal, extract the dried zinnia, and hold it out on my palm. "I found *this* tucked into an account of the battle when King Callahan obtained his power. The moment he claims the strength of the earth sank into his *blood, flesh, and bone*. Do those words mean anything to you?"

Instead of answering, Von Nevus reaches wistfully for the zinnia in my palm. "Gods of the mountain, I've missed those little pops of sunshine."

I close my fingers around the flower. "Answer the question."

He scowls at my clenched fist before raising his gaze to mine. "Are you asking for a lesson in basic human anatomy? Because blood is the red liquid that seeps from a wound when you—"

"You know what I'm asking," I cut him off.

"Calm down. I'm just having a bit of fun."

"Nothing about this is *fun*!"

"Yes, you're making certain of that," he mutters.

He gestures for me to sit in the same dark leather chair as my last visit, but instead of taking the chair opposite, he perches on the arm of mine. He's so close, his burgundy waistcoat brushes my cheek and the spicy musk of his cologne tickles my nose.

I shift uncomfortably and lean away, hoping he'll notice and give me space, but he continues looming over me, peering down with a smile, as if this should be the most natural thing in the world. And maybe it should be. Maybe this is how allies act. Maybe this is the level of trust required, and he's testing me before he reveals more.

I clear my throat, open the journal, and point to the words *blood, flesh, bone*. "I found these same words cut into the wall of a closet in Rowenna's bathing room. I think she may have carved them herself, after reading this account. Do you know anything about that? Perhaps she told you what she was doing? You were clearly her closest confidant."

"Sadly, I was never invited into your sister's bathing chamber," Von Nevus laments coyly. I spear him with a glare, and he raises his hands. "Fine, fine. Rowenna and I never spoke of her scheming outright. As one of Soren's advisors, I needed to keep my integrity somewhat intact. I simply made offhanded suggestions that she pursued as she pleased."

That would imply you had any integrity to begin with, I want to snarl, but I hold my tongue.

"I'm no fool, though," he continues. "I presumed Rowenna was searching for a way to undermine Soren's power. Or channel it for herself." He flips his hand, as if stealing his king's power source is a trivial offense.

"And you still chose to help her?" I ask, bewildered. "What if she'd succeeded?"

"I knew she wouldn't. Soren and Alaric's power resides in their *blood, flesh, and bone*—as you so sagely discovered. There was nothing she could do to change that. I knew she'd eventually have to accept her place here, and as I said before, I wanted to be in her good graces when that happened. I pointed her toward Callahan's journal as a way to prove my worth and earn her trust."

"And you presumed you'd do the same with me?" I scoff. "Unfortunately, leading me to a dead end is the last way to earn my trust."

"Who said anything about a dead end? There's much to be learned from Callahan's journal beyond where his power lies." Von Nevus leans even closer, reaching across me to tap the cover of the book. I smell the garlic on his breath, feel the tassel from his hat bobbing against my cheek.

I want to shove him away and run from this oppressive room and his unsettling company. But I want answers even more, so I force myself to hold my ground and adamantly shake my head. "What are you talking about? Callahan's account is nothing but a long-winded excuse. A convenient tale to justify his decision to steal power from the earth and use it to enslave my people."

"It seems you weren't paying attention," Von Nevus tuts. "If you had been, you'd know what fuels Soren's power—in addition to its origin. He didn't steal anything from the earth that fateful day. It was a fair trade."

"What did Callahan have to trade for power, other than the lives of the men who died in that battle against the Marauders?" I ask. "Are you telling me *blood* is the cost of moving the earth?"

On the one hand, it would explain at least part of Rowenna's fixation with *blood*, *flesh*, *bone*. But if blood was key to moving the earth, the Marauders would be more powerful than all of us.

"Not blood. *Memories*, Little Ro. Memories are the cost of moving the earth."

"'Memories'?" I skeptically repeat. "You mean all that purple prose about Callahan's life flashing before his eyes and sliding away? That was clearly metaphorical."

"Or you *clearly* misunderstood."

"But bagrava fuels Soren and Alaric's power," I cry out in exasperation. "Or at least greatly enhances it," I add when Von Nevus's eyebrows rise and his lips quirk—just like Alaric's. Making me feel like a pitiful little gardener with her head in the dirt. Like I'm the butt of a joke that I've never even heard.

"Callahan didn't know of your people's existence, let alone the bagrava," Von Nevus points out, "so how could it have fueled his power?"

I shrug helplessly. "Maybe it didn't fuel their power initially, but it certainly does now."

"Why do you think that?"

"Because Soren's strength keeps increasing according to the size of our tributes!" I explode, shooting to my feet.

Von Nevus outright laughs. "It's funny how much credit you give your precious fruit. King Soren's strength has nothing to do with your plants. It's all for the courtiers in the queen's salon and always has been. You saw how they guzzle their tea like fish."

"NO!" I cry, cursing the wobble that's crept into my voice. "They couldn't possibly drink so much."

The only thing more intolerable than the thought of Soren using our life-giving bagrava to move the earth is the thought of it being wasted so frivolously. At least, if he used it to erect the protective mountains around our border, it's still *ours* in a way. It still benefits Tashir.

But this?

"You're lying," I say in a low growl.

"I'm afraid not. Our king's power has always been fueled by memories. That's why everyone prays so frequently and fervently—to deposit memories into the earth for Soren and Alaric to use as fuel. Just as Callahan did so many years ago. Think about everything you've learned and seen since you arrived on the mountain, and you'll find it makes perfect sense."

It irks me to admit it does.

How else could the queen and her ladies have forgotten our argument so quickly? How could Alaric seem to know nothing about Rowenna, despite being married to her for a year? How could courtiers, who supposedly saw her every day in the queen's salon, not know my sister has been dead for weeks?

I pinch the bridge of my nose and pace back and forth in front of Von Nevus, trying to make sense of it. "*If* you're telling the truth, how does it work? How many memories are you required to sacrifice? Do you choose what to give, or are they taken at random? How can you be sure not to forget something, or *someone*, important? And how do you ever know what's actually true?"

Questions pour from me like grain from a silo spigot until Garitt reaches out and catches my hand, pulling me to a stop before him.

"Look at you. Suddenly so curious about my country." Garitt flashes a gratified smile. "I *want* to tell you everything, of course, but I can't give away *all* of my nation's secrets in one night. Or without proper payment."

"'Payment'?" I jerk back, but Von Nevus doesn't let go. "I thought you wanted to curry favor, for when I'm queen of Vanzador someday?" The same as you did with Rowenna."

"That will be the bulk of my reward, yes, but can I really be expected to wait so long, especially when I'm risking so much? Rowenna was more than happy to compensate me for my trouble now. I was hoping you'd feel the same. We can pick up right where she and I left off…"

Still holding me fast with one hand, Von Nevus stands and gently traces his fingertips up my bare shoulder and across my collarbone with the other. He might as well be wrapping his fingers around my throat. I can't breathe. Can't wrap my mind around what he's insinuating.

I've had to grapple with a host of inconsistencies about Rowenna's time on the mountain, and most of them, I've been able to rationalize. But not this. She never would have allowed *this*, no matter what Councilor Garitt Von Nevus was offering.

I wrench my arm free from Von Nevus and clutch it against my chest as I stumble back. "I don't believe you. If you had relations with my sister, it's because you forced yourself on her."

Von Nevus laughs. "We both know no one could force Rowenna to do anything against her will."

My shoulders bump into the back wall of the study. Has the room always been this small? How can the door feel so impossibly far away at the same time? I suddenly wish I hadn't marched in here quite so brazenly.

As if he can hear my thoughts, Garitt moves between the door and me. "You're coyer than your sister. I like that."

Dread floods my belly, but I grit my teeth and lift my chin. "Let me pass. I'm not interested in your help if *this* is the cost."

Von Nevus chuckles. "*You* sought *me* out—you literally pounded on my door. No need to be bashful now."

"It was obviously a mistake."

I should have listened to Elodie. She tried to warn me. But that would have required disregarding Rowenna.

You knew I would never agree to this! I silently cry out to her. *Please tell me you didn't agree to this.*

But Ro doesn't answer, and as the seconds grind past, her silence feels prickling. Almost purposeful. Like she expects me to do *whatever* it takes to liberate Tashir and avenge her. Like she wants me to endure this torture because she had to.

I squeeze my eyes shut.

These are Von Nevus's poisonous lies. The Rowenna I know and love would never want me to suffer. In fact, she'd do everything in her power to *keep* me from suffering a similar fate. She was my staunchest protector.

But you're not dealing with the Rowenna of Tashir anymore, my own small, terrified voice whispers. *You're dealing with the Vanzadorian version of your sister, and whatever she chose to do in this horrific situation, she isn't here to save you now. You have to save yourself.*

"I want to leave," I say with a deliberate side step.

Von Nevus mirrors me, blocking the way again. "You can't go now, Little Ro. The fun is just beginning."

He takes another step toward me, and my heart flies into my throat, pounding, pounding, pounding as I cast about for something, anything I can use.

There.

I snatch a letter opener off the table beside the armchair and aim the tiny blade at Von Nevus. "Let me pass."

My hand is shaking so hard I almost drop the pen, and Von Nevus chuckles. "Put that down before you hurt yourself."

He reaches out, like he expects me to just hand over my weapon, but I flex my wrist and the tip of the letter opener grazes the side of his smallest finger. It's hardly more than a paper cut, but the way his eyes flare, you'd think it was a killing blow.

He watches a single bead of black-red blood slide down his finger; then his eyes flick to mine as he slowly licks the crimson trail. When he finally moves aside to let me pass, my thoughts are so frantic, my sobs so racking, I almost fail to hear his parting words.

Once they register, I wish I hadn't heard at all.

"You'll regret this, Little Ro," Von Nevus promises as I stumble into the hall. "Unlike most Vanzadorians, I'm not quick to forgive—or forget."

NINETEEN

RUN.

Down the crowded, twisting halls, past blurs of horrified faces. Several of them are palace guards, but I don't bother asking for help or reporting Von Nevus. They won't believe me over one of King Soren's councilors. They won't punish him for the same reasons. In fact, they'd probably encourage him.

Men like Garitt Von Nevus are untouchable.

I don't stop running until I'm locked inside the walls of my chamber, surrounded by impenetrable stone. But even then, I feel too alone and vulnerable. I trip frantically through the sitting room and grapple the protrusions of emerald and quartz until I find the hidden knob and shove through the heavy door.

It isn't until I stumble into the echoing solarium and see

Alaric's empty desk that I realize how desperately I hoped he'd be here. But of course he isn't. He's been avoiding me since our first and only encounter in this space. And it's not like he'd believe me or care that I'm being harassed.

I break into erratic laughing sobs, fall to my hands and knees, and vomit all over the rug. Just because I no longer believe Alaric killed Rowenna, it hardly makes him safe. That's how utterly alone I am on this mountaintop. Somehow, *he's* my best option. My most tolerable enemy.

Still whimpering, I curl onto my side and stare out the wall of windows, watching the sun paint the snow-dusted mountains purple and pink. But I don't actually see any of it. Just as I don't realize I'm compulsively clawing at the tattoo on my wrist until my nails break the skin.

Our clovers were supposed to be a promise. A vow to love and protect one another. But I've never felt more lost and terrified and alone. I want to find a sharp piece of shale to scrape off every layer of green-dyed skin.

How am I supposed to believe Rowenna caroused with Queen Tessa, drank bagrava tea, and traded intimate favors with men like Garitt Von Nevus? How am I supposed to accept that our precious bagrava is used for nothing more than idle recreation, and watch the Vanzadorians fawn over Soren, when I know his kindness and generosity are an act—so they'll happily supply him with memories?

It's all so wrong.

And makes horrible, perfect sense.

I'm so lost in my spiraling thoughts, I don't realize someone else has entered the hidden solarium until they ease down beside me.

There's a featherlight touch on my back. "Shh. Don't be afraid. I want to help."

I flinch and lash out, wild and wounded like the foxes we find in the traps dotting our fields. "Don't touch me!"

The stranger holds up their hands, and as my gaze travels upward, I'm shocked to find the face of my maid looking down at me.

"What are *you* doing here?" I demand.

Her expression is almost as fearful as mine, but she tucks a strand of golden hair behind her ear and attempts to smile. "I'm here to help."

I let out an incredulous laugh. "You expect me to believe that? After everything? Why are you really here?"

She frowns but doesn't back down. "I came because I heard what happened. My friend services Councilor Von Nevus's chambers, and he overheard the, um, commotion when he came to deliver fresh linens. He saw you flee the room." My maid shudders and weaves her skinny arms around herself. "Did Von Nevus hurt you?"

I shake my head and look away from her pitying gaze.

"I'm glad of that, but you shouldn't have been in his rooms at all. Von Nevus is a disgusting pig. I should have warned you about him."

"That would have required you to occupy the same room as me for more than five seconds," I snip.

"I know." The girl lets out a weary breath, and her entire body sags. I expect this to fill me with vindication, but annoyingly, her guilt doesn't make me feel better.

"It isn't your job to look out for me," I mumble. "I wouldn't have listened anyway."

Not with Rowenna encouraging me to seek out Von Nevus.

I still can't believe she'd lead me to that pig. Maybe he's changed. Or I somehow misunderstood her instructions.

"Has Von Nevus hurt *you*?" I ask my maid, my voice so low, it's almost a whisper. "I'm not trying to pry. You just said you should have warned me; does that mean—"

My maid cuts me off with a decisive shake of her head. "I was lucky. Others warned me to keep my distance when I came to work in the palace."

"Good." I busy my hands with the letter opener I'm still clutching, hoping the girl will scamper off like she has before. But now that I want her to go, she continues sitting there, watching me with her large blue eyes. And I don't know if it's residual stress from my encounter with Von Nevus, or if the discrepancies about Rowenna's time here are slowly driving me mad, but the knots in my stomach cinch tighter and tighter until I suddenly blur, "I-I also want to apologize for whatever Ro put you through. I don't know what to believe, and I don't want to make excuses for her—I know an apology from me isn't the same—but she must have been so scared, so desperate. The sister I know would never have..."

My voice trails off. Because, the truth is, I don't know what *this* version of Rowenna might have done.

My sister's stricken face fills my mind, as if summoned by my betrayal. *Is that truly how you feel?* she asks, but her voice is soft and oddly far away. Far enough, I don't feel compelled to answer right away.

My maid clears her throat, not trying to hide the fact that she's watching me.

I laugh because what else is there to do? "You think I'm out of my mind, don't you?"

She shakes her head, and her eyes soften. "You're really nothing like her, are you?"

I don't have to ask who she means, and under any other circumstance, this would be the worst sort of insult. To be nothing like my sister is to be everything witless, spineless, and weak. But after all the lies and inconsistencies, and my visit with Garitt Von Nevus, I can't deny this declaration fills me with the smallest bit of relief. Which brings yet another wave of guilt crashing down on my head.

"I'm Delphine, by the way," my maid offers.

"Indira," I say, though I'm certain she knows this.

Delphine leans back on her hands and stares out the window, watching the swooping birds and the skiffs of white snow billowing off the peaks. "I have a sister too," she says. "So I know how confusing and infuriating they can be. But I also know there's nothing I wouldn't do for Cloudia, so I understand why you feel the need to defend Rowenna—and why you're so determined to figure out what happened to her."

This unexpected acknowledgment, this sliver of genuine understanding, makes tears spring to my eyes. Which makes me feel even more ridiculous and pathetic. A testament to how lonely and desperate I am. Rowenna is probably rolling over in her grave.

I clear my throat and try to discreetly wipe my tears on my sleeve. "Does Cloudia work in the palace too? Is she older or younger than you?"

"Cloudia is three years younger—sixteen—and she's an incredibly talented seamstress. She beat out a dozen more experienced craftsman to apprentice with the Fortress's finest modiste. And this was two years ago, when she was just fourteen. But this past year, she became too ill to work."

"I'm sorry to hear that," I say, and I truly am. I don't know which is worse: to have your sister ripped away without warning, like Rowenna, or to watch her suffer. "What does Cloudia have? Is it treatable?"

A pained expression flits across Delphine's face before she steers the conversation back to *my* sister. "Rowenna wasn't always horrible, you know. She had many friends here, and she told the most amusing stories at dinner. And she kept her things tidy, never making extra work for me. But she had another side too. It's almost like she was two different people stuffed inside the same body. I never knew which version to expect: the silly courtier or the snarling beast."

"'Snarling beast'?" I repeat.

Delphine's face reddens. "That's obviously an exaggeration, but that's what those of us who caught her prowling the halls at odd hours called her because she always flew into a rage and started hurling accusations."

I still can't imagine Rowenna doing any of this, but I want to keep Delphine talking, so I nod. "I'm beginning to understand why you weren't thrilled to meet me. I've been stalking around the palace just like her."

"Except, unlike Rowenna, you have every reason to be hostile and suspicious. Your sister *died*, and you were dragged here as her replacement. Rowenna was treated like a queen from the moment she set foot on the mountain, yet she was always spinning, always meddling. It's like she was possessed—consumed with something that took her out of her chambers almost every night. I think that's the true reason she banished me to the balcony. So she could sneak about more easily."

Goose bumps prickle the backs of my arms, and I sit up straighter. "Do you know what she was doing? Where she was going?"

From the time we were young, Ro loved sneaking out of our bedchamber under the hill—mostly to play pranks and make mischief in the fields with Haddesh. But she wouldn't have been gallivanting about here or trying to escape. She would have been looking for clues. Cracks. Perhaps she was visiting the Vanzadorians' gemstone mines at night, hoping to find a way to destroy their economy as they've destroyed Tashir's. Or she could have been searching for the caches where they keep our bagrava tributes—to stop the courtiers from wastefully guzzling it. Or maybe she was trying to find and access the memories the Vanzadorian people deposit into the ground—to keep Soren and Alaric from using them as fuel.

Whatever she was doing—whatever she discovered—was damning enough to cost her her life.

"Did you ever question her? Or follow her?" I ask Delphine, practically humming with a new surge of energy. For the first time since arriving on the mountain, I feel close to *something*. Some clue or revelation that will change everything.

"Of course I didn't follow her," Delphine says with a huff. But then she sighs and scrunches her eyes. "I mean, technically, I suppose, I followed her once—but not on purpose. I was just doing my job. Rowenna was wearing a white dressing gown, and I knew the head housekeeper would skin me alive if the garment came back soiled. So I grabbed a more suitable cloak and ran after her. I assumed she was going to meet a gentleman friend, so imagine my surprise when she slipped out a window, lowered herself down the castle wall, and slunk toward the sleeping city.

"I'll admit, I followed out of curiosity then—and duty too. Rowenna wasn't allowed to leave the palace. Especially not at night. And especially not by herself. I figured she was going to meet an accomplice some Vanzadorian traitor who was secretly assisting her—and I couldn't just let that happen. But then, instead of following the paved road that leads from the palace to the grand square, Rowenna veered off onto an overgrown trail. One of the old mining routes that lead to the highest reaches of the mountain."

"What's up there?" I lean closer, eyes huge, not bothering to pretend I'm not completely in her thrall. She could easily be making all of this up as punishment for Rowenna's supposed cruelty. But I don't think she is. The way Delphine spoke about her own sister, and how she came to my aid despite the actions of *my* sister, feels genuine. Empathetic in a way that can only come from a soul-deep understanding of the bond between sisters.

"That's the thing," Delphine continues. "There's nothing up there but abandoned mines and empty caves. Our ancestors excavated those veins of gold and copper decades ago. No one has had any reason to return since they closed. It didn't make sense."

The *thump-thump-thump* of my heart quickens,

because abandoned mine shafts seem like an ideal place to store things Soren doesn't want anyone else to find.

Like memories.

Or bagrava.

"Did you see what she found?"

Delphine shakes her head. "We never made it to the caves. I'm not the most sure-footed, and I stumbled over a boulder in the dark. A wash of pebbles rolled down the trail, straight into the boots of a night watchman. Rowenna told him I forced her out of bed and dragged her into the wilderness. She said I'd been threatening to shove her off a cliff if she didn't pay me extra wages under the table. I've never seen anyone lie so quickly and smoothly. It wasn't natural."

Delphine shudders. "I told the guard Rowenna was lying, but who do you think he believed? He beat me with a tree branch so soundly, I couldn't work for an entire week. Seven days without pay, which meant I couldn't afford Cloudia's medication or a nurse to look in on her."

Delphine bites down on her trembling lip and takes two deep breaths. "When I returned to work, *I* was forced to apologize to Rowenna. She then commanded me to sacrifice my memories of that night. And I wanted to. I would have loved to forget your sister's existence entirely. But I refused to put myself in such a dangerous position. I didn't want to make the same mistake and attempt to follow her again, or let down my guard around her even slightly. So I pretended to sacrifice the memory and continued serving Rowenna with a cheery smile, as if I had no recollection of that night and no animosity toward her. It almost killed me," Delphine murmurs darkly, only realizing the gravity of her statement when she catches my appalled expression. "But I swear, in the name of the kings, I didn't kill her," she adds.

I lean back on my hands with a deflated sigh, weary to the bone of these terrible accusations against Rowenna and seething with frustration to have hit yet another dead end.

Delphine never made it up the mountain, which means she can't tell me what Rowenna was doing up there. But, perhaps, I could convince her to take me there now, if I offered the right incentive.

Fear and excitement battle for hold of my stomach. Part of me knows it's dangerous, asking her to take me to such a remote location. Everything she's told me could be a lie. She could be responsible for Rowenna's death, and I could be inviting her to lead me to my own grisly end. But I don't think that's the case. This serving girl is like me—a bit timid and out of her depth, but determined to do the best for her sister.

I reach out and place a tentative hand on Delphine's bony shoulder. "Would you be willing to sneak me out of the palace and guide me up the mountain? So I can see for myself what Rowenna was up to?"

Delphine's face goes white, and her head's shaking before I've even finished. "I-I couldn't—"

"I know I'm asking a lot, especially since your last journey up the mountain ended so painfully, but I would never sell you out to the guards. And I'll help you in return, of course."

Delphine's head stops shaking, and she cocks a skeptical brow. "How can you help me?"

"I know a lot about plants. There could be remedies to treat your sister's illness the Vanzadorian healers have never even heard of, since so little grows on this mountain. I always keep a stash of dried herbs in my haversack that I'd be happy to experiment with. And if that doesn't work, I have dozens of seed packets I could cultivate in the growing beds Soren has provided. If you take me up the mountain, I won't stop until we find a cure for Cloudia."

Delphine's mouth falls open. "Y-you'd be willing to do that?"

I hold her gaze and nod. "I'll help you with your sister if you'll help me with mine."

Delphine studies me, anxiously fingering the end of her braid for what feels like an eternity.

"*Please*," I beg. "This is the only lead I have to go on."

After a long searching look, Delphine lets out a shaky breath. "Fine. I'll take you tomorrow night. Secure an alibi for yourself—and ensure it's ironclad. Soren has guards and councilors everywhere, and none of them can know we left the palace."

"Not a problem," I say. "In fact, I know just the thing.

Can you bring a tray of lavender tea, a plate of scones, and a bowl of nutmeg when you return tomorrow night?"

Delphine gives me an incredulous look. "Be serious, Indira. This won't be a picnic. We'll be in real danger. We need a real plan."

"Trust me," I say with a blossoming grin. "A picnic is precisely what we need."

TWENTY

WE KNOCK ON ELODIE'S CHAMBER DOOR JUST after sundown the following day. She looks so different from the glamorous, giggling courtier I'm used to, I almost don't recognize her. Her braids are wrapped up in a silk bonnet, her eyes have been scrubbed clean of kohl, and instead of a glittering gown, she's dressed in an old floral robe that makes her looks like the younger sister of the noblewoman who flounces about the queen's salon.

"Indira!" She fingers her bonnet self-consciously. "Did we have plans? I confess, it must have slipped my mind." She glances from me to Delphine, who's carrying the tray of tea and scones I requested, to the pair of guards I asked to escort us here—so there's no debate about where I spent my evening.

"No, this is a surprise visit," I say with an apologetic smile. "I've brought sweets in exchange for advice. Turns out I don't know the first thing about being a wife or pleasing a prince." I shrug helplessly and make a pleading face. "But if it's a bad time, I can come back."

"Don't be silly. I always have time for my dearest friend—especially when you need *this* sort of advice." Elodie ushers me in with a wink and an excited clap, and her genuine enthusiasm to help me at a moment's notice prods me with an unexpected finger of guilt.

Don't forget, she could have ulterior motives, I remind myself. I still don't have proof that she wasn't part of Rowenna's demise. She could be the most cunning threat on this mountain. The wolf, masquerading as a lamb.

Elodie ushers me into a gaudy sitting room with pink-striped wallpaper, delicate crystal statues, and half a dozen framed portraits of Elodie and her mother. She seats me on one of the enormous lounge pillows covering the floor and flounces down beside me.

"Tell me everything."

I launch into a dramatic tale about my wifely failings all while stuffing Elodie so full of pastries, and my specially concocted tea, that she's snoring soundly in less than an hour and should remain that way until midmorning.

Delphine melts away from the wall and helps me lug Elodie into bed. Then we raid her closet for heavy boots and fur-lined cloaks before crossing to the nearest window.

The sun set hours ago, and the moon looks like a sliver from my bitten nails, making the shadows deep and impenetrable. Elodie's rooms are closer to the ground and far more conducive to sneaking out than my solid-rock chamber. There's even a ledge to shuffle along, which leads to a turret we can use for cover as we climb down to the street.

Delphine opens the casement and leans out, glancing right and left. "The guards should be busy chasing chickens that just so happened to escape their coop and wander into the courtyard where King Soren keeps his hunting dogs. So the coast should be clear—if you're ready?" She peers back at me.

I nod once, afraid the roiling anxiety in my stomach will spew out if I open my mouth.

There are so many ways this could go wrong.

After a deep breath and a trepidatious look of her own, Delphine slips out onto the ledge.

I follow, keeping my eyes fixed on a far-off watchtower so I'm not tempted to look down. It isn't the drop that grabs me by the throat and makes me shudder, though. It's the frigid mountain air. When you spend all day cocooned in glass and stone, it's easy to forget these breathtaking views come at the cost of punishing wind and cold. My teeth instantly begin to chatter, and my legs are slow and shaky, despite the extra clothing I borrowed from Elodie. I only manage to shuffle one step in the time Delphine takes five.

I don't know how she's moving so swiftly or easily, especially since she didn't borrow any extra clothing for herself. She insisted she didn't need it, and judging by her easy progress, it's true. But it contradicts everything Alaric taught me about their culture. Someone as physically weak and low in status as Delphine shouldn't be able to withstand such bitter cold. And wasn't her supposed clumsiness the thing that got her and Rowenna caught the night Delphine followed my sister up the mountain? Yet, here she is, navigating the turret wall as effortlessly as a salamander climbing a rocky embankment.

A full-bodied shiver grips me, and I stop shuffling.

"What's the matter?" Delphine asks when she realizes I've fallen even farther behind. "Do you need help?"

I don't have a clue how to answer because, once again, I don't know if my worries are legitimate or if I'm so paranoid and jaded, I'm sabotaging a perfectly good opportunity to find answers.

There could be logical explanations for every little discrepancy. My perception of cold and climbing ability obviously aren't the same as the Vanzadorians, for starters. But I could also be so desperate for answers and assistance, I'm willfully overlooking warning signs.

There's a very real possibility I am following Rowenna's killer to my own demise.

What should I do? I silently ask my sister. *Can this girl be trusted?*

Rowenna doesn't answer for a long moment, and when she does, her voice sounds even softer and farther away than the last time we spoke. *Why ask me? You've decided you can't trust this version of me, remember?*

It isn't like that! You have to understand...

Delphine snaps my name, bringing me back to the ledge. "Do you want me to take you up the mountain or not? The longer we stand here, the more likely we'll be caught." She points to the city streets below, where shadowy men and women bustle between lamplit homes and shops. Right now, their heads are bowed against the wind, but they could look up any second and spot us.

"This was *your* idea," Delphine adds with a frustrated huff, and that's what finally uproots my feet. She didn't lure me out here. *I* begged *her* to take me up the mountain. Even if she somehow manipulated me into thinking it was all my idea, it's still my best chance to learn about Rowenna.

Potentially my only chance.

I set my teeth and force myself to move, following Delphine closely as we pick our way down the turret wall. Once our feet are on the ground, she allows me exactly one minute to catch my breath before she sets off at a breakneck pace, leading me through the maze of snow-dusted streets.

I expect the wealth and opulence of Vanzador to decline, now that we're no longer within the palace walls, but even the broader Fortress is far more lavish and inviting than I could have imagined. Lovely stone cottages line the well-manicured lanes, each home painted a bright pastel with coordinating shutters and a neat little gravel yard. Some even have small stone tables and slides for the children. There are streetlamps on every corner, and the shops are tidy and clean, built one on top of the next like children's blocks. It has a homey feeling. The type of city where neighbors say hello and borrow eggs and sugar. The sort where a person would feel safe walking alone after dark. A far cry from the bleak, inhospitable slums Rowenna described in her letters.

Yet another glaring lie.

Delphine stops suddenly as a group of weary, soot-streaked miners trudge through the cross street. I slam into Delphine's back, which is surprisingly solid given her bony frame. I'm even more surprised when she claps a hand over my mouth and easily drags me into the shadow of the nearest shop, pressing my shoulders against the freezing stones.

"Pay attention! If you do that on the switchbacks up the mountain, we'll both fall to our death."

Like Rowenna.

We're both thinking it, and Delphine's face immediately softens. "I'm sorry. That was insensitive."

"Do you really think that's what happened?" I don't know why I ask. Her opinion doesn't matter, and I know better than to trust it. I guess I'm just desperate for validation. I need someone else to tell me Ro didn't fall. That I'm not doing all of this for nothing.

Delphine's golden braid sways with the sharp shake of her head. "Do you think I'd be out here if I thought she fell? The Rowenna *I* knew was far too nimble to make such a careless mistake. Everything she did was measured, calculated. There's a reason she was sneaking up the mountain, a reason someone wanted her dead, and we're going to find it. Then you're going to find a cure for Cloudia."

She says this so definitively, it almost sounds like a threat.

I swallow hard against the swelling knot in my throat. I fully intend to do my best for Cloudia. If I can keep anyone from suffering the all-consuming grief of losing a sister, I will. But I'm no healer, and I'm beginning to worry I've promised too much.

Delphine watches me for another long moment, and it's all I can do not to crawl out of my skin. At last, she turns and climbs a steep road leading to the outermost wall of the Fortress. A pair of guards are playing dice near a gate, and we slip past them to a section of wall conveniently hidden behind a laundress shop. It happens to be quite a bit lower here, to allow a pipe to vent steam out into the dark, and the constant hiss dampens our footsteps. The thick haze conceals us as we scramble over the wall.

It's all so disconcertingly convenient. So perfectly

planned. Like this is something Delphine has done a hundred times rather than somewhere she followed Rowenna once.

Stop, I reprimand myself. Paranoia helps nothing. And who's to say Delphine *hasn't* done this a hundred times? Or that this is even the route Rowenna took? The citizens of Vanzador aren't forbidden to leave the Fortress. That rule only applies to me, the captive bride. Delphine probably played out here as a child, ran errands to the mines, or crept out here to kiss boys under the stars. There are a thousand explanations.

Unfortunately, none of them help me feel calmer.

"This way." Delphine brushes off her hands and gestures for me to follow her higher still, into the boundless shadowed wilderness. "We can speak freely up here. We shouldn't see a soul."

There isn't a tree or shrub in sight, only moss and scree. Which means, if someone is waiting up here, they have nowhere to hide.

And neither do we.

"Tell me more about Cloudia's symptoms," I say in an effort to distract myself. "When did they begin?"

"I first noticed the change several months ago. She began having nightmares, which hadn't happened since she was a little girl. She also grew moodier and kept to herself more than usual. I didn't worry, though. She's sixteen. It would be strange if she wasn't moody. Her best friend,

Nenia, had also recently run off with a traveling minstrel who passed through Vanzador with his troupe.

"I felt sorry for Cloudia, of course, but I was secretly glad Nenia was gone. She was always skipping work and sneaking off with boys or trying to worm her way into the palace. She thought herself above the doldrums of common life and insisted she would become a courtier one day. And she nearly managed it. Nenia somehow found her way into your sister's good graces—to the point I was certain I was going to be replaced as Rowenna's maid."

"How did she manage that?" I ask, perplexed. "Why would my sister spend time with a random Vanzadorian girl?"

"According to what Nenia told Cloudia, it's because Rowenna said Nenia reminded her of herself. And, honestly, I have to agree. Both girls were so vain and entitled and—" Delphine catches herself and clears her throat awkwardly. "But then Nenia met that minstrel boy, and that was that. She was on to her next flight of fancy."

"She gave up her courtly ambitions so easily?" I ask.

"The boy *was* handsome," Delphine admits, pausing our ascent to catch her breath. "Maybe he convinced her that being a maid in the palace would never be the same as being a courtier. Or maybe Rowenna grew tired of Nenia's company, and that's why she left in such a hurry. Whatever the reason, she was gone, and I tried to give Cloudia space to mourn her friend. I let her sleep late and didn't ask her to do as many chores. But instead of improving, Cloudia grew noticeably weaker and more exhausted. She missed several days of her apprenticeship, then stopped going all together, often remaining in bed until late afternoon, staring at the wall."

"Sounds like melancholia," I say, trying not to sound relieved. It isn't a pleasant illness, but it's common enough I know a few different herbal remedies to try.

"That was the doctor's initial diagnosis too." Delphine resumes climbing. "He prescribed vigorous exercise and sunshine. And I tried to make as much time for Cloudia as possible when I wasn't working. We'd take walks to her favorite overlooks, and I'd smuggle her treats from the palace. But she continued to get worse. Eventually, she remained in bed all day. That's how it's been for months now. She lies there, as still as the dead, aside from random fits when her arms and legs suddenly jerk and her eyelids fly open, searching the room without actually seeing anything. Sometimes she whispers in a strange, scratchy voice until she runs out of energy and appears to faint."

Delphine shivers, and it's all I can do not to follow suit.

"I see," I say with a contemplative nod, careful to keep my expression neutral and my breath steady—like the healers under the hill do. So she can't see the fingers of anxiety slowly tightening around my throat. "That sounds horrible."

"It's terrifying," Delphine agrees. "The only thing it

reminds me of, even slightly, is the foaming sickness some animals get. The one that drives them mad."

At last, the ground levels off, and I double over to catch my breath. My relief is short-lived, though. When I glance up, Delphine is staring at me expectantly, awaiting promises and reassurance I can't give her. On top of this, the mountaintop is nothing how I imagined.

For some reason, I expected the abandoned mines to be vast open pits Soren greedily scooped from the earth, in order to extract every useful gemstone and mineral as quickly as possible. But it's actually an intricate system of caves and crevasses riddling the mountaintop like mouse-eaten cheese. Some shafts are so narrow, I'd have to wriggle on my belly to crawl inside. Other caves are so large and black, they could easily house entire families of mountain lions.

I curse under my breath as I take it all in. It will take weeks to simply find and catalogue every cave, let alone search them for Soren's secrets or clues to what Rowenna was up to.

I want to sit down hard and bury my freezing hands in my hair. I want to shout into the velvety-black sky and berate my sister for making every step of this process so difficult. For leaving me to do this all alone.

"Come on." Delphine takes my arm and gently tugs me toward a shallow cave entrance near the trail. "It won't be so bad. We'll start here and proceed in a clockwise fashion. It shouldn't take too long."

But after five long hours of combing through dripping walls and mossy floors, we haven't found a trace of my sister. Or bagrava. Or anything even slightly out of the ordinary. Just spiders, muck, and old rusted mining tools.

Delphine wipes her sweaty face on the inside of her blouse and glances at the trail leading down the mountain. "We need to get back before the sun rises and someone notices you're gone."

I'm bone-weary and half-frozen, but the thought of returning without anything to show for our efforts feels even more painful and exhausting. "Just a little while longer," I beg. "Elodie is the only person on the mountain who pays me any mind, and she'll be asleep for several hours yet, thanks to my special tea."

"She's the only one who *openly* pays you mind," Delphine corrects me as she tugs me back down the trail. "Don't think for a second Soren's inquisitors aren't watching your every move. They're always watching all of us."

"What are you talking about? What inquisitors?" I ask as we slide down a steep field of scree.

"Those of us who work in the palace and have witnessed their machinations firsthand, like to call King Soren's councilors *inquisitors*, since they do far more than simply offer advice. They're always sniffing about for trouble and watching over our prayers, compelling us to get rid of inconvenient memories."

"*What?*" I grind to a halt, forcing Delphine to stop

too. "Von Nevus told me that memory tithes fuel Soren and Alaric's power, but he didn't tell me you don't get to choose which memories to sacrifice when you pray."

"In theory, each person chooses what to remember and what to give to the land, but that doesn't mean we aren't heavily *influenced*. Soren and his inquisitors often make *suggestions* or offer *incentives* for purging certain memories that might be problematic or paint them in a bad light. Then they watch us like hungry wolves, ready to pounce if we haven't followed through."

It feels like Soren is here, yanking the ground out from under me. This must be what Alaric was referring to when he said his people weren't the most forthcoming. When he insisted I was wasting my time hunting for the truth about Rowenna's death.

There *is* no truth—only King Soren's carefully curated version of it.

This must be why his people still love him. And why no one seems to remember anything substantial about Rowenna. And why I'll never be able to piece together the truth about her death.

"But how is it enforced?" I ask Delphine. "Soren and his councilors can't possibly know if you've purged specific memories, *right?*"

Delphine sighs. "Like it or not, our actions reveal our thoughts. Even if you're careful and try to play along, it's impossible to be perfectly vigilant. Every day, I'm terrified

I'll slip and reveal something about Cloudia's illness. After her initial visit with the healers, I lied and said she was getting better. I'm *still* making up stories and excuses to explain her absences because I'm terrified the king and his minions will take her away if they know the truth. They'll say they need to isolate her to keep the illness from spreading. They'll claim they're doing us both a kindness—Cloudia is clearly suffering and watching her decline is affecting my nerves, distracting me from my work. But what then? Will they lock her away for observation? Use her for experimentation? Kill her outright, even? I'd never know because they'd order me to forget it all."

"I'm sorry," I say. "That's...*horrifying*."

I feel suddenly guilty for asking her to hide even more. Risk even more.

"Sometimes, in my weaker moments, I want to be done with it all," Delphine admits. "It would be such a luxury to purge my problems and flounce around the palace like the giggling courtiers."

I nod with understanding. "The truth can be heavy, but remembering the good and the bad makes us *real* in a way the vapid courtiers will never be. It makes us strong. I would never choose to forget Rowenna, not even if the pain of losing her feels like having my innards scraped out with a spade. Not even if my efforts to avenge her never amount to anything. I don't expect you to continue putting yourself and Cloudia at even greater risk by helping me, though," I say, meeting Delphine's gaze in the moonlight. "The less you know about my machinations, the better. I'll still do everything in my power to help Cloudia, even if you choose not to continue searching the caves."

Delphine studies me with a strange, almost perplexed expression. Then she turns abruptly and resumes her descent. She doesn't utter another word as we wind through the city streets and climb back up the turret wall. Only once we're back in Elodie's rooms, standing over the courtier's prone form, does she speak.

"I take back what I said before—about you being nothing like Rowenna. You're just as brave, just as determined. But you're also kind, perceptive, and empathetic. You're exactly what we need—"

"I don't think Elodie would agree with your assessment," I interrupt in a strained whisper, looking down at the courtier in her bed. "Especially since I'm going to have to drug her again in order to continue searching the caves."

But Delphine continues as if I haven't spoken. "I want to join you back up the mountain. I'm willing to risk my life and go behind my king's back, because I see it now. You really are the answer. For the first time since Cloudia fell ill, I feel a bit of hope."

The answer to what? I want to ask. But Delphine throws her arms around me, and it's been so long since anyone has truly embraced me, I don't remember where to put my hands. Or how long to linger. I can't even tell if the warmth and tightness feel safe and reassuring or if I feel trapped and suffocated.

In the end, I simply stand there, rigid and reeling, while a girl who used to loathe me cries onto my shoulder.

TWENTY-ONE

WAKE WITH A START SEVERAL HOURS LATER, MOMEN-tarily confused by the midday sunlight casting rainbows around my geode chamber, and the fact that I'm wearing a fur cloak in bed.

Then it all comes rushing back: my midnight trek up the mountain with Delphine, the staggering number of caves, and collapsing into bed, too exhausted to even change into a nightgown.

I sit up, stretch, and consider burrowing back into my blankets. I could easily sleep the rest of the day. It would be so nice to hide from the impossibility of my task. But Delphine has probably been hard at work for several hours already, running on even less sleep, and the debt I owe her nags at me like a hard-to-reach itch. She's sacrificing so much, risking so much, to help me. The least I can do is uphold my end of the bargain.

I change into a shirt and pair of trousers I brought from Tashir, grab my haversack, and make my way into the hidden solarium. The glass room is hot and bright, and I squint as I inspect the planter and tools King Soren provided. The shovels and hand rakes are clearly mining implements that have been repurposed—iron hammers and picks that were melted and reformed—but they'll do the job. And the floor-to-ceiling windows provide an ideal amount of light. A small cluster of bagrava fruit sits in a basket, so shiny, purple, and perfect. Calling to me like an old friend.

My fingers twitch with longing. My heartbeat throbs in my ears. It would feel so good to scoop the seeds from the flesh and start humming the incantations. I'd give almost anything to feel the familiar swell of strength that flows between me, Earth Mother, and the newly sprouted plants.

But that's exactly what Soren wants—the reason he placed the basket here in the first place,, hoping I wouldn't be able to resist its siren song. I kick the basket across the room to prove a point and breathe a sigh of relief as the bagrava roll under Alaric's desk. Out of sight. Then I reach for my haversack and upend it. Everything I brought from Tashir spills around my feet and I kneel down to pick through the contents. There isn't much: two pairs of socks, a few scraps of fabric to tie back my hair, three bottles of plant food, a dropper of neem-oil, and a leather packet that contains dried herbs, seeds, and cuttings from our foundation crops.

Every gardener in Tashir carries a packet like this, even us master gardeners, who rarely help with common plants. We've found it best to let most crops grow at their natural rate, during their natural season, so we master gardeners can focus our energy solely on the bagrava. But every once in a while—like after a particularly brutal storm or in case of infestation—we step in to reseed and speed the growing process, so the timing of the harvest is unaffected.

I comb through the packet, sifting through sachets of wheat, barley, and corn until I come to the collection of herbs at the back of the bundle. It's nothing earth-shattering. Just hyssop, lavender, chamomile, calendula, rosemary, and St. John's wort. Basic ingredients you'd find in any cupboard in Tashir. But these things *could* be earth-shattering in a place like Vanzador. For patients like Cloudia, who has only been prescribed sunlight and exercise.

I tie back my hair and get to work, pressing my thumb into the dirt to form evenly spaced holes. Then I snuggle seeds into each bed, cover them up, and give them a good drink of water. Once the entire planter is prepared, I press my hands to the earth and lower my head until my cheek brushes the dirt.

The incantations we use to nourish common plants is different from the words we sing to the bagrava, and the tingling in my chest isn't nearly as intense. But it's still so comforting, empowering, and *normal*, I burst into tears.

Of course, Alaric strides into our solarium at that very moment.

He looks as immaculate as ever in a black jacket that nearly brushes the floor. The high collar and thick cuffs are embroidered with golden filigree, and the contrast of the glittering gold against the inky black makes his long lean frame almost glow in the harsh sunlight.

When he spots me, he halts in the doorway and stares as if I'm covered in blood rather than dirt. "What in the name of the kings are you doing? You're supposed to be in my mother's salon."

"I wasn't aware I had a schedule to keep," I snap. "Or that you watch my comings and goings so closely. I'm flattered." I bat my eyelashes and smile sharply, hoping my bravado hides how fast my heart is hammering.

Gardening is a sacred experience. With Earth Mother's incantations on my lips and her soil in my palms, it's the closest I can come to being part of the land itself. A moment far too personal and intimate for any Vanzadorian to witness, let alone the crown prince. I feel even more exposed than if he walked in on me naked.

Alaric rolls his eyes, strides to his desk, and rummages around until he finds a pair of scrolls. "You *wish* I kept a closer eye on you."

I bark out a laugh. "That's the last thing I want."

"Are you sure? Because your expression when I walked in said otherwise." Alaric lets his mouth fall open dramatically and blinks at me with wide fluttering eyes. As if I looked anything like that.

"You surprised me! And interrupted a sacred moment! Of course I was a bit flustered. But it has nothing to do with—" I gesture up and down his flashy visage, hoping to seem dismissive and unimpressed. But Alaric's smirk broadens, and my cheeks feel like they've been burned by the blistering sun.

I can't believe I sought him out after my confrontation with Von Nevus, even subconsciously. He would have mocked me just like this. The glimpse of vulnerability I saw at the end of our previous encounter in this room meant nothing. It was a carefully choreographed act, like everything else in Vanzador.

I silently thank Earth Mother for sending me Delphine instead—a true ally with an actual heart. Someone who understands the bond between sisters.

"I'm just pleased to see you're finally getting to work," Alaric says as he saunters toward the planting beds.

"Speaking of, don't you have somewhere else to be?" I mutter. "You're always nattering on about your important princely duties." I wave my trowel toward his door, but Alaric continues stalking closer.

"No one will miss me for a moment. In fact, Father would want me to survey your progress."

"I hope you're prepared for disappointment, because I'm *not* growing bagrava. None of this is for you—or your father."

Alaric's perpetual smirk finally falters, and it brings me an inordinate amount of joy.

"What are you doing, then? What are you growing, if not bagrava?"

"I don't see how it's any of your business," I say archly.

"I'm the crown prince. Everything is my business—especially if it has to do with my meddlesome wife."

"I thought you weren't going to address me as such."

"Believe me, I don't want to. But your actions now reflect on me, so I don't have a choice. Now, tell me what you're doing, or I'll come over there and dig around myself."

I let out a long beleaguered sigh. "I'm helping a friend who's ill."

"But you don't have any friends here."

"How would you know that unless you've been watching me?" I challenge.

Alaric sputters, and it's even more satisfying than honey mead at harvest time. The sweet, sweet taste of victory.

"Run along, back to your important business." I give another dismissive wave of my trowel, but instead of retreating, Alaric stubbornly perches on a chair near my planting bed and cants forward so he's hovering over me.

His cloying scent invades my nostrils—the same hint of wind and leather I remember from the Tomb Flats, but now it's accompanied by something spicy too. Cardamom, perhaps? The combination is far too heady and intoxicating, and I force myself to cough loudly.

"Must you sit so close?"

"I need a good view. I've never known a master gardener who's also a healer. I must bear witness to such talent."

"Fine." I stab my trowel into the soil and breathe deeply, so the loamy scent covers up his stink. Then I push the dirt around, pretending to be busy, while I wait for Alaric to get bored and leave.

As expected, he sighs after just a few minutes. "Aren't you supposed to use magic? Anyone can plant seeds and wait for them to grow."

"Even *I* can't grow something from nothing. The seeds must first be planted before they can be coaxed. But that never crossed your mind, did it? You think you're above the laws of nature."

"No," Alaric says with surprising vehemence. Then he adds, more softly, "I don't, actually."

I bark out a laugh. "Have you seen this glass solarium? Your opulent palace? The entire Fortress is extravagant and excessive, carved out of the mountain without thought for the integrity of the earth *or* the well-being of your own people—whose precious memories fuel your power."

Alaric's eyes darken, and he shakes his head. "You're oversimplifying. Just because you don't understand something doesn't make it wrong. I can use my power to widen the mine shafts and provide work for my people while still preserving the mountain's natural integrity. Just as I can reroute an avalanche to stop it from obliterating innocent lives and homes without redirecting so much snow that the rivers and water supply are affected. My power isn't at odds with nature. I work *with* the earth—like you," he adds, and the statement is so ridiculous, his expression so unexpectedly earnest, I want to tilt my head back and howl with bitter laughter.

His power is nothing like mine. *He* is nothing like me. But before I say these things, I think better of it. I consider what my sister would do. An emotional outburst will help nothing. But seeing how Soren and Alaric's powers work and govern the Fortress will make it easier to find and exploit their weaknesses.

"Prove it," I challenge my husband. "If your power is truly in harmony with the earth—*like mine*—let me watch you work."

Alaric appraises me with a furrowed brow. "My father wouldn't like that."

"And you'd never dream of upsetting dear old Daddy," I goad.

"However"—Alaric narrows his eyes at me—"I'd be willing to take you to a jobsite, if *you're* willing to show me how your power works." He jabs his chin toward the planter.

"It's not bagrava, so why do you care?" I ask suspiciously.

He shrugs. "I find plants fascinating."

"*You're* interested in plants?"

"Of course. They're beautiful and strange. Something so foreign, up here on the mountain. My few trips to Tashir are the closest I've ever come to anything green, and I couldn't very well plop myself in the middle of a cornfield and examine it then, could I?"

The thought of Alaric sitting in a cornfield is so ridiculous, I burst out laughing.

His cheeks redden, and the splash of warmth makes his face look more flesh than stone. Almost human. It's so disarming, I don't immediately look away when our eyes meet. But then Alaric opens his big mouth and shatters the illusion.

"Plants draw strength from the earth—just as I do."

And there it is. The real reason behind his *interest*. He doesn't care about all the ways plants can be used as food or medicine. Or how they can beautify a space and cleanse the air. Or how they literally saved my people from starving to death on the Tomb Flats. *No*. To him, plants are just another potential source of power. Something else he can steal from the ground, since he and his father apparently don't have enough power already.

Allowing him to watch me work would be a terrible

idea—a betrayal to Earth Mother and the plants themselves. It could give him ideas. He could try to replicate my incantations, and with the luck he and Soren have, he'd probably succeed.

Except he isn't asking to watch me grow bagrava. And the knowledge I stand to gain from watching him manage the mines could be far more useful than anything he might glean from watching me grow a few common herbs.

"Fine," I tell Alaric. "I'll show you a bit of plant magic *after* you've taken me to a jobsite."

"But you're literally knee-deep in the process now." Alaric points at the planter again. "And it will take some time to arrange a visit to the mines without my father present—and with the right foremen on duty, who won't alert the councilors."

"Hopefully not too long. I won't let you weasel your way out of your end of the bargain," I warn as I lower my face to the earth and quietly begin to sing.

In Tashir, people often watched me work—Lewis, of course, and the other master gardeners—but it was also commonplace for other planters to lean over the stone walls and listen to the incantations as they passed. Their presence never gave me a second's hesitation. On the contrary, it strengthened my performance and intensified my connection with Earth Mother—as if they were adding their voice to my prayers. But now, as I stumble through the opening stanza, I'm acutely aware of the tremor in my voice. I can feel Alaric's judgmental gaze searing my back, and it's all I can do to force the words through my clenched teeth.

It's too much. Far too intimate a moment to share with someone like him. But before I can sit up and shoo Alaric away, the familiar tingling floods my bloodstream, and Alaric, the Fortress, and the rest of the world melts away, leaving only me, Earth Mother, and the newly planted seeds, trembling to life beneath the soil.

Even though I can't see them, I *feel* them writhing against their fleshy casings, swelling as Earth Mother's strength pours through me like a sieve. With every stanza, the pressure builds until a soundless *pop* judders through my body, and I know, beneath the soil, the shoots have broken free from their pods.

I imagine the tiny plants curling to life like snakes. I picture them surging upward through the soil, hungry for that first glimpse of sun and sky. When I reach the chorus of my song, they punch through the surface in an explosion of green, and I know I've done more than enough to appease Alaric. His gasp of surprise fills the entire solarium. But still, I keep singing. Still, I keep coaxing. Urging the shoots to stretch higher until the song is over and fully grown herbs populate the entire planter.

I sit in their midst, sweating and panting, breathing in the sweet evergreen aroma of the lavender and the earthy-apple fragrance of the chamomile. For the first time since I arrived on the mountain, I feel at peace. My fingertips flutter through the velvety buds and down the ridged leaves, reveling in the thrum of new life in this cold, dead place. Savoring this beautiful reunion with Earth Mother after a long week apart.

It isn't until Alaric gently claps that I remember he's sharing in this sacred, private moment.

I wrap my arms around my chest and keep my gaze fixed firmly on the plants, mortified that I let myself get so carried away. But Alaric continues clapping, and when I finally glance up, he's wearing an expression I've never seen before. His eyes are soft, his lips slightly parted. It's the way you'd look at something impressive and fascinating and *beautiful*, even.

The opposite of everything I am in his eyes.

I turn away to hide my burning cheeks and try to dredge up something terrible to say. Anything to shatter this moment. I'd much rather he slap me with a spiteful scowl and snide remark. I know how to defend against those attacks. But this. This feels even more insidious. Even more dangerous.

"Indira." Alaric murmurs my name with too much reverence. "That was—"

"Quite enough for one day." I stand abruptly and brush off my pants. "Find me when you've arranged my visit to a jobsite."

"But—" Alaric's vexingly handsome face contorts into

a wounded frown that must render most women on the mountain into beet pulp. But not me. I turn and march across our solarium to my chamber door, praying he can't hear my galloping heart.

"Indira, wait! I have so many questions!" he calls after me.

I slam the gemstone door behind me and lean against the sharp protrusions, gulping back air. Certain I've made a fatal mistake.

Sharing my gift was supposed to help me break through Alaric Alaverdi's defenses. But I have a terrible, overwhelming feeling he somehow broke through mine.

TWENTY-TWO

"M ISS INDIRA? ARE YOU UNWELL?" DELPHINE calls through the door after knocking a second time. "You missed dinner."

I missed breakfast and lunch too. I haven't left this chamber all day. I told myself it was due to exhaustion; cultivating an entire planter of herbs from seed requires a staggering amount of energy. *That's* why I can't bring myself to change out of my dressing gown or leave this warm cocoon of blankets. It has nothing to do with that look of wonder on Alaric's face or the terrifying prospect of passing him in the halls.

"That's it. I'm coming in," Delphine calls out. A moment later, she bursts through the door with a tray full of food and darts worried glances at me as she arranges the saucers and bowls on the table. "Did something happen yesterday after we returned from the mountaintop?"

"I'm just tired. I spent the day cultivating herbs for Cloudia," I tell her, conveniently omitting Alaric's presence.

He was nothing but a fly on the wall. An annoyance.

"Really?" Delphine's entire countenance brightens. "I didn't expect you to start on Cloudia's treatment so soon. I figured you'd wait until after we finished searching the caves, when you have answers about Rowenna."

I firmly shake my head. "Living sisters should take priority. And it would be unwise to sneak out again so soon. Someone might notice if I'm suddenly spending every evening in Elodie's chambers. Which is just as well, since I'm worried the sleeping herbs will affect her mind. Drugging her once felt like a regrettable but necessary risk. Doing it again—potentially many times—feels wrong."

"It's not as if it could make her more frivolous and silly," Delphine cuts in with a tiny giggle. "And you have nothing to worry about. I have it on good authority that Elodie Tomasko was prancing about the queen's salon this morning as if nothing was amiss."

"Was she truly?"

"The queen's attendants told me she looked even more rosy cheeked than usual. Undoubtedly a benefit of such deep sleep. Really, we're doing her a favor."

Delphine's eyes meet mine, and I join in her giggling, unsure if I'm more grateful for the feel of laughter in my belly or the word she used.

We.

I'm no longer alone on this quest.

You've never been alone, Ro huffs indignantly.

You know what I mean.

No, I don't, my sister argues, but I'm not in the mood for bickering. Not when I have a planter full of herbs to show Delphine— who actually seems to appreciate my efforts.

I grab Delphine's sleeve and pull her through the hidden solarium door. "Come on. I have something I want to show you."

If Rowenna protests, I don't hear her over the sound of Delphine's delighted shriek when the blooming planter comes into view. Her hands fly to her mouth. "Indira! It's space incredible! You did all of this *today*?"

She approaches the bed reverently, the way you would a sacred altar, and glides her palm across the tufts of lavender. It reminds me a bit of Alaric's reaction to my work, but unlike my power-hungry husband, Delphine's interest is selfless and sincere, her gratitude tangible.

"It's nothing, really," I say with a modest shrug. "Common plants are much easier to cultivate than bagrava. Here, help me harvest them. If we work quickly, we can have a medication ready for you to take to Cloudia tonight."

I show Delphine how to run her fingers along the stalk to collect the fragrant buds, and once the bucket is filled, we begin grinding the lavender into a pulp.

"I want to know more about Cloudia," I say as we work. "Not her illness, but who she is as a person—as your sister. I want to remember what it's like to have someone who shares your blood and experiences. Someone who knows your worst qualities and darkest secrets, and loves you anyway."

I glance down at the clover on my wrist and slowly trace the three round leaves. I miss Rowenna so much it hurts, but I've never been more frustrated with anyone in my life.

Delphine considers me thoughtfully before answering. "Cloudia is hilarious but also painfully shy, so few people get to see that side of her. And she's brilliant with numbers. She started helping me with my lessons when she was only ten, and I'm ashamed to admit I was never as grateful as I should have been. But Cloudia didn't hold it against me. She continued tutoring me—after only a bit of groveling on my part."

I squeeze the reddish compound from the stamens of St. John's wort into a jar. "She sounds lovely."

"She is. Some might even say she's *too* lovely—far too warm and gentle for this cold, inhospitable place. Our parents died in a mining accident when Cloudia was eleven and I was fourteen, so I've done everything in my power to shield and protect her since then."

"As any good older sister would," I say with reverence. "That's exactly what Rowenna did for me. She spared me from attending council meetings after each Marauder attack, knowing the damage and loss of life would upset me. And she steered me away from toxic friendships with noble children who only wanted to befriend me for my status. She even helped me make the best alliances among Father's councilors, since I was always working in the fields and not privy to their hidden agendas."

Delphine cocks her head and studies me with a furrowed brow. "I'm not sure that's the same at all. The way you describe Rowenna…" Delphine bites her lip, choosing her words with care. "She sounds a bit manipulative."

"*Manipulative?*" The word lands like a physical blow, and I reel back, shaking my head. "Ro could be bossy at times, but what older sister isn't? I'm sure Cloudia would say the same about you. You just don't understand because you're the oldest."

Delphine shrugs and musters a smile, but it doesn't quite reach her eyes. "Thank you for sharing your perspective. You younger sisters can be a headache, but there's nothing we wouldn't do for you. No sacrifice too great."

"And we younger sisters feel that devotion. It's why we worship the ground you walk on—even if we don't always show it. If we acted too grateful, we'd never hear the end of it. Older sisters can be completely insufferable, you know."

Delphine laughs, and we continue trading memories

as we grind the herbs into a simple sleeping draft. I'm not naïve enough to think it will work miracles, but even a slight improvement in Cloudia's condition would feel like a victory.

But night after sleepless night, we're met with failure.

I make every remedy I can recall our healers using and send them off with Delphine, along with a silent prayer to Earth Mother for success, but none help Cloudia's condition in the slightest. And our slow and excruciating search of the abandoned mines is even more fraught.

Every few nights, we find a way to sneak up to the highest reaches of the mountain, but there's nothing up there but depleted veins of silver and empty tunnels. And every time we leave the palace, our odds of being caught increase. One of these days, the guards will spot us scaling the turret. Or poor Elodie will keel over dead from the repeated drugging. Just yesterday, she was complaining of headaches in the queen's salon. Or, most terrifying of all, King Soren will run out of patience.

I've managed to avoid him for the better part of the week by taking my meals in my chamber instead of the great hall and never venturing too close to his council rooms, but last night, my luck ran out. He sent a pair of guards to check my progress in the planting beds, and they nearly gave me a heart attack, pounding on my chamber door in the dead of night, demanding to know if I'd started cultivating bagrava, and reminding me, in no uncertain terms, what would happen to the mountains surrounding Tashir if I failed to produce something soon.

I huddled in the corner, biting my fist to stave off a scream. I was out of time. I would have to betray my people, Earth Mother, and the bagrava itself, and for what? So the courtiers could continue guzzling their tea? It didn't make sense. Why was Soren so desperate to grow bagrava on the mountain if it didn't directly benefit his power? There had to be more to it.

"We've been ordered to break down the door if necessary!" one of the guards bellowed, throwing his weight against the wood. It groaned and crackled, and just when I was certain it would splinter, another door, farther down the hall, slammed open.

I listened, frozen with shock, as Alaric's voice rang out, threatening to end the guards' lives if they dared to bother me again.

After a few tense moments and several unsavory words, the guards clattered away, but my panic didn't abate. If anything, I felt even more frantic because my husband now stood on the other side of the door, and he was far more volatile and dangerous than the guards. They were mindless brutes, merely carrying out Soren's orders. Alaric, on the other hand, had chosen to come to my aid—*again*—and I couldn't fathom why. Especially after our last encounter in the solarium, when I'd met his interest in my plants with hostility.

It's obviously a trap, Ro interjected. *He'll expect something in return.*

But her voice was oddly muffled, as if *she* was the one standing on the other side of the door, while Alaric's presence loomed all around me despite the actual physical barrier.

I swore I could smell his spicy scent. And picture how he'd be raking his hair out of his face with impatience. I could even *feel* his eyes on the doorknob, staring with the same intensity I experienced in the solarium—when our gazes briefly met across the herbs.

He was clearly waiting for me to do something—*say* something. But what? *Thank you* felt inadequate yet entirely too vulnerable at the same time.

Eventually, Alaric sighed and I heard his hand press against the door. "I'm trying to buy you time—so you can ease into these responsibilities—but I can't hold my father off forever."

My own fingers rose to the door, drawn by his confession. My throat burned with the urge to thank him.

Don't! Rowenna interjected at the last second, and I snatched my hand back as if the door were aflame. *Luring flies with sugar water is no different than smashing them with a swatter. In fact, I'd say the swatter is kinder. At least it's swift and straightforward.*

I nearly choked on a burst of bitter laughter. How dare she speak of straightforwardness when everything about her time here was a contradiction?

Delphine's awful accusation pounded like a drum in my head:

She sounds a bit manipulative.

I let my head thud against the door, hating Delphine for putting such wicked thoughts in my head. And hating even more that she might be right.

Unbelievable, Rowenna seethed.

Before I could apologize or explain, a ferocious chill rattled through me, and the air that had been brimming with my sister's presence felt suddenly hollow and flat. It was as shocking as having the quilts ripped off on a winter's night, and I clutched my arms around myself, desperate to call her back, wanting, more than anything, to burrow back into her warmth and affection. But I held my tongue. She couldn't just punish me with silence every time I disagreed. Of course I valued her opinions, but how was I ever supposed to trust and rely on myself if she was the loudest voice inside my head?

I don't know how long I stood there, silently cursing my sister and myself, before I regained enough composure to offer a mumbled thanks to Alaric.

But like Rowenna, he was gone.

TWENTY-THREE

AFTER THE VISIT FROM SOREN'S GUARDS, Delphine and I redouble our efforts up the mountain. We risk the journey two nights in a row, totaling four nights in one week, yet still we find nothing.

"What in all the green hills of Tashir were you *doing* up here?" I yell as if Ro is out there in the swirling snow.

The night is howling and vicious. Delphine hangs back in the mouth of yet another empty cave, but my frustration is too blistering to notice the icy wind tugging my hair or the snow pelting my cheeks.

"M-maybe Rowenna wasn't *doing* anything," Delphine says through chattering teeth. "M-maybe she just needed an escape from the palace. A place to think."

I shake my head resolutely. Rowenna wasn't like that. She was most comfortable in the thick of it, tackling problems head-on and basking in the admiration of our people. If she was trekking all the way up to this remote location, there was a reason.

The reason behind everything.

"I think, perhaps, we should pray," Delphine offers gently. "I'll show you how. You'll immediately feel calmer and more centered." She settles down cross-legged in the cave and offers me her hand.

I stare at it like a venomous snake. "That's a terrible idea. We'll forget which caves we've searched. And I refuse to strengthen Soren's power even more."

"We won't forfeit the specifics of our search, obviously. I'll teach you how to keep that information barricaded in your mind. But there's no reason we can't use the memory sacrifices to release the useless frustration and fear you feel now. The small amount of energy it gives Soren will pale in comparison to the clarity and relief it brings. It's what I give to the land almost every day, for my required tithes." Delphine offers her hand again, along with an earnest smile. "I think you'll find our memory tithes are quite similar to the contract Tashiri gardeners keep with the land. A give-and-take to strengthen the whole."

I adamantly shake my head. "Your tithes are *nothing* like our bond with Earth Mother and the land. Vanzador is the opposite of Tashir in every way," I declare, but even I can hear the shiver of uncertainty in my voice. And Delphine is staring into my soul like she knows about the traitorous thoughts I had when I first arrived on the mountain and saw the familiar hustle and bustle of the square. The children playing in the streets and the hardworking, dirt-streaked people.

"You can't go on like this, Indira," she persists. "You won't be able to help either of our sisters if you run yourself into the ground. Don't you trust me?"

I don't—not fully. But I can't deny that I *want* to. It would be so nice to fully trust someone.

I'm about to step forward when Rowenna's voice howls past on a gust of wind. *Have you completely lost your mind?*

Instead of bringing comfort and relief as it always has before, though, I feel my hackles rise. She can't just vanish in a huff when I fail to follow her orders, then expect me to listen the next time she graces me with her presence. That's not how alliances work.

That's not how *friendship* works.

I'm doing this because you've left me with no other choice, I say, even though I know, on some level, she's right. Participating in Vanzadorian prayers would be reckless—dangerous, even—but I'm out of ideas. And patience. And part of me wants to make Rowenna mad. Part of me wants her to feel even a fraction of the frustration I've felt, trying to navigate her riddles and contradictions.

You know she can't actually feel anything, my darkest inner voice whispers. *Just like you know, deep down, it isn't her voice you've been hearing.*

I immediately banish the thought. Rowenna has always been the voice inside my head. She'd never leave me alone or let something as inconvenient as death come between us.

I wait for her affirmation, but once again, she's gone disconcertingly quiet, and as I strain to hear her through the silence, I hear something else instead. Something that sounds unnervingly similar to the tread of boots on rock.

I stiffen and glance at Delphine. "Did you hear that?"

"Hear what?" she asks.

Instead of answering, I creep to the cave opening and squint into the snow-swept darkness. "Look! There!" I point at a smear of shadow that could be nothing more than a crooked tree waving in the wind. Except trees don't grow up here, and they definitely don't wear coats with golden buttons that reflect the snow and moonlight.

The wind feels suddenly colder and the hairs on my arms stand at attention. "Why would Alaric be up here, where Rowenna just so happened to be exploring?"

"Maybe he followed her?" Delphine whispers shakily. "Or maybe *she* followed *him*, and he killed her because she saw something incriminating?"

"Only one way to find out," I say as I step out of the cave and into the wind, which dampens the sound of our footsteps on the scree. Boulders provide adequate cover as we tail Alaric through the rocky maze until he eventually ducks into a cave that looks no different from all the rest.

Delphine and I share a nervous glance, then follow,

chasing the sound of his boots through the dark. The tunnel seems to go on forever, and the deeper we wind, the lower the ceiling gets, eventually forcing us to crawl on our bellies. Just when I think I might suffocate, the ground beneath us shudders and heaves. A deluge of dirt and pebbles rains down, and I cover my head with my hands, braced for the entire cave to collapse. That's probably why Alaric led us here—to squash us from existence like bugs. But then the earth stops bucking, and the low murmur of Alaric's voice fills the silence. A second later, a shaft of moonlight spills into the tunnel, pouring through a gash in the ceiling that wasn't there before.

Alaric's shadow climbs through the hole. I sink my fingertips into the dirt and drag myself down the narrow passage, not about to let him get away. By the time we emerge through the hole at the back of the cave, Delphine and I are sweaty and panting, and the blast of frigid air is a welcome reprieve. Compared to the blackness of the claustrophobic tunnel, the night no longer seems as endlessly black either. In fact, I easily spot Alaric's shadow, weaving through a series of boulders.

We seem to have emerged *behind* the system of caves, in a small clearing accessible only through a tunnel that doesn't usually exist. Which means, if we hadn't spotted Alaric, I could have spent my entire life searching without ever finding a trace of my sister—assuming she has anything to do with his sneaking around up here.

But she must.

It's too much of a coincidence to believe they were trekking up here separately. Ro must have followed him. Or he followed her. Or I suppose they could have been working together and meeting in secret.

The thought turns my stomach, but I have to consider every possibility, even if it seems completely out of character for Rowenna and contradicts all of Alaric's assurances.

Up ahead, he scrambles nimbly across the slick rock, faster than Delphine and I can manage. Mercifully, the clearing is almost as barren as the Tomb Flats, so it isn't hard to keep him in our sights. This will also be our downfall if Alaric senses our presence and turns around, but for now, he plows ahead, not stopping until he reaches a particularly large boulder, where he drops to his knees and gingerly removes his gloves.

All the air whooshes out of me when I realize that he's digging.

The only reason he'd have to dig is if something's buried up here.

Something he doesn't want anyone else to find.

Even though it's completely irrational—I *saw* Rowenna's body in Tashir—my mind still conjures images of her broken bones and decaying flesh beneath the frozen soil.

"Quiet!" Delphine elbows me in the ribs, which is when I realize I'm whimpering.

To my immense relief, Alaric stops digging when the hole is still relatively shallow—much too shallow for a body—and whatever he extracts fits inside his fist. He uncurls his fingers and stares down at the object for a long moment before glancing back over his shoulder.

Delphine and I flatten ourselves against the ground, waiting for him to call us out, but Alaric returns his attention to his treasure. He seems to be whispering to it as he settles cross-legged in the dirt, one hand over his eyes while the other hand holds the object flush against the ground.

A minute passes. Then two. And the longer I watch, the more my jaw clenches. There's no way Alaric Alaverdi came all this way just to pray.

But after five full minutes, Delphine gives an exhausted sigh and pushes to her knees. "Let's go. This is a waste of time."

I shake my head and hold my ground. "Rowenna wouldn't have trekked up here if it wasn't important. Could you tell what Alaric dug up? That must be the key."

"*Or* this could just be how Alaric harnesses his power to move the earth, and Rowenna had nothing to do with it."

"Shouldn't Soren be up here too, then?" I point out. "It's too much of a coincidence."

Delphine casts me a pitying look, and I know how desperate I sound—like an exhausted climber, dangling from a cliff by my fingertips.

"We'll think of something else," Delphine assures

me, offering a hand up. But before I can take it, a flare of golden light blooms around Alaric, and we drop back to the ground with a gasp.

TWENTY-FOUR

Golden light unfurls around Alaric like petals of fire, growing taller and brighter until he's completely consumed.

"What is that? What's happening?" I whisper to Delphine.

She shakes her head, gilded light dancing in her frightened eyes. "I don't know."

We watch, mouths agape, as the light flickers and jumps, burning so hot and bright, we're forced to look away. Alaric, however, sits calmly in the middle, seemingly uninjured.

After a time, the bright yellow and gold flames cool to deeper shades of ocher and umber, and swirl into an image of sorts. The walls of a phantom room erect themselves around Alaric, who hasn't moved from his prayer position.

The details of the room are impressive: walls made of dark-paneled wood, a vast collection of books fill the floor-to-ceiling shelves, and a long black carpet slashes through the center of the room like a crevasse.

"That's the king's council chamber," Delphine whispers. "I've cleaned it before."

The room is every bit as imposing and austere as I'd expect from King Soren, but even more unsettling are the floating wisps of shadow that drift across the strange apparition world and form into people.

"Is this real?" I ask. "A projection of the room in this very moment?"

"How should I know?" Delphine shrugs. "It certainly looks real."

I turn back to the scene, feeling more uneasy by the second. If Soren and Alaric have somehow learned to manipulate time and space, in addition to the earth, they could be everywhere at once. Always watching. Eternally a step ahead.

I drag myself through the sharp pebbles until I'm just a few lengths from where Alaric sits. Close enough to parse out more details of the room and the people within. But that only makes me more confused.

Instead of Soren and his blue-robed councilors, a little boy, no older than five, sits on a wheeled ladder attached to the bookshelves. He's chubby and red cheeked with gorgeous black curls that hang in his stone-gray eyes.

It's so clearly a younger version of Alaric, I gasp.

Thankfully, grown Alaric doesn't stir from his prayer pose in the center of the light.

A second boy, slightly older, with paler skin and a thatch of brown hair pops up on the other side of the ladder, grinning.

Delphine slithers up beside me and stammers, "Th-that's Besnik. The king's eldest son who died years ago."

"So this is the past?" I whisper. "Like a memory?"

Delphine shrugs again, and we watch as phantom Besnik throws his weight against the ladder, and the two boys giggle as it zips down the track, crashing to a stop at the far end of the shelf.

"Again, again!" little Alaric cries, and Besnik happily obliges, pushing them back and forth until they both topple off onto the rug, laughing.

From the center of the light, grown Alaric says something, and the glowing images smear. When they reassemble, the boys are still running wild around the same wood-paneled room, but now they're noticeably older, leaping from armchair to armchair and chasing each other with swords that look disconcertingly real. They laugh and parry, taking turns attacking and defending. A harried-looking man without a speck of hair watches from the corner, begging them to calm down and keep quiet—their father is in meetings on the other side of the wall. But that just makes Alaric and Besnik shout louder and laugh harder.

When they finally slump onto a settee to catch their breath, their eyes are wild and exuberant, their bodies a tangle of smiles and laughter. They are happiness and completeness. Friendship and solidarity. Two parts of the same whole.

Like Rowenna and me.

The tightness in my throat is almost strangling, and I breathe a sigh of relief when grown Alaric mutters again, causing the scene to blur and reform.

This time, it depicts the two boys as adolescents, but now neither is smiling. And no one is laughing.

A leggy, long-haired Alaric stands in the center of the same room, staring down at his hands, which are cupped around a walnut-sized gemstone the color of an apricot.

"It was an accident," he whispers frantically. "I didn't mean… I would never!" His hands tremble around the jewel, which is riddled with spiderweb cracks.

Besnik paces in front of Alaric, glancing nervously from the gemstone to the double doors. "It's fine. The stone is *meant* to be divided. That's how Father received his portion, and Grandfather before him. It was going to be split again soon for me anyway."

"It's going to be *carefully chiseled* for you." Alaric's voice cracks. "Not splintered like the stained-glass window we broke in the music room when I was four."

"The Flesh isn't going to shatter like that." Besnik

waves a dismissive hand, though his eyes dart back to the double doors. "We'll sneak it back into the royal coffers and never speak of this again. No one needs to know you took it or that it fractured in your care. When Father eventually discovers the damage, he'll think it must have split naturally. Maybe he'll finally admit we're excavating the mines too quickly and carelessly. Far more than a single gemstone will crumble if we continue carving up the mountain without thought for its long-term stability."

Alaric still looks pale and stricken, but he nods as he considers the damaged gemstone. "Do you think its power remains intact?"

"Of course," Besnik says—a little too quickly. "And, anyway, the Flesh is only one third of the triad. The others will make up any difference."

My ears snag on the words *Flesh* and *triad*, but I don't have time to work out their importance. The council room doors fly open with a *bang*, and King Soren strides into the room.

At the sight of his sons, he skids to a halt. His eyes fall on the apricot gemstone in Alaric's hands, and his craggy face twists and reddens. A vein on his forehead bulges like a bloated leech. He levels a finger at Alaric, but he doesn't bellow his accusation. He whispers, which is far more terrifying.

"It was *you*?"

"It-it isn't what you think." Alaric stumbles toward his father, his fear so visceral my own hands feel damp with sweat.

I can't imagine being so frightened of my own family. Mother and Rowenna could be a bit ruthless and single-minded, and Father was often overly emotional and disappointed, but I never had cause to fear any of them. I never doubted, for even a second, that they would meet my mistakes with compassion rather than anger. With love rather than threats.

Poor Alaric is so focused on his garbled explanations and apologies, he trips over his ungainly legs and the gemstone bobbles in his grip. I hold my breath as he dives to catch it, but the jewel slides through his fingers and hits the ground with a *crack*. Daggers of tangerine light slash across the walls—flash across Soren's livid face—as the pieces scatter and spin.

"What have you done?" King Soren roars as he lumbers across the room.

Alaric flops about like a fish on land, frantically trying to gather the shards into a pile.

Soren thunders closer. "You know the sacrifices my grandfather made!"

Besnik darts between them, holding up his hands. "Father, have mercy. This is a misunderstanding—"

Soren flings his oldest son aside and looms over Alaric. "The Flesh of Callahan goes missing—no, is stolen from the royal coffers—and I find it in the possession of my own son? Irreversibly damaged!"

"Father, I can explain." Alaric scrambles back, wincing as fragments of the stone dig into his palms.

"There's no good explanation for stupidity." Soren bellows and raises a hand.

The room begins to shake, infinitesimally at first, like hundreds of dancers in a hall. Then it builds to a rush of galloping hooves and, finally, to earth-wrenching tremors, like the quakes that shook the fields of Tashir the day Soren raised our protective mountain range. Quills and inkpots rattle and the bookshelves lining the council room walls spit their massive tomes to the floor.

Alaric yelps with each heavy *thwack*.

"Father, stop!" Besnik pleads. "The structural integrity of the palace—"

"You disrespect our ancestors!" Soren booms over his sons. "You spit upon our most sacred relics—the very source of our power. Power *you* have no right to wield as a second son." He stabs a quivering finger at Alaric.

"It isn't like that," Alaric wails. "I wasn't trying to take it. I just wanted to look at the stones and feel close to the power, just once, before it's rightfully given to Besnik."

Soren's laughter is loud and merciless. "If you're so desperate to feel *close* to my power, I'll happily oblige."

He thrusts both hands toward Alaric, but Besnik moves at the same time, crashing into Alaric's side and sending the younger boy sprawling into the ladder they rode as children. The floor crumbles at the same moment, directly beneath where Alaric stood.

Where Besnik stands now.

Each second plays out in slow, excruciating detail. Splinters of wood explode into the air, Besnik's arms pinwheel, and his feet churn as if running. For an impossible moment, he seems to hang there, suspended like a bird, before the laws of nature reclaim him.

I scream as he plummets, and Delphine slaps her palm over my lips. We watch in silent horror as the tail of Besnik's velvet jacket catches on one of the jutting, broken floorboards. Unfortunately, it isn't strong enough to stop his fall—only to change his trajectory. The snagged garment pitches Besnik heels overhead, flinging him down, down, down into whatever lies below.

Before I can ask Delphine which room lies beneath the council chambers, the sharp sounds of smashing china and tinkling flatware ring out, followed by a wet, heavy thud.

Then silence.

Complete and utter silence when Besnik should be howling in agony after such a nasty fall.

Alaric flings himself toward the gash in the floor, shouting Besnik's name, and in that moment, his screams are my screams. His horror is my horror. He's me, throwing myself across Rowenna's coffin.

I swipe at the tears filling my eyes just in time to watch

Soren catch Alaric around the waist and drag him back from the hole in the floor.

"What are you doing? Do you wish to fall too?"

"Let me go!" Alaric writhes and thrashes against Soren's hold. "Let me fall! Isn't that what you wanted?"

Soren says nothing. He simply stands there, dispassionately holding his frantic son, until Alaric eventually sags with exhaustion.

"Now that you're no longer hysterical and a danger to us both," Soren says with derision, "you need to see the outcome of your poor decisions."

No!

The urge to throw myself into the golden scene and stop them is so visceral and overwhelming, Delphine has to stop me again. She digs her nails into my forearm and sternly reminds me none of this is happening in the present, but still I struggle and squirm.

I tell myself it's because I never want to see another dead body. But deep down, I know it's more than that. Seeing Rowenna's battered corpse almost killed me. Those gory images are forever emblazoned on my brain, marring the actual memory of her face. It's a horror I wouldn't wish on anyone. Not even the Vanzadorian prince.

Which begs the question—why is Alaric choosing to relive it?

Soren leans out over the gash, Alaric locked tight in his grip, until Besnik comes into view. He lies motionless atop a wreckage of wood that must have been a banquet table. Splinters as long as my arm impale Besnik's stomach and chest, and one side of his head is malformed and tacky with blood. He must have hit the enormous chandelier on his way down, because the bent frame swings eerily and pieces of broken glass still fall around his body, creating a horrifying mosaic of glitter and gore.

Beside me, Delphine gags and looks away, and I desperately want to do the same. But I can't. It feels wrong to leave Alaric to face this alone.

"Such a needless tragedy," Soren murmurs with a grim shake of his head. "The result of your selfish betrayal."

"No," Alaric whispers. "I'm not the one who obliterated the floor. I don't even have the ability to move the earth—and never will as you so love to remind me."

"But you *did* take the Flesh of Callahan. None of this would have happened if you'd left it in the hands of those meant to wield power. Clearly, I must keep the triad somewhere safer. Away from people like you, who can't be trusted."

With a growl, Soren flings Alaric back into the corner—into the same ladder he hit when Besnik saved his life. I expect that to be the end of the argument, but after several painful breaths, Alaric pushes up to his hands and knees, jaw set with determination.

"Are you going to kill me too? Will you leave our people without an heir and protection? Wouldn't that be far more traitorous and selfish than merely holding a sacred relic?"

"Silence!" Soren thunders toward Alaric, who flinches and looks down, clearly waiting for the ground to fall out from under him. But Soren's bejeweled fingers crash into his cheek instead.

"*You* are to blame for all of this," Soren shouts as Alaric collapses once more. "And it's well within my rights to sentence you to a traitor's death for killing Vanzador's future king. But as you so kindly pointed out, that would leave me without an heir, so I shall be merciful. *More than* merciful. I'll forget this heinous crime, and so will you. I'll declare Besnik's death a tragic accident. We'll say he was training in the council chamber and pushed his fledgling power too far. He lost control, and the ground dissolved beneath him. It's miraculous all three of us didn't plummet to our deaths."

"No one will believe you." Alaric spits out a mouthful of blood. "Besnik didn't even have power yet. The ceremony wasn't for another month—"

Soren waves a hand. "I'll say we did it sooner—because he was showing such promise. No one will question me."

"Because you don't let them!"

"I *can't* let them! This is what it takes to be king! Sacrifices must be made, our own feelings put aside. We will mourn this tragedy and move forward—for the stability and strength of Vanzador." Soren glares at his youngest son—now his *only* son. "You'll see this is for the best once you've purged these horrors from your mind. Quickly, now. Help me collect the pieces of the gemstone so we can pray. The guards will be here any second to investigate the crash."

Soren drops to his knees and uses his large hands to scrape the pieces of their sacred rock into a pile. He motions for Alaric to join him, but Alaric shakes his head and steps back, laughing wildly. "You can't honestly expect me to *forget* you tried to kill me! And *did* kill Besnik! I would never dishonor him by forgetting how he saved my life."

"You'll do as I command." Soren glances at the door and lowers his voice. "Think of your mother. Besnik's passing is going to crush her. Imagine if she learns *you* are to blame? The grief and disappointment will kill her. Are you strong enough to carry that guilt too?"

"It isn't my guilt to carry—" Alaric starts, but both men freeze at the sound of boots in the hall.

Heavy fists pound the council chamber doors. "Your Majesty!" A deep voice calls out. "We felt the tremors. Is the Fortress under siege?"

"If you wish to protect your mother and honor your brother, this is the only way," Soren says through his teeth. "*This* is the truth. Otherwise, Besnik's death will have been for nothing."

"Your Majesty!" the guard yells again. "Please confirm your status."

Alaric glances back at the gaping wound in the floor. Tears course down his face, and he wraps his jacket around his chest so tightly, a silver button pops free. While he fumbles to catch it, Soren places a forceful hand on Alaric's shoulders.

"We pray together. *Now.*"

Alaric looks like he's going to scream, but he clenches his fists and allows his father to pull him to the ground.

Once they're both in position, the King of Vanzador begins to sing.

TWENTY-FIVE

THE GOLDEN LIGHT FALLS AWAY, WHISKING THE phantoms of young Alaric and Soren into the starswept darkness of the mountaintop. Grown Alaric, however, remains curled over his knees, sobbing. I don't realize I'm crying, too, until Delphine reaches over and wipes an icy tear off my cheek.

"It's just the cold," I whisper. "I'm not..." But I can't finish. I'm too wounded by the ragged ache inside my own chest. It doesn't matter that Besnik died years ago. A loss like this never gets easier to bear. You just learn to live with the bone-deep pain. You go on dressing the infected wound, knowing it will never fully heal.

Alaric rocks back and forth, howling his brother's name, and it's the saddest thing I've ever seen.

But undeniably convenient, Rowenna says.

I'm surprised and relieved to hear her voice again after our little disagreement. It was wrong of me to purposely make her mad. Clearly, I need her help to see things from a strategic, rather than emotional, perspective.

It's almost uncanny, how perfectly this new information about Alaric could work to my advantage. Soren commanded Alaric to purge the memory of Besnik's death, and not only did Alaric disregard Soren's request, he somehow found a way to relive the event. A way to *prove* Soren killed Besnik—a revelation that would be devastating for both men, should the truth come to light. The Vanzadorian people would never look at Soren the same. They might even hesitate to give him their memories if they feared his temper and lack of control. At the very least, his reputation as a strong, compassionate ruler would be shattered. And if he learned Alaric's disobedience was to blame for his fall from grace, Soren would ensure no one ever looked on his son again. *Period.*

A shiver overtakes me, lifting the hairs on my arms.

This could be the answer—a way to weaken, or even eliminate, both men—and I know, deep in my bones, Rowenna arrived at this same conclusion. It's why she was sneaking up the mountain. Why she was murdered. She must have caught Alaric reliving these forbidden memories, and he must have killed her to keep his secrets safe. It would have been so easy. No one would have seen or heard Ro fall from such a remote location.

But could Alaric really have taken another life so soon after reliving Besnik's death? I consider him, still curled in on himself like a pill bug, too distraught to even notice a threat, let alone overpower one. And his cryptic words from our argument in the solarium come back to me, rife with new meaning:

You know nothing about the blood on my hands or how it haunts me.

There's no question Alaric Alaverdi is haunted, but I'm beginning to think it's by his own demons. Not my sister's ghost.

But if he didn't kill Rowenna for discovering his secret, who did?

I suppose Alaric *could* have gone to Soren for help, but that would have required admitting he'd kept the memory of Besnik's death. Something he's clearly unwilling to do, seeing as how he treks all the way up the mountain to view it. So maybe Rowenna bypassed confronting Alaric and took her knowledge straight to Soren? She could have tried to blackmail the Vanzadorian king in exchange for better terms for Tashir. He wouldn't have hesitated to kill her to extinguish such a threat.

But if that were the case, wouldn't Soren have come down on Alaric too? He would have destroyed the memory of Besnik's death at the very least.

"What do you make of all this?" I whisper to Delphine. "What did we just witness?"

"I don't know." Delphine slowly shakes her head. "It felt like a memory, but I didn't know it was possible to *relive* them like that. We can recall the memories we choose not to give to the earth, of course. And it's popular among the courtiers to pay a siphoning tax that allows them to store important memories in prized possessions—in addition to keeping them in their minds—for added assurance they won't be lost to the tithes. But as far as I know, siphoned memories can't spring to life in glittering detail. If they could, the courtiers would be obsessed with replaying their proudest moments for all to see."

I think of my own most cherished memories—all the moments I'd relive if I could—and every one includes my sister: dancing in the apple press during the harvest festival, racing barefoot through the wheat beneath the summer sun, and ordinary nights in our bedchamber when we'd whisper and giggle in the dark until our bellies ached. Bringing those memories to life would be the next best thing to resurrecting my sister—the *real* Rowenna, not the mercurial ghost she's become on this mountain.

What if they're one and the same? My irritating inner voice resurfaces. *What if Rowenna has always been deceitful and self-serving, but you were too blinded by devotion to see it?*

I vehemently shake my head, but another parade of memories is already marching across my mind: Rowenna flirting mercilessly with Middeon Kalendi in order to get invited to dinner with his family so she could gauge his mother's opinion on her proposal for the planting rotation, as she was one of the only ministers whose vote was undecided. After the vote was cast, Ro never spoke to Middeon again. Or the time she purposely told Janesa Ofa the wrong time for their debate on irrigation techniques, so she'd win by default. Ro claimed she'd been too busy cleaning up one of Father's messes to properly prepare, and she refused to be publicly humiliated due to someone else's mistake.

I was quick to defend her both times. Middeon had led on his fair share of girls over the years and deserved to be humbled a bit. And Janesa was a know-it-all who was determined to best everyone in the classroom—my sister especially. If Ro wrote a three-page report on the merits of pest control, Janesa wrote six pages. If Rowenna volunteered to help a primary child learn to read, Janesa would take on two pupils and ensure they were sounding out words twice as fast. She needed to be put in her place. They both did. That's something all of Rowenna's "enemies" had in common. If my sister was cruel or deceptive, it was always with reason. More often than I care to admit, that reason was defending me.

So you're admitting she could be cruel and deceptive? The maddening voice of doubt persists, twisting my words.

No.

Yes.

It's not like it happened often. These are just a few moments across an entire lifetime.

That you could recall at a moment's notice?

Say something to defend yourself! I silently beg my sister.

But she's glaringly quiet. Probably too incensed to answer.

Perhaps because she isn't there at all...and never has been, my deepest fears whisper.

What if I invented her voice to fill the Rowenna-shaped hole in my life? Because I didn't trust myself and my own judgment?

I double over, feeling like I'm going to be sick.

Delphine places a gentle hand on my back. "I'm in shock too. When King Soren said Besnik's death was a tragic training accident, we had no reason to question him. Soren adored Besnik. Though I do remember some rumbling from Besnik's valet after the accident. The boy insisted Besnik was too responsible and meticulous to have requested power early or to have pushed that fledgling power too far. But we all attributed his claims to shock and grief."

Delphine fiddles with the end of her braid before continuing. "If that's really what happened, and not some alternate reality Alaric invented, I can't fathom how Alaric has maintained such a close relationship with his father all this time. The anger and resentment would be crushing. Alaric would *never* be able to show a hint of remembrance or a sliver of resentment—not with his father and the inquisitors watching."

"But *would* they be watching?" I ask. "Soren was supposed to purge the memory of Besnik's death too."

"Do you really think King Soren would put himself in such a vulnerable position? Leave his fate in the hands of the son he just tried to kill?" Delphine shakes her head. "I think it's much more likely he also retained the memory, and the excessive praise he heaps on Alaric now is a way to ease his guilty conscience—and test his son."

I try to swallow, but my throat has gone drier than the Tomb Flats. I can't fathom living like that. Forced to love a monster, knowing every word out of Soren's lips was a lie.

Alaric's cryptic refrain makes so much more sense now.

You'd drink this much, too, if you were me.

I rest my forehead on my tented knees, wishing I could purge the memory of Besnik's death. But that just makes my stomach churn with guilt and disgust, because it's precisely what the Vanzadorians do with unpleasant and inconvenient memories. Not to mention, it's the crack I've been searching for since I arrived on the mountain. The fracture that could set the kingdom of Vanzador to crumbling.

Like the fractured gemstone that set all of this in motion.

Those scattered, spinning pieces are an important piece of the puzzle too. Soren called the broken jewel the *Flesh* of Callahan and said it was part of a triad. A group of three.

Like the three words written in Callahan's journal.

And the three words carved into the walls of Delphine's chamber.

Blood, flesh, bone.

If the Flesh is a gemstone, might they all be? Could the key to Soren's power be hidden in jewels that could be potentially stolen? If young Alaric was able to get his hands on the stone of Flesh, who's to say others haven't tried?

That *Rowenna* didn't try.

Cold certainty drips down my back like freezing rain.

This is how she planned to save Tashir. I know it as well as I know the twisting halls of the hillock palace. She planned to steal the gemstone triad and command the earth herself. If Ro possessed Soren's ability to move the earth, we wouldn't need him or his seeds-forsaken treaty. She could protect us herself and return home to take her rightful place as queen of Tashir.

But she must have gotten caught. Soren said he'd be keeping the gemstones somewhere safer than the royal coffers going forward, and Rowenna must have figured out where. Then Soren made her death look like an accident because he knew he'd never be able to bring me back to Vanzador in Rowenna's place if they were responsible for her death.

It's all so painfully, laughably clear.

And it makes my next steps so perfectly, brutally clear. I need to finish what Rowenna started. I need to steal the gemstone triad and return to Tashir with Soren's power. But I have to be extremely careful. If he suspects I'm searching, he'll send me to join Rowenna in the Great Fields Beyond. I must come at this from a completely different angle.

One they'd never suspect.

I scramble back across the scree and stare at Alaric, still quietly rocking back and forth. It's difficult to watch—difficult not to feel compassion for him, when I know exactly how he feels. That's part of the reason I don't stride over there, spewing threats and making demands. The rest is more strategic. If Alaric hasn't already cracked under the weight of his secrets and Soren's scrutiny, I'm not likely to break him. If I approach him with empathy and understanding, though—if I offer the kind of support he's never had—I might be able to earn his trust and trick him into leading me to the gemstone triad.

The smallest pang of guilt pricks my conscience at the prospect of capitalizing on his grief, but Vanzador has never hesitated to use our weaknesses against us.

I have to put Tashir first. I have to be the leader my people need.

Yes, yes, yes! Rowenna's voice bursts back into my mind, as fierce as the swirling wind. She feels closer and more alive than she has in days. *There's the sister I know and love. I knew you'd figure it out.*

But for some reason, her praise doesn't feel as frothy and fortifying as it used to. On the contrary, a wave of queasiness grips me as I push to my feet and make my way across the clearing toward Alaric.

TWENTY-SIX

TWENTY-SIX

"WHAT ARE YOU DOING?" DELPHINE SAYS WITH wide petrified eyes. "Get down! He'll see you!"

"That's precisely what I want," I say, beckoning for her to follow.

After a moment of dithering, Delphine scrambles after me, tripping on the loose pebbles. "I don't understand what you hope to accomplish by confronting him."

"Who says I'm confronting him?"

"What else could you possibly do?" Delphine sputters loudly, but Alaric is still so lost in the past, he doesn't seem to register our voices. He doesn't even glance up until we're looming over him—like a boot poised to squash a beetle.

"*Y-you!*" He gapes at me as he scuttles backward. "What are you doing here? And who's that?" He points at Delphine,

With his darting eyes and tear-streaked cheeks, he looks nothing like the steely prince he portrays on the outside. Just the lonely, broken boy he hides within. Especially as he brings his fist to his chest, protecting whatever he unearthed from the ground. My fingers itch to grab it—to force him to reveal what it is and how it works—and Alaric notices. He slips the object into an inner pocket of his jacket and hurriedly yanks his gloves back on, hackles up and teeth bared like a guard dog.

I smile pleasantly and plunk down in the dirt beside him.

I don't know whose eyes bulge wider, Alaric's or Delphine's.

"This is my maid, Delphine." I pat the dusty ground beside me, but she shakes her head, blinking like I've completely lost my mind.

Maybe I have.

"Your maid?" Alaric repeats. "The same maid you begged me to protect you from just last week? The one you blamed for the disturbing carvings in your closet, who you were ready to condemn for Rowenna's death?"

Delphine sucks in a breath, and I feel her wounded gaze.

"I was wrong." I shoot her an apologetic smile. "We worked all that out."

"How nice." Alaric's voice drips with sarcasm. "Unfortunately, I can't *work out* what either of you are doing up here now."

"We want to know what *you're* doing up here, surrounded by all that golden light?" I gesture around, as if recreating the scene. "It's a memory, isn't it? The truth about what happened to your brother?"

"I don't know what you're talking about. I was only praying," Alaric snaps.

I raise a skeptical brow. "Why hike all the way up here just to pray? It doesn't make sense. Seeking privacy to watch such a harrowing memory, however, makes perfect sense. Especially since it paints your father in such terrible light."

Alaric's face grows redder with every word. "You followed me up here, didn't you? You plan to blackmail me, is that it?"

"Indira, this is too much," Delphine cuts in. "This isn't what I agreed to—"

"Actually, our trip had nothing to do with you," I continue calmly. "Delphine and I have been sneaking up this mountain most nights to look for clues about Rowenna's death."

Behind me, Delphine lets out another strangled breath—as if I'm betraying her, like Rowenna did—but I keep my focus on Alaric, praying my blunt honesty will catch him off guard. Maybe even encourage him to follow suit.

"We were searching a cave when we saw you slink past," I explain. "It seemed suspicious that you were creeping around the very same mountaintop my sister was searching when she died. It seemed more like *you* had been following *her*, and I wanted to know why."

Alaric blinks several times, as if I'm speaking a different language. "Rowenna came up here? When? Why? How do you know any of this?"

"Unfortunately, I still don't have a clue why my sister did most of the maddening things she did on this mountain, but I'm beginning to realize it doesn't matter. Knowing won't bring her back. Just like watching that awful memory won't bring Besnik back. So why do you torture yourself?"

Alaric scoffs and shakes his head. "You wouldn't understand—" he starts to say, but I cut him off.

"Actually, I know *exactly* how it feels to lose an older sibling—like a limb has been severed from your body. Like the scaffolding that holds up the sky has crumbled. You don't know who you are or where to go without them, and you're terrified you'll never be able to fill their shoes. You don't even *want* to fill their shoes. But, most of all, you're terrified it was all your fault. That everyone secretly wishes you had been the one to perish. Sometimes you secretly wish it yourself...."

The words rush out of me faster than I intended—and far more vulnerable. I brace for Alaric to mock me, but he simply blinks with large glassy eyes, which make him look younger, softer, and, aggravatingly, even more attractive.

"Except Besnik's death *was* my fault," he eventually whispers.

I scoot a tiny bit closer, pleased when he doesn't shrink away. "You shouldn't blame yourself. If what we saw is true, your father is to blame, no one else."

"My father wouldn't have lashed out if not for *my* mistakes."

"You're not responsible for his temper. No mistake, no matter how grave, justifies murder. He was the adult—the king, for seed's sake. He should have been able to control his power and emotions."

I expect my little speech to bolster Alaric, but his expression darkens, and he purposely leans away, reestablishing the distance between us. "Why are you trying to comfort me? What are you really after?"

The gemstone triad and your power, I think.

But I say, "Honestly, I don't know anymore. Nothing about Vanzador is what I expected—including you," I add, looking up at him from beneath my lashes.

Alaric searches my face through the dark, and I'm struck by how the moonlight paints the contours of his cheeks silver. How starlight gilds the blackness of his hair. It shouldn't be possible for someone so outwardly intimidating to be so small and shattered within. The disparity is unsettling. That's why my stomach dips. Not because I like the way he's looking at me. Or because my opinion of him has changed because of our shared trauma.

"How does it work?" I nod down at his coat, where he hid the mysterious object. "Delphine told me memories can be siphoned into objects, but how do you bring them to life?"

Alaric tosses his head back, and his acidic laughter echoes around the mountaintop. "You honestly expect me to open up and share my secrets after you ran out of our solarium when I expressed interest in your magic?"

"I'm sorry. You caught me off guard," I try to explain. "I wasn't ready to share then."

Alaric stands and folds his arms over his chest. "Well, I'm not ready now."

A flare of irritation burns through me. I've been bending over backward to appease him, yet he's still acting like a petulant child.

I could do the same. I could pester and pressure him or threaten to tell Soren about Alaric's siphoned memory if he refuses to cooperate. But neither of these plans will earn his trust or get me closer to the gemstone triad, so even though I'm screaming on the inside, I bow my head and step back.

"Very well. I'm sorry we disturbed you. Let's go, Delphine." I take her hand and pull her forward.

We only make it a few steps before Alaric calls after us. "Where are you going? The Fortress is back that way."

"We came all this way. It would be a waste not to scour the mountaintop for clues about Rowenna. But don't worry. We won't disturb you again." I smile sweetly and bob a curtsy, which makes Alaric splutter.

Delphine's gaze bounces back and forth, torn between duty to her prince and her desperation to find a cure for Cloudia.

Alaric starts after us with an exhausted sigh. "I'm serious. You can't go that way. It isn't safe."

"Because we're physically in danger, or because we might find something that incriminates *you*?" I can't stop myself from needling him, just a bit.

"Stop, Indira. We're near the cliff's edge, and the ground up here is unstable from overmining. It could give way any second."

"Wouldn't it be convenient if I fell?" I ask, taking another deliberate step.

"*Stop!*" Alaric lunges forward with shocking speed and drags me back several paces. "I refuse to let anyone fall on my watch. Even *you*."

The emphasis he puts on the word *you* drips with disdain, but the expression on his face is terrified, his breath ragged as he holds me against his chest.

Delphine loudly clears her throat. "We should be getting back, Miss Indira."

Alaric lets go, and we fly apart. But even when I'm several paces away, I still feel the press of his arms around me. Still feel the dangerous buzz of electricity zapping through the air.

I rack my brain for something snappy to say, to prove his heroics didn't affect me. Or something contrite, to remind him I can be kind and trustworthy. But my brain can't seem to form a coherent thought. Even if it could, my teeth are clenched too tight to speak. So I settle for an awkward half bow, before Delphine tugs me sharply back toward the caves.

"You shouldn't goad him like that," she scolds once we're out of earshot. "What were you thinking?"

I don't answer.

Because I honestly don't know.

TWENTY-SEVEN

WAIT UNTIL THE SUN IS SHINING HIGH IN THE SKY before knocking on Alaric's chamber door the following morning. After such an eventful night on the mountaintop, I figured a good night's rest would do us both well. Plus I needed more time than I cared to admit to prepare for his razor-sharp looks and cutting remarks.

Alaric won't be happy to see me. Which is fine. I don't give a fig what he thinks. I do, however, need him to open up and trust me, which means I need to extend another olive branch. A much larger olive branch.

One heavy enough to crush me if things go awry.

"Alaric?" I call out, trying to ignore the worms of anxiety writhing in my stomach. If this plan was a grave mistake, surely Rowenna would intervene?

Like she intervened with Von Nevus? the new needling voice inside me argues.

Rowenna's methods with Von Nevus were undoubtedly flawed, but her intentions were noble. She was willing to do *anything* to take Soren down, and she expected me to do the same. Her sky-high expectations were nothing new. My sister always pushed herself to be the bravest, boldest, shrewdest version of herself, and she expected the rest of us to follow suit. She knew how to draw out potential we couldn't see in ourselves. It's one of the things I admired most about her, and I know she's pleased with me now, for uncovering the secret of the gemstones and developing a plan. *Her* plan.

Why give her all the credit? the meddlesome voice persists. *Not every brilliant idea is Rowenna's.*

"Alaric?" I knock again. "Are you in there?"

At last, the door creaks opens, and Alaric fills the frame. He looks even more exhausted and exposed than he did last night on the mountain. Surprisingly, this has less to do with his chest, which is, of course, bare, and his low-slung pants, which fall scandalously below his hip bones, and more to do with the beaten-down look on his face. I have the strangest urge to reach out and comfort him—until he opens his mouth.

"What now?" He drags a gloved hand through his messy hair. "You've decided to blackmail me, haven't you?"

My hackles instantly rise. "Why would you think that?"

"What else could you possibly want?"

"I don't *want* anything."

"Then why are you here?"

I pull a deep breath in through my nose and exhale slowly. "I wanted to make sure you were okay after last night... And to thank you for looking out for my safety, despite my belligerence."

His scowl doesn't budge. "Is that all?"

Is that all? I almost shout back. *I'm throwing myself at your feet, bridging ninety percent of the gap between us. Would it kill you to come ten percent?*

"No, actually, that's not all," I say through a rictus smile. "May I come in?" I try to step forward, but Alaric braces his hands against the doorframe.

"Whatever you have to say, you can say it out here."

"What if it isn't something I want to say but rather show you?" I poke my finger into his chest.

When he jerks back with surprise, I push my way inside.

Alaric's rooms are a mirror image of my own. A four-poster bed stands to the right of the door, and his bathing chamber branches off to the left. A sizeable wardrobe, flanked by dressing tables, dominates the space between, and a few armchairs are arranged around a cold hearth. But where my room radiates color and warmth from the gemstone walls, Alaric's space is cold and gray. At first I think it's because his walls are made of harsher, more masculine stones like onyx and obsidian. But as I venture deeper, I realize it's because there *aren't* any stones set into his walls. Not anymore. Every gemstone has been cleaved away, leaving deep gouges and unsightly scars in the bedrock.

A shiver moves through me as I picture Alaric furiously swinging a pickax, taking out his rage and frustration on the walls since he can't unleash them on his father.

"You can't just barge into my rooms!" He stomps after me.

"Get dressed. I have something to show you in the solarium."

Alaric stands there gawping like I hoped he would, giving me the opportunity to make my way to his chest of drawers. Unlike young Alaric, who had to steal the apricot gemstone I saw in his memory, grown Alaric rightfully has the power to move the earth, which means he must have unfettered access to the stones. His gaudy bejeweled jackets and chains seem like the most logical place to keep them—something he wears every day, hidden in plain sight.

"I can't believe you don't know how to dress yourself without a valet," I mutter under my breath as I yank open the drawers. My eyes quickly scan his collection of extravagant jackets for inlaid jewels the color of blood, flesh, or bone. Then I trail my fingers across the top of the dresser, assessing dozens of decorative chains that range in size and splendor, from simple links of silver to diamond-studded strands of braided gold.

Curiously, all of Alaric's accoutrements feature only crystal-clear diamonds, cerulean topaz, and jade green.

"Stop pawing through my things!" Alaric yells.

"Then kindly dress yourself so we can go to our solarium."

He steps between his drawers and me, arms folded and expression defiant. "What if I don't want to get dressed?"

"You're acting like a petulant toddler, but if you prefer to garden in loungewear, that's your choice. Just don't blame me when your underclothes get filthy." I turn on my heel and march toward his solarium door, which is much less hidden due to the desecrated walls.

"You're taking me to *garden*?" Alaric asks, jogging after me.

"That's the plan, if you stop throwing tantrums."

"I'm not throwing tantrums," Alaric grumbles as we step into the blinding light and heat.

I say nothing, letting his whiny declaration prove my point.

I cross to the nearest planting bed, filled with the healing herbs I've been growing for Cloudia—none of which have done a bit of good—and drop to my knees in an open stretch of dirt. I pat the soil beside me and gesture for Alaric to join me.

He holds a gloved hand to his chest with exaggerated shock. "I'm allowed to touch your precious planting beds?"

"Get in here before I change my mind," I say with a roll of my eyes.

But Alaric stands his ground. "Why now, when you were clearly against this just a few days ago? What's changed?"

"Everything," I say softly, and it isn't wholly a lie. "I didn't know we shared a similar loss. That you're just as captive bound to Soren as I am…"

I allow my gaze to tentatively wander up to Alaric's, but instead of grateful understanding, I'm met with a pop of bitter laughter.

"I don't want your pity."

"Good. Pity would imply I feel something for you, which I don't. Now, get in here before I change my mind. And take off those frilly gloves. I promise you won't die if your hands get dirty."

Alaric steps into the planter, careful to avoid the knee-high lavender and balsam, and eases down beside me. He doesn't remove his gloves, but I let it go with a sigh and shake of my head.

"So, what will you be *allowing* me to watch you grow?" He tries to sound aloof, but I can feel his body vibrating with excitement beside me— and he doesn't even know what I have planned.

With a dramatic flourish, I reach for the basket of bagrava fruit, which has sat untouched in the corner since my arrival, and place it between us.

Alaric's gaze immediately darts to my face, and the way he's blinking at me, lips parted with surprise, makes my stomach do an absurd little flip.

I clench the basket tighter. "I thought we'd grow this."

I expect Alaric's face to bloom with delight, but because he lives to make my life difficult, his features harden. "You didn't want me to watch you grow ordinary herbs, and now suddenly you're willing to do *this?*" He shakes his head. "It's too much. You swore you'd never grow bagrava in Vanzador."

"That was when I thought you were a complete monster," I say.

"And now what? I'm just a partial monster?"

Instead of answering, I take a plump purple fruit in my hand and make an incision around it with the tip of a trowel. Then I pull the halves apart to reveal clusters of seeds nestled within like a pomegranate.

I hold one half toward Alaric. "Take some."

He sputters and stares at the fruit. "Are you sure?"

Once again, his childlike wonder makes my stomach flip-flop.

"I wouldn't have invited you here if I wasn't certain." I wave the bagrava half in his face.

After one more deep breath, Alaric digs his fingers into

the flesh and collects a handful of seeds. Red juice drips from his creamy leather gloves and onto the dirt, turning it black. It looks like he recently murdered someone, and I almost point out this "proof" of the blood on his hands. But then images of Besnik's body sprawled across the banquet table bombard me, and I press my lips firmly back together.

"They're beautiful." Alaric gazes down at the shiny seeds, tipping his hands back and forth so they catch the light. "Like tiny jewels."

It's the perfect comparison—and makes for a perfect trade. A glimpse of my bagrava for his gemstone triad.

"Help me plant them," I say, showing Alaric how to press his thumb into the damp soil, drop a seed into the hole, and cover it with the proper amount of dirt.

"Am I doing it right?" Alaric asks as he makes a line of careful thumbprints. "I don't want to ruin anything."

I give a haughty flick of my hair. "I'm Tashir's most powerful master gardener. You couldn't ruin my work if you tried."

Alaric chuckles, and the deep, rumbling sound steeps in my belly like warm tea. And the feel of his hands, even through his gloves, as I press my palms to the ground and encourage him to place his hands over mine, makes me gasp.

I scramble to think up an excuse. I'm unused to being touched, unused to being anything but despised on this mountain. I didn't expect him to actually follow my orders. But a breath passes, then two, and Alaric doesn't tease me. He simply waits, his hot breath tickling my cheek, making me even more flustered.

This was a terrible idea. Allowing him to watch me grow ordinary herbs was bad enough, and bagrava is a different beast altogether—the way it makes me *feel* is different. Every time I try to start the incantations, my tongue feels as thick and slow as a slug.

"Is something wrong?" Alaric glances up from beneath his long lashes. His shimmering gray eyes are uncharacteristically soft—a prism of shifting greens and silvers, like granite polished smooth, rather than raw stone.

"I'm not used to doing this in front of an audience," I admit.

"Do you want me to leave?" Alaric starts to pull away.

"*No*," I say sternly, surprising us both. "I want you to see."

I need you to trust me.

I grit my teeth, close my eyes, and focus my energy into the ground, blocking out everything but the feel of my fingers in the dirt and the pulse of the newly buried bagrava seeds. They call to me from their soil beds, reaching for me like mewling babes, and I picture my fingers growing downward like roots, branching wider and deeper until my fingernails touch the delicate casing of a seed. With a gentle touch, I peel back the skin and set the purple seedling free. Then I release another, and another, coaxing them toward the surface with my incantations.

As the seedlings rise, I sink into the rhythm of the words and the cadence of the melody, repeating the well-worn notes until, at last, the shoots break ground in a surge of glorious energy. The power is dizzying and euphoric, pouring through me and cycling back into the ground like a fountain, making it impossible to tell if I'm feeding the bagrava or if it's feeding me.

Alaric sucks in a wondrous breath, but I don't stop singing. Can't risk losing my concentration.

I've never cultivated bagrava behind glass walls or without the help of a planting partner, and the added strain is taking its toll. Sweat trickles down my face, and my arms begin to tremble. It feels like I'm drilling through rock instead of soil, which I suppose isn't far from the truth. Just when I fear I'm going to collapse, the plants reach their mature height, and tender leaves unfurl, followed by small balls of fruit that deepen in color until they're as big as my fist and as rich and dark as wine.

At last, I release the ground and sit back on my haunches, smiling and exhilarated but also panting and exhausted—and, apparently, crying.

Alaric reaches over and gently swipes his fingers cross my cheek.

My hand flies to my face and I scramble back, uncertain if I'm recoiling from his touch or what I've done. I betrayed myself and my country by growing bagrava in Vanzador—even if it's just a means to an end.

"I'm sorry." Alaric retracts his hand, and his cheeks redden. "I didn't mean... I got caught up in the moment." His voice is soft and full of even more wonder than when he watched me grow common herbs. He can't stop looking from my face to the stalks of perfect bagrava and back again. "That was incredible."

"More like incredibly stupid," I deflect with a hoarse laugh. "You'll probably take this crop straight to dear old Daddy as soon as I'm gone."

"It *would* get him off your back," Alaric points out, "but I won't tell him yet—not until you're ready."

"What if I'm never ready?" I chance a look up and find Alaric gently gliding his fingertips across the top of the bagrava. "Who will you side with then?" I ask, even though we both know the answer.

Alaric clears his throat and changes the subject. "Thank you for sharing this with me. I know how sacred it is to you. There's something I want to share with you in return."

"Oh?" I say casually, though on the inside, I'm pulled tighter than bailing twine.

My plan is actually working.

Alaric reaches into his waistcoat pocket and reveals a small silver button that glitters in the intense sunlight.

I immediately recognize it. "That's the silver button from your memory—the one that came loose from your coat."

Alaric nods. "When my father tried to force me to purge the memory of Besnik's death, I siphoned it into this button instead."

"So does the memory exist only in the button? Is it like learning the truth anew every time you watch it?"

Alaric rolls the button through his fingers. "For now, I have it in my mind and in the button. But it's only a matter of time before I slip up and my father discovers I didn't purge the memory. The button ensures the truth will never be lost, and it's far more detailed. Our natural memories fade over time, and I want to remember every detail of Besnik's sacrifice. It's the least I can do to honor him."

"How does it work? How do you bring the memory to life? Delphine said she's never seen anything like it."

Alaric looks down and lets out a long, slow breath before answering. "I hadn't either until late one evening, several years ago, I was returning to the Fortress from a jobsite and noticed an old woman creeping into a mine shaft that had been permanently closed. A pocket of gas had caused an explosion that collapsed several tunnels and killed dozens of miners. I didn't want the old woman to meet a similar end, so I followed her into the abandoned shaft. I presumed she was senile and had wandered in by accident. My only intention was to bring her back up to safety. But as I descended into the gloom, I heard her singing—a sad, strange song I'd never heard before.

"I tried calling out to her, but the woman was singing

too loudly, and before I could reach her and carry her to safety, she was surrounded by a burst of golden light. I watched in awe as the light formed into the visage of a man with a scraggly beard and three younger boys, ranging in age from perhaps twelve to thirty. They danced to life around her, laughing and embracing each other, blowing out birthday candles, and singing songs around a cookstove. It was like a dream, only more detailed, and it wasn't until I watched the man and boys don mining boots and hats, collect their lunch pails, and blow kisses to the old woman, that I understood what I was seeing.

"This was a memory. These men—her family—must have died in the accident, yet here they were, so real and alive. As if she'd found a way to bring them back to life. It was what I wanted more than anything—to see Besnik happy and alive, rather than a bloodied corpse strewn across a banquet table—and I was willing to do anything to get it.

"I'm not proud of what I did next." Alaric looks down and sheepishly rubs the back of his neck.

I almost laugh. I didn't have a high opinion of him to begin with, so it's not like he has much to lose, but I force myself to hold my tongue because he's finally opening up. And because I can't deny that my opinion of him is changing.

I'm not sure what, exactly, I think of Alaric Alaverdi, but it isn't all bad.

He clears his throat and continues. "I waited for the memory to end and confronted the woman. I accused her of trespassing, of conjuring sorcery and stealing memories from the earth. When she insisted they were her own memories that she never gave as tribute, I refused to believe her unless she showed me how she brought them to life. I made her teach me the song, which was a promise to the earth—a sacrifice of moments of joy—in exchange for not reporting her suspicious activity to my father.

"I exploited her pain," Alaric says miserably. "What kind of person does that?"

"The grieving kind. I would have done the same to see Rowenna again. It doesn't make you a bad person."

"It doesn't make me a good person either. But I needed to know the truth. By that point, it had been several years since Besnik's death, and the loving way my father treated me, the way the people adored him, and how assuredly he spoke of his version of events, I was beginning to question my own sanity. I wondered if I had invented the tragedy to absolve my guilty conscience. If there was a way for me to witness the truth, I needed to see it."

"For what it's worth, I don't think you did anything wrong. You didn't take the old woman's memories of her family or report her to Soren."

Alaric shrugs and turns his attention back to the bagrava, skimming his fingers along the fruit.

"I'm glad you shared this with me," I say after a beat. "But if I'm honest, I'm not sure *why* you did."

Without any warning, Alaric lobs the silver button at me. "Catch."

I'm so surprised, I barely manage to grab it. Then the instant the metal hits my palms, I shriek and almost drop it again.

The button pulsates with energy—an intense thrumming, like an angry bee buzzing in my hands.

I gasp and look up at the Vanzadorian prince. "Is it *alive*?"

"In a sense," Alaric says. "Memories are made of energy. They encapsulate the vitality of the time they represent. So when we give our memories to the earth, that energy is converted into power that funnels into my father and me. But when that energy is siphoned inside an object, it has nowhere to go, so it builds and brims, waiting for release. All siphoned memories emit this thrum. Someone in the Fortress might possess a memory of your sister, and now you know what to look for."

I don't know what to say, and the longer I stare at Alaric in open-mouthed shock, the more his cheeks redden.

Objectively, the odds that anyone saved a crucial memory of my sister are low. And the odds of me finding said memory are even lower. But the fact that Alaric shared this information is monumental. He's letting me in. And he's given me an ideal excuse. I can hunt for the triad gemstones under the guise of hunting for hidden memories. All the places people might choose to hide precious memories—like in the finest salons or personal chambers—could also be places they'd hide precious gemstones. Maybe Alaric will take me to these places if he believes I'm only hunting for memories.

"Thank you," I murmur, reaching for his hand.

Surprisingly, he lets me take it. And that's how Delphine finds us—hands clasped in a planter of newly grown bagrava—when she bursts through the solarium door a moment later.

TWENTY-EIGHT

"What's all this?" She gapes from me to Alaric, her eyes settling on our clasped hands.

"Nothing," I say, yanking free. "Just a bit of gardening."

"A bit of gardening?" she sputters.

Alaric frowns at his empty hand before addressing Delphine. "Is there a problem with that?"

"No, forgive me, Your Highness." Delphine bows and backs toward the solarium door. "My business can wait."

But her puffy red eyes and shuddering breaths tell a different story.

"Delphine, wait! What's wrong?" I call. Seeing me with Alaric clearly surprised her, but that couldn't possibly be what's making her so upset.

Delphine doesn't answer or slow, and when I jump to

follow her, Alaric's frown deepens. Who leaves a prince alone in the dirt to chase after a maid?

I'm navigating this all wrong—offending them both—but I don't have a clue how to juggle so many tenuous alliances.

I catch Delphine by the shoulder before she disappears into my chamber. "Tell me what's going on. *Please*," I beg.

Delphine casts a wary glance back at Alaric before quietly uttering, "It's Cloudia. She's taken a turn. I've never seen her this bad. I'm worried she's going to—to—" Delphine crumples to her knees, and I awkwardly collapse with her, trying to break her fall. "I need you to come see her." She squeezes my hands painfully tight. "There must be something you can do, some herb or poultice you haven't tried?"

I nod, even as I mentally comb through the inventory of herbs I've grown these past weeks—all the failed remedies. I'm not a healer, and I'm out of new seeds. Out of ideas.

Except for one. There's *one* plant we haven't tried. The same plant I just so happened to cultivate with Alaric.

I look back at the tall stalks of bagrava, heavy with fruit.

It feels wrong to even consider disobeying Earth Mother by administering bagrava to Cloudia, but if bagrava tea can soothe Queen Tessa and her courtiers without driving them mad, perhaps a small dosage might be able to calm Cloudia too. It may not cure her illness, but it might offer a little relief. Surely, Earth Mother would be willing to overlook my disobedience this once, since it's a matter of life and death? Especially if I beg her forgiveness and serve her with perfect devotion going forward.

To my surprise, it isn't Earth Mother who condones or rejects my decision.

It's Rowenna.

You need to stay focused, Indira! You can't flit off to help a worthless maid and her sick sister when Alaric is finally opening up.

Her use of the word *worthless* makes me bristle. Just because she and Delphine didn't get along, it hardly makes Delphine worthless. And who's to say I can't do both? Alaric revealed so much just now. I don't want to press too hard and make him suspicious.

Careful, sister, or I'll grow suspicious of your priorities, Rowenna whispers darkly.

"Who's Cloudia?" Alaric asks, bringing me back. "And what's the matter with her?"

Delphine casts me a terrified look, and I scramble to explain in a way that won't put Cloudia in more danger. The last thing I want is for Soren to take an interest in Cloudia's strange illness and separate the sisters thanks to my "help."

"Cloudia is Delphine's younger sister," I say. "She's been ill recently, so I've been making simple remedies for her."

"*This* is the friend you've been helping with your herbs?" Alaric asks with a note of surprise. "Your maid?"

Delphine tries to shrink back, but I clasp her hand and force her to remain at my side. "Yes. She's been helping me, so I'm helping her. Do you take issue with that?" I raise my chin defiantly.

Alaric studies us for a long beat before shaking his head. "No, actually. I find it oddly refreshing."

I'm certain he's being sardonic, and I wait for him to mock me and forbid me from going to Cloudia, but he continues watching Delphine and me with curiosity rather than contempt.

"Does this mean I'm allowed to leave the palace to go to her?" I cautiously ask. "And may I take a bit of bagrava?"

Alaric tilts his head back and laughs, making Delphine and me jump. "*Now* you're concerned with asking for my permission to sneak out?"

"This is different—" I start to say, but surprisingly, Alaric reaches for my satchel, which was propped against the planting bed, and holds it out. "The bagrava doesn't belong to me—as you so love to remind me. Take whatever you need."

Our fingers brush as I take the strap, and I feel it again: that sudden jolt of electricity. The tickle of his stare dances across my skin as I pluck a few ripe bagrava and stuff them into the satchel. I still can't believe he's allowing this. There must be a catch, some angle of attack I'm missing.

But then I think of the feel of his hands atop mine in the dirt, the buzzing silver button he willingly shared.

"Ready?" Delphine asks.

I nod and hurry toward the door, eager to get away from the unsettling swooping in my stomach. But before we slip out, Alaric clears his throat.

Delphine stiffens and looks to me with panic, but I'm almost relieved. I knew he wouldn't let us go so easily. Alaric Alaverdi is as cold and unrelenting as always. Nothing between us has changed. The sporadic glimpses of softness are just a ruse—a tactic to throw me off-balance.

Alaric clears his throat again and says, "Do you think... do you think I could come with you?"

"*What?*" I nearly trip over my feet as I whirl back around.

Alaric looks up hopefully from his fidgeting hands, and the swooping in my stomach increases a thousandfold.

"Perhaps there's something I could do to help your sister," he says to Delphine. "I have access to healers, books, and ingredients."

It's a terrible idea for so many reasons, but I find myself inexplicably wanting to say *yes*. After helping me grow the bagrava, it feels strangely right he should come with us.

But Delphine blurts out a more sensible answer. "Surely, you have more important things to do? I-I mean, it would be an honor, of course, but my house isn't fit for royalty. And Cloudia would be so embarrassed to be seen in such a state."

"Of course." Alaric stands, brushes off his breeches, and offers a pleasant smile, but the light is gone from his eyes, and the butterflies in my belly are still. "Go. I'll ensure no one notices your absence."

I try to catch his gaze—to communicate what, I'm not sure. I know better than to trust his motives. But I also feel a strange surge of protectiveness. I don't want him to feel rejected, yet again, when he's finally let down his guard.

"Alaric?" I call out softly, but he's already fallen back into the arrogant stride he uses around the Fortress, disappearing into his chambers without a backward glance.

"Come on." Delphine pulls me through my own chamber and out into the hall, where we weave down corridors I've never seen and into the chill of an extravagant and secluded courtyard. She skirts around a reflecting pool and behind a stone obelisk that conceals a gate leading out into the broader city.

As her blond braid disappears through the gap, I marvel yet again at how she seems to know every nook and cranny of the palace—even places like this opulent garden, where a chambermaid would never have cause to visit.

It's suspicious, Rowenna agrees. *Yet another reason why you should be listening to* me *instead of her*.

I don't answer. I'm not in the mood to argue, especially

over something like this. How could helping an innocent, suffering girl ever be wrong?

Delphine leads me through the winding, snow-dusted streets until we reach a gray stone cottage with fresh thatching and a door painted a merry mint green. It isn't half as dreary as I expected, and I'm about to say so, when Delphine bypasses the green door and continues around the side of the house, down a staircase, and into a basement that smells of standing water. The door creaks loudly and emits a gust of dirty straw and beetle carcasses.

"I know it's bleak," Delphine apologizes, "but we can't afford anything nicer on my wages alone. We used to live a few streets over, in a second-floor apartment that was bright with sunshine, but Mrs. Higgens wouldn't let us stay when Cloudia lost her job. Said half of us had to go if we could only pay half as much, so of course, we left together."

Delphine keeps her eyes on the ground and gestures for me to enter. As I pass, I place a hand on her shoulder. "I know you're accustomed to serving the courtiers in the palace, but my people are humble too. Dreadfully poor by Vanzadorian standards. And like you, we live underground. So believe it or not, I feel more at home here than I ever have in Soren's glittering palace."

A small grateful smile lifts Delphine's face as she follows me inside.

It's a single room with a wooden table in one corner,

a basin filled with both the dishes and the washing in another corner, and a squat coal stove burning hot in the third. Heat pours into the room, and the sudden shift from freezing to stifling makes me queasy.

I yank at the already low neckline of my gown. "Why is it so hot in here?" I start to say, but my voice falls away when I spy the white-faced, blue-lipped girl lying on a straw mattress in the final corner.

Cloudia looks to be captured in ice—so deathly pale she's almost translucent, staring up at the ceiling with vacant, unseeing eyes. Her body, however, twitches and jerks. Her back arches while her arms twist and her legs flail. All the while, her face remains blank and still. It's unsettling. Unnatural. And I have already retreated a step when a scratchy voice spills through Cloudia's chapped lips.

"I don't want to see!" she wails. "Not again, not again!"

After repeating herself three times, Cloudia falls quiet, though her body continues to writhe.

It might be the most horrifying thing I've ever seen, and I'm no longer surprised my herbal remedies did nothing. But I can feel Delphine's eyes on me, so I try to keep my expression calm and neutral—like the healers in Tashir—even though I've never felt more out of my depth. "Has she always thrashed about like this?"

Delphine wipes her tears with the back of her sleeve. "Yes, but it's gotten worse lately. Her speaking is the real change, though. She never used to say anything, which was worrying in its own way, but this is so much worse. I can't imagine the torture that must be playing across her mind. She doesn't even sound like herself. That strange, rasping voice is so—so—*wrong*."

I catch one of Cloudia's flailing hands and gently stroke her fingers as she squirms. "Cloudia, my name is Indira. Your sister brought me here to help you."

No response.

"It's clear you're suffering. If speaking is too difficult, squeeze my hand to let me know you hear me. Or even just blink your eyes."

Nothing.

Delphine gulps back a sob and covers her mouth. "Do you think the bagrava will truly help?"

I don't have a seeds-forsaken clue how to answer, so I don't. Instead, I wrap my arms around Delphine's bony frame and hold her for several long seconds while she cries. Then I shrug out of my satchel and pretend to be confident as I remove the freshly picked bagrava. I may not be able to heal Cloudia, but I can be strong for Delphine—like she was for me after my encounter with Von Nevus.

"Put a kettle on," I instruct. "And bring me a knife and a chopping board."

When Delphine brings the supplies, I mince the bagrava and steep it in water until the room fills with the horrid scent of burning flesh. After it has cooled a bit, I ladle the purple liquid into a bowl, and Delphine spoons it into her sister's mouth. Cloudia continues to twitch, and purple spittle dribbles down her chin onto her sheets, but Delphine gets the majority down her throat.

"Now what?" Delphine asks anxiously.

"Now we wait," I say. "It will calm her, make her even more agitated, or have no effect at all."

Delphine musters a bleak smile, and we both stare into the shadows, sweat rolling down our cheeks as the minutes pass.

"What you saw back there, in my chamber," I begin awkwardly. "Between me and Alaric. It's not how it looked."

Delphine flushes and looks away. "He's your husband. You don't owe me an explanation."

"But I do. You're my closest ally. I don't want you to get the wrong impression. I wasn't falling for his witty banter or charming smile."

"I wouldn't blame you if you were. I'd melt straight into a puddle if he put his hands on me like that," Delphine says with a small giggle.

As our laughter fades, I find myself wanting to tell her the rest. I want someone else to look at all the puzzle pieces and assure me they see the same image taking shape, and Delphine is the closest thing I have to a friend. The closest thing I've *ever* had to a friend, other than Rowenna. I always thought it would feel unnatural to confide in or rely on anyone else, but it's actually kind of nice. Kind of freeing.

"Alaric was telling me more about his memory of Besnik's death. He stores it in the silver button that tore from his coat that night. He said he brings it to life with a song—one he blackmailed an old woman into teaching him when he caught her reliving memories of her deceased husband and children."

"He told you all this?" Delphine stares at me in awe.

"He said it was to help me potentially find memories about Rowenna. Apparently, these siphoned memories emit a sort of vibration, and he thought I might be able to locate them around the Fortress."

"That's..." Delphine blinks slowly several times. "Shocking," she finally says. "Are you going to start searching? Do you really think someone might possess something related to Rowenna's death?"

"No," I say, and Delphine looks perplexed all over again.

"But that's what you've been searching for since you arrived on the mountain. The entire reason you came to Vanzador."

"I'm much more interested in the other part of Alaric's memory—the part he didn't explain—about the broken gemstone they called the Flesh of Callahan. I'm fairly certain that's what *blood, flesh, bone* refers to. I think they're all gemstones, and I think they're the source of Soren's power. So *that's* what I'm going to look for—under the guise of looking for hidden memories."

I hold my breath and wait for Delphine's reaction. I've essentially just admitted to the highest form of treason. I'm conspiring to steal her king's power. She could run straight back to the palace and tell Soren or his ministers, and I'd be sentenced to death—just like my sister. But I don't think Delphine will rat me out. Not for a king and system that have failed her and her sister so horribly.

"Why are you telling me all this?" Delphine splutters with wide terrified eyes. "I don't want to know these things, Indira. I don't want to have to turn you in."

"So don't. Come with me when I find the gemstones and leave Vanzador—Cloudia, too, of course. I promise you'll both be far happier in Tashir than you've ever been here."

"You'd be willing to take us with you?" she asks before remembering herself and shaking her head. "This is utter madness. We couldn't possibly." But after several more minutes of dithering, her delicate features settle into a thoughtful expression. "You continue to surprise me, Miss Indira," she whispers.

I teasingly nudge her shoulder. "In a good way, I hope?"

"Almost *too* good," she answers quietly.

By sundown, Cloudia's thrashing has slowed, and my eyes are so bleary with exhaustion—or maybe it's the oppressive heat of the stove—the walls seem to shiver and spin.

I stand and brush off my skirts. "I'm going to head back," I whisper.

Delphine stirs from where she nodded off to sleep, leaning against Cloudia's bedside. She groggily moves to follow, but I wave her back down. "Stay with your sister and rest tonight. I remember the way."

With a grateful nod, Delphine nestles back down. I tiptoe toward the door, but before I'm halfway across the room, Cloudia speaks again—and not in the frantic, rasping voice that's haunted us all day. Her voice is calm and level, her body perfectly still.

"The people...the children...are dying."

I whip around and lock eyes with Delphine, who's already on her feet. She takes Cloudia's hand and leans close to her face, stroking her hair. "Who's dying, Cloudia? What are you talking about?"

Cloudia doesn't answer or even seem to register Delphine's presence. She simply repeats herself again, then drifts back to sleep.

Her sudden stillness and composure are even more unsettling than all the shouting and thrashing. Ice trickles between my shoulder blades, and I shiver despite the heat.

Delphine continues whispering to Cloudia, tearfully begging her to say more. When she finally gives up, Delphine gestures for me to follow her to the corner by the stove.

"Do you think this means the bagrava is working?" she asks. "Cloudia sounded so calm, almost like her old self. Except the words. They were so macabre."

I shrug helplessly. "It could be the bagrava, or it could be nothing more than a bad dream. The only way to know is to continue giving her the tea twice a day and monitor the results. Make sure someone stays with her while you're working, in case she suffers any adverse effects or speaks again. We need to write down everything she says, especially in her seemingly more lucid moments. It might give us insight into what's happening in her mind."

"Thank you." Delphine's eyes brim with tears as she walks me to the door. "I know you didn't come to Vanzador under happy circumstances. Rowenna's death was a terrible tragedy—one I wish I could reverse, despite our differences—but the one silver lining is it brought us *you*. And your friendship has been nothing short of miraculous for Cloudia and me. I thought knowing this might bring you a small measure of comfort."

Delphine squeezes my hand, and now I'm getting choked up because it *is* comforting. I hope Rowenna can feel it too. I hope she sees these new green shoots, springing up from the ashes of her death.

Forgive me if I'm less than thrilled my greatest legacy is helping a Vanzadorian servant and her ailing sister, Rowenna grumbles.

I want to shake her and make her see sense. *Why do you insist on being so discontent when we're making good progress and gaining more allies?*

Because you don't need other allies, she says, and I sigh.

I have to trust and rely on someone who's actually here. But that doesn't mean I've turned my back on you. I'm doing all of this for you. Surely, you see that.

As quick as it appeared, the familiar crackle of my sister's presence is gone—blown out like a candle—and I don't rush to call her back.

She'd see right through my groveling anyway.

It's difficult to apologize when you're not actually sorry.

TWENTY-NINE

WHEN DAWN BREAKS THE FOLLOWING MORNing, I find myself in the same unlikely place as the day before, knocking on Alaric Alaverdi's chamber door.

"*Why* is this becoming a regular occurrence?" he groans through the small crack.

I'm so flustered and unsure how to act after everything that transpired in the solarium the day before, I babble and fidget nervously.

"I let you run off with your maid, precisely as you wished—shouldn't that buy me at least one morning of peace?" he demands.

"I'm sorry. I didn't mean to disturb you. I just thought you'd want to know what happened with Delphine's sister."

I venture a smile and wait for the curious boy who sat

beside me in the bagrava bed and asked to join us to visit Cloudia to reappear and invite me in, but Alaric's scowl deepens, and he closes the door another fraction.

"Well, you thought wrong. Why would I care about a random servant's sibling?"

His voice is pure ice, and it slaps me across the cheek.

"B-because you were there," I stammer.

"And then I was dismissed," he says flatly. "Like always. You'd think I'd be better at sensing where I'm not wanted by now."

"It isn't like that. I wanted you to come, but it wasn't my place—"

"Are we done here?" Alaric snaps. "I have things to do."

"No," I say, taking a breath for courage. "I was hoping you might accompany me to your mother's salon this morning."

Alaric's face contorts with horror. "Why, in the name of the kings, would I do that?"

Because I need to search for the gemstone triad, and I can't bear to face Garitt Von Nevus without, at least, the illusion of protection.

But I'm not about to explain my encounter with Von Nevus. Alaric may not see eye to eye with Soren's councilors, but he'd surely have to side with a high-ranking official over me, so I say, "To look for hidden memories, as you suggested. The courtiers and your father's councilors seem like the most logical place to begin, but I'm a stranger—the enemy princess. They'll never allow me to get close enough to properly search them."

"And you think they'll let me get close?" Alaric laughs bitterly. "You've been here long enough to know better. I might as well be the Tashiri captive for how little they respect me. My own mother can hardly bear to look at me. Half the time, I think she doesn't even remember she has a second son."

It's exactly how I felt after Rowenna went to Vanzador, and I swallow hard against the lump of emotion that clogs my throat. "Your mother isn't shutting you out on purpose. People deal with grief in different ways. And your people respect you far more than you think. I've seen how they watch you and call out with admiration. The only reason your father's ministers don't trust you is because they didn't spend a lifetime grooming you, like they did your brother. They fear you because they can't control you, not because you're lacking in any way."

"I will always be lacking because I'll never be Besnik." Alaric's voice cracks on his brother's name, and I bite my lower lip.

I've never had to deal with comparisons between me and Rowenna. We had separate identities and responsibilities in Tashir—me with the bagrava and her the throne. We each earned the respect of the people in our own right. If I ever did feel inadequate, it was due to my own insecurity and idol worship of my sister, not something our people said or did. I can't imagine how it would feel if that judgment came from them—even if it was only a small number of them. Or if I didn't have power of my own. If I had always been viewed as less than and excess. A shadow son or daughter, suddenly thrust into the light.

"Trust me, you'll have better luck searching for memories if I'm not with you," Alaric says, shutting the door with a decisive click.

I'm tempted to continue banging on the door until he opens up and sees the truth—until he sees himself the way the majority of Vanzadorians see him. The way his brother undoubtedly sees him, looking down with pride at how Alaric has stepped into this role. Alaric shouldn't give a fig what a few worthless ministers think. But I know these assurances will mean nothing coming from me, so after several fruitless minutes of staring at the door, I give up and make my way toward Queen Tessa's salon.

I tell myself it's for the best. The less Alaric sees me searching for the gemstone triad, the less likely he'll figure out what I'm up to. But the familiar churning in my stomach that always seems to plague me after an encounter with Alaric continues eating me from the inside out.

I hate that I added to his self-doubt by excluding him the day before, but what was I supposed to do? I couldn't force Delphine to bring him into her home—especially when we couldn't know how he'd react to Cloudia's illness. While I suspect he'd approach it with concern and understanding, he has an entire country to consider. It would be perfectly understandable to quarantine one ill person to potentially protect thousands. Prudent, even.

I'm still stewing when I reach the queen's salon and push into the crush of colors and finery. I quickly scan the crowd for Von Nevus, unable to breathe until I'm certain I don't feel the weight of his hungry eyes.

Next, I look for Elodie's intricate braids and bright smile, praying she'll appear at my side like always, but before I can find her, I'm surrounded by a swarm of unfamiliar faces, whipping fans, and waves of competing perfume—lily, then lilac, then rose. It's all so cloying and close, so demanding and loud. I want to pull out my trowel and cut the courtiers back like life-sucking weeds, but I force myself to take a deep breath, nod, and smile pleasantly.

I need to find the gemstone triad, and if there's one thing the courtiers know, it's jewels. Each of them is bedecked in sparkling finery, from the pins in their hair down to the polished buckles of their boots. So I plaster a smile on my face and reach for a gold and ruby chain clasped around the wrist of a copper-haired courtier.

"Your bracelet is breathtaking," I say.

She blushes and brings it to her chest to better display it to the crowd. "Thank you. It was my mother's and my grandmother's before her."

"Such a treasured family heirloom. You *all* have such

beautiful pieces," I say to the broader group. "Where do you store them for safekeeping? You'd each need a king-sized vault."

Several of the men and women titter. Others shake their heads behind their fans.

"I know you're used to a crude farming lifestyle," the copper-haired girl says, "but we don't have to worry about such poverty and lawlessness here. Even the lowliest miners make a livable wage, and gemstones are abundant and accessible to all. No one has to steal anything."

"So you all keep your prized jewels in your homes? Lying about for all to see?"

"That's the entire point," a girl with soft curls and a square chin cuts in. "We want everyone to admire our collections. Some even make window arrangements with the pieces they're not currently wearing. There's an entire street in town that's particularly festive around the holidays. Dazzling displays in every window."

"So there are no vaults? No coffers or the likes in Vanzador?" I ask with astonishment and growing dismay. While this development might remove concerns about locks and guards, it also reduces the odds of me ever locating the triad gemstones. They could be anywhere on this mountain.

While I inwardly spiral, the courtiers giggle and whisper about how disorderly and dreadful Tashir must be. How tiresome it must be, constantly fighting off thieves and brigands.

"It isn't like that," I try to explain, but they're not listening, and their opinion of my country doesn't matter anyway.

"Where is that husband of yours?" the copper-haired girl asks, batting her eyes with innocence, though her question is anything but. She can barely contain her gleeful grin as she casts her gaze dramatically around the room. "You couldn't convince him to accompany you? Pity."

"Don't feel bad," another girl with garishly bright cheeks puts in. "He has never been willing to accompany any of us publicly. It would pull him away from his one true love."

She eyes me expectantly, as if waiting for me to flush with outrage and jealousy, but I wanly ask, "And who is his *one true love*?"

"Not who. *What*," another girl whispers conspiratorially. "Alaric Alaverdi loves only his work."

The swarm of ladies laugh and shake their heads, as if this is a bad thing.

"Shouldn't the future king be devoted to his country?" I ask, feeling an odd swell of protectiveness.

The women share a meaningful look, as if I'm completely clueless. "Not if you're his wife," one of them says, and they all begin to snicker.

"If he's so aloof and inattentive, why have you all been vying for his affection?" I ask.

"I presume you have eyes," the copper-haired girl drawls, and the rest of the group giggles and fans themselves.

"And since the council believes he is ill-equipped to rule, they have always made it clear that Alaric's wife will be instrumental in ruling Vanzador—something many of us found appealing," a girl in a frilly white gown explains.

"He isn't ill-equipped," I argue.

But the girl continues as if I didn't speak, smiling with all the sweetness of a snake. "Then *you* came."

The hairs prickle down the back of my neck. "You mean Rowenna came," I correct her. "*She* was Alaric's first bride."

The first to strip these girls' of their ambitions.

Any one of them could have killed my sister. Just like any one of them would leap at the chance to use Alaric. And I can't stand to be in their company a moment longer.

"Queen Tessa!" I say with an exuberant wave. "Excuse me, my mother-in-law is calling," I tell the gaggle of monstrous girls as I flit away with a forced smile.

The queen is not, in fact, calling for me. She's sitting on her usual settee, her eyes hazy and her smile vacant, but I make a beeline toward her anyway. I refuse to believe that no one on this mountain keeps their prized possessions in a secure location. Particularly the royal jewels. Soren *must* keep them under lock and key after the incident with Alaric and Besnik. The courtiers just don't know where they're hidden and are too proud to admit they're not in the king's innermost circle of trust.

"Your Majesty, you look lovely today," I say, sweeping into a low curtsy that would make Mother and Rowenna proud.

Queen Tessa slowly turns to face me. For a second, it seems as though she's looking through me, and I wonder, yet again, how the Vanzadorians can possibly believe their bagrava tea has no ill effects. But then she shakes herself and squints at me—with curiosity or suspicion, I can't tell.

"Indira, you've returned to my salon. Does that mean you've decided to accept our *lifestyle*?"

I will never accept their abhorrent tea—it's an insult to Earth Mother and destroying my country—but I lower my chin demurely. "Of course you're able to do as you see fit with our tributes. I'm sorry I reacted so defensively before. I was exhausted and overwhelmed by so much change."

"And now?" A bemused smile flits across my mother-in-law's lips. "Have you settled into life on the mountain?"

"Yes, I believe I have—for the most part. One thing's still troubling me, though. It's actually what I came here to discuss with you."

Queen Tessa quirks a brow.

"I've been meaning to ask about your jewelry," I say shyly. "It's all so lovely. And the other ladies at court are always adorned in gemstones too. I'd very much like to wear some—to fit in among you—but I'm afraid I don't own any. We don't have such luxuries in Tashir."

The queen's face immediately softens into a smile. "Of course you should wear jewels. You're Vanzadorian now. Join me before dinner, and I'll select a few pieces from my own collection."

"That would be wonderful, Your Majesty." I lower into another curtsy. "Shall I meet you at the royal coffers? I'm afraid I don't know where they're located."

Queen Tessa cocks her head and frowns. "I keep my jewelry with me, in my personal chamber. Come there. And bring my delinquent son. He goes to such great lengths to avoid me, I'm beginning to think he's allergic to my presence."

"It isn't you he's allergic to, Your Majesty," the waspish old councilor, who seems to be Alaric's most vocal opponent, proclaims loudly. "Prince Alaric has always been allergic to a good time!"

More than half the crowd snickers, and I want to shout at them all: *He's clearly allergic to failure, you idiots. And grief! He avoids this salon to spare himself the headache of interacting with vapid courtiers and judgmental councilors, and because he can't bear to see his mother reduced to this empty husk. Can't bear to lose another person he loves.*

I can't imagine being forced to stand face-to-face with the baffling version of Rowenna who lived on this mountain. I don't know how I'd cope if that was all that remained of her. If she was technically present but gone in all the ways that mattered.

If anyone is 'gone in all the ways that matter' it's you, Rowenna grumbles. *I hardly recognize you, fretting over the feelings of an entitled prince. He doesn't deserve your pity. Don't let him play the oppressor and the victim.*

But after witnessing his living memory, I don't think Alaric Alaverdi has ever been anything but a victim, and it's all so infuriating and unfair, I don't realize I'm shouting until the words have tumbled from my lips.

"Or perhaps Alaric is *allergic* to all this useless idle chatter. If he wasted more time among you, I fear Vanzador would cease to function!"

The hum of laughter and clinking of teacups immediately ceases, and every eye in the salon blinks at me with shock.

Strangely, this doesn't bother me. I stare brazenly back at them, even Queen Tessa, until I feel a hand slip through the crook of my arm and squeeze my elbow tight.

"Indira! You're always such a comedian!" Elodie says with a loud laugh. "Forgive the princess; she gets this way when she's hungry. Never come between a gardener and their next meal." She laughs gaily, playing to the crowd, and the tension in the room instantly dissipates—order restored now that I am, once again, the butt of their jokes.

"Let's get you some refreshments." Elodie pulls me

toward a banquet table laden with meat pies. As I watch her trembling hands make a plate for me, waves of gratitude and unexpected fondness course through me.

She always appears exactly when I need her, always comes to my defense, despite the potential damage to her own reputation.

I can *feel* Rowenna rolling her eyes, but I'm not in the mood to doubt one of my only allies just because Rowenna feels jealous and insecure. Instead, *I* fall silent and pretend not to hear her reminders to stay vigilant.

Ignoring her isn't easy. Every passing second feels more excruciating than the one before it. The wrenching in my chest is so heavy, I'm certain it will crush me. But as seconds turn to minutes, I realize there's something empowering about being the one to wield the silence. I feel a bit like the gemstones the Vanzadorian miners cleave from this mountain. Simple rock, transformed by the crushing weight. I, too, am changing. Growing harder, sharper, and clearer. I don't have to give in to anyone's demands—not even my sister's.

Assuming the voice in my head was ever hers to begin with and not just a way to fill the Rowenna-shaped hole in my life.

As soon as I think these traitorous thoughts, the space around me crackles with cold, and the feel of my sister's presence vanishes faster than the morning dew. Once again, I don't immediately call her back. She can no longer manipulate me with the threat of being left all alone because I'm not alone.

I glance up at Elodie, who sets my food on a small table and drops into the seat across from me with a heavy sigh.

There's no denying the toll our "friendship" has taken on her. Her braids fall lank around her shoulders, and her makeup creases in the bags beneath her eyes. Even still, she musters a smile as she pushes the plate in front of me.

"Thank you for coming to my rescue back there," I say.

She shakes her head and touches her temple. "I don't know what you were thinking. You haven't had a single nice thing to say about Alaric all this time, then suddenly you're going toe to toe with the queen to defend his honor?"

"I didn't mean to." I wince. "It just came out."

"You know I'm all for you falling madly in love with your husband—that's why I've been instructing you in the art of seduction." She winks and I shake my head with horror.

"I'm not falling in love with him!"

Elodie rolls her eyes and continues… "But you still have to use your brain, Indira."

The irony is almost laughable—this seemingly frivolous courtier is telling *me* to use my brain. Rowenna would have a heyday with this reversal, and I feel another odd surge of satisfaction that she left. That I'm allowed to feel how I want to feel. Trust who I want to trust.

I stab a large bite of pie and bring it to my lips. "It's completely unfair, how some of them treat Alaric. How they judge him."

"Lots of things on this mountain are unfair," Elodie says gravely, as if she's ever experienced suffering or injustice.

Once again, my mouth spews out words before my brain thinks better of it. "What about your life could possibly be unfair?"

Her pretty face crumples, and I immediately hate myself for being just as small-minded and judgmental as the rest of the courtiers.

"I'm sorry, I didn't mean that." I reach for Elodie's gloved hand. "It's just everything about you, and your life, seems so perfect."

"Did you know they won't let me compete in the stone-throwing contests?" she says with surprising bitterness. "Not even as an alternate. This week two competitors failed to show, and they chose to refund all of the bets rather than letting me step in."

I don't know what shocks me more—the fact that she wants to compete in the brutish competitions or that she's ever been denied anything.

"You want to compete?" I ask with surprise.

She nods firmly. "More than anything. I've been practicing in private for years, but women of my status aren't permitted to 'debase' ourselves in the ring. Noblemen aren't denied such privileges, but because I wear dresses and enjoy salons, they assume I'm incapable of working hard and getting dirty. They insist I'll injure myself, which is offensive and infuriating."

I'm so surprised by Elodie's admission, I can't think of a single thing to say, which ends up working in my favor, because she keeps on talking, spurred on with conviction I've never seen before.

"You know what else is unfair? Certain council members are petitioning to have my mother removed from her position due to her recent illness. They're acting as if she's done something wrong—like we all don't fall ill from time to time."

"I didn't know that your mother was unwell," I say with a frown. "What does she have?"

Elodie shrugs. "Just a fever of some sort. The healers insist she'll turn the corner soon."

"How long has it been?"

"A few weeks."

I nearly choke on the pie in my mouth. Elodie's mother has been ill for the entirety of my time in Vanzador, but it has never come up in our hours upon hours of conversation.

Because I never asked.

Not about Elodie, her family, or anything beyond my sister and my agenda.

I'm just as selfish and self-absorbed as the courtiers.

Shame burns my cheeks as I gaze across the table at Elodie, who's always there to offer help, advice, and friendship, even though I haven't reciprocated.

"I'm so sorry I didn't know—that I didn't ask," I say in a rush. Elodie tries to wave off my apology, but I don't let her. "If you ever need help tending to your mother, I'm more than willing to lend a hand. I know a lot about herbal remedies."

Elodie laughs to disguise a sniffle. "Don't be ridiculous. You're the princess. You haven't time for such things. My mother is in good hands, besides. The king's personal healers have been caring for her round the clock. They said I should be able to visit her soon and assured me she'll be back in the king's council chambers in no time."

"We're all praying for her swift recovery," a deep voice cuts in behind me, and my entire body stiffens. It feels like ice water is pouring over my head—so shockingly cold, I can't move as Garitt Von Nevus saunters into view and leans casually against our table.

THIRTY

"Forgive the intrusion," Von Nevus says to Elodie, "but I overheard your conversation and had to offer my support. The entire council is beside ourselves with worry for your mother."

His tone is gentle, and his hands are clasped fervently at his chest, but the glint in his eyes is far from sympathetic. He reminds me of a grinning jackal, and I want to climb up on my chair and shout his crimes for all to hear. So everyone knows how he cornered me. What he tried to *take* from me. What he *has* taken from other girls.

I have no doubt he's leading the charge against Elodie's mother, but when I try to voice this accusation, my jaw won't move. It's shut tighter than a rusted padlock. I gaze desperately across the salon, praying someone will see my panic and intervene, but Elodie is cornered with me, and none of the other Vanzadorian nobles would notice my discomfort, let alone accuse a high-ranking councilor like Von Nevus of anything untoward. Even if they suspected he was harassing me, a good portion of them would probably applaud him for seizing the opportunity and taking what he wants.

"I see I've rendered you speechless," he chuckles when neither Elodie nor I reply. "I tend to have that effect on people."

Only because your victims are too traumatized to speak! I want to bellow, but all that comes out is a gasping wheeze.

Elodie narrows her eyes at Von Nevus. "Thank you for your prayers, Councilor, but you should know it's impolite to eavesdrop," she says sharply.

He gallantly removes his tasseled cap. "It's also criminal for two ladies, as lovely as yourselves, to be sitting alone with your grief. Allow me to lighten your spirits. Shall we take a turn about the room, Miss Indira? I've been hoping to continue our previous conversation."

Von Nevus offers me his hand, and all I can see, smell, and even *taste* is the blood I drew with the letter opener. That trail of red, snaking down his wrist, and his disgusting tongue, lapping it up.

Elodie flashes me an insistent look, compelling me to dismiss him, but the harder I try, the more the words get lodged behind a wall of panic, sealing off my throat.

With a concerned frown, Elodie addresses Von Nevus

herself. "I'm afraid we must pass on your kind offer. We're engaged in an important *private* conversation."

Von Nevus doesn't even blink at her dismissal. He keeps his attention fixed on me. "Let the princess speak for herself. What do *you* say, Little Ro?"

No!

I scream it. Shout it. So loud, my throat feels raw and ripped open.

But still, I don't make a sound.

I'm a prisoner in my own body.

Taking my silence for assent, Von Nevus reaches for my hand.

I squeeze my eyes shut and brace for the brush of his clammy fingers. But another hand comes down on the back of my chair and drags me out of Von Nevus's reach.

"I'm afraid I must whisk my wife away," says a voice that sounds like Alaric's. But it can't be. He refused to come. "I've shared her long enough," the voice continues, and a gloved hand adorned with fine white embroidery takes me by the elbow and helps me to my feet.

I'm so panicked and surprised, my wobbly legs give way, but surprisingly, I don't hit the ground. The scents of leather and cardamom invade my nose as muscular arms encircle me.

"I've got you," the voice that can't be Alaric's whispers. But when I glance up, he's there, glaring at Von Nevus with his dangerous, beautiful eyes

I'm hallucinating. In the throes of a panic attack. It's the only explanation.

"Miss Tomasko." Alaric nods politely at Elodie, who's glancing between my husband and me with giddy delight. Then he ushers me away, across the salon, and I'm so stunned, I can do nothing but trip along as he drags me past Queen Tessa and dozens of courtiers.

They wave and call out to him, but Alaric ignores them all, escorting me out of the salon with long confident strides. Once we're down the hall and around the corner, I expect him to drop me like a scalding pot. Maybe even wipe his hands on his waistcoat to remove the stain of my touch. But he continues gripping my arm until we reach my chamber door. Then he shocks me again by letting himself in—as if he's joined me in my private quarters a hundred times before.

"Indira?" Delphine's voice chimes from the adjoining bathing chamber. "I didn't think you'd return so soon. Did you have any luck finding—" Her head pops around the corner, and when she sees Alaric, her eyes grow round. "Your Highness! I-I didn't realize..." She folds into a clumsy bow and curiously watches Alaric help me across the room.

What's going on? she mouths when he turns to help me onto the sofa.

I know how this must look—me, draped all over him, the two of us stealing into my private quarters—but I'm still incapable of speech. Incapable of doing anything but dropping onto the sofa and melting into the cushions.

The longer I remain silent, the more urgently Delphine looks between Alaric and me, then down to the bowl in her hands—as if judging its heft. She makes a beeline across the sitting room, past Alaric, and stops in front of me, wordlessly asking if this encounter is the same as my ill-fated encounter with Von Nevus. If I'm with Alaric against my will.

For the second time today, my chest swells with gratitude for another brave girl who, against all reason, cares for me. Delphine is willing to face down the crown prince on my behalf, armed with nothing but a washbasin. No one, other than Rowenna, has ever stood up for me like this. Partly because I didn't allow it. I thought it would diminish my and Rowenna's connection to let anyone else in. But it turns out love isn't finite. A portion isn't taken from one recipient when it's shared with another. It simply grows.

"Thank you for escorting her here, Your Highness," Delphine says to Alaric. "That was most kind, but I can take it from here. Indira looks unwell, and I don't want you to catch—"

"Actually, I'd like to stay," Alaric says.

Delphine looks to me with panicked eyes.

"It's okay," I manage to whisper.

"You're certain?" She flicks another suspicious glance at Alaric.

I reach for Delphine's hand and squeeze it tightly. Gratefully. "Yes. Why don't you spend the night with Cloudia? I made another dose of the bagrava tincture. It's ready to go in the solarium. Be sure to note any changes."

Delphine thanks me graciously and moves toward the hidden door, but before she vanishes, she throws Alaric an unmistakable look of warning.

"I see why you like her," he says once the door has closed. "Good friends are hard to come by around here."

He pours a glass of water from a pitcher on the side table and hands it to me. I gratefully gulp it down, so thirsty I hardly notice the silty flavor.

"So," Alaric says, easing down next to me. "Do you want to talk about what happened back there?"

"Nothing happened. I don't know what you're talking about," I say, but my voice is still wispy and weak.

"You looked like you were going to be sick. And you were so quiet."

I snort. "Isn't that a good thing? You made it clear you have no interest in speaking with me."

"Yes, but this was *too* quiet. Disconcertingly quiet. What did Von Nevus do?"

"Why were you there at all?" I volley back.

"Why did you defend me to my father's councilors?" Alaric asks, his voice soft.

Mortifying heat spreads across my cheeks. "You heard that? How long were you in the salon?"

"Not long. Though I probably didn't need to be there at all. I think I could have heard you shouting from my chamber."

"It's a new development—since Rowenna died. I can't seem to keep my opinions to myself when I'm passionate about a subject."

"Are you saying you're passionate about *me*?" Alaric raises his too-perfect brows.

I glare at him and shove his shoulder. "The things the courtiers were saying were cruel and untrue. I couldn't just listen to their lies."

Alaric nods, his gaze softening into the same expression he wore when he watched me grow the bagrava. "That's why I came to your defense too. I couldn't just stand by and watch Von Nevus torment you. I'm the only one who gets to do that."

I shove his shoulder again. "That still doesn't explain why you were there in the first place."

"I came to help you look for hidden memories. I felt guilty for brushing you off after you kindly tried to relay news of Delphine's sister."

Being kind was hardly all I was trying to accomplish, but I keep that to myself.

"So, did you find any memories you want me to bring to life?" Alaric presses.

I shake my head. "Sadly, no."

"Then do you want to tell me what happened with

Councilor Von Nevus? Why did you panic like that?"

"You'll never believe me, so I see no point telling you."

"I never would have believed you'd publicly defend me, either, so we've already left the realm of plausibility far behind." When I still refuse, he adds, "Take your time. I'm more than happy to sit here all evening…together." He shimmies deeper into the sofa and throws me a needling smile.

I tilt my head back with a groan. "Fine. Councilor Garitt Von Nevus approached me not long after I arrived on the mountain, claiming to be Rowenna's mentor and ally. He offered to be the same for me. Said he'd help me look for answers about her death and teach me how to navigate life in the Fortress. But his offer didn't come without a price. H-he made advances. He cornered me and tried to…"

My hand drifts to where he caressed my arm, and a sob escapes me.

I expect Alaric to roll his eyes at my theatrics and dismiss the accusations outright. Or pick apart my story and tell me it was somehow my fault—I must have enticed Von Nevus and invited his advances. I wait for him to tell me I should be flattered men can't control themselves in my presence. Or at the very least, to tell me there's nothing to be done because of Von Nevus's position.

But Alaric Alaverdi says none of these things.

His eyes go hard as flint, and he mutters words like

pig and *castrate* as he paces the sitting room for five solid minutes. Finally, he stops in front of me and crouches low, so we're face-to-face—like we were during our wedding ceremony on the Tomb Flats.

Somehow, this is even more intimate.

"I'm sorry you were assaulted in my home. I would never condone such behavior. Did he harm you? Do you need a healer?"

I give my head a small shake. "I defended myself."

Alaric's mouth curves into the smallest of smirks. "Of course you did."

"Is it that hard to believe?" I demand. "Or will I always be the girl who shrank in silence when you and your father took Rowenna? The girl who crumpled across her coffin like a wet rag when you returned her body?"

"*No!*" Alaric says with surprising alarm. "That's not how I see you at all. You're the girl who made a *bomb* to save your storehouse. The girl who's been searching and scheming since the moment you arrived at the Fortress. The girl who followed me up the mountain and learned my darkest secrets, but instead of blackmailing me, you've treated me with kindness and compassion. You are a force to be reckoned with."

I don't know if it's the declaration itself, how he says it, or the way he's looking at me, but my insides suddenly feel as light and floating as a dandelion seed.

Really? Rowenna cuts in, and I nearly fall out of my

chair. I expected her to punish me with silence after I willfully ignored her earlier. But she's here—her voice small and scratchy, yet unmistakable.

I had to say something, she continues. *I've been giving you these same compliments, but I suppose it means more coming from a handsome, brooding prince.*

"You don't need to say anything more about your encounter with Von Nevus if it's too difficult," Alaric says, mistaking my silence for pain. "Thank you for trusting me with this. I can't imagine how difficult it must have been to see him again. Most people in this palace would have chosen to purge the ordeal immediately."

I stubbornly shake my head. "Forgetting would let him off the hook and give him the opportunity to prey on me again. I don't regret my memory of the incident. I regret that I froze in his presence just now. I had a chance to confront him, but I quite literally choked on the words. I hate that I let him have that kind of power over me—especially when there are other girls who have suffered far worse at his hands."

"There are others?" Alaric's fists tighten, and I swear a shudder passes through the gemstone walls. My breath catches as I glance up, searching for fractures. Alaric's eyes dart upward too, and he immediately shakes out his hands.

"If it were up to me, I'd strip Von Nevus of his title and cast him into the icy wilderness beyond the Fortress—condemn him to a long cold death. But, since he technically serves my father, I can't. I can, however, ensure you're never made to suffer his presence again. I won't let him come within five paces of you," he promises.

The relief of being believed and supported is so overwhelming, I nearly burst into tears again. But Alaric has already seen too much of my soft underbelly today, so I hide behind a shield of humor instead.

"That's a very noble offer," I say, "but in order to ensure Councilor Von Nevus doesn't come within five paces of me, it will require you to *always* be within five paces of me. Are you sure you'll survive that?"

Alaric scrunches his face dramatically, but when he clears his throat, his expression turns solemn. "It seems a fitting punishment, actually, for allowing someone so vile to hold a position of power. It would be my honor to escort you anytime."

"*Anywhere*?" I shamelessly press. "Because you still owe me a trip to your mines, to witness your power in exchange for showing you my gardening magic—twice now."

I am suddenly, deliriously happy Alaric refused to take me to a jobsite the first time I asked. Back then, I would have only thought to look for hidden stores of bagrava or ways to exploit their mining operations. Now I know to look for so much more.

Like stones of blood, flesh, and bone.

Perhaps other magical deposits were formed the day

Callahan obtained his power, and Soren and Alaric have been steering the miners away from these caches, to ensure they alone have access? Or they could have hidden the original gemstone triad in an old, abandoned mineshaft for safekeeping, where no one ever has cause to visit. It would be so brilliant to keep the key to moving the earth within the earth itself. Hidden in plain sight. Much safer than royal coffers that could be infiltrated by a curious young prince or vengeful captive bride.

Alaric shifts uneasily, pinning me in place with his storm-cloud eyes. A few short weeks ago, I would have accused him of trying to manipulate me with that roguish stare. But now I see the dazzling flecks of silver for what they really are—a mask to hide his doubt and uncertainty.

"Unless there's a reason you don't want me to see your mines or your magic?" I goad.

Alaric closes his eyes and sighs loudly. "Fine. I'll take you to visit one of the mines. Be ready to go before dawn tomorrow. We need to be finished before the miners arrive for the day."

With that, he stands and heads for the door.

I surprise myself by calling out, "Thank you—for believing me about Von Nevus. And for coming to your mother's salon. I didn't realize how much I was asking when I begged you to escort me. It can't be easy, seeing her like that."

Alaric shrugs stiffly. "She's been that way for so long,

I should be used to it. Besnik's death broke her—just like my father said it would. I lost all of them that day."

Scenes from his golden memory bombard me, and it's all so tragic, so unfair, and so achingly *familiar*.

"That's how it happened for me too," I blurt. "You might as well have taken my parents the day you took Rowenna, because they've never recovered. It's like the best parts of them only existed in my sister. Like they had nothing left to live for when they were left with only me."

The way Alaric is appraising me makes my stomach flip. I feel like I'm standing on the edge of a cliff, heart hammering, feet tingling, but instead of fearing the drop, my body buzzes with the inexplicable urge to jump.

Look away! Rowenna commands from the depths of my consciousness.

But I don't look away.

Neither does Alaric.

His lips slowly bend into a smile that isn't smug or smoldering. It's timid and raw and, quite possibly, the most beautiful thing I've ever seen.

THIRTY-ONE

THE CASTLE HALLS ARE THICK WITH QUIET, AND darkness still blankets the sky when Alaric collects me the following morning.

I have to force myself to count to five before reaching for the doorknob—so he doesn't know I spent most of the night waiting for him, obsessively nervously pacing and obsessively dissecting every moment of our interaction.

I pull up my hood and pretend to yawn as I open the door, but the charade falls away the moment I lay eyes on him.

He looks like a Tashiri planter: shirtless, with low-slung trousers, working gloves, and hair in a wild tangle. It's startling and wrong and appealing. So very, *very* appealing. Especially when the ghost of a smile touches his sleepy eyes and he murmurs a gravelly greeting.

"Ready to go?"

"I think the better question is if *you're* ready," I blurt awkwardly. "You're not even wearing a jacket today."

Alaric chuckles. "Always so concerned with my wardrobe."

"Because you're always missing half of it."

"The mines are dirty," he says with a shrug that draws my gaze to his sculpted shoulders. "And my work is strenuous," he adds. And now I'm thinking of sweat sliding through the grooves of those muscles.

I shake my head and pin my eyes to the ground. Stress and lack of sleep are clearly addling my senses. Just because he saved me from Von Nevus and we share similar trauma doesn't mean we share anything else. Anything deeper.

I'm using him to find the gemstone triad.

Nothing more.

I repeat this like a mantra as Alaric leads me through the deserted halls and down a twisting staircase, to the base of a circular turret. He runs his fingers across the stones until there's a distinct click. Then the wall rotates, and the next thing I know, we're expelled from the castle and skirting around a watchtower, into the twists and turns of the walled city.

Alaric moves at a breakneck pace, leading me in the opposite direction of the trail that took us to the highest reaches of the mountain. Instead, we wind down streets full of sleeping stone houses until we reach another Fortress wall—this one built into a cliff's edge. A wooden sign indicates the Kirana mineshaft lies below, down a steep flight of stairs carved into the mountainside.

"Watch your step," Alaric whispers over his shoulder. "The stairs can be slick. And keep close. We won't be able to see more than a few paces ahead."

He doesn't have to tell me twice. I am more than willing to huddle close to the tantalizing warmth of his body.

At the bottom of the stairs, he takes a lantern from a peg and ducks beneath a wooden archway set into the rock face. It's hardly large enough for a person to pass through, and I take a breath for courage before fisting my skirt and following Alaric into the dark.

I shouldn't be nervous. I'm accustomed to living belowground. This mine shaft should feel familiar and comforting compared to Soren's austere palace. But the deeper we shuffle into the oppressive blackness, the more the air dampens and sours—so opposite the dry clay hallways of the hillock palace, which are always spread with spicy cedar rushes and lit with glowing sconces.

"How do the miners see what they're doing?" I ask, tripping over my own feet for the third time in as many minutes.

How am I supposed to hunt for Callahan's gemstones in pitch-blackness? is what I really want to ask.

"The drilling site is brighter, you'll see," Alaric assures me.

We round another tight corner and emerge into a

high-ceilinged cavern that's only marginally brighter, even after Alaric hangs his lantern in an iron fixture. It would take dozens of lanterns to counteract the sheer size and oppressive gloom of the cavern.

"Wait for it," Alaric says, sensing my skepticism

A moment later, the lantern light catches on a thick vein of silver ore striating the cavern ceiling, which reflects back onto another deposit near my feet and jumps to a glittering streak just above Alaric's shoulder. On and on, the silvery glow bounces from one vein of silver to the next until the cavern glows almost as bright as midday.

"It's stunning," I murmur as I trace a vein of silver along the outer wall to where picks and shovels and helmets are arranged in neat rows. In the center of the space, wooden handcarts wait to be filled with excavated silver ore, all of it well-lit. "It's ingenious," I continue, "but also completely inefficient."

Alaric, who's been gazing up into the cathedral-heights of the ceiling with a proud smile, turns to glare at me. "Excuse me?"

"You're unable to excavate all this silver ore because you need it for light." I gesture overhead.

Alaric shrugs stiffly. "It's too dangerous to have more than one open flame down here—too many volatile gases are released during excavation—but it doesn't matter. There's plenty of silver ore in the mountain. We don't need it all."

"*You* might not need it all, but what about the rest of us?" I ask as I inspect the walls, which are literally bursting with riches, a fraction of which could change the circumstances in Tashir beyond recognition.

Their silver doesn't matter, Ro reminds me. *Focus on finding the gemstones.*

But it *could* matter. I feel it in the deepest parts of me—the same places Earth Mother's power takes root when I'm gardening.

"What's your part in all of this?" I ask Alaric. "The operation seems pretty straightforward." I mime swinging a pickax at the wall. "I see no need for power."

Alaric scoffs and places a possessive hand against the cavern wall. "I can feel which portions of the mine are stable enough to excavate—and how deeply to follow a vein. I open and reinforce new shafts before sending miners down, and stop cave-ins before they cause too many injuries. We've only lost three miners in the five years I've overseen the work down here."

I give an appreciative nod. "That all sounds quite impressive, but I'm afraid I'm having a hard time picturing it. Will you *show* me your power in action?"

"You asked me to bring you to the mines, not put on a show."

I smile and bat my eyelashes. "Please? I showed you far more than simple gardening. We're hardly even."

"You are the most galling and demanding person I've

ever met," Alaric says, but there's a smile in his voice "And you're in luck because I've been meaning to create a new access tunnel to an older shaft on the other side of this wall anyway."

He closes his eyes and digs his fingertips into the wall

Within seconds, a palpable surge of energy crackles through the stone—like a hive of bees buzzing back to life after a long winter. I instinctively widen my stance, half expecting a sinkhole to swallow me. Or for the ground to crest into a wave and toss me across the cavern, the way King Soren flung Haddesh across the courtyard of the hillock palace. But the trembling remains steady, and a sound like a deep-bellied sigh fills the cavern. A moment later, a divot appears in the wall just above my shoulder. I watch in horrified wonder as the hole slowly widens and deepens, as if a large invisible worm is tunneling through the solid rock.

It reminds me a bit of the stakes we twist into the soil of certain planting beds to support vining vegetables. Except those stakes churn out messy clumps of dirt as they spiral into the earth. Alaric's power slices through the rock like butter. Not a speck of mud or shard of stone breaks loose. It's as if the earth is happy to bend to Alaric's will—just like he claimed. Like his changes are as natural as if they'd been formed by battering wind and rain over thousands of years.

I tear my gaze away from the growing tunnel and

squint suspiciously at Alaric, who looks more relaxed than he has since I arrived at the Fortress. The tense set of his jaw and rigid line of his shoulders has finally gone slack. Which makes no sense. Changing something as solid as rock should be difficult. Sweat should be dripping down his face. His forearms should be quivering with effort. But Alaric and the earth appear to be sharing the load. Blending in perfect harmony, like the notes of a familiar song.

Like the incantations I sing to the bagrava.

Nausea grips my throat, and even though I can see Alaric's tunnel widening before my eyes, it feels like the cavern walls are pressing in, threatening to crush me and everything I thought I knew about the Vanzadorian's power.

I need it to stop. Need *him* to stop.

"That's enough!" I shriek, startling Alaric from his trance.

He blinks and leans over his knees, finally looking as dizzy and drained as I feel. "Are you duly impressed?" he asks through panting breaths.

I don't answer because I don't have a clue what I'm feeling. Watching him move the earth was supposed to confirm the wrongness of his power and reveal Earth Mother's resistance. But instead of certainty, a cold lump of dread is settling in my stomach.

Don't let him distract you! Keep your focus on blood, flesh, and bone, Rowenna reminds me. But her voice sounds weak and far away again. Perhaps because we're so far underground?

"Well?" Alaric asks, "What do you think?" He holds out his hands and flashes a confident grin, but it doesn't conceal the yearning in his voice, the desperation in his eyes for a scrap of approval.

"It's incredible," I whisper with unabashed awe. "Is it safe to enter?"

Alaric huffs out a breath. "Of course it's safe. Did you forget this is my *job*?"

I roll my eyes and slip inside.

The new tunnel is small, barely higher than my head. Colder and darker, too, lit only by the light leaking in from the cavern. It even smells different—like the mineral tang of wet rock and something oddly floral. The smell gets stronger as I leave Alaric's tunnel and enter a wider cavern that must be the old shaft Alaric mentioned. The walls here look rough and ragged, all but stripped of silver ore, but when I brush my fingers across the stone, it's strangely warm and velvety soft. I snatch my hand back with a gasp.

"Please tell me you haven't hurt yourself already," Alaric calls from the mouth of the tunnel. "Wait there. I'm coming to get you."

I ignore him and bring my fingers to my nose, sniffing the soft fuzz clinging to my fingertips.

"Are you *smelling* the walls?" Alaric asks as he rounds the corner.

Again, I ignore him and inhale deeply, shivering with excitement when I finally place the light floral scent.

"It's goblin's gold! The walls of this old shaft are covered in a thin layer of goblin's gold," I say.

"Goblin's *what*? If you're trying to convince me there are monsters down here—"

"It's bioluminescent moss!" I cut him off. "One of the only plants capable of growing in extremely low light. But this tunnel is almost *too* dark. It's barely surviving."

Alaric blinks at me for several long seconds. "Why should I care about moss?"

"Because it's the answer to all of your problems!"

"Our mines don't have problems."

"*Watch.*" I burrow my fingers into the sparse growth and close my eyes, allowing Earth Mother's power to flow through me and into the moss. Within minutes, a thick layer of goblin's gold has spread across the tunnel walls and ceiling, shining a bright golden green. Perfectly illuminating Alaric's dumbfounded expression.

"When properly nourished, it glows!" I say with a triumphant wave. "It's more than bright enough to light your tunnels, which means you wouldn't need to rely on hazardous open flames at all. And you could excavate the strains of silver ore you're currently using to reflect light."

Alaric peers at the glowing ceiling, his sharp cheekbones and strong jawline awash in the ethereal glow. "It's beautiful," he whispers. "And it's been down here all this time?"

I nod. "It just needs a bit of help to thrive so far below the surface. But that's simple enough. I could visit the mines every few days to nourish the moss and—"

"You'd do that?" Alaric's voice is laced with skepticism. "You'd *willingly* assist our mining operations?"

NO! Rowenna shouts.

But I bob my head, certain my sister will change her tune once she understands the breadth of my plan. "I would be happy to nourish the moss so long as the outcome benefits Tashir too," I tell Alaric.

"And how would it do that?" he asks.

"I want a percentage of the additional silver ore you're able to extract as a result of using goblin's gold for light."

Alaric's mouth pinches. "What need do farmers have for silver ore? Your people don't wear jewelry or finely embroidered clothing."

"Maybe we *would* if we had access to such luxuries," I retort, though I can't imagine my people caring about silver-buttoned trousers or luxurious blouses that will only make us sweatier. But they *would* be interested in the supplies I could purchase from the isles across the sea with my own allotment of silver.

"I don't plan to keep my portion," I explain to Alaric. "I would use it to purchase new plows and tools. We're in desperate need of younger, stronger animals and higher-grade feed, as well as stores of dried food to sustain us through lean harvest years. If I had a stake in these mines,

I could use my profits to import everything my people need."

We don't need to work with the Vanzadorians, Rowenna snaps. *We need to cut them out, like a malignant tumor.*

A malignant tumor Tashir needs to survive, I remind her.

Not if you find the stones of blood, flesh, bone.

I don't have a seeds-forsaken clue where to find them, I silently shout. *And there's more than one solution to every problem. Maybe we don't need to bring the entire mountain down to save Tashir.*

We do, Rowenna maintains—as confident and unrelenting as ever, and I can't take it anymore.

Why do you always do this? I snap.

Do what?

Pop up out of nowhere and make me doubt my decisions as soon as I find a bit of footing.

Several silent seconds pass before Ro says in a wounded voice, *Have you considered that I 'pop up out of nowhere' because your 'footing' is crumbling? But I'll stay quiet if you'd prefer I let you fall.*

And maybe that's the problem. Letting Delphine and Elodie—and even Alaric—in doesn't feel like falling but rather like being lifted up.

If that's how you feel, I won't bother you anymore, Rowenna's voice is rough and ragged. *You clearly don't need me.*

She waits for me to recant and beg her to stay, but I don't. Because she's right. I *don't* need her voice in my head anymore. I've found my own way to navigate life on this mountain, and just because it isn't how Ro handled things, doesn't mean it's wrong. It doesn't mean I can't lead Tashir just as effectively on my own terms. Maybe I never needed her guidance as much as I thought I did. Certainly not as much as she wanted me to believe.

Rowenna gasps, like I physically struck her, and vanishes in a huff.

Instead of guilt, though, I feel an immediate flood of relief. An intoxicating sense of freedom.

"Well?" I turn back to Alaric. "Will you give me a stake in your silver ore in exchange for cultivating the moss?"

"How large a stake?" he asks.

"Sixty percent—but only of the excess you gain through mining what was used for light," I remind him when his eyes narrow.

"Forty," he counters.

"Fifty is as low as I'll go. It's the least I deserve, considering you'd have *none* of the silver ore you use for light without my help."

"Fine." Alaric agrees. "Light my tunnels with your moss, and you can have half of the additional output. Purchase donkeys and wagons to your heart's content."

The way he says *donkeys* and *wagons* makes them sound so frivolous. Like something as trivial as his courtiers' lavish gowns rather than essential supplies that will literally ensure my people survive the winter.

Not to mention it will help his people too.

"You do realize that by providing for the basic needs of *my* people, we will have more time and energy to devote to producing bagrava for *you*?" I point out. "Though I still can't fathom why you need so much if it's truly only used for *tea*."

I expect Alaric to come back with a wagonload of excuses, but he silently traces his fingertips through the lustrous moss. "I honestly don't know why we need so much bagrava," he admits. "Or why my father keeps demanding larger tributes."

"You're the crown prince. How could you not know?"

Alaric's shoulders hitch up. "I've never enjoyed drinking Mother's foul-smelling tea, and I'm always so consumed with my work in the mines. It's possible I've missed something. But I promise to look into it now. If my father is hoarding or misusing your bagrava in any way, I'll put an end to it."

Despite our very different motivations and goals, I genuinely believe he will.

"Thank you," I say, "for bringing me here and showing me all of this. All of *you*," I add in a breathy whisper. I step closer to Alaric, unable to stop my hand from rising toward his face. I fully expect him to stiffen and lurch back, but to my surprise, he leans in, eyelids fluttering closed as my fingertips glide across his cheekbone

Behind us, a gravelly voice coughs. "I hope we're not interrupting."

I shriek and clutch my hands to my chest.

Alaric whips around, staring back into the larger cavern we came from, which somehow filled with miners while we were arguing. Or negotiating. Or whatever it is we've been doing here in the dark.

"Not at all. Your timing couldn't be better," Alaric says with a bit too much enthusiasm. "I've just opened a new connecting shaft." He gestures to the small tunnel, but the miners don't look convinced.

"What is *she* doing down here?" a man with a scraggly beard points at me. "What business does a gardener have in a mine shaft?"

"More than you think," Alaric explains. "Indira has kindly agreed to use her abilities as a master gardener to light our shafts with a type of glowing moss rather than lanterns. It's much safer and will allow us to excavate the silver ore we currently use to reflect light."

"Why would she do that?" a middle-aged woman asks, eyeing me with suspicion. A chorus of voices agree—their dubious expressions cleaving away my confidence the same way the picks in their hands shatter rock.

Alaric appraises me too, but the softness in his expression is even more unsettling. Even more dangerous. "Indira has agreed to help us because she's kind, savvy, and invested in this relationship—between our countries," he clarifies with an awkward cough.

My toes curl inside my boots, and I stare at the ground, certain my cheeks must be glowing brighter than the goblin's gold.

"Follow me, and see the moss for yourselves." Alaric gestures down the new tunnel. "If you're still skeptical then, we'll put it to a vote."

For what feels like the hundredth time today—which is a lot, given it's barely sunrise—the Vanzadorian prince has surprised me. It would be so easy for him to bark orders and impose his will on the miners. But he doesn't. And they clearly respect him for it. A good many workers pat his shoulders as they shuffle into the tunnel, and he patiently answers their questions, which feel endless.

I hang back to give them space—so they feel comfortable sharing their worries and opinions. And so I have time to scour the larger cavern for the gemstone triad. This might be my only chance. I should take advantage of every second. But I keep getting distracted by the echoes of surprise and delight coming from the tunnel as the miners admire the otherworldly beauty of the goblin's gold. And when I hear Alaric recount how I nourished the moss—making the process sound far more exciting than it was—I linger near the tunnel, grinning stupidly, and before I know it, my opportunity is gone.

And I'm not even mad about it.

The wondrous smiles on the miners faces as they reemerge are worth every wasted second. They're mesmerized by *me*. By something other than bagrava.

Alaric's beaming brighter than them all—almost brighter than the moss itself—and it completely transforms the harsh angles of his face. For the first time, I see flashes of the confident, carefree boy from his earlier memories—before Besnik's death—and I know I'm staring, but I can't seem to look away. Not even when he catches me.

To my surprise, he doesn't smirk or tease me. He simply grins back—a wide, genuine smile that's far more enticing than the seductive looks he flashes around the palace.

"As suspected, everyone is most eager for you to cultivate goblin's gold in all of our mines," he says proudly.

The miners shout and stomp their agreement, the echo near deafening as it rattles around the chamber. And rattles around my soul.

Men and women eagerly reach for my hands and clap me on the back, thanking me for my generosity and compassion. And with every kind word, the lump in my throat swells larger and hotter because I didn't come here to help them. I came to find and steal the source of their power. They're giving me everything I've secretly longed for: adoration like my people had for my sister, acknowledgment of my abilities beyond the bagrava. But I've never felt more undeserving.

Tears pulse behind my eyes, but I'm not about to let them fall in front of Alaric and so many people, so I turn and sprint back through the twisting tunnels of the mine, praying I'm fast enough to outrun my guilt.

THIRTY-TWO

'M SLIPPING DOWN AN ICY STREET, HALFWAY BACK TO the palace, when Alaric catches up with me.

"Indira, what's wrong? Why did you sprint away like the tunnel was on fire?"

"I'm just tired," I say, which isn't a lie. "I need to return to my rooms and rest. Cultivating such a large amount of goblin's gold took a lot of energy."

Alaric nods with understanding, but he continues stealing worried glances at me as we walk. "Are you sure you're okay? We can stop and rest if you need." He bites his lower lip, and I find myself wondering how I failed to notice how full and soft and utterly enticing his lips are.

My boot catches on the edge of a cobblestone, and I curse myself for noticing his lips at all. This is complete and utter madness. I need to squash it. Or outrun it at the very least.

Alaric reaches out to steady me, but I brush him off and trudge ahead faster, looking anywhere but at him.

The city around us is beginning to wake. Curtains pull back from windows, sleepy-eyed people emerge to sweep ice and snow from their walks, and hordes of miners make their way to work. Their eyes widen, and they immediately begin to whisper and point when they realize who we are. I expect Alaric to pull on his confidence like armor and slip back into the cliched role of how he thinks a strong leader should act, but he continues chasing after me, seemingly oblivious to our audience.

"Indira, wait! I don't understand." He jogs alongside me. "Is it something I said or did? I know we were supposed to be gone before the miners arrived, but I lost track of time. I wasn't trying to make a spectacle or force your hand."

I keep marching, determinedly ignoring Alaric, who's wringing his gloved hands, growing more agitated by the second—wringing his gloved hands and pulling at his hair, willing me to look at him.

"You're regretting your offer to grow goblin's gold, aren't you?" he blurts out, his voice unexpectedly rough.

I'm regretting a lot of things—like letting him get this close, and opening my eyes to the Vanzadorians' struggles, and mostly for thinking I could help. For allowing myself to picture how it might be to have a place among them.

"Help me understand," Alaric persists. "You were so

excited to discover the goblin's gold and propose a trade. But then the miners arrived, and your whole demeanor changed." His voice trails off, and he stops abruptly in the middle of the road. "It's me, isn't it?" he says with horrified realization.

Yes, I want to exclaim. *You and your tender, bleeding heart are* precisely *my problem*.

But Alaric keeps spiraling. "You completely shut down when you saw the miners interact with me. And I can see how it must look from the outside. What kind of ruler lets their subjects question them like that? You don't think I have enough control—"

"Alaric, stop." I finally turn to face him.

"No. I can take it. Say what you truly think of me. Everyone else does."

The people in the road are blatantly staring at us, and I can feel a hundred more eyes watching through the cracks of their shutters. I grab Alaric's wrist and tug him toward the palace, not allowing him to stop or speak until we're back in our secluded wing of the castle.

"Why do you always assume the fault lies with you?" I ask, hoping the walk gave him time to clear his head. But his face crumples miserably.

"Because it does! No matter how hard I work, I will never be able to give my people the perfect future they would have had with Besnik. It's why my father's councilors look down on and despise me, why the courtiers pity and patronize me. And why you refuse to work with me." He levels me with a devastating look.

I shake my head. "Have you ever considered that *you* are strapping yourself with these unrealistic expectations? Not your father or his councilors or anyone else?"

"What are you talking about? You've been here long enough to see their animosity firsthand! How can you deny—"

"What *I've* seen are miners who trust and respect you because you get down in the dirt and work beside them as an equal. And courtiers who may not understand your work ethic but are more than happy to reap the benefits of your labor. As for your father's councilors, they're clearly jealous of the pride and confidence Soren has in you. They don't think you're less than Besnik—they're worried you're *more*. They're trying to control you by stripping your confidence and making you think you need them. But you don't need their help or approval. Vanzador will be the strongest and most prosperous it's ever been with you as its king."

Alaric gapes at me, mouth bobbling open and closed. "You don't actually believe that."

"I've spent most of my life despising you, so if I'm giving you a compliment, you know it's done begrudgingly."

Alaric laughs, but his eyes take on a glassy sheen, and he lets out a long breath. "It's just hard to believe I'm ever good enough when *everything* I've ever known is a lie."

"Why do you assume everything is a lie? Just because your father killed Besnik back then doesn't mean he can't be proud of you now. Those things don't have to be mutually exclusive."

"I shouldn't want him to be proud of me. I shouldn't care what he thinks," Alaric chokes out. "He tried to kill me."

"Unfortunately, caring is part of being human. It's what makes you better than your father. It's what convinced me to trust you—when I was determined not to."

Alaric cocks his head and regards me for a long minute. "Who knew gardeners could be so wise? Guess you don't have peas for brains after all."

"Who knew princes made of stone could be so sensitive and emotional?" I fire back, playfully shoving his chest.

Alaric catches my wrist and guides me gently back, until my shoulders press against my chamber door. "You say that like it's a bad thing."

"It's definitely good," I say, a little breathless.

"Then what's the problem?" He leans in closer, and his voice drops to a husky purr that I feel in the lowest part of my stomach. "If you no longer think I'm terrible, why the sudden hesitation regarding the goblin's gold?"

"It isn't you I distrust," I admit, tilting my face up to look at him. "It's myself—when I'm around you."

Alaric's gaze darts between my eyes and down to my lips. And now *I'm* looking at *his* lips again, and our chests are heaving, every nerve ending in my body zinging, as he slowly brings a gloved hand to my face. His fingertips trace the line of my cheekbone and slide into my hair, making me shiver.

"Is this okay?" He leans even closer, eyes still locked with mine, giving me every chance to pull away. But I don't. For the first time in a long time, I'm certain I want this. And not out of duty or vengeance, or on behalf of someone else.

I want this for *me*.

Alaric's lips brush mine—rose petal soft—and I wait for Rowenna to roar into my mind like a whirlwind and obliterate the moment. To insist I stop this foolishness and remind me kissing our enemy will ruin everything. But the only sounds I hear are my and Alaric's mingled breath and the erratic thumping of my heart.

When it comes to Alaric, my sister's opinion no longer matters.

I lean up on my toes and press my lips more firmly against his, which are warm and wet, and taste of honeysuckle. With a groan, he eases me back against my door, surrounding me with his cardamom scent, and my body comes alive in the same way the earth awakens to my incantations.

I grapple with the doorknob behind me, unsure what's come over me. I've never felt so out of control yet wholly unafraid, and I want more of this feeling. More of him.

With a click, the door swings inward, and we tumble into the soft rainbow of light of my chamber, laughing as we trip over a pair of slippers and fall onto the rug, me on my back and Alaric kneeling on either side of my hips, gazing down at me with a look that can only be described as ravenous.

Again, I expect Rowenna to intervene. To drag herself back from the Great Fields Beyond and physically wrench me away from Alaric if necessary. But there's nothing. No voice in my head nor hum of her presence.

Alaric bends over me, covering my mouth with his, and I close my eyes as his tongue sweeps across my lips and his stubble tickles my face. My fingers trace the grooves of muscle from his shoulders to his trousers, and I thank the Vanzadorian gods that he isn't wearing a shirt. That I get to explore so much of him without the impediment of clothes.

"We've been married for weeks. Why haven't we been doing this all along?" he says between kisses.

"Because you were determined to avoid me."

"Only because you wouldn't stop accusing me of murder."

"I'm going to murder you now if you keep on talking." I bury my fingers in his hair and pull his face back to mine.

"So bossy and demanding," he mumbles playfully.

"I do what I must to get what I want."

Alaric pulls back and looks at me searchingly. "And am *I* what you want?"

He says it so hopefully, with such fragility, and without Rowenna's voice in my head, I realize I want a lot of things—like this boy, and the way I feel when I'm with him. I want the miners to continue looking at me the way they did today. I want to help maximize their output so I can ride back to Tashir with a wagonload of supplies and earn my peoples' and my parents' gratitude and admiration. I want them to see I accomplished this impossible task and made peace with Vanzador. Maybe not in the way I initially planned or how anyone could have expected, but in my own way.

"Yes," I close my eyes and whisper against Alaric's lips, "I want you."

THIRTY-THREE

"How thrilling!" Elodie claps with delight, beaming like a proud parent when I relay every detail of my kiss with Alaric the following day, as we take lunch in my chambers. "I knew you had a seductress inside you," she continues. "You just needed the right tutor to set her free."

She giggles and taps my nose with her fan, and even though Delphine doesn't make a sound from the corner where she stands, I feel her scoffing.

My maid was considerably less thrilled to learn of the developments between Alaric and me.

I spewed the details as soon as she returned from tending to Cloudia, and she looked like she was going to faint.

"You realize it's a calculated distraction, right?" she scolded. "He's trying to keep you from finding the gemstones."

"He doesn't even know I'm searching for the gemstones," I reminded her.

"And are you—still searching?" Delphine folded her arms. "Because it sounds to me like you're letting him manipulate you with his charms—like every other woman on this mountain."

Her assertion made me flinch. "Our connection is different."

"I'm sure."

"Can't you just be happy for me?"

"No. Because I don't want to see you hurt. Or forget what's most important. Don't let a man distract you from your goals," she said, waving the empty bottle of Cloudia's medication still clutched in her hands.

Suddenly all made sense.

"This doesn't change anything for you and Cloudia," I said, reaching for her hand, but she pulled away.

"How can it not? If you're *in love* with Alaric, you won't be returning to Tashir, and you certainly won't be taking my sister and me with you."

I wrapped Delphine in a tight hug. "You don't need to worry about that. If things work out how I think they will, you won't need to flee Vanzador. And I won't need to steal Soren and Alaric's power. We can all help each other. Alaric wants me to continue using my magic to help in the mines. I wish you could have seen the goblin's gold—how excited Alaric and the workers were. I'm going to receive a percentage of the output from the mines, which I'll use to purchase supplies for Tashir, so we're not so burdened by the bagrava tributes. And Alaric promised to look into why Soren needs so much bagrava in the first place. I think...I think our nations can actually work together. That we'll be stronger together. And I promise, wherever I go, you and Cloudia will be with me."

Delphine still looked like she was going to cry, but she nodded and agreed to support me. I obviously couldn't giggle and gush about the kiss with her, though—not how I am now, with Elodie. And it's so refreshing to feel happy, hopeful, and *free* for a change.

"When do you plan to see him again?" Elodie asks. "Will he accompany you to the queen's salon? I can't wait to see the faces of all the girls who pined for him when the two of you walk in arm in arm. What will you wear? Can I dress you?" I have the most divine midnight blue gown that will accentuate your golden skin."

It feels more than a little silly and frivolous, but I do let her dress me. And I revel in our shared smiles as the noble ladies glare at me and Alaric.

Days pass, and life on the mountain develops into a routine of sorts. Mornings are spent in the queen's salon, where Alaric and I dare the courtiers and councilors to disparage us. In the afternoons, I work in the gardening beds, visit Cloudia, or watch the stone-throwing contests with Elodie. Evenings are spent cultivating goblin's gold in the mines or tangled in Alaric's arms, reveling in the rightness of it all. This partnership that doesn't make sense and shouldn't work but somehow does.

I still keep an eye out for gemstones the color of blood, flesh, and bone, but I never find a trace—not among Queen Tessa's personal jewels or in the throne room. I even search unlikely places like the kitchens and library.

But nothing.

We do, however, come across a few hidden memories. Alaric and Delphine—and even Elodie, on occasion—pluck a buzzing brooch or a humming bracelet from an unsuspecting courtier, and we howl with laughter when Alaric brings the memory to life, exposing the courtiers' darkest desires and most scandalous secrets.

Alaric tells Soren about the goblin's gold I'm cultivating in the mines, hoping it will get his father off my back and maybe even ease his obsession with bagrava altogether. If Soren sees there are other ways I can contribute to Vanzador, perhaps he won't focus so intently on the one crop my people desperately need to survive. We hope it might encourage him to open up to Alaric about why they need so much bagrava in the first place.

Days pass without hearing from Rowenna. Then weeks. And even though I miss my sister as a person, I don't miss the version of her I conjured in her absence. I can admit that's all her voice ever was now—a coping mechanism. A crutch. I was so used to following her lead,

I was terrified to trust my own instincts and make my own decisions.

But not anymore.

Against all odds, I've found happiness on this mountain—with real friends and a purpose for my magic. With hope for Tashir and a love I never dreamed possible. I'm so happy, sometimes I almost forget Rowenna was murdered here. I even allow myself to entertain the idea that she truly did fall. After all this time, that feels more likely than a killer lurking in the shadows.

"I have a surprise for you," I whisper in Alaric's ear during dinner in the great hall several weeks later.

He scowls at me warily, but his eyes gleam with mischief—so warm and confident. So opposite the boy I married on the Tomb Flats.

"What sort of surprise?" he asks.

"The sort I can only show you in the privacy of my chambers."

His fork clatters against his plate, and I cackle wickedly.

"Does that mean you're finished eating?" I ask, batting my eyes.

Alaric pushes back from the table, grabs my hand, and practically drags me out of the banquet hall, heedless of the courtiers' giggles and Queen Tessa's knowing smile.

"I hope you're on your way to harvest more bagrava!" Soren calls after us with a wink, which elicits even more laughter from the dinner guests.

For once in my life, though, the pull of the bagrava isn't as strong as another force, pulsing in my chest and steadily working its way lower.

We're kissing before we're even down the hall, and Alaric carries me, legs wrapped around his waist, all the way to my chambers. We crash into the door, laughing when it slams open, and I hungrily unfasten the chains across his chest, shucking his jacket to the floor as he places me on the bed.

When he tries to lay me back, though, I hold a hand against his chest and wriggle out from beneath him. "Be patient, or you'll ruin the surprise."

He growls with frustration, the hunger in his eyes tantalizing as I slowly slide the lacy sleeve off my right shoulder, then my left.

I'm wearing another gown Elodie selected—emerald green with a low square neckline and a split skirt that cuts clear to the tops of my thighs. It's provocative and revealing, but tame compared to the tiny strips of fabric underneath.

Alaric's breath catches as I let the gown slip farther down my torso, and I feel my cheeks flame. I have never let anyone see me so bare and vulnerable. I want to clutch the dress against my chest or make a joke to ease the tension pulsing between us, but I force myself to hold Alaric's gaze as I take the dress lower and lower still, until I'm standing before him in nothing but bejeweled strips of velvet and lace—the traditional costume Vanzadorian brides wear on their wedding night.

"What do you think of your surprise?" I whisper. "I know I'm not technically Vanzadorian, but Elodie assured me this was—"

"Perfect," Alaric says, his eyes roving up and down my body.

I feel like I'm burning from the inside out, hotter than the fires that scorched Tashir, and the only thing that will douse the flames is his lips on my lips. His skin on my skin.

My need must be written all over my face, because he finally removes the bothersome gloves he always wears and cups my chin in his bare hands. His fingers are warm and deliciously smooth as they glide down my throat and into my hair. His mouth is hot and insistent as it covers mine.

We fall to the bed in a tangle of arms, legs, lips, and sheets. Two broken people finding wholeness in the pieces of the other. Coming together to form an image like stained glass—far more beautiful pieced back together than if the glass had remained a solid pane.

We taste and touch, shiver and sigh, neither pausing to doubt or question. Just feeling. Moving. Savoring. Until we break apart, sweaty, gasping, and breathless, somehow lying on the floor.

"Who could have guessed that growing bagrava isn't your greatest talent?" Alaric murmurs into my hair.

I swat his chest, but he catches my hand and brings my fingers to his lips, softly kissing each one.

"I have a surprise for you too," he says quietly.

"Please tell me they make scandalous bejeweled outfits for men," I say with a coy grin. "I'm furious you didn't put it on sooner."

"It isn't an outfit," he laments, "but it is something I should have shown you sooner—so you know every part of me."

He swallows hard, eyes filled with sudden gravity, as he rotates his arm to expose the underside of his wrist, where three small stones are embedded in his skin.

A crimson ruby, an apricot diamond, and white quartz.

Blood, flesh, bone.

THIRTY-FOUR

I GAPE DOWN AT THE GEMSTONE TRIAD—THREE PERfect jewels that have been, quite literally, at my fingertips all this time.

I sit up, clutching the blankets to my chest, unsure if I want to recoil from Alaric and this deception—if it can even be considered that, since he has no clue I've been hunting for the gemstones—or if I should grab his wrist and hold it tight. Sink my nails into his skin and claim the prize that's been eluding me for months.

"This is the gemstone triad—the source of my and my father's power," Alaric explains, running his fingers across the line of stones. "It was forged from the earth by my great-grandfather Callahan and has been embedded in every Vanzadorian king since. He referred to them as his own blood, flesh, and bone, which I know you asked about, and I'm sorry I waited so long to explain. I just didn't know if I could trust you." Alaric ducks his head sheepishly. "I was worried you might try to use me, but now I know better. We want the same things and we'll work together to accomplish them."

He smiles and reaches for me, and I feel like I've been kicked in the chest.

He was right to doubt and mistrust me. If he'd explained the meaning of blood, flesh, bone when I first asked, I wouldn't have hesitated to drag him back across the Tomb Flats to Tashir. I would have been thrilled to see our roles reversed, so *he* was the captive husband—tortured and starved until he agreed to wield his power for the betterment of *my* country. And if he'd refused to cooperate, I would have lopped off his arm or scraped the stones from his flesh. I would have found a way to implant them in my own skin, because that's what Rowenna would have done—what she would have told me to do—and I would have listened without question.

It would have been the perfect way to avenge Rowenna and prove I was a competent heir for Tashir. More than just a second-born sister or a gardener. But now the thought's unfathomable. Unbearable. Especially when Alaric's looking at me with those hypnotic eyes and hopeful grin. When I can still taste his mouth on my lips, feel his fingertips on my skin. I would sooner cut out my own heart than rip the stones from Alaric's wrist, and I don't know what that says about me and my duty to my country or my ability to lead them.

I blow out a breath and thank Earth Mother Rowenna's no longer speaking to me. Her disappointment would be crushing, her demands more adamant than ever, reminding me it isn't too late to do the right thing. I could still use Alaric and the gemstone triad.

Alaric reaches for me and gently tilts my chin up. "Hey, what's going on in that brilliant head of yours?"

"I understand why you kept this from me," I finally say. "I can't fault you for guarding your biggest secret when I was just as hesitant to share mine. It took me weeks just to accept that you're not a murderer. That doesn't exactly inspire confidence," I say with a self-deprecating laugh.

Alaric laughs too, and all the tension melts from his shoulders. "I don't want there to be any more secrets between us. If we're going to rule Vanzador and Tashir side by side, as true and equal partners, you need to know everything. All of me."

He holds out his arm, inviting me to touch the stones. "The king of Vanzador has always embedded the triad in his skin, but after the memory you witnessed, when I broke the stone of flesh and Besnik died, my father destroyed the larger stones to keep our power safer and closer. These pieces are all that remains of the triad, so someday, I will pass them on to my own son or daughter. *Our* son or daughter—I hope."

He looks at me from beneath his thick lashes, and my heart might burst from pumping so hard. My hand shakes as my fingertips skim across the triad, because this feels like a promise—a thousand times more sacred than our wedding vows—and I'm determined to honor it.

Honor *us* and the future we will make.

"Thank you for trusting me with this," I say.

"I'd trust you with my life," Alaric answers, pressing his forehead to mine.

My eyes flutter closed, and I wait for the warm brush of his lips, but my chamber door bangs open instead, and we fly apart.

Delphine shrieks and holds her arm over her eyes. "You really need to start tying a ribbon on your door, so I know if it's safe to enter."

"Or you could try knocking," Alaric says with a good-natured laugh.

"Of course," Delphine splutters, "and normally I would, but I wasn't thinking straight." Her big blue eyes find mine, wide and terrified. "Cloudia's been speaking more, and there's something you need to see."

"Of course." I leap to my feet, rummaging for my clothes. "I'll be ready in a moment. You don't mind, do you?" I ask Alaric, who starts to shake his head, but Delphine cuts in.

"I think His Highness should come too."

Alaric glances at me with surprise and delight, and my

heart melts at his eagerness—and Delphine's acceptance. These different people and parts of my life are starting to come together.

As soon as we're dressed, Delphine leads us out into the cold fortress city. I assumed she'd take us back to her home and Cloudia's bedside, but she marches briskly in the opposite direction, past homes, shops, and schoolhouses until we're in an entirely different quarter of the city with densely packed buildings.

When she stops in front of a sign that says Vaynir's Fine Furs and Exotic Textiles, Alaric and I share a confused look.

"*Fashion* is your sister's pressing concern?" he teases.

"Don't pretend it isn't your top priority too," I say, brushing invisible dust off the lapels of his emerald-green jacket.

"Quiet, both of you," Delphine whispers harshly, shocking us both into silence. She glances furtively down the street before tugging us around the corner of the building. "Not everything is as it appears."

She guides us to a nondescript door and, after rooting around in the flower bed, produces a key. Holding a finger to her lips, Delphine eases the door open and motions for us to follow her inside.

The hallway is long, dark, and dusty, and I instantly want to retreat back into the cold fresh air. This desire quickly becomes a need when I venture a few steps farther and an unmistakable stench invades my nostrils. My throat spasms, and I catch myself against the wall, looking around for the source of a smell that has no place in a Vanzadorian textile factory. No place anywhere on this mountain. Yet the fetid aroma of rotting flesh wafts down the hallway, even more potent than the tea in the queen's solarium. Almost as noxious as the smoke-filled sky the day our bagrava fields burned.

I shoot a horrified look at Delphine, who has buried her mouth and nose in her shirt.

I do the same.

Behind me, Alaric coughs and then full-on gags. "What in the name of the kings?"

"This way." Delphine points toward a glowing doorframe at the end of the hall, and we tiptoe toward it. Once we're huddled outside, she points to the keyhole.

Alaric's eyes find mine, silently asking if I want him to look first. As much I appreciate the offer, I shake my head. Whatever's happening here clearly has to do with my bagrava.

I bend toward the keyhole, heart hammering so loud it sounds like a fist against the door in the unnatural quiet. I half expect someone to fling open the door and catch us.

I hold my breath and peer through the keyhole into a large open room. It's as vast as any of our storehouses in Tashir, except instead of being filled with animals and produce, it's filled with beds. Row after row of steel beds are crammed side by side, and each bed houses a body—old and young, infants to the elderly, boys and girls alike. The strange conglomeration of people lie stiffly on their backs, staring blankly at the ceiling, even the babies.

The wrongness of it feels like spiders creeping down my shirt. Babies are supposed to coo and cry. Children are supposed to giggle and chatter. Adults are always yelling and arguing over something. But everyone in this room is as still as a corpse, aside from a handful of men and women in white smocks, who weave through the narrow paths between beds, blotting foreheads and fluffing pillows.

"I don't understand. Is this a hospital?" I ask Delphine, but it's Alaric who answers, shaking his head as he nudges past me to look for himself. "Of course it isn't a hospital. We have two *actual* hospitals in the Fortress. Why would anyone need to hide in a warehouse for treatment?"

He squints into the room, and I swear I feel the muscles down his back stiffen one by one. "What is this?" he turns on Delphine. "How did you find this place?"

Delphine takes a shaky step back. "It-it was Cloudia. She became more lucid last night, after another dose of Indira's bagrava tincture, and she started talking about people dying again. I still didn't think anything of it until she began reciting an address. *This* address. We've never had any business on this side of the Fortress, so I found it odd and decided to investigate. *This* is what I found, and I came to inform you immediately."

"How did Cloudia know about this?" Alaric demands.

Delphine shrugs helplessly. "I haven't a clue."

"I haven't a clue."

I chew my lip, trying to make sense of it. "Do you think these people have the same illness as Cloudia? Perhaps it's catching. Maybe there's an outbreak, and that's why they've been quarantined?"

"Maybe..." Delphine nervously twirls the end of her braid. "But Cloudia isn't silent and still like this. If anything, she's the opposite. Consumed by fits and outbursts. You saw her."

"No one is quarantined," Alaric interrupts. "I would know if there was an epidemic among my own people."

He returns to the keyhole, and I squeeze in beside him. For several minutes, we watch the nurses make their rounds—tucking blankets and changing sheets. They work with cold, clipped efficiency, never talking to their patients or even looking at them, really. For their part, the patients offer no acknowledgment or thanks to their caregivers.

All of it is deeply unsettling. I want to look away, *run* away, but then a pair of swinging doors open, and even more nurses enter the room, carrying trays of steaming soup. This wouldn't be noteworthy if not for the purple steam rising from the broth and the putrid smell, which intensifies a hundredfold.

Beside me, Alaric gags.

I do the same as the nurses begin spoon-feeding every patient.

They're basically poisoning them. These patients are too unresponsive to stop the soup from dribbling down their chins, let alone refuse to drink it. Such high doses of bagrava will drive them mad, if not kill them entirely.

I'm about to crash through the door like a raging bull to stop it when, all at once, the silence breaks, and the patients begin to yawn and sit up, stretching as if it's the start of a new day.

All around the room, babies cry and children chatter. The elderly moan and creak, while middle-aged men and women share quiet conversations.

I jerk back from the keyhole, my voice shaking with disbelief, awe, fear, and a dozen other conflicting emotions, because this can't be what it looks like.

It can't.

I had a hard enough time believing Queen Tessa and her courtiers could sip small doses of bagrava tea without becoming wild and unhinged. But this is another development entirely. If I didn't know better, I'd think the bagrava *healed* these people.

We take turns watching through the keyhole. Every minute, I expect the effects of the bagrava to overpower the patients and stir them into a frenzy. But an hour passes, maybe more, and they never lose themselves. Instead, their smiles and conversations gradually fade until each patient is once again lying still and catatonic on their cots.

"I don't know what this is, but you have to stop it," I tell Alaric. "It isn't right. These people will be permanently damaged. Addicted."

"I'm more concerned with *who* these people are and how they got here," Alaric says, pointing to a red-cheeked baby with dark curls. "That one looks eerily similar to Lady Hawthorne's child, the one that died suddenly in its sleep several months ago. And I'd swear that's Lord Fillibus's daughter." He nods at a girl who looks around my age. "She supposedly got lost while foraging outside the walls. We presumed she froze to death."

"Is that Elodie's mother?" I point to a woman with long silver braids who looks like the skeletal twin of the smiling woman I saw in the portraits adorning Elodie's walls. "Where are their families?" I wonder. "Isn't it odd there are no visitors? That no one has stayed to sit with or care for their loved ones—especially the younger children?"

"What's *odd* is that this facility exists and I was unaware of it." Alaric's voice quivers with rage.

"It must be an illegal establishment, acting outside the law," Delphine suggests, but Alaric shakes his head, his nostrils flaring wider with each breath.

"There's no way they would have access to this much

bagrava without the knowledge and support of my father and his councilors. Which means this facility isn't operating illegally. I've just been kept in the dark."

I place a gentle hand on Alaric's shoulder, but he brushes me off, and before Delphine or I can stop him, he grips the knob and charges through the door.

THIRTY-FIVE

"WHAT IN THE NAME OF THE KINGS IS GOING ON here?" Alaric roars.

The nearest caretaker, who was collecting empty soup bowls, shrieks and fumbles her tray. Dishes clatter noisily to the floor, and several of the other nurses scream. The patients, however, blink slowly at the commotion—if they notice it at all. Most are staring silently up at the ceiling, returned again to stone.

Delphine and I slink into the room, keeping our backs against the wall, as Alaric shouts and stomps down the long rows of beds.

"Under whose orders do you operate? Who gave you the authority to open this facility and use bagrava in this way?"

The ground noticeably shudders with each of his steps, and for the first time since arriving on the mountain, I see a glimpse of Soren's temper in him. I see how easy it would be for them to lose control of their power in a fit of anger or outrage.

"Someone had better start talking!" Alaric bellows when none of the nurses come forward.

"Settle down," a familiar voice drawls from the far side of the room, and a wave of revulsion washes over me. I want to run—far, far away—but Delphine reaches for my hand and squeezes it tight as Garitt Von Nevus emerges from the shadows. His velvet robes and glowing complexion look especially ridiculous here, in this sea of plain white sheets and sallow faces.

"Von Nevus," Alaric spits. "Somehow I'm not surprised to find you here. Who are these people, and why wasn't I aware of this facility?"

Von Nevus smirks and casts his eyes about the room, breaking into a full-blown grin when he spots me. "Ah, good. You brought Indira."

The sound of my name on his lips makes me want to scream.

"Answer me!" Alaric roars. "*Now!*"

"It's so unbecoming for a prince to throw a tantrum like a toddler." Von Nevus tuts and leans casually against a bed frame. "And yelling will do no good. I don't take orders from you."

"You'd better start if you want to leave this warehouse alive," Alaric warns, raising his hands.

Beneath our feet, the stone floor shudders even harder.

"Alaric!" I cry out with alarm, but his attention remains fixed on Von Nevus.

"Tell me!" Alaric commands.

When Von Nevus still doesn't answer, fractures zigzag up the plaster walls of the warehouse. The bed frames rattle and clank, and the nurses who haven't already fled bolt without a backward glance at the helpless patients.

The thought of taking even one step closer to Von Nevus makes me want to vomit, but I force myself away from the wall. I refuse to let Alaric lose control the way his father did. And I refuse to let Garitt Von Nevus have any power over me.

I stride down the row of beds, catch Alaric by the elbow, and yank him backward. "*Think* about what you're doing!" I shout, giving him a meaningful look when he snarls down at me.

His hands drop to his sides with a thump, and he falls back a few steps, the fury on his face morphing into horror and shame. Before he spirals too far, I tighten my grip on his arm, like Delphine did for me, and tell him to look at me. Breathe with me. Slowly, in and out.

"Thank you, Indira," he whispers.

"Yes, thank you, Indira," Von Nevus interrupts, wiggling his fingers in a mocking wave. "So nice of you to intervene on my behalf."

"It had nothing to do with you," I snap. "I would have

let Alaric level the building and bury you alive, if not for the patients."

Von Nevus lets out an exaggerated huff. "Why is everyone so touchy today? If you had let me finish"—he turns to Alaric—"I was going to say, *I don't serve you* yet. But I will someday, which is why I'm willing to compromise now. So long as it's of future benefit to me."

"You're despicable," Alaric says. "We're in a warehouse full of sick Vanzadorians, and you're thinking of how it can benefit you."

Von Nevus shrugs. "I'm not responsible for their condition. I'm simply taking advantage of an opportunity—which doesn't harm them further, I should add. If that's despicable, so be it. I personally think it would be worse to squander the opportunity to make some good come from this awful situation."

"What do you want?" Alaric bites out.

"To be lead advisor under your rule," Von Nevus says without a breath of hesitation.

Alaric barks out a laugh. "You're daft to think—"

I step down hard on Alaric's boot and shoot him an insistent look. Von Nevus is the only person who can tell us what's happening here, so for now, we need to appease him.

Alaric closes his eyes and sighs. "I'll take it under consideration—*if* your information proves useful. And truthful," he adds sharply. "Who are these people? Where did they come from, and why are they ill?"

"*These*"—Von Nevus holds out his arms—"are the people—or, in some cases, the children of the people—who have chosen to sacrifice the largest quantities of their memories to the earth. Many courtiers do it for the wealth and status born of a large endowment. While commoners do it for appealing incentives like lower taxes, repaying debts, and educational opportunities. For whatever reason, these people poured so much of themselves into the ground—in order to fuel *your* power, I want to remind you—that there's nothing left," Von Nevus says with a theatrical frown.

Alaric's face crumples with confusion. "I don't understand."

"We aren't made of an infinite amount of memories. If a person sacrifices too much, they no longer have enough life essence to support themselves or the children they create. Nothing left with which to sustain or make a soul, leaving bodies without proper substance to animate them, as you see here." Von Nevus turns a slow circle.

"No." Alaric staggers back. "That can't be true."

I want to agree, but it explains why the courtiers are so distant and distractable, why people are mysteriously vanishing, and why Soren needs more and more bagrava.

Of course sacrificing one's memories would have long-term consequences. The Vanzadorian people are draining their vitality more every day. Every hour. And minute.

"No," Alaric growls with more vehemence. "Our people choose which memories to give—and how *much* to give. They would never sacrifice more than is sustainable."

"Tell me, Your Highness, how are they supposed to know when they've reached their limit? Is there a bell that rings to let them know their social climbing days are over?"

Alaric looks pale and dazed. He fumbles to respond.

Von Nevus fills the silence with another devastating blow. "We tried to mitigate the problem by adding bagrava to the water supply, which has helped to slow the epidemic, but it's like trying to dam a river with a twig."

I clutch my throat, feeling sick. How much bagrava have I unknowingly consumed? I should have realized, should have recognized the flavor. But how could I when I've never tasted it before? When Rowenna's letters blamed the flavor on mineral deposits?

"We bring the worst patients here," Von Nevus continues, "so as not to frighten and upset the rest of the population."

"But don't their families notice they're missing?" Delphine speaks up for the first time.

Von Nevus shakes his head. "The majority of families have *chosen* to forget their ailing loved ones, rather than live with the pain of losing them in this harrowing manner."

"You mean the families have been compelled to forget,"

Alaric says through clenched teeth. "My father forces them to purge the truth about their loved ones, doesn't he? To ensure everyone continues depositing memories."

"It's not our place to question or criticize the king," Von Nevus says. "If you are unable to move the earth, we won't be able to keep the Marauders from scaling the mountain, and our mines won't yield half as much. Not to mention our society as a whole will collapse. It's built around rewarding those who give the most."

"What happens to these people who have already sacrificed too much—or never had enough to begin with?" Alaric gently leans over to touch the cheek of a boy no older than five. The boy doesn't look up or even flinch, and it reminds me of the hollow shell cicadas leave behind when they molt.

"They die," Von Nevus says gravely. "Most of these people would be dead already, if not for this rigorous bagrava treatment—which I suggested, by the way." He straightens his robes proudly. "When I saw how the bagrava tea soothed and stabilized the queen and her courtiers following a memory sacrifice, I hoped it would help these people too—fill the void where memories should be. And it does, to an extent. It prolongs their lives for months, sometimes even years, and allows them a few hours of normalcy each day, as you just witnessed."

I look from one vacant face to the next, my heart throbbing painfully.

"What's the point?" I sputter. "This isn't sustainable. Surely, Soren must see that. My people can't produce enough bagrava to meet your demands now, and if what you claim is true, the number of ailing Vanzadorians will only grow. Even if Tashir *could* produce enough bagrava without sentencing ourselves to starvation, it doesn't actually give these people a good quality of life. A few hours a day is hardly enough."

"So should we just let them perish?" Von Nevus asks. "You're beginning to sound even more stonehearted than us, Princess."

"*No*. Of course not. That's not what I meant." I blink around the dismal space. "Their suffering should be eased, of course, but the greater problem needs to be addressed. People need to stop giving memories."

Von Nevus laughs. "Don't try to solve problems you know nothing about. If you want to be useful, cultivate more bagrava."

"But no matter how much bagrava we have, won't there eventually come a time when everyone is ill?" Delphine asks. "When no healthy children are born? What does King Soren plan to do then?"

Von Nevus gives a full-bodied shrug. "King Soren says we must focus on the present, and the best way to serve and protect Vanzador *now* is by keeping his power as strong as possible."

"He doesn't care about the bleak future because he

plans to dump it on me," Alaric says, gazing at the rows and rows of cots with a haunted look in his eyes.

I slump against the wall, overcome with exhaustion. For so long, I thought Soren used our bagrava to fuel his power, but the truth is so much worse. Keeping sick people alive might seem like a nobler cause, but by nursing these people with bagrava, it allows Soren to continue collecting memories and amassing power without consequence.

"Did Rowenna know?" I ask Von Nevus. "About this place? About the sickness?"

"I brought her here once, so she'd know the full breadth of our situation when she became queen."

If Rowenna knew Vanzador was imploding, would she still have tried to steal the gemstone triad? Especially if she knew *our* people would have to sacrifice memories in order to fuel its power? Or would she have been content to stand by and watch Vanzador consume itself? Rowenna was never a patient person, and she would have seen the flaws in that strategy too—without Soren feeding power into our mountain range, we would be left exposed to the Marauders.

So what did she choose? And how, exactly, did that choice result in her death?

When I first arrived in Vanzador, I would have twisted myself into knots trying to untangle this complicated web. I wouldn't have been able to move forward unless I knew I was following in her footsteps with exactness. But, as I look at Alaric and Delphine standing beside me, and all the people in need of help in this hospital, I realize I have options Rowenna never had, because I've let people in when she never did. Unlike her, I am willing to pivot from my original plans and admit my way isn't the only way—or even the best way.

My sister and I may have hiked the same treacherous path leading up this mountain, but we arrived at two very different destinations. One an ending, the other a new beginning, and I am choosing to build rather than burn.

I turn my back on Von Nevus and the dreary hospital, and charge back toward the palace, my mind racing as fast as my steps. There have to be other sources of power. Other means by which Alaric can move the earth without draining the life essence from his people and depleting our bagrava stores. A way Tashir and Vanzador can both thrive, as true allies.

Alaric and Delphine chase me back through the streets, demanding to know where I'm going and what I'm doing, but I don't stop until I'm back in the solarium, sinking into the soft soil of my planting beds—my sanctuary. The only place I can make a difference.

"We shouldn't have to live like this—with our people suffering and dying on both sides," I say, looking up at my panting maid and bewildered husband. "We're all sacrificing so much and still losing. It's madness."

"What other choice do we have?" Alaric asks with an exhausted sigh.

I raise my chin and confidently say the very words I swore I never would. "I'm willing to cultivate bagrava in earnest for the sick Vanzadorians, if *you're* willing to search for alternative ways to fuel your power. There has to be something more sustainable than memories. If we work together instead of against each other, we can all prosper instead of limping along, clinging to half the life and opportunity our people deserve."

Alaric fiddles with the chains on his jacket. "You know I would happily agree, but I doubt my father will."

"So we'll make him," I say resolutely.

THIRTY-SIX

"**N**O ONE CAN *MAKE* MY FATHER DO ANYTHING," Alaric says bitterly. "That's his area of expertise—you saw my memories."

I shake my head. "I saw him *try* to force you to forget Besnik's death, but you found a work-around. That's what we need now—another work-around."

"Changing his entire mindset isn't going to be as simple as siphoning a memory into a silver button."

"It's too bad we can't put thoughts and memories *into* his head rather than siphoning them into objects or the ground," Delphine says as she slumps beside the planter box.

"That's it!" I cry, grabbing her face with my dirty hands. "Delphine, you're brilliant!"

She laughs nervously and exchanges a look with Alaric,

who gives a sad shake of his head—like a parent about to disappoint a child.

"I don't want to sound pessimistic, but it isn't possible," he says. "We can't control my father's thoughts."

"But we *can* make him relive memories he'd rather keep in the past," I insist. "Things he wouldn't want his adoring subjects to see. Memories he'd do *anything* to keep hidden."

"Are you suggesting we blackmail my father, the king of Vanzador?" Alaric splutters.

Delphine pales and lets out a whimper, but I sit taller in my planting bed, a devious smile playing across my lips. I'd prefer to think of it as a nudge in the right direction."

The mountaintop is colder than I remember it being the night Delphine and I followed Alaric into this secluded clearing. Darker too. I tell myself it's the howling wind and thin crescent moon, casting everything in freezing shadow, but I know the cold seeping into my bones is much more literal.

King Soren Alaverdi is making his way up the mountain, billowing ever closer.

I shiver and wrap my jacket more tightly around my shoulders. Then I sink my fingers into the planting box I reassembled up here. I hum a few refrains of Earth

Mother's incantations, even though the planter doesn't contain a single bagrava seed. I would never subject my plants to such torture; they'd perish up here in these hellish conditions.

But Soren doesn't know that.

So I sing to fool him, and to soothe my nerves, as the minutes pass with excruciating slowness.

My fingers lose feeling first, despite the thick gloves I borrowed from Elodie, and my toes follow not long after. The tips of my nose and ears begin to burn, and as the soil in the planting box hardens, the lumps dig into my backside.

I shift uncomfortably and glance back over my shoulder, down the mountainside.

It wasn't supposed to take this long.

Alaric promised Soren would eagerly follow him up here when he learned it was where I finally agreed to cultivate large amounts of bagrava.

"He won't be able to resist seeing it for himself," Alaric said. "And he wouldn't miss an opportunity to punish you for making him wait so long."

I shiver again, but now it has little to do with the cold. Soren is volatile. Unpredictable. Instead of submitting to our terms when backed into a corner, he could lash out in rage—like he did when he killed Besnik. We might all die on this mountaintop tonight.

An echo of distorted voices rises from the cave Alaric

uses to access this summit, and I almost drop the two tiny buttons as I remove them from my cloak pocket. One is the silver button containing Alaric's memory of Besnik's death. The other is a golden button I tore from my own dress, containing a new memory of my own.

Two small buttons that will decide the future of our two nations.

"This is preposterous," Soren mutters as he and Alaric emerge into the punishing cold. "Couldn't you have convinced your wife to grow bagrava *inside* the walls of the Fortress? Even *I* know these conditions are inhospitable for growing. It's freezing and there's hardly any soil. The ground has been excavated to the brink of collapse."

"The girl likes it up here. She says it reminds her of Tashir." Alaric plucks the lie out of thin air—so quickly, so seamlessly, it leaves me blinking. "Her people transformed the barren Tomb Flats into lush planting fields. Indira believes she can do the same here, on the mountain. She also believes she's safe from you up here," Alaric adds.

"Yet fool enough to believe she's safe from *you*." Soren chuckles darkly.

That's the story Alaric told his father—that he wooed me with his charms and tricked me into falling in love with him, so I'd agree to grow more bagrava. But I would only do it up here—where I thought Soren couldn't find me. The truth is we needed to get Soren away from the watchful eyes of his councilors and guards in order to threaten him.

"I'll convince the girl to move her operations to the palace soon," Alaric assures his father as they hike into view. "She's so smitten, she'll give me anything I ask. Poor girl's head is full of nothing but dirt." Alaric's laughter is even colder than the wind, his face a mask of brutal indifference. He's so convincing, so good at playing the role of Soren's doting son, I would almost believe it was genuine if I didn't know better. If I hadn't seen the warm, beating heart he hides beneath his stony exterior.

Soren bobs his meaty head. "You've done well with the gardener. Much better than the disastrous union with your first wife. Such a useless girl."

I clench my teeth so hard, it feels like they're going to crumble out of my mouth, and force myself to stay hunched in the planting bed, pretending to be oblivious to their approach.

I feel the moment Soren's greedy eyes find me. The hairs on my neck lift one by one, and I'm overwhelmed by the oily feeling of being watched.

I mouth a silent prayer to Earth Mother and clench the buttons even tighter, but I don't whisper the song Alaric taught me. Not yet. Soren must be close enough to be enveloped by the golden light of the past, yet far enough not to see my planting bed is actually empty.

Their boots scuffle through the scree. My heart throbs in my throat. Still, I wait. Second after excruciating second, until the overbearing musk of Soren's cologne fills my nose. He barks my name, as if I'm a dog, trained to leap to his call, but instead of answering, I press the golden button to my lips and whisper the words in a rush.

Dazzling yellow light explodes from my fist, even brighter than when I watched it envelop Alaric. I'm pretty sure I scream, but it's swallowed up by King Soren's frightened bellows.

He drops to the ground and frantically tugs on Alaric's trousers before covering his head. "Get down, boy! We're under attack! The girl is using her infernal magic against us!"

But Alaric remains on his feet, tall and stoic, as the golden light shifts and eddies, slowly taking shape. "Who says it's magic, Father?"

"What else could it be?" Soren demands.

"Memories." Alaric leans forward, looming over his father. "I know about the hidden hospital, about the dying people. I discovered your little secret yesterday."

As Alaric speaks, my memory of the warehouse with its rickety beds and despondent patients swirls into focus, enraging me all over again.

"I can't believe you thought you could keep this from me," Alaric continues, voice quivering with fury. "I can't believe you're willing to continue taking memories from our people when *this* is the cost!"

"How are you doing this?" Soren stands and staggers in a circle. "How have you brought the hospital here?"

"The hospital shouldn't exist at all!" Alaric roars, causing the ground beneath us to tremble.

"You act as if we have another choice," Soren snaps. "Of course I'm not pleased to see a few of our people deteriorating, but we need memories to fuel our power. And we're treating their symptoms with bagrava. It's the best we can do."

"You can't honestly believe that!" Alaric cries. "And it's more than a few people—it's an entire warehouse! Soon, it will be all of Vanzador. This isn't sustainable, Father. You know that."

"What I *know* is that Vanzador needs our power to be safe and prosperous, so that is what I provide—what *we* provide. Have you forgotten you're just as guilty of using their memories?"

"Only because I didn't know any better," Alaric bites back. "But now I do. If we continue draining our people's life essence, there will be no one and nothing left of Vanzador to protect and serve. We need to find another way to fuel our power."

"There *is* no other way!" Soren bellows, and the ground heaves in response, pitching me sideways. "We will continue doing what we've always done and use as much bagrava as necessary to keep our most important citizens in good health," Soren says resolutely.

But Alaric shakes his head. "How do you determine whose lives are most important? And how do you know there's no other way? Have you ever experimented with alternative tithes?"

"Of course I have! I've tried pouring every part of myself into the ground, but nothing works. The earth won't accept any other form of payment."

Alaric flinches like he's been struck. "Why didn't you tell me? I could have been helping you, sharing the burden. We have to keep trying until we find another way. It's our responsibility to—"

"Enough!" Soren shouts. "I'm returning to the Fortress, and it would be in your best interest to join me. Forget this ill-conceived intervention that was clearly the idea of your scheming wife."

Soren sets off with brisk, angry strides—in the entirely wrong direction. It's easy to get turned around up here on the summit, surrounded on every side by endless scree and sky, and Alaric doesn't redirect him.

"I'm not going with you, and I'm not going to forget any of this. We can't bury our heads in the dirt and pretend nothing's wrong, Father," Alaric calls, his eyes ablaze with fire and determination. He's never looked more beautiful and brave, standing up to the man who's given him everything—and taken just as much.

"If you refuse to do what's best for our people," Alaric continues, "I'll be forced to reveal the hospital. I'll show them where their loved ones have actually disappeared to instead of the stories you've invented, and the memories you convinced them to purge. Do you think our people will still eagerly give their memories to the earth when they know what's truly at stake?"

Soren wheels back around. "How can you disrespect and undermine me like this, after everything I've done for you? After all the years we've spent working side by side? I've been nothing but kind and loving and supportive. Don't I deserve the benefit of the doubt?"

"There's no doubt what's happening to our people," Alaric points out. "And we both know you've only loved and supported me to hide your own guilt."

Soren's face contorts into an unrecognizable mask of fury. "You don't know what you're talking about."

"Yes, Father, I do."

Soren holds up a quivering finger. Spittle flies from his lips as he speaks. "If you proceed with this madness, I'll tell them it was you. I'll tell everyone *you've* been keeping the hospital a secret from *me*. That you're the one who callously takes their memories. I'll make them believe you're responsible for it all, and you know they'll believe me. They'll always trust me over you because you're weak and dithering and have never had what it takes to rule. I know it, my councilors know it, and deep down, you know it. Soon the people will know it too—how inept you are, how much I've coddled you."

Soren's hateful words stab my flesh like thorns. I can only imagine how deeply they stab Alaric, having his fears and insecurities laid bare like this.

Alaric stands completely still and in a low, calm voice says, "Our people only trust you because they've never seen the truth. But I have other memories, too, Father. Much older memories I can share if I need to."

"I don't know what you're referring to," Soren blusters.

Alaric nods at me, and I whisper to the silver button, launching the second wave of our attack.

Another whoosh of light explodes from my hands, and Soren's council room materializes over the hospital, creating a dizzying convergence of scenes.

"How are you doing this? Stop at once!" Soren stumbles and shakes his head, swatting at the glittering images the way you would a swarm of flies. But his blows strike nothing but air, and the erratic swinging sends him lurching across the narrow summit.

"Do you remember this day? Because I do—despite your commands to purge it," Alaric says as the flecks of gold and copper coalesce into a face.

Besnik's face.

Soren flinches away from the specter, but he's confronted on the other side by a phantom of himself. He lets out a guttural cry as memory-Soren charges across the council room and levels an accusatory finger at young Alaric, who's holding the broken Flesh of Callahan in his shaking hands.

"How is this possible?" Soren babbles. "You shouldn't remember any of this."

He watches in open-mouthed horror as the golden visage of Besnik falls through the crumbling floor.

Alaric sneers at his real father while memory Soren forces young Alaric to his knees, commanding him to expel all evidence of the crime.

"I knew you wouldn't sacrifice the memory," Alaric says. "You had to remember to ensure I didn't—to make certain I never told anyone the truth about Besnik's death. But I kept the memory too. I never wanted to forget how my brother saved my life, so I siphoned the memory into an object and discovered a way to bring it to life. Do you know what that means? I can show our people the truth about Besnik's death. They can witness your crime firsthand."

For the first time in all the years I've known him, King Soren looks afraid. He mumbles and staggers back again, trying to put more distance between himself and the golden rendering of Besnik's corpse on the banquet table and the equally terrifying, and very real, version of Alaric, prowling closer.

For every step Alaric takes, Soren retreats two, drawing nearer and nearer to the cliff's edge.

"Stop running from this," Alaric says. "There's nowhere left to go. All you have to do is agree to stop draining our people's vitality and help me find another way to fuel our power, and all of this will go away."

Soren's jowls quiver, and he drops his head to his chest. For a moment I think he's going to relent, but then he raises his hands and bellows, "Enough!"

The ground shudders so violently, Alaric crashes to his hands and knees.

Shock waves roll across the summit, and there's a loud crack—like the sound of snapping bone. A moment later, the earth rumbles again, though Soren's hands haven't moved. It isn't until plumes of dust fill the air that I realize what's happening. A disconcertingly large shelf of rock has broken away from the mountain and is tumbling down the cliffside.

"Come away from the edge, Father," Alaric commands, just like he did when I ventured too close to these unstable cliffs.

Soren shakes his head. "Shouldn't you want me to fall? Vanzador will be better off without me. You think you will be a superior king. Isn't that what you're trying to prove with all of this?"

Alaric reels back with shock. "That isn't at all what I'm saying."

"You think I'm unnecessary. You're trying to overthrow me." Soren snaps, and Alaric shrinks lower with each accusation, like a scolded dog.

It's horrifying to watch the swift reversal of roles. Soren knows just how to twist Alaric's words and exploit his kind heart so Alaric turns the doubt and guilt back on himself. Just like he did when Besnik died.

"I would never conspire against you," Alaric continues babbling. "I need you. Vanzador needs you. I only want your help."

Every apologetic word makes me want to reach out and shake him. Force him to stop groveling and stay on the offensive. But Alaric continues spiraling, deeper and deeper into Soren's trap.

"You couldn't have known the memory tithes came at such high cost," Alaric insists. "And accepting that something no longer works doesn't mean you've failed. It just means we need to find a new solution, another way." Alaric extends a hand to his father. "Help me fix this, Father. Please."

But Soren laughs bitterly and takes another step back. "All I've ever wanted is to lead and protect our people—to live up to the legacy handed down to me by my father—but I'm clearly lacking."

"You're not lacking," Alaric cries. "You're even stronger than the kings who came before you. That's why you were chosen to rule now. The Gods of the Mountain knew you were up to this task."

But Soren shakes his head sadly and steps back again, teetering at the edge of the world. Tears slide down his bearded cheeks. "Even if I was, there's no way for me to come out of this unscathed. Like you said—once our people see the hospital and realize what I've allowed to happen, they'll despise me. They'll never forgive or trust me again.

And if they discover what I did to Besnik..." He shakes his head again. "I couldn't bear it. I'd rather be dead."

"I don't have to show them," Alaric says quickly "If you agree to find other ways to fuel our power, they never have to know." He carefully steps out onto the ledge and places a gentle hand on Soren's arm. "Come back with me, and we'll work all of this out."

"I'm sorry." Soren's watery eyes look from Alaric to the ledge they're standing on, and I suddenly realize what he's going to do.

I leap from the planter with a scream and slam into Alaric's legs, knocking him sideways. Soren lunges at the same time, but Alaric is no longer standing, and Soren cries out as he trips over our crumpled bodies. His head makes a terrible cracking sound when he hits the rock, and a second later, the ground makes a crack of its own.

"Get away from the edge!" Alaric shouts, but Soren doesn't move or respond, and before Alaric can scramble out to retrieve him, the ledge sloughs away—into the midnight sky.

I can't help but think Soren looks eerily similar to Besnik tumbling end over end through the floor as he falls.

Alaric scrambles to the edge, screaming his father's name. He even thrusts his hands out, as if to move the earth and save him, but I place a heavy hand on his arm.

"Don't."

He flinches and throws me off. "I have to!"

"You have to save yourself and your people," I argue, squeezing his arm even harder. "How many times will you allow him to almost kill you? He's shown you who he is. Believe him. Then let him go."

"But he's my father," Alaric wails. "Vanzador needs him. I'm not strong enough—"

"You are," I cut in. "Vanzador needs a king with the power to move the earth. That doesn't have to be your father. Don't let him be the downfall of your country—and mine," I add quietly.

Alaric's eyes are wild and wet, and he's shaking so hard his legs give way and he crumples to his knees. But he doesn't lift his hands to move the earth. Instead, he allows me to lace my fingers through his and we watch, together, as Soren vanishes into the darkness below.

THIRTY-SEVEN

DON'T KNOW HOW LONG WE SIT THERE, STARING into the abyss. The bottom is too far below and too shrouded in darkness to see the moment of impact, but it must have happened, because the ground is eerily quiet and still. If Soren had survived, he would already be climbing up the switchbacks to punish us. These precarious cliffs would be crumbling beneath our feet. But the night is perfectly calm. Clouds roll lazily across the star-swept sky. And for the first time in ages, I release a full breath.

Alaric, on the other hand, makes painful gasping noises as he struggles for air. "I can't believe he's really gone," he mumbles over and over again.

I squeeze his fingers tight and let him cry until he eventually runs out of tears and lowers his forehead to my shoulder.

"I'm sorry for your loss," I begin, choosing my words carefully, "but isn't there a small part of you that's relieved he's gone? Or vindicated, perhaps? Didn't you ever dream of getting justice for Besnik?"

"Sure, I *thought* about it, in my darkest moments," Alaric admits. "But I never would have actually hurt my father. Like I told you a thousand times: I'm not a murderer. Or I wasn't," he corrects himself.

"You still aren't. Soren drove himself over the ledge trying to kill you—for a *second* time. Even if you shoved him, it would have been warranted. You have no reason to feel guilty."

Alaric's face is moonstone pale, the shadows beneath his eyes amethyst purple. "I know it doesn't make sense. He killed my brother and lied to me, manipulated me, but he was still my father. He taught me everything I know, and I do think he loved me, in his own way. He undoubtedly loved our people. The Fortress has always been safe and prosperous under his rule. Our people have job security and steady incomes."

"A good king doesn't strip his people of memories and life essence, then hide the dying bodies in a makeshift hospital," I say flatly.

Alaric's face is pained. "He was obviously far from perfect, but so am I. I should have noticed how the memory deposits were affecting our people. I should have asked why we needed so much bagrava. Who's to say I won't be an even worse ruler than my father? His councilors clearly don't think I'm up to the task. They'll never accept me as king."

"Look at me." I reach over and gently touch the side of Alaric's face, turning his head until our eyes meet. "They won't have a choice. You're Soren's rightful heir and the only one with the ability to move the earth."

"There's no law that states the person with power has to be the one *in* power. It's just always been that way, since my father and grandfather were strong, natural rulers. But I'm not. The council will find ways to undermine and control me. They'll keep me caged like the beasts in the traveling minstrel shows. Force me to perform on command."

"No, they won't. We won't let them—."

Alaric lets out a shuddering cry. "How can I be the king my people need when I was never meant to rule Vanzador?"

I tighten my grip on his hand, trying to squeeze strength and confidence into him. "But what if you *were* meant to rule?" I ask softly. "What if you were *always* meant to be king, and that's why the Gods of the Mountain blessed you with such a wonderful older brother—to teach you how to be kind and selfless and brave? To show you a different way to lead so you'd be prepared to save your people from the memory sacrifices?" I lower my voice to a reverent whisper. "What would Besnik say if he were here? What would he want—for you and for Vanzador?"

Alaric is silent for so long, I fear I've overstepped. Then he says, "He would support me without question."

I nod my agreement. "You're more than up to this task. Most of your people have never doubted you, and the ones who have will come around once they open their eyes and see how dedicated, passionate, and hardworking you are. It's impossible not to love you," I add.

Alaric's eyes slowly lift, finding mine from beneath his thick curtain of lashes. "What about you? Do *you* feel up to the task? If *I* am king, it means *you* are the queen of Vanzador."

I swallow hard, hoping it will calm the anxiety churning like a sickness in my stomach. The thought of ruling any country makes me nauseous. I never thought I'd be queen of Tashir, let alone Vanzador. Ruling isn't something I ever wanted, but maybe, like Alaric, I'm the unexpected queen Vanzador needs. There are good people on this mountain. People like Delphine and Elodie, who readily extended their friendship. Who showed me it's okay to trust and let people in. And there are so many people *I* can help here, like the people drained of their life essence, in desperate need of bagrava. And the miners, who have safer working conditions, thanks to my goblin's gold.

Against all odds, I do believe I can be Vanzador's queen—if I am brave enough to throw myself into the task wholeheartedly.

"Come on." I brush off my skirt, haul myself to my

feet, and extend a hand to Alaric, determined to be the strong one. Ready to lift him now, as he's always lifted me. "We need to find your father's body and carry it back to the Fortress before the city wakes."

Alaric's face goes ashen. "I can't bear to see it. What will the guards say? They'll think we killed him. They'll—"

"They'll thank you," I interrupt, "when we show them the horrors of that makeshift hospital. When they learn the truth about Besnik's death."

"It feels so wrong, destroying everything he built," Alaric whispers, staring off into the distance, at the sky slowly graying with dawn.

I lean up on my toes and press a gentle kiss to his lips. "He was the one destroying Vanzador. *You* are saving it."

Hot tears slide down Alaric's cheeks as he kisses me back. Then he takes my hand, and we wend our way down the mountain in thoughtful silence.

The search for Soren's body is slow and arduous. For some reason, I imagined finding him on an outcropping of stone, lying peaceful and unscathed, as if on a funeral pyre. As strong in death as he was in life. But even with the power to move the earth, he was no match for its brutal strength in the end. Jagged rocks ripped the king of Vanzador limb from limb as he fell, and the final impact obliterated everything that remained.

Alaric falls to his knees, retching, so I force down my own queasiness and collect what I can in my skirt. Then we make our way back up to the Fortress as the first rays of coral sunlight streak the sky.

Alaric's breaths quicken and his steps falter as the spires of the castle take shape through the low-hanging clouds. He looks like he's marching to his execution, but I feel the opposite. Without the threat of Soren looming over us like a storm cloud, the Fortress doesn't look nearly as intimidating. The palace, buildings, and even the behemoth wall are just structures made of stone. The streets are pebble-packed earth. All of it as real and natural as the soil and grasses of Tashir.

We slip through the city wall and back inside the palace, which is thankfully still quiet with sleep.

"Go make yourself presentable," I tell Alaric. "You need to address the people as soon as possible. I'll have them gather in the industrial sector, near the secret hospital."

Alaric blinks dazedly. "How will you manage that?"

"Delphine and Elodie will help me spread the word among the courtiers and servants. Then we'll send runners into the city to inform the rest of the people."

"What about my Father's councilors? They won't come if they know I'm the one that's calling."

"I'll alert them myself. I'll tell Von Nevus you and Soren got into an argument last night and lead him to believe the announcement has to do with Soren reprimanding you. They will happily gather to witness that."

"And what happens when it doesn't play out like that? When they realize..." His eyes drift down to the remains of his father in my skirt.

"They'll have no choice but to fall in line. Now go."

In less than an hour, the last of the miners are filing into the crowded streets, looking irritated and bewildered. Word reached them just in time. A few minutes later, and they would have descended into the depths of the earth. It would have taken hours to bring them all back to the surface, which would have left too much time for Soren's councilors to start asking questions.

They stand in a line of blue robes at the head of the square, arms crossed and faces stern, pretending not to be as curious as the sleep-tousled courtiers, who are too busy whispering to worry about their rumpled gowns and mussed hair for once.

Behind the courtiers, vendors and shopkeepers chatter amongst themselves, while Delphine and the other palace servants exchange whispers and furtive glances.

I shoot my maid a grateful smile from where I stand beside Alaric and Queen Tessa, on the balcony of a factory adjacent to the hospital. I search out Elodie's face, too, and blow her a kiss. None of this would have been possible without their quick feet, far-reaching connections, and unwavering trust.

I didn't know what I was missing when my world was so narrow. I never knew how good it feels to have people who love and trust you enough to leap to your aid without hesitation. And as I look fondly on these two Vanzadorian women—the last people I would have sought for friendship—I silently vow to follow their example going forward. I want to be a queen who reaches out instead of retreating in. Our lives are meant to be shared—like the sun, spreading its life-giving light across the planting fields. If we share ourselves with only a select few, they risk being scorched by the heat and intensity—the way I was burned by Rowenna's love. I was so close to her fire, I didn't even realize I was burning until she was gone.

"*Where* is your father?" Queen Tessa asks Alaric for at least the sixth time. "What on earth could the two of you have to say that's more important than my morning salon? I requested cheese soufflés today, and now they'll have fallen flat."

I watch Alaric's jaw work. He's about to take the biggest leap of his life, and neither of his parents are truly here to witness it.

I grab his hand and hold it tight. "You can do this," I whisper.

He nods, his eyes wide with fear, but he gives a small squeeze in return. "*We* can do this."

He kisses me and his mother on the cheek—the signal for Delphine and her helpers to get into position—then he strides to the front of the balcony and grips the rail with both hands. I'm struck by how strong he looks with his back straight and chin lifted, wearing a silk jacket so fine it's nearly translucent. His face is freshly shaven, his boots polished to a high shine, and his wild hair has even been oiled back, making him look less boyish and brooding, and more serious and competent. More like a king.

A wave of overwhelming pride and admiration surges through me. A feeling dangerously close to love.

Alaric clears his throat and raises his hands. "Thank you for joining me this day," he begins, but he's instantly cut off by shouted questions and demands for King Soren.

Each word makes Alaric flinch, but he rolls his shoulders back and forges on. "My father's absence is exactly why I've called you here."

"What do you mean *absence*?" Von Nevus steps forward. "Where's the king?"

Another councilor quickly joins in. "*You* called us here? I thought we were summoned by King Soren."

"If you would let me explain—" Alaric says, but the crowd begins to murmur and roil.

The cantankerous gray-haired councilor barks out, "We want the king's explanation, not yours!"

The rest of the council shouts their agreement, infecting the crowd with their fear and suspicion, until the entire congregation is calling for answers.

Alaric looks around helplessly. He waves his hands and demands silence, but no one listens. The councilors continue yelling and stoking the hysteria until Alaric slams his hands down hard on the railing and bellows, "You can't hear from my father because he's *dead*!"

For one protracted moment, the square falls quiet. Sweat beads down my cheeks, and I'm gripped by a wave of nauseating heat. This is *not* how we planned to break the news. The announcement was supposed to be calm and controlled, methodically revealing the sick in the hospital followed by the memory of Besnik's death, to highlight Soren's crimes and instability compared to Alaric's quiet strength and control.

Instead, Queen Tessa lets out a bloodcurdling wail and collapses on the balcony, and the already riotous crowd devolves into chaos.

Attendants fly up the metal staircase to assist the queen, while the councilors charge forward, shouting words like *traitor* and *murderer*. Servants and courtiers dart this way and that, unsure where to go, which way is safe.

It reminds me of the hysteria the day I left Tashir—when flames were devouring our fields and Soren could have used his power to stop the destruction.

"Alaric!" I shout. "Use your power!"

His horrified gaze snaps to mine. "Against my own people?"

"Just to command their attention. Show them you're every bit as powerful and capable as your father."

Alaric stares into the chaos with a pained expression. Then he raises both hands, and tremors rattle down the balcony and roll down the teeming streets. The cobblestones crest and sink like waves, making it impossible for the people to stay on their feet.

At first, this causes even more terror and confusion, but slowly, the cries begin to fade as the people of Vanzador are forced to sit on the ground and look up at Alaric, directing the stones from the balcony the way a conductor leads an orchestra.

Soon, only Soren's councilors remain on their feet, still hurling accusations and shaking their fists. With a weary sigh, Alaric moves his arm in a slashing motion, and a deep gash splits the earth, severing the councilors from the rest of the crowd. The blue-robed men and women stumble and flail, desperate to keep themselves from tumbling into the abyss, and I'm more than a little disappointed when Von Nevus doesn't fall to his death.

Alaric straightens, adjusts his waistcoat, and calls out in a firm voice, "Listen! And I will relay all that has happened." No one moves or speaks, and after several deep breaths, Alaric continues. "Last night, I confronted my father about a troubling discovery I made recently with the help of my wife." Alaric slides his arm around my waist and pulls me against his side—his heartbeat hammering through me in a frantic staccato.

"There is a hospital, hidden in *that* warehouse"—Alaric points to the textile factory—"and it's filled with Vanzadorian citizens on the brink of death. Your very own mothers and fathers, sons and daughters, have been wasting away in agony without your knowledge."

Von Nevus's head snaps up, eyes blazing. "Lies! If Vanzadorians were missing, don't you think their families and friends would know? Stop trying to divert our attention from your crimes! Tell us what you did to King Soren!"

I tighten my grip on Alaric's waist, willing him to feel my strength and support.

After only a slight pause he shouts, says in his loudest voice, "If you don't believe us, see it with your own eyes!"

He points again to the textile factory, and every head turns at the sound of metal doors opening. Several moments later, Delphine and the servants she recruited to help emerge into the square, each of them carrying or escorting a weak, hollow-eyed patient. I made sure to include prominent figures like Elodie's mother, Councilwoman Tomasko, and innocent babies, like Lady Hawthorne's supposedly deceased child, to make it clear no one was safe from Soren's treachery.

The crowd silently parts for the grim procession, and

as the sick are carried through the throng, teary-eyed families rush forward.

"Where have they been all this time?"

"How is this possible? I was at the funeral!"

"What have you done to them?" a noblewoman demands, pointing between Alaric and the council, unsure where to lay the blame, which feels like our first step toward victory.

"This is the unforeseen consequence of sacrificing our memories!" Alaric says before Von Nevus or other councilors can cut in and spin their lies. "My father encouraged all of us to give our memories abundantly in order to secure our borders and increase the output from our mines. He even offered incentives, like promises of wealth and status to those who sacrificed the most. He made us believe there was no reason to hold back—no ill effects from giving away these trivial moments. In fact, he convinced us the tithes were a blessing—a way to forget tragedies and blunt our pain and suffering. But *this* is the true cost of the memory tithes."

Alaric gestures sadly to the parade of sickly patients, still unresponsive despite the deafening commotion.

"My father was knowingly taking far more from us then we ever dreamed—or consented to," Alaric continues. "When we give too much of our past to the earth, we no longer have enough life essence to support our souls—or to pass on to our children at birth—creating bodies that are too weak and depleted to survive on their own. Bagrava, from Tashir, is the only thing keeping these patients alive.

"Soren *knew* this was happening, but instead of finding more sustainable ways to fuel our power, he hid the sick away, manipulated you into sacrificing your memories of the truth, and invented stories of their death or disappearance so you'd carry on depositing more memories."

Von Nevus breaks rank from the other councilors and stands at the edge of the gulf Alaric created to contain them. "Do you know what you're saying? What you're *doing*?" he snarls up at Alaric. "You need their memories just as much as your father did—even more so, since your power is fledgling and weak!"

"I don't want your memories if this is the cost," Alaric booms for all to hear. "I didn't think my father would either. But when I confronted him, he refused to accept responsibility. Not only that, he lashed out and tried to kill me to keep me from sharing this information with you. Just as he killed my brother, Besnik, in a fit of rage, years ago…"

Alaric nods at me, and I release the memory from the silver button once more. Instead of watching the past, though, I watch the crowd, their eyes wide with shock as the golden light of the past surrounds them. It's so quiet, I swear I can hear every beat of Alaric's thundering heart.

Once Besnik is dead and memory Soren has

commanded young Alaric to forget, real Alaric speaks again, no longer needing to shout to be heard.

"Despite these heinous crimes, I did not harm my father. He tried to shove me over a cliff edge and lost his balance, resulting in his own demise. I'll admit, I didn't use my power to save him. It seemed better for one man to perish than for the entire nation of Vanzador to lose their life essence. Better that I should be your king, inexperienced though I may be, than a man who was willing to lie and take advantage of you in such an appalling manner."

"Traitor!" Von Nevus yells. "You might as well have pushed him!"

But unlike before, very few citizens take up his cries.

Flutters of hope take flight in my rib cage and I urge Alaric on. "It's working. Keep going!"

Alaric grips the rail in both hands and stands even taller. "Being King of Vanzador is never what I wanted or planned—my brother would have made a far better king—but I am what you have, and I vow to do everything in my power to lead and protect you in a way that doesn't compromise your well-being. I won't stop searching until I find an alternative means to fuel my power and a cure for those already affected by the memory sacrifice.

"My wife, Indira, has agreed to aid us in this cause." Alaric looks down at me, and his tender, proud expression makes the butterflies beat their wings even more erratically.

Thousands of eyes are watching me, but I see only Alaric's.

"Her bagrava is the only reason these people are still alive," he admits gravely, "and she has generously offered to grow even more bagrava on the mountain to sustain their condition, but this comes at great cost to her and the people of Tashir. The amount of bagrava our sick require is so great, her own people are suffering on the brink of starvation. But Indira has agreed to help us nonetheless, because she has seen the goodness and strength of Vanzador and its people. She believes we are worth saving and that we can work together to sustain each other."

Alaric raises both arms high in the air, signaling the end of his speech.

I wait for the crowd to erupt with cheering. For people to throw themselves at his feet and offer their admiration and loyalty forevermore. But no one says a word. Not even the councilors. Alaric's panting as if he just sprinted across the Tomb Flats, and the smile plastered across his lips grows even wider, bordering on desperate, the longer the silence stretches.

How can they stand there and say nothing? How can they possibly deny this man as their king?

Mercifully, Queen Tessa clears her throat and hobbles forward. I completely forgot she was there, standing behind us throughout Alaric's speech.

"Is it true?" Did your father really kill Besnik?" She

sobs the name of her firstborn. "Was he truly responsible for this sickness?"

Alaric nods and reaches for her hands. "I'm sorry, Mother, I know you loved him. And I know you would have counseled him to make different choices, had you been aware."

Queen Tessa pries her hands free and collapses in a heap, wailing as she tears at her skirts. It's heart-wrenching and horrifying. The entire square is captivated.

Alaric eases down on one knee and tries to help her to her feet, but Queen Tessa swats him away.

"Don't help me up." She wipes beneath her eyes and places a gentle hand on Alaric's cheek. "I want to be the first to kneel before the rightful king of Vanzador."

She prostrates herself on the ground before Alaric, and goose bumps flash down my body as a deafening cheer rises from the square below. One by one, the multitude follows her lead, dropping to their knees, until only Garitt Von Nevus and a handful of sour-faced councilors remain.

"How do we know the king is truly dead?" Von Nevus demands. "We should bow to no one else until Soren's body is found."

"We recovered his body for those who wish to see and pay their respects," Alaric announces, but other voices are surging up from the crowd.

"I never want to see Soren Alaverdi again!"

"Even if he lived, he's no king of mine!"

The shouts of agreement are instant and deafening.

A palace guard draws his sword and aims it at Von Nevus's chest. "You will bow before your king."

Grudgingly, Von Nevus and the others sink to the ground until the entire nation is on its knees before me and Alaric. A Tashiri gardener and an unwanted prince. Somehow the rightful king and queen of Vanzador.

THIRTY-EIGHT

For the second time in our brief relationship, Alaric and I march in a royal funeral procession. Though, this one feels wildly different from Rowenna's because Alaric walks beside me. He wears a jacket of bagrava-purple silk that was made to match my gown, and our hands remain tightly clasped the entire time. Even in his grief, he makes certain to never get even a hair's breadth ahead of me, so we're equals—stride for stride.

A stone pyre has been erected in a large public square, and I feel myself getting unexpectedly emotional when Alaric touches a torch to the kindling and sets alight the remnants of Soren's body we recovered.

Initially, I was horrified to learn they burned the dead in Vanzador, rather than burying them. But now, as I watch the dancing orange flames and curling black smoke, it feels right. Like an ending and a beginning. Our journey started on the burning fields of Tashir. It feels right it should end with fire too.

"It's beautiful," I whisper, and I don't know if I'm referring to the pyre itself or the overwhelming sense of peace I feel, acknowledging that people can be both good and bad. The smiling, laughing Soren who chatted with his people in the square was every bit as real as the merciless tyrant who allowed Tashir to burn. Just as the sister who told me bedtime stories and ran with me through the cornfields was the same woman who lied to me in her letters and made alliances with Von Nevus. We all contain multitudes, and it's okay to mourn and celebrate both.

"It is beautiful," Alaric quietly agrees.

Once the fire has burned down to embers, we turn away from the blackened altar and the painful past it represents, and move toward banquet tables and stone-throwing courts that have been arranged around the perimeter of the square. Toward Alaric's coronation, which deserves a celebration all its own.

The dancing is vigorous, the wine free-flowing, and the number of people who drop into a curtsy or kiss the back of my hand is staggering. They praise my generosity and willingness to grow bagrava, despite the toll it has taken on my people. They thank me for supporting Alaric in his bid to expose the truth about Soren. And they thank me for the jubilant celebration and how it's lifting their spirits.

Even the healers who are back at the palace tending to the sick sent letters of approval and thanks before the event.

I make certain each of them knows none of this would be possible without Alaric, our new king, and Delphine, my new head of household and organizer of the festivities.

It was her idea to have a memorial and coronation all rolled into one.

"The people need a chance to grieve, but also a reason to celebrate," she insisted, and she couldn't have been more right. She also couldn't have planned a more perfect event.

I've felt like a proud parent watching her these past few days, boldly collaborating with Queen Tessa and the courtiers on decorations and menus, and bustling around the palace to direct florists and chefs like she's been doing so all her life.

Delphine's been so busy, I've hardly been able to steal a moment with her, and I squint through the throng now, hoping to catch a glimpse of her new silk gown with her golden hair tumbling down her back, instead of her old maid's uniform and customary braid. But she must be ushering in the next course of food or performers because I don't see her anywhere.

"There you are!" A horde of dancers whirls past, and Elodie Tomasko takes me by the hands, spinning me into the chaos before I have a chance to say no.

Just like the first time I met her, it's impossible *not* to be swept up in her warmth and enthusiasm. Though it's a different kind of enthusiasm than when I first arrived at the Fortress. Like Delphine, my noble friend has transformed before my eyes. Instead of worrying over every wrinkle in her gown, she spins with reckless abandon, completely unaware of the filth marring the hem of her rose-pink skirt. Unbothered by the braids falling from their pins and sailing around her head like a windmill. She has never looked more radiant—free from courtly pressures and gossip.

"I love seeing you like this," I shout in her ear as we sashay through a tunnel of dancers.

"Not as much as your husband loves seeing *you* like this," she replies, looking me up and down with a wicked grin. "He can't take his eyes off you. I told you this gown was perfection."

I glance over at Alaric, who's been on a raised dais in the center of the square for the whole of the celebration, reassuring councilors and negotiating with merchants and entertaining courtiers. But finally, now, he's coming.

"Do you mind if I steal my wife for one dance?" Alaric's voice is as thick and rich as freshly tapped syrup, and I imagine it dripping down my body.

"Of course, Your Majesty," Elodie says with a playful curtsy. "She's all yours."

Alaric offers me his hand, eyes glittering brighter than the veins of silver in his mines. "It's been killing me to stand up there and watch you dance with everyone else," he murmurs in my ear.

"Maybe you should stop being such a patient, empathetic king," I say with a playful wink.

I rest my head against Alaric's chest and listen to the rhythm of his heart, calm and steady, as we sway beneath the blazing torches and glittering stars. One song bleeds into the next, and the musicians and dancers around us change, but I could stay here forever, locked in Alaric's embrace.

I'm so blissfully content, I yelp when someone taps my shoulder.

I shake my head and laugh as I pull away. "I suppose I shouldn't hog every dance with the king." But when I step aside, there's no new partner to take my place. Frowning, I turn to find Delphine standing with her head bowed, her new gown rumpled and torn.

"What's wrong? Are you hurt?" I take her hands and lift them to inspect her. "I told you you've been working too hard—"

"I'm sorry to interrupt," she chokes out, "but I need you now, Indira."

She looks up, her face stricken and pale. A look of unspeakable loss.

"Cloudia?" I whisper. "Is she…?"

I can't bring myself to say the word. She can't be dead. Not now, when we had plans to move her into the palace as soon as the healers situated the sick from the factory. Cloudia was finally going to receive proper care, and Delphine was going to have more time to sit at her sister's bedside.

"But she was doing better. "She was having more lucid moments. She led us to the hidden hospital!" I point out, like that somehow precludes her from dying.

"I'm afraid it's the end," Delphine whispers, "and I don't want to be alone."

"Let's go to her at once," Alaric agrees, pushing through the crowd. "I'm sure there's something more that can be done."

"*No!*" Delphine shouts so loud, the nearest revelers turn to stare. She steps nearer and lowers her shaking voice. "You can't leave your own coronation festivities. It would send the wrong message to the people. And if this is truly the end, I'd like it to be just the three of us—just family." Delphine's watery eyes find mine, and I feel my own eyes burning, with tears of empathy, of course. But also with gratitude—and love.

She considers me part of her family.

With Alaric's blessing, we weave through the crowded courtyard and pound down the twisting streets to their damp little cottage that smells of mold and sickness.

Delphine drops to her knees at Cloudia's bedside and strokes her sallow, sweaty face. The girl's entire body writhes and jerks as unintelligible words dribble from her lips.

"I've tried everything," Delphine says with a defeated

sigh. "I used the rest of the medication you made, along with every other remedy the healers ever prescribed, but they only seem to weaken her. She's slipping away, and there's nothing I can do to stop it."

Each of Delphine's cries tears through my heart like a blade, but I force myself to remain calm. We can't both fall apart.

"I'll make a new batch of medication," I say resolutely. "I'll use twice as much bagrava as before. That has to strengthen her."

It will also likely wreak havoc on her body and mind, since she isn't an empty vessel like those affected by the memory sacrifices. But there's no point worrying about long-term consequences when the next few minutes aren't guaranteed.

I move to the other side of the bed, lean down close, and speak in a slow, soothing voice. "Stay strong, Cloudia. I'm going to help you," I promise. But when I reach for her hand, she jerks violently. Her fingers close around my wrist, squeezing to the point of pain. I cry out and try to free myself, but Cloudia's other hand joins the fight, crushing my fingers in her vise grip.

"What are you doing?" Delphine reaches across her sister. "Stop this! You're hurting Indira."

As she struggles to remove her sister's clawlike fingers, I feel a familiar pulse of vibrating energy.

"Wait!" I shout, and instead of trying to pull away from

Cloudia, I place my hand on top of hers. The vibrations immediately intensify. "There's something in her hand," I tell Delphine. "Something that feels like the hum of a siphoned memory."

Delphine's eyes widen and dart down. "What's in your hand, Cloudia? Show us."

At last, Cloudia stops moaning and writhing and falls back to her pillow. She's so stiff and still, I start to fear we've lost her to oblivion, but then, finger by finger, her left hand uncurls to reveal a length of broken chain—the kind Vanzadorian men wear to fasten their jackets. This one is platinum and inlaid with enormous obsidian jewels, but the final link is bent and wrenched open.

"Do you recognize this?" I ask Delphine. "Is it a family heirloom or something?"

Delphine shakes her head. "Our family has never owned anything so fine."

"Then where did it come from? Could someone have given it to her?"

Again, Delphine shakes her head. "No one visits except me and the occasional friend who checks in when I'm working late. But none of us have riches like this." She studies the chain and glances around the room, bewildered. "Unless…" Delphine's gaze settles on a trunk in the corner. "That's where Cloudia keeps her sewing kit and tools. She often did alterations and embroidery work for the nobles. Maybe this is from one of her projects. Maybe she retrieved it because she wants me to sell it to cover the cost of her funeral. It's so like her to be thinking of me, even in her final moments," Delphine says on a shaky whisper.

It's a nice thought, but wholly improbable. "Won't the damage diminish its value? And how did Cloudia retrieve it from her sewing trunk when she can't rise from bed? What are the odds it would also contain a memory?"

Dread swells in my belly like black bloated roots in stagnant water as I point out each inconsistency. Something about Cloudia—and all of this—feels very, very wrong.

"I don't know, I don't know." Delphine wrings her hands through the bedclothes. We both sit there, staring down at the foreboding chain. "Do you think we should try to view the memory?" she eventually asks. "It feels like Cloudia's trying to tell us something."

Heart pounding, I nod, free the chain from Cloudia's slackened grip, and murmur the words Alaric taught me before I lose my nerve.

All at once, the room fills with glittering light, and I think I must be hallucinating because the swirls form a face I recognize. Eyes lips, freckles, and hair that could only belong to one person.

My sister.

THIRTY-NINE

"Rowenna?" I croak, reaching for her even though I know it's just a memory. But it's the closest I've come to seeing my sister alive in over a year, and every part of me screams to grab her. Hold her.

Save her.

She's running at full tilt, hair tangled across her face, features twisted with fury—or is that fear?—as she weaves through the darkened streets of the Fortress.

I dart a glance at Delphine. "What is this? Why would Cloudia have a memory of my sister? What is she running from?"

Delphine shakes her head, gaping at Rowenna's apparition.

My sister careens down a residential street, leaping over stone fences that separate each yard. The moon is high, and the houses are dark, but she peers over her shoulder every few seconds, as if someone is chasing her.

In one hand, she clutches a drawstring bag to her chest, and she fists her skirt with the other, gathering speed and gazing up with determination—like she plans to leap over something impossibly high.

Like the city wall?

Right before she jumps, a shadowed figure moves in her periphery.

She crashes into the wall and fumbles to steady herself. "*You!*" she cries. "H-how did you know? You're supposed to be—"

"I know everything." The shadowed figure cuts her off, and every hair on my arm rises because I *know* that voice. It's the same voice that whispered in my ear not ten minutes ago.

I watch in open-mouthed shock as Alaric materializes in the glittering haze, stepping out from a pool of shadow near the base of the Fortress wall. He looks so much darker, so much more sinister than the boy I just danced with—like the cruel, detached version of Alaric I met on the burning fields of Tashir. It's almost hard to believe they're the same person.

"I was aware of your plans as soon as you started making them," he says with a reproachful shake of his head. "You weren't exactly stealthy."

Ro makes little choking noises before setting her jaw

and lifting her chin. "I'm going home, and you can't stop me. I've seen the hospital. I know your dirty secrets. You have no future without Tashir, which means *I* now have the upper hand."

Alaric snorts. "We will *always* have the upper hand. Even with this new unfortunate sickness, you and your people will perish far faster. All I have to do is demolish the mountains and allow the Marauders to resume their attacks."

Rowenna takes a bold step forward. "What if I told you we don't need your protection anymore?" She holds up the drawstring sack and rattles the contents within.

It sounds like jangling coins.

Or rattling stones.

Alaric waves a dismissive hand. "You could have stuffed anything in there."

Rowenna continues swinging the bag back and forth. "When you're the smallest, weakest plant in a gardening bed, you have to grow twice as fast—and branch out in unexpected ways—to capture enough sunlight to thrive. So while you and Soren have been gloating in your superiority, ignoring me and the rest of your 'inconvenient problems,' I've been working myself near to death—down to my *blood, flesh, and bone*, you might say—to find a way to free my people. And I have."

Alaric's face goes pale as Rowenna rattles the bag again, her smile sharp and glinting.

My pulse beats against my temples, pounding so

hard my entire head aches. Could Rowenna really have found more pieces of the gemstone triad? Alaric insisted his father destroyed the larger pieces when the Flesh of Callahan was damaged. But what if he was lying?

What if he's been lying about other things?

Everything?

"Let's see, shall we?" Rowenna loosens the ties and overturns the bag.

My hand flies to my mouth as three small stones plunk into her palm. Red, pink, and white. A crimson ruby, an apricot diamond, and a sparkling white quartz—identical to the stones embedded in Alaric's wrist.

I want to drop the chain and stop the memory.

Alaric promised there were no more stones. Just like he promised he had nothing to do with my sister's death. And how he also claimed to know nothing about the makeshift hospital and people drained of their life essence. I was with him when we discovered the hospital; I saw the horror and disgust on his face. No one could be such a convincing liar.

Could they?

As if in answer, memory Alaric lunges for the stones in Rowenna's fist. He's as lithe and swift as a garden snake, fast enough to catch most opponents off guard.

But not Rowenna.

She dodges easily, slides the stones back into the pouch, and leaps up the Fortress wall.

I marvel at her strength, speed, and sheer brilliance as she scrabbles up the stones, creating handholds by driving two blades from her belt into the cracks.

Alaric tries to follow her, but he's sputtering and flustered, and even though he's stronger than Rowenna, he's also heavier—too heavy to support his body weight with just his fingertips.

She looks down at him as she swings one leg over the top of the wall. "You and your father are fools," she calls. "You brought a grain beetle into your storehouse and assumed I'd no longer eat wheat, that my appetites would change simply because you took me from my home. Then you ignored me and underestimated me, left me to poke around at my leisure, and now you're shocked to learn I stole your precious triad." She shakes her head and clucks her tongue. "I can't wait to see how lovely the stones look embedded in *my* wrist."

Rowenna holds out her arm as if inspecting a bracelet, and I want to shake her, shout at her for being just as reckless and arrogant. She needs to run and maintain her slight lead. Even then, it likely won't be enough. Alaric could level the wall with a snap of his fingers or snatch the earth out from beneath Rowenna's feet. This couldn't have been her entire escape plan.

"Embedding the stones in your own skin won't work," Alaric says through gritted teeth. "You're not a descendant of Callahan. The stones won't give you our power."

"I'd like to test that theory myself," Rowenna says as she swings her other leg over the wall and drops to the ground.

"Give me the gemstones, Rowenna!" Alaric roars after her. "If you cooperate, I'll convince my father to be merciful. Perhaps we can renegotiate the terms of the treaty."

"Except you no longer have anything to negotiate with," she calls back over her shoulder as she bounds down the moonlit path.

Alaric lets out an exasperated growl and raises both hands. A door-sized hole blasts through the city wall, and he shouts my sister's name again as he storms through the wreckage. "You know you can't outrun me. It's like trying to outrun the mountain itself!"

Rowenna glances back, finally looking properly scared.

She should be. I don't know how she ever thought this would work. She's smarter than this, more cunning than this.

With a wave of his hand, Alaric rips the frozen path out from beneath Rowenna's feet. She hits the ground with a painful grunt, looking from her bloody palms to Alaric. He strikes again before she can regroup, chipping away at the rock beneath her, forcing her closer and closer to the edge of the mountain until there's nowhere left to go.

Except down.

Ro doesn't beg or sob. She stares defiantly at Alaric. "Do it," she dares him. "It might be my end, but it will be yours as well. Mark my words."

Alaric leans forward, his face a hair's breadth from Rowenna's when he whispers, "Your words will never be marked. They'll be forgotten."

Then he clenches his fist, and the ledge Ro's standing on breaks away.

I scream and Rowenna does too—a horrible, discordant harmony. She claws the air, grasping for solid ground, and against all odds, her fingers snag on the chain of Alaric's waistcoat—the same obsidian-studded chain I hold in my hands now.

Ro stares at it hopefully, as if it might somehow save her.

But then the chain snaps, and my sister falls.

And all my hopes for the future plummet with her.

FORTY

HURL THE CHAIN ACROSS THE ROOM AND MELT TO the dirty floor of Delphine's home, crying so hard I can't breathe.

"What was *that*?" I gasp out, even though I know the answer. There's only one thing it can be.

The memory.

The truth I've been searching for since I arrived in Vanzador.

Except everything about it is *wrong*.

Or maybe *I've* been wrong all this time, and my initial fears and suspicions were right.

No.

There has to be another explanation. One that doesn't involve Alaric lying to my face from the second I arrived on the mountain. One that doesn't involve me falling in love with Rowenna's murderer. He never would have killed someone the same way his father killed Besnik. It would have destroyed him.

Delphine stumbles across the room and collapses at my side, tears spilling down her cheeks as she wraps me in a hug. "I'm so sorry, Indira. I hate that you had to see that. And that Alaric isn't who we thought he was. He fooled us all."

"Maybe it isn't true." I mean to say it with conviction, but my voice pitches up into a question, and Delphine's looking at me with so much pity, I have to squeeze my eyes shut.

I sink into the blackness of my mind, trying to calm my breathing as I sift through every interaction I've ever had with Alaric Alaverdi—from our wedding on the Tomb Flats to our fights in the solarium, from our visits to the mines to defending each other in the queen's salon, from our secret stolen moments in my bedchamber to dancing in his arms at our coronation—desperate for some sort of proof that it was real.

It *had* to be real.

I would have known if it was an act. I wouldn't have felt the things I felt. His explanations and excuses wouldn't have made so much sense. Alaric had nothing to do with Rowenna's death or the Vanzadorian people in that hospital. He was blindsided, like me. Used, just like me.

But then how can I explain the memory—this physical, indisputable truth?

Another sob rips through me, and a tiny part of me is grateful Rowenna died never knowing the full extent of my betrayal. Even from beyond the grave, she was trying to warn me and guide me, but I refused to listen. I chose a *boy* over my own sister.

"I'm sorry," I cry out, but of course she doesn't answer. Why would she when I gave up on her a long time ago?

"Did you know?" I look to Delphine. "Have you seen this memory before?"

She shakes her head, tears still flowing down her cheeks. "Of course not. I would have told you immediately."

"Where did the memory even come from? I don't understand how Cloudia has it. Or how it exists in the first place. Alaric would never have kept proof of his guilt."

"Unless he wanted to watch it back and revel in his triumph," Delphine points out.

"He isn't vindictive like that," I start to say, but I bite my tongue.

Why am I defending him? How can I possibly know what he would or wouldn't do when I clearly don't know him at all?

I drag my fingers through my hair, pulling to the point of pain. Then I look down at Cloudia, who's still staring blankly up at the ceiling, unable to answer a single question. Unaware she just shattered the framework of the life I've been building here.

"I obviously don't know anything for certain"—Delphine reaches out and moves a sweaty strand of hair away from my face—"but I think it's much more likely the memory was Rowenna's. Not Alaric's."

"But in order for the memory to be Rowenna's, she would have had to siphon it into the chain as she was falling."

Delphine nods. "You saw her expression in those final moments. You know how brave and determined she was. Rowenna wasn't going to let Alaric kill her *and* have the final word. This was her only chance to tell the truth about her death."

"But the broken chain was still attached to Alaric's jacket," I babble. "And he's familiar with the buzz of hidden memories. He would have felt it."

"Would he have?" Delphine asks contemplatively. "He was so furious. He'd just murdered his wife. I bet he ripped off the ruined jacket, stormed back to the palace, and tossed it in the laundry without noticing the faint buzz. Especially since he had no reason to believe Rowenna knew about siphoning memories. He never knew she followed him up the mountain and saw his memories. The coat must have been sent to Cloudia for cleaning and repairs. It all aligns."

I push up to my wobbly feet, needing to move, to think. "Except Alaric was so vehement he had nothing to do with Rowenna's death. You didn't see the look on his face."

"People lie all the time," Delphine says softly, "and liars can have beautiful eyes and soft lips." After a beat she adds, "Or maybe he doesn't know he's lying. He might honestly believe he's innocent. He could have purged the memory of killing Rowenna, assuming the truth about her death would die with her."

I feel like I'm going to vomit. I bend over, head between my knees, and take big gulps of air, but my heart continues pounding. The room is suddenly stifling—even hotter than the Tomb Flats. "He wouldn't do that. It's too similar to how Soren tried to manipulate him after Besnik's death."

"I don't want to believe it either, but you have to admit, it all fits," Delphine persists, and I can't argue because, now that I know what to look for, it's easy to see how Alaric used me to get everything he wanted. He must have tried to woo and manipulate Rowenna first, but she was too savvy and strong-willed to fall for his tricks. So he killed her and decided to try again with me—the weak, naïve sister.

Once Alaric had me in his pocket, he set his sights on Soren—to avenge Besnik and clear his path to the throne. And like a fool, I helped him carry out the perfect assassination, making Alaric look strong and capable while ruining Soren's legacy. Then I handed him the last thing he needed—the final piece of his elaborate scheme:

Unlimited access to bagrava.

If I offered it willingly, I wouldn't be able to accuse him of bleeding me and my people dry. If I loved him, I'd be too blinded by affection to notice that he never really looked for other means to fuel his power.

I grab fistfuls of my blue velvet skirt—this ridiculous Vanzadorian gown that was chosen with *him* in mind—and twist the fabric until my fingertips are bloodless and throbbing. My head still screams not to jump to conclusions. There could be other logical explanations. But I can't think of a single one, and my heart is too shattered to keep searching.

Alaric's deception is even worse than Soren's. At least Soren never pretended to be anything he wasn't. He knew his people were dying, he knew my people were suffering, but he believed the need for his power justified the cost. But Alaric pretended to be broken like me. He tricked me into believing he was truly invested in a new and different future.

It's just like what Rowenna said about grain beetles. I *knew* who Alaric was and what he's always wanted, but I convinced myself I was different. Special. That he'd change for me. But he didn't hesitate to strike as soon as the opportunity presented itself.

"What do we do now?" Delphine asks, unable to hide the tremor in her voice. "I'm scared."

I continue twisting my skirts, winding the fabric like

wet laundry. But instead of wringing out dirty water, I'm wringing out my feelings, purging every smile, laugh, and touch I ever shared with Alaric Alaverdi. Until my insides are as dry and desolate as the Tomb Flats. Until my heart is as cold and hard as stone.

Even harder than Alaric's.

"What do we do?" Delphine asks again. "We obviously can't voice these accusations. No one will believe us after we just helped Alaric take the throne. Especially since he's the only one with the ability to move the earth now. Vanzador needs him. So does Tashir."

"No," I say darkly. "We need a ruler with the ability to move the earth. That doesn't necessarily have to be Alaric."

It isn't lost on me that these are the same words I said to Alaric just a few days ago, to convince him to depose Soren.

"Rowenna showed us exactly what to do," I say. "We need to steal the gemstone triad, harness the power of the earth ourselves, and put an end to all of this corruption. The stones must work in other people's flesh, or Alaric wouldn't have chased Rowenna across the Fortress and hurled her off a cliff to get them back."

Delphine nods, but her fingers worry the embroidery on her bodice. "We don't even know if he recovered the gemstones from Rowenna. Or where they're hidden if he did. According to Alaric, they no longer exist."

"Thankfully, a perfectly good set is just waiting to be carved from his flesh," I say.

Delphine regards me with a searching, almost pitying expression. "You know you won't be able to simply carve the stones from his flesh, right? Are you prepared to—"

"Yes," I snap.

She continues staring, like she can see the infected thorn buried in my chest, but I set my jaw and raise my chin.

"I'm sure."

"Okay," she murmurs, but it sounds forced. Worried.

"You don't have to assist me with this part. You've already done more than enough. All I need you to do is pretend nothing is amiss. If Alaric realizes we know the truth about Rowenna's death, he'll try to silence us too. We need to say and do all the right things. Make Alaric believe we're still aligned. Then I'll strike when he least expects it."

Delphine nods and bids farewell to her sister—who continues lying deathly still—while I retrieve the broken length of chain and slip it into my bodice. It's cold and pointed, and I secretly like how it bites my skin, how it sharpens my focus, as we make our way back across the Fortress to celebrate the coronation of my sister's murderer.

FORTY-ONE

ALARIC SPOTS ME AS SOON AS WE RETURN TO THE crowded square, as if he'd been waiting like a lost, lonely puppy.

Less than an hour ago, this would have sent a thrill zinging through my chest. He's the most magnificent person on this mountain, the king of this great nation, and he's looking for *me*. Less than an hour ago, I would have darted through the crowd, folded myself into his arms, and shared my worries and fears about Cloudia's condition.

But less than an hour ago, I was a fool.

Now, rage crackles through me like lightning at the sight of him. I want to bluster through the crowd and rain down vengeance on my husband. But I force myself to meet Alaric's gaze and even muster a wave as Delphine and I make our way toward him.

"How's Cloudia?" he asks, glancing between Delphine and me, looking so genuinely concerned I could slap him.

"Still alive—for now," I say. "We were able to stabilize her."

"Thank the kings." Alaric cups my face in his hands, regarding me as if the sun itself shines through my eyes. "You're amazing, you know that?"

His gaze slides down to my lips, and despite all his lies, despite the harrowing memory of Rowenna's death emblazoned on my brain, my traitorous heart still flutters.

It's all an act, I sternly remind myself. But my body doesn't want to believe it. It leans closer to him, like a plant following the sun, craving his light and warmth.

Delphine loudly clears her throat, and I flinch back.

"Thank you for letting me steal Indira during your big celebration," Delphine says to Alaric. "It was most kind."

"You know I'd do anything to help you or your sister. Is Cloudia coherent? Did she say anything more?"

On the surface, Alaric's questions seem innocent. He cares for Delphine and me, so of course he'd care for Cloudia too. Especially when her previous mutterings proved so helpful. But I find myself analyzing his curiosity, picking apart his tone and expression. Is he too eager? Is he genuinely curious, or is he probing to see how much I know? I don't think Alaric could possibly know that Cloudia found the memory of Rowenna's death—assuming he knows the memory exists at all—but at this point, nothing would surprise me. He could be responsible for Cloudia's strange sickness for all I know. It could be his way of keeping her quiet.

"Sadly, Cloudia didn't speak," Delphine says when it becomes clear I'm not going to. "But she's resting peacefully again."

"Good," Alaric says, and I might be imagining it, but I swear his shoulders slacken. Whether that's because he's truly glad, or if he's just relieved his secret's safe, there's no telling.

I squeeze my eyes shut, so frustrated and terrified, I want to run back to the palace, cover my head with my pillow, and forget all of this. I want to purge every moment since I arrived on the mountain.

But that's exactly what the courtiers do, and I refuse to be like them. I refuse to forget the past just because it's difficult or inconvenient or, in my case, proves how wrong I was. How badly I betrayed my sister.

Alaric drapes his arm over my shoulders, enveloping me in the spicy scent I used to find so intoxicating. Now it just makes me nauseous.

"Shall we dance?" He gestures to the revelers. "You look like you could use a distraction. Visiting Cloudia clearly upset you."

I hate how well he knows me, how easily he reads me, when I know nothing about him. But most of all, I hate my body's reaction to him. Despite everything, it still wants to be swept up in his traitorous arms.

"Are you feeling all right?" Alaric murmurs as he spins us in a slow circle. "You seem distracted. Or upset."

I shake my head—perhaps too fast—because Alaric raises a brow.

"It's nothing." I force my lips to smile while inwardly berating myself. Alaric has been deceiving me for weeks. Surely, I can pretend everything's normal for a single dance? "I'm just tired," I continue. "It's hard to see Cloudia so ill and Delphine so worried."

Alaric's frown deepens. "What about *you*? How *are you* feeling? You're so pale. And we still don't know what's ailing Cloudia. I'd hate for you to catch her illness."

Or uncover her memories, I think darkly.

But I say, "I'll be fine." Then I broaden my smile, kick up my heels, and pretend everything's perfect. When the song ends, though, Alaric is still considering me with a frown.

"You know you can talk to me about anything," he offers. "I *want* you to talk to me about everything, especially if something's bothering you."

He always says the right things, knows precisely when to flash his smoldering smile to bend people to his will. And since I'm apparently incapable of hiding my emotions from this man, I decide to tell him the truth—at least a portion of it.

"I'm just missing Rowenna. I wish she could be here to see everything we've accomplished and take part in the victory."

I carefully watch Alaric for a slip in his composure—for a twinge of panic or remorse at my sister's name. But there's nothing.

He truly remembers nothing.

Which means it's time to remind him.

─── ✑ ───

Three days later, Alaric stands at the head of my planting beds in our solarium, admiring the mature crop of bagrava I've been tending night and day since the moment I left the coronation festival.

"It's so beautiful," he says with hushed reverence.

I nod because it's true. The yield is almost flawless: thick green stalks, as tall as my waist; bright indigo flowers, softer than velvet; and delicate serrated leaves, sharp as a razor.

It's as fine a crop as any I've grown in Tashir, not due to perfect growing conditions, but because I've spent every minute of the past three days coddling the seedlings. Anything to speed the process along so I don't have to stay on this mountain a second longer than necessary.

Anything to avoid Alaric.

The less time I spend with him, the less likely I am to get re-ensnared by his calculated charm and devastating beauty.

Thankfully, growing bagrava for the sick has been the

perfect excuse. Every time he's come to talk, I remind him bagrava needs silence. Every time he tries to take my hand and lure me away for a stolen moment, I remind him the crop could wilt if I step away. As king and queen, we have to put the well-being of our people above our own desires.

If I'm honest, the bagrava has always been my excuse—even back in Tashir. Tending plants has always been easier than cultivating relationships. Keeping my head down and my hands in the dirt always yielded better results than sticking my nose in political matters where it didn't belong. I have no business trying to lead. I'm as pathetic and useless as my father. The one time I decided to trust my own judgment and rely on other people, I ended up aligning with Rowenna's killer.

What about Delphine? a tiny voice cries from the rotten, soggy compost of my heart. *And Elodie? You don't have to cut them all out.*

But I do. I've been keeping both girls at an arm's length since the celebration—declining Elodie's invitations and being purposely vague with Delphine about the next steps of my plan to steal Alaric's gemstones. I have to protect them.

If I fail, I'll fail alone.

"How many people will this treat?" Alaric asks, bringing me back to the solarium. "Can we reseed these planters immediately? I'd like to see if we can give the sick more than a few hours of relief each day."

Each question makes my hackles rise higher, and I barely stop myself from slapping his hand away when he strokes a rounded bagrava fruit. Now that I'm no longer blinded by his charming smile and clever lies, I can't believe how transparent he is, how I didn't see through his act.

I reach for the reaping scythe propped against the wall, more than a little tempted to swing it at his neck and take my vengeance immediately, but, since I'd never make it out of the Fortress covered in his blood, I lop off an entire row of bagrava with one artful swing and flash a sweet smile over my shoulder instead.

"The first thing we need to do is process the bagrava to preserve its potency. Then I can churn the beds and replant. I'm sure I can cultivate enough to experiment with the dosages—especially if it's combined with the tributes my people send."

"Can't we just take the crop straight to the healers?" Alaric asks with a frown. "Why process it if it doesn't have to be transported across the Tomb Flats?"

"The fruit can be used right away, but the leaves and flowers must be pressed and baled in damp conditions to help the cuttings retain moisture. Otherwise, they'll quickly lose potency."

Lies. All of it. The leaves and flowers are useless, but Alaric doesn't know that.

"I didn't realize the cuttings could be used in addition

to the fruit," Alaric muses. "You've never sent them as tribute."

I shrug. "Your father only demanded the fruit. So that's what we sent. But now that we're truly unified, I'm willing to give everything we have to offer."

More lies. I just need an excuse to get Alaric away from the palace and his guards. Somewhere remote and secluded—like the mountaintop where Soren died. It seems fitting both father and son should face their reckoning there.

Alaric glances around the blindingly bright solarium and frowns. "Damp conditions will be difficult to find. The air in the palace is drier than a bone from all the hearth fires."

"That *is* a problem." I furrow my brow and pretend to think hard. "What about the caves up the mountain? They are spacious and damp, and no one will disturb us there," I say, as if the idea just occurred to me.

Alaric peers out the window, at the pelting wind buffeting the cliffs with snow. "It will be a difficult hike, especially carrying all of this bagrava, but if you think it's best…"

"I do." I bend over and begin gathering the sheaves into my arms.

"You want to go *now*?" Alaric asks. "In this weather?"

"The sooner the better. The sick are counting on us. We can't let a little snow slow us down."

Alaric blows out a breath and helps me gather the cuttings. Every few minutes, I catch him looking between me and the bagrava with the same perplexed expression he wore during our dance at his coronation—and every time he's visited me here. I know he senses a shift, but he can't pinpoint what it is because I've been careful not to say or do anything that would make him think I've lost faith in our plans—or each other.

As Alaric is packing the last of the bagrava cuttings into satchels, Delphine bustles into the solarium.

"What's all this? Can I help?" She takes several packs from the pile near my feet, and I'm too surprised to stop her.

"What are you doing here?" I ask in a panic. "? I thought the queen mother needed your help preparing the ballroom for the gala tomorrow?"

I'm the one who whispered the idea in the queen's ear, insisting she should host an event of her own, to personally prove her loyalty to her son over her husband. It was absurd, given the coronation festivities just ended, but of course Queen Tessa jumped at the chance to host a party of her own and nodded eagerly at my suggestion to let Delphine help. I needed to ensure she and the rest of the palace staff were busy and distracted.

Yet here she is, pulling another bag of bagrava over her shoulder and refusing to meet my eyes.

"Elodie offered to take over the party planning. She

was very excited about some feathers she planned to use in the centerpieces." Delphine rolls her eyes. "So I thought I'd see if I could be of use here. What exactly are we doing?""

"Great," Alaric says, handing her another sack, "we're going up the mountain to process this bagrava."

"Which is really only a two-person job," I interject.

Alaric's brow crumples with confusion, but I pretend not to notice. Just as Delphine pretends not to notice my insistent stare.

She knows me so well. She must have suspected I'd have something planned. Something she can't have anything to do with.

I can't outright tell her she can't come. It would instantly raise Alaric's suspicion. So, even though I'm screaming on the inside, I have no choice but to swallow my frustration and follow them out of the palace.

Delphine leads the way up the frosty switchbacks, followed by Alaric, with me at the rear. I wanted to lead, but Delphine refused. I'm certain it's to stop me from sending her away or demanding to know what she's doing here, when I tried so hard to shield her from this part of my plan.

The wind is hellacious, stealing each breath as it ghosts from my lips. I'm shivering as much as I did when I first arrived on the mountain, despite being the only one wearing a cloak. I have a feeling I'd be shivering right now even if it was as scorching hot as summer on the Tomb Flats.

When we finally reach the caves, I set Alaric with

the meticulous task of laying the bagrava cuttings out in an intricate, and wholly needless, pattern, while I snatch Delphine's wrist and pull her to her knees beside me, so it looks like we're discussing the satchels.

"What are you doing here?" I ask.

I know you're up to something, and I can't let you do it by yourself," she says resolutely.

"But what if something goes wrong? Who will care for Cloudia? It's not too late to go back. I'll think of an excuse."

"Indira." Delphine places her calloused hand over mine and looks me straight in the eyes. "I have to be here."

The surge of love and gratitude I feel for her almost brings me to tears. Having her here complicates everything, and I hate that she's putting herself at so much risk, but I'm undeniably grateful.

We get to work, helping Alaric spread the bagrava across the cave floor, conveniently sending him deeper and deeper, until the ceiling is too low to stand. Until there's no escape—except through the rocks themselves.

Alaric brushes off his hands, looking across his handiwork with a pleased smile. "What's next?" Before, I would have considered his enthusiasm endearing. Now, all I can see is the obvious pleasure he's taking in this. How clever he thinks he is.

I dart a sideways glance at Delphine, and, together, we move forward, cornering Alaric in the narrowing space.

"*Now*, you're going to tell me the truth about what

happened to my sister," I say, purposely grinding a purple bloom beneath my boot.

Alaric frowns at the ruined flower, then at me, sputtering with disbelief. "What are you doing? What are you talking about?"

I bend over and remove a knife from my boot—which I stole from dinner the night before—and level the blade at Alaric's chest. "I'm going to give you one more opportunity to tell me the truth about what happened to Rowenna. What I do after that depends on your answer."

A burst of incredulous laughter escapes him. When I fail to lower the knife, an awkward silence settles between us. "You're serious?" He blinks at me with confusion and something akin to grief. But I won't fall for his sad-eyed act this time. He clears his throat and folds his arms. "Why are you bringing this up again? You know I had nothing to do with Rowenna's death."

I give a terse shake of my head. "I know nothing of the sort."

He turns to Delphine. "Tell her she's being ridiculous." When Delphine says nothing, he laughs again, only now it's bitter. Broken. "I've been honest from the start. I told you everything I know. I-I thought we we're friends—allies. So much more than that."

He looks directly at me as he says the last part, and waves of longing and loss roll through me. The knife wobbles in my grip.

"I know we love each other," Alaric continues. "Or at least, I love you..." He pauses, clearly waiting for me to bare my feelings, but I don't have any. Not anymore. My heart has been turned to stone just like the layers of sediment pressed together over thousands of years to form this mountain.

I shake my head. "You've only ever cared about what you can get from me. You used me to get rid of your father, win over the council, and get unfettered access to bagrava. You're just like Soren. Worse, even! At least he didn't pretend to love me."

Alaric's eyes are big and round with hurt—as if he's actually capable of feeling emotions. "Where is this coming from? What in the name of the kings are you talking about?" His voice rises with each word. "I thought we moved past all this."

"We only 'moved past' Ro's death because you assumed the truth died with her, but I found this." I hold out my hand and unfurl the chain, letting it dangle from my fingertips.

Alaric squints at the spinning platinum. "What does a chain have to do with anything?"

I step closer, hold the chain higher. "This is *your* chain, from the waistcoat *you* wore the day you murdered my sister. Rowenna siphoned the memory into the chain in her final moments. Then the garment was sent to Cloudia for repair after you returned to the palace. She accidentally discovered the truth." I wave the chain again. "Did Cloudia confront you about it? Is that the real reason she's deathly ill? Did you induce some kind of sickness to keep her silent?"

"*No!*" Alaric shouts. "What are you talking about? I haven't made anyone ill. That isn't even possible. And Rowenna couldn't have siphoned the memory of her death into that chain because *I didn't murder her.* I've never even seen that chain!"

I prowl closer, both arms extended—one holding the chain, the other the knife. "Just because you don't remember killing Rowenna, doesn't mean you didn't do it. We both know how easy it is to *forget* things on this mountain."

Alaric vehemently shakes his head and steps back, but there's nowhere to go. The cave has grown so low and narrow, his arms easily span both walls, fingertips digging into the wet rock. It occurs to me he could bring it all crashing down on our heads. He could silence Delphine and me and these accusations forever, but the walls don't tremble in the slightest.

Alaric lets out an exhausted sigh. "You *know* me, Indira. You *know* I'd never do any of that."

His words slice through me like a dagger, because I *did* believe I knew him. And I thought he knew me—*loved* me, even.

"That's not to say I don't believe *you*," Alaric hurries

to add. "I'm not diminishing your experience—or what Cloudia believes she found," he says to Delphine. "I have no doubt you've seen something terribly upsetting. But there has to be another explanation. I didn't do this."

"Then where did this memory come from?" I demand, waving the chain in his face.

Alaric reaches for it. "Let me see the memory, and we can figure that out."

I snatch the chain back with a laugh. "Do you really think I'm going to hand over the only proof of your crime?"

"I haven't committed a crime!" he bellows. When I flinch, he does, too, holding his hands up as he looks between Delphine and me. "If you don't trust me with the memory, call it forth yourself. At least let me see what you're accusing me of and give me a chance to explain. Cloudia is sick. Maybe the 'memory' is a hallucination."

"Like the 'hallucination' of a warehouse full of dying Vanzadorians?" Delphine retorts.

Alaric groans with frustration. "Someone is setting me up. It's the only explanation. My father's most loyal councilors are still reeling from his death. Maybe they planted a false memory to incriminate me and—"

"Have they planted false memories before?" I interrupt. "Is that even possible?"

"Not that I know of," Alaric says miserably. "Look, I know I've made mistakes. I'm not claiming to be innocent by any means. But I do know I didn't do *that*." He gestures to the chain. "If you ever felt anything for me, Indira, please, let me see my supposed crime before you execute me for it."

Alaric reaches out again, eyes locked with mine, willing me to coil the chain in his palm. And I almost do. The foolish, lovesick part of me still wants to believe this is just a terrible misunderstanding and everything we've said and felt and accomplished together was real.

But then I think of my sister's face as the ledge crumbled, of her hands grasping wildly for purchase, and I lunge, slashing my blade toward the tender flesh of Alaric Alaverdi's throat.

FORTY-TWO

SQUEEZE MY EYES SHUT AND WAIT FOR THE KNIFE TO glide through flesh. For blood to pour over my fingers. But Alaric is too quick.

He ducks, and the blade slams into the cave wall instead. Delphine's scream is almost as loud as the metallic clang.

Shock waves judder up my arm as sparks fly through the darkness, illuminating Alaric's horrified expression.

"You actually tried to kill me!" he shouts.

"It's what you deserve," I cry, slashing sideways.

This time, my knife tears through Alaric's waistcoat, narrowly missing his side. He clutches the shred of velvet with a shaky hand and looks at me aghast. "Please, Indira! This is madness!"

"No, this is retribution," I growl through my tears, which makes me even madder. I shouldn't be crying. The boy I'm mourning never existed. It was all a lie. An act. "You let me trust you!" I slash again. "Made me believe you cared for me and the future of my people! And your people too! You're no better than your father. You *knew* about the sick people in that warehouse and did nothing to help them!" Another slash. "You listened to me grieve for Rowenna and pretended to know the same sorrow when you were responsible for her death all along!"

"What are you talking about?" Alaric explodes. "I *do* care about both of our people! I knew nothing about the sick in that warehouse until I stepped through the door alongside you, and I am not, in any way, responsible for Rowenna's death. You *know* this. You know *me*."

"It's impossible to truly know anyone on this mountain when the truth can be forgotten and rewritten at will," I say, readjusting my grip on the knife.

The look of utter heartbreak that crosses Alaric's face steals my breath. I didn't know it was possible for my chest to hurt this much. I feel like I'm trapped underwater, lungs screaming, but I can't rise to the surface and save myself because *he* was the source of my air.

"Delphine." Alaric turns to my maid with wild, pleading eyes. "Help me. She'll listen to you."

Delphine shakes her head, and Alaric lets out a pitiful, gut-wrenching sob.

"Stop trying to manipulate me!" I shriek. "I'm so sick of everyone using me!"

I swing my blade again, and sparks dance around us like fireflies as I drive Alaric back, my blade striking stone with each erratic swing.

Bang, bang, bang.

Flash, flash, flash.

The ceiling pitches lower, and the walls press closer until there's nowhere left for Alaric to go. He drops to the ground and curls in on himself like a dead beetle, which makes me even more incensed.

"Why won't you fight back?" I yell. "Why won't you move the earth to protect yourself?"

"You know why." Alaric's frantic eyes soften when they lock with mine, and it feels like I've been kicked in the stomach and skewered through the heart all at once.

"Stop saying things like that! We both know you won't fight back because you think I'm weak and pathetic. You don't believe I'll kill you, even as I'm in the act of doing it!"

"Fire!" Alaric shouts, and I think he's goading me until Delphine says it too and points over my shoulder.

"Indira, the bagrava is on fire!"

That's when I notice the wisps of purple smoke swirling around my feet. When I realize the oppressive heat at my back is fueled by more than just my rage.

Flames fill the front half of the cavern—where my blade first struck stone—and they're burning hungrily toward us, devouring the bagrava we laid out in a convenient pathway. I thank Earth Mother the smoke from this part of the plant isn't noxious as it billows around us, invading our eyes, noses, and mouths, The last thing I need right now is to lose my senses.

"Indira!" Delphine cries, spinning frantically. "What do we do?"

I scan the cave for branching tunnels that might lead to another entrance. I study the walls and floor for crevasses that might be deep enough to take cover in. But if there's a place to take shelter from the inferno, I can't see it through the thickening haze. My lungs feel coated in soot, and my vision swims. When I try to scream, I'm gripped by a pummeling cough.

It's one thing for Alaric and me to perish in this cave—the final battle of the war our people have been waging for years—but Delphine doesn't deserve to die like this. She wasn't supposed to be here at all.

I cough into my cloak, and it gives me an idea. Yanking the ties loose, I drop to my knees and spread the fabric out across the damp rocks, pressing it into the little puddles until it's heavy with water. Then I lift it up and swing the cloak over Delphine's head and shoulders.

"Run!" I tell her. "Go back the way we came in. You might get a few burns on your legs, but the wet cloak should shield you from the worst of it."

"What about you?" she yells. We both look down at the dripping cloak. The only one we have, since Delphine and Alaric are accustomed to the cold.

"If I have to burn alive, at least he'll die with me." I nod back at Alaric, still curled into a trembling ball. "And Rowenna will be avenged."

And I'll finally be with her, I realize. The thing I've wanted most since the Vanzadorians returned her in that box.

I close my eyes and try to picture our reunion in the Great Fields Beyond, but the image is blurred and distorted, making it impossible to tell if I'm dissolving into her embrace or shoving her away. I'm still so furious about her lies and deception—how she manipulated and controlled me—but she isn't the only one who lied to me. And I know, deep down, everything she did was out of love. She was fighting for Tashir and me in the only way she knew how. We'll have eternity to mend what was broken and find our way back to each other.

"I won't leave you," Delphine says.

"You have to. Think of Cloudia."

Her eyes well with tears. She holds my gaze for a few excruciating seconds then says, "I'm so sorry, Indira. I wish I could go back and do so many things differently. You weren't supposed to be so—"

"*Go!*" I shove her toward the fire.

With a ragged cry, Delphine stumbles forward, screaming as she runs through the smoke and flames.

I send a prayer up to Earth Mother, begging her to protect my friend. Then I wipe my tears on my wrist and return my attention to Alaric, who's still lying on the ground, shielding his face with his arm.

"Are you going to confess before we die?" I shout over the crackle and whoosh of the fire.

"I have nothing to confess—other than my love for you," he chokes out.

It's so sappy and ridiculous, I scream, "Stop it! Just stop with all of these lies and games, and let me die in peace."

I drop to the ground and lie on my back—making the cave my makeshift funeral pyre.

"What are you *doing*?" Alaric finally gets up and stomps over, yanking me up by my arm.

"What does it look like I'm doing?" I strain against his grip, waving the knife wildly behind me, cursing this infuriating boy who is always complicating everything. "I'd rather die than be part of your tyranny!"

Alaric wrestles the knife from my grip and tucks it into his belt. Then he clutches me tight against his chest. The sweat dripping down my back fuses with his sweat-soaked jacket, cementing us together.

"What are you talking about?" His breath is hot against my ear, even hotter than the fire. "*You're* the one who turned on *me*, remember?"

"Only because you betrayed me first!"

"I never betrayed you!" Alaric tries to yell, but he's gripped by a violent cough. "Give me the chain, and I'll get us out of here," he rasps.

I shake my head. "I'd rather perish."

"No, you wouldn't. The bagrava smoke is clearly addling your senses."

"The cuttings don't induce hallucinations. They have no magical properties at all!"

Alaric lets out a bewildered laugh that sounds more like a cry. "Please, Indira. You know I deserve to see the memory." He slides his hand down my arm, grasping for the chain, but his fingers are too slick with sweat to pry mine apart.

"The only thing you deserve is a painful death," I snarl over my shoulder.

I expect him to hurl equally ugly words back at me, but his voice is unexpectedly gentle when he says, "What about you? What do *you* deserve, Indira? Is dying for vengeance really what Rowenna would have wanted for you when you could choose to live for something greater?"

I laugh at his audacity. "Rowenna would never consider an alliance with her murderer *something greater*."

"What do *you* think? What do *you* believe? Aren't you ready to trust your own instincts and choices? Don't you want to live your own life instead of skulking around in Rowenna's shadow? It's okay to choose yourself. To choose to live. To choose *me*," he adds, whisper soft.

I open my mouth to argue, but the smoke strangles me. At least I tell myself it's the smoke. The burning in my eyes and chest can't be tears. I have no reason to cry, because

Alaric's wrong. I will never have to choose between my sister and myself because we are two halves of the same whole. Rowenna's cause *is* my cause. She came here and sacrificed everything, trusting I would pick up the pieces, so that's exactly what I'm going to do.

It's what I *want* to do.

I may have gotten caught up in a few distractions along the way, but I will always choose her—choose *us*—over everything else.

Alaric will never accept this, though, so I show him what he wants to see—deceiving him how he deceived me.

Summoning my best, most anguished whimper, I melt into him and finally open my shaking fingers. This time, when Alaric reaches for the chain, I let him take it.

As soon as he has the memory, Alaric tucks me against his chest and tears a hole in the back of the cave.

It isn't smooth and seamless, like the first time I followed him to his hidden memory grove. Nor is it perfectly controlled, like when he opened the new mine shaft. This is a bloody gash, ripped open by ravenous claws. I swear I can *feel* the earth shudder with pain as we tumble through stone and sediment. I scream and brace for debris to pummel me. Crush me. But Alaric shields me with his body, bearing the brunt of the violent collapse.

We tumble out into the frigid dark of the mountaintop, retching and coughing, flames still dancing in my eyes. We lie there, gulping back the clean air, until Alaric says in a scratchy voice, "For a second there, I thought you were really going to choose the fire."

"Me too," I say, which makes him chuckle, even though I have never been more serious.

Alaric rolls onto his side, staring at me so adamantly, so fondly, my skin begins to prickle again. I sit up and look away. If I don't keep my traitorous body in check, I won't be able to do what needs to be done next.

"I'm still not convinced I made the right choice," I say archly, and Alaric's expression immediately sobers.

"Thank you for giving me this chance. I know it wasn't easy, given what you've seen—what you think I've done. But I'm sure I'll be able to explain after I've seen the memory."

"I hope so," I say, even though I have no intention of listening to any of his convoluted explanations.

Alaric gets to his knees and holds the chain across his open palm. "Do you want to watch it with me?"

I don't even have to force the shiver that overtakes me. "No, I don't want to watch my sister die again. I'll wait over there," I point to a boulder behind Alaric.

"Of course." He watches with a patient smile until I'm out of sight.

I press my back against the cold rock and count each thunderous heartbeat, waiting for the golden light to appear. When it finally blooms around the edges of the boulder, it reminds me of the sun rising over these peaks—gorgeous and glittering, like the dawning of a new day. Which feels appropriate since this will be the dawning of a new era.

As soon as I hear the far-off strains of Rowenna's voice, I palm my knife, which I easily snatched back from Alaric's belt while he saved me from the collapsing cave—then I slip soundlessly out from behind the boulder and slink toward Alaric's kneeling form.

He looks as small as he did when Delphine and I caught him replaying Besnik's death. Like a scared little boy, not a murderer. Thankfully, the golden memory is the perfect reminder.

My eyes catch on Rowenna's face, and I'm torn between wanting to watch it all to strengthen my resolve and the very real fear I might not survive the heartbreak of experiencing her final moments again.

In the end, I look away and focus on the knife in my palm and the rage in my heart as I pad through the scree. When I'm less than a length away, Alaric flinches and lets out a curse, and I silently scream.

My ragged breath and thumping heart must have given me away. He's going to whirl around and catch me stalking him like a mountain lion. He'll sweep the ground out from under me and kill me like Rowenna. But several seconds pass, and instead of looking back, Alaric leans forward—further into the memory.

I let out a shaky breath and position myself directly

behind him, close enough to feel the warmth of his body and the subtle shake of his shoulders. Close enough to hear burbles escape his throat—almost as if he's crying.

For half a second, I allow myself to believe they're tears of regret. He knows the bone-deep pain of losing a sibling and killed my sister anyway. But then I gaze into the golden scene and see the vicious expression on memory Alaric's face as Rowenna empties the gemstone triad into her hand, and my resolve hardens. Hatred burns like coals in his eyes. His face twists into a cruel smile, reminding me that any regret Alaric feels in this moment is only for himself—because I uncovered his treachery and beat him at his own game.

It's the final push I need.

As memory Alaric raises his hand to rip the ground out from under my sister, I raise my knife, take a breath, and howl Rowenna's name as I plunge the blade into his back.

FORTY-THREE

ALARIC HEAVES FORWARD WITH A WET, GUTTURAL cry, and the chain slips from his hands as he collapses. The golden glimmer of the past dissolves, leaving us in total darkness, but not even the black mountain sky can conceal the deep red stain spreading through his jacket and snaking down his sides.

It's horrifying and mesmerizing. It doesn't seem possible one body could hold so much blood. As it soaks into the ground, I wait for vindication and relief to wash over me. For feelings of pride and victory to raise me up above the carnage. But it feels like my insides have been scraped out with a rusted trowel. Which doesn't make sense.

I won. Alaric had every advantage—including the power of the earth—but I emerged victorious. *I* struck first, before he could strike me.

And that, right there, is the problem, I realize.

Alaric didn't strike at all. He never tried to defend himself.

"Are you really going to just lie there and accept defeat?" I shout, kicking dust at his face.

With an agonized grunt, Alaric raises his arm.

I scramble back, waiting for the ground to shift, for the battle to truly commence. But the earth remains still. Hauntingly so.

"Take them," Alaric begs, arm still raised.

I narrow my eyes and take another step back. "Take what?"

He overturns his wrist. "The gemstones. That's what you're after, right? Pull the knife from my back and use it to cut them out. I don't know if the power will transfer to someone not of Callahan's bloodline, but you have to try. It's the only way to maintain the mountain range and protect your people. I just ask you to think of my people too. They didn't know any better. I thought a small part of you was beginning to care for them," he adds, his voice rough and wet.

A sour lump rises in my throat because, despite years of lies and exploitation, I *do* care for the Vanzadorians. Not their rulers, obviously, but the people themselves: the shopkeepers and courtiers, who danced in the square during the coronation; the miners, who smiled with awe and gratitude when they saw goblin's gold; and brave girls like Delphine and Elodie, who helped me time and again, despite the danger. When they had no reason to do so. When Rowenna gave them every reason *not* to trust or befriend me.

I want to help them. I *will* help them. And the first way I'll do so is by removing this boy—who's been lying, manipulating, and misusing their memories, just like his father—from the throne.

I stare down at the ruby, diamond, and quartz embedded in Alaric's flesh. Three shiny berries, ripe for the picking. Yet, for some reason, my hand refuses to move.

I already stabbed him in the back. Cutting the gemstones from his wrist will hardly injure him more. But taking them doesn't feel right. Not when he's just lying there, offering them.

This was supposed to be a battle. I was supposed to be fighting for my life and country. Not stomping on a flower already snapped off at the stem.

"Fight me!" I scream down at Alaric. "Defend yourself!"

He chuckles, low and rattling. "How can I defend against a piece of my own heart?"

"Don't say things like that. You don't truly feel that way about me."

"Don't tell me how I feel," Alaric volleys back with surprising vehemence. The effort makes him collapse to his side, and he lowers his head into the puddle of gore seeping out around him—so red it's nearly black.

In an almost inaudible whisper, he says, "Cut the gemstones out, or cut off my arm entirely. It doesn't matter. It couldn't hurt more than it already does."

Tears fill his beautiful, infuriating eyes, and the way he's staring up at me—with so much love and anguish, with so much admiration and disappointment—it's clear he's not only referring to the pain in his back.

My throat clogs with emotion, and for a moment I am frozen. Torn.

"If you won't cut them out, I will." With a painful wince, Alaric pushes up onto one elbow and reaches back with his other hand. Little flecks of blood wet his lips as he stretches and strains, panting with effort.

I watch him struggle in rapt horror, certain he won't be able to free the knife. He's too weak. The angle's too awkward. But once again Alaric proves me wrong. With an anguished cry, he pries the blade free, unleashing a gush of even darker, faster-flowing blood.

Before my mind can process what my body's doing, I lunge forward and knock the bloody knife from his grip.

"What are you *doing*?" he roars with frustration. "This is what you wanted! What you planned! Finish the job."

His fingers grapple for the knife, but it landed just out of reach. And the effort of freeing it took the last of his strength. He collapses into the spreading puddle of blood.

"Please, Indira. Do me this last kindness. Carve the

gemstones out and end my suffering. I don't have long, and their power could be affected if you wait until I'm dead."

My eyes dart between my husband and the blade on the ground.

"Do it," Alaric says again. "Make all of this mean something."

Now I'm crying. Sobbing. Covered in his blood.

Do it, the logical part of my mind orders.

"Do it!" Rowenna roars.

She sounds so close, like she's standing right behind me, and I've never been so glad to hear her voice. I've finally earned her forgiveness.

I press the blade against the soft underside of Alaric's wrist, angled toward the stones. Red as blood, pink as flesh, and white as bone.

"Now, Indira!" Rowenna bellows, and the strangest thing happens.

Alaric stiffens and turns his head.

And my entire world goes still.

Because, somehow, impossibly, he heard Rowenna too.

FORTY-FOUR

I WHIRL AROUND, CERTAIN I'M HALLUCINATING. I have to be.

"Ro?" I whisper, blinking furiously. I must have been wrong about the bagrava cuttings. Clearly their smoke can addle your mind. It's the only way I could be watching my dead sister stride across the mountaintop when I know for a fact her body's decomposing beneath the fields of Tashir.

I shake my head and close my eyes, but when I open them, she's still there—a specter made of moonlight and shadow, prowling closer. She's paler and thinner than I remember, with eyes as dark as charcoal and tattered clothes hanging from her bony frame. The biggest difference, though, is in the way she moves. Instead of long confident strides, her gait is jerking and off-kilter, like a scarecrow come to life.

Or a corpse, risen from the grave.

"Y-you've returned from the Great Fields Beyond to punish me, haven't you?" I whisper. "B-because I stopped listening. I'm sorry I was so foolish—"

Alaric's disbelieving laughter cuts me off—wet and chilling as if his throat is filling with blood. Though, still not as chilling as what he says next. "The only place your sister has returned from is the hovel she's been hiding in these past months. Now do you *finally* believe I didn't kill her?" Alaric looks at me sadly and shakes his head.

My mouth falls open as I look between Alaric and my sister's ghost. "You can see her too?"

I've never heard of two people sharing the same bagrava-induced hallucination. The Marauders move in packs, but they only look out for themselves and their own needs. But the smoke in the cave was so thick, so choking. Maybe if we inhaled enough…

"Of course he can see me," Ro says with a dramatic eye roll. "I may be dirty and underfed, but I don't look dreadful enough to be *dead*. And if I do, you're to blame, little sister, since you took ages to catch on and carry out my plans. I suppose I must forgive you, though, since you came through in the end—like I knew you would."

Ro winks and cuffs me under the chin, like she's done since we were kids. As if nothing is amiss. As if I haven't been mourning her death and hunting her killer. As if I didn't just stab Alaric in the back to avenge her.

"I don't understand." It feels like someone is driving a stake through my temple. I grip my forehead and double over, but that makes everything worse because now I'm staring down at Alaric's blood and the platinum chain lying in the rocks. A chain that supposedly contains the memory of Rowenna's death. Except she's very much alive.

"I don't understand," I babble again.

Alaric laughs, even though it clearly hurts him to do so. "She played you, Indira. Like she played all of us."

My eyes dart back and forth between Rowenna and the chain, which is looking more like a snake every second. "Explain. Right now!"

Rowenna clutches her hands to her chest. "I thought you'd be happier to see me. You can't imagine how much I've missed you, how hard it's been to watch you struggle and spin. But now I don't have to hide anymore. We can finish this together—return home together. All we have to do is take care of this last loose end." She wrinkles her nose as if Alaric is a slab of rotting meat. "Then I'll happily explain everything during our journey back to Tashir."

Ro opens her arms, as if she expects me to rush into them—the very thing I've imagined doing for over a year. But I step back numbly and drop to my knees beside Alaric instead, frantically pressing the shredded remains of his coat against the knife wound.

"I'm so sorry," I whisper as I lean over him, using my

weight to apply pressure. "You're going to be fine. I'll get you to the healers."

He musters a nod, but we're both staring at the wad of fabric in my hands, already soaked through.

"Help me, Rowenna! We have to get him down the mountain."

When she doesn't move, I slide my hands beneath Alaric's arms and try to move him myself. I manage one step—one tiny step that makes Alaric cry out in pain—before he slips back onto the rocks.

I look back up at my sister who's just standing there, watching dispassionately, and for the first time, a small part of me wishes she *had* died all those months ago.

"How is any of this possible?" I cry. "You were *dead*! I saw your body in Tashir—I prepared you for burial myself."

"Yes, thank you for dealing with all of that," Ro says with a flip of her hand—as if her thanks is all that was needed, not an explanation about where the body came from, since it clearly wasn't hers.

"Who was she?" I demand. "The girl you sent to Tashir in your place?"

"Some poor soul *Rowenna* shoved off a cliff," Alaric rasps. "If I wasn't dying already, the irony might kill me."

Rowenna shoots Alaric a lethal glare.

"Is it true?" I ask my sister. "Did you…?"

Rowenna bristles. "*No*, I didn't kill anyone. Honestly, Indira! Is that how little you think of me?"

I don't answer. I don't know what to think anymore.

Rowenna sighs heavily and looks down at the clover on her wrist, tracing the green leaves. "The girl was a friend from the village."

"A 'friend' who just so happened to look like you?" Alaric grinds out. "With the same distinctive tattoo? Who conveniently died of natural causes right when you needed to disappear?"

My stomach twists tighter with every glaring coincidence.

"*Yes!*" Rowenna snaps back at Alaric. "Vallista was desperate to make a better life for herself. She dreamed of working in the palace and becoming a courtier one day. I liked her tenacity, so I pulled some strings and found her a position."

Something about Rowenna's story prods at my brain, tickling with familiarity, but I can't put my finger on what.

"I changed her life," Ro goes on. "*That's* why Val wanted to be like me—and why she had the same clover tattooed on her wrist. She was always commenting on how lovely mine was and how she adored the sisterly connection it represented. She longed so desperately for that kind of closeness, and it seemed like another simple thing I could give her—especially since I wasn't sure I'd ever see you again." Rowenna glances at me sheepishly. "So I found an artisan to etch a replica onto Vallista's wrist."

"You replaced me?" My voice cracks painfully.

Ro adamantly shakes her head. "Of course not. I just widened our circle. We're allowed to have friends beyond each other, you know."

"*You* were allowed to have other friends," I argue. "But you groomed me to be completely dependent on you."

Rowenna rolls her eyes. "Shutting out the world was your decision. Don't blame your lack of social skills on me."

I shake my head because the more I think about it, the more I'm certain most of my decisions were actually Rowenna's in disguise. She knew how to frame ideas to make me believe they were my own. How to make me believe I needed her and no one else.

"What happened to Vallista?" I demand. "How did she end up dead in Tashir with such fortuitous timing?"

"Val left Vanzador of her own accord," Rowenna says. "Or she tried to. She became completely besotted with a traveling minstrel and left with the boy and his troupe, despite only knowing him for a few days—and despite all the trouble I'd gone to securing her employment," she mutters. "I was offended, of course, but I would never kill someone over hurt feelings."

The prodding in my brain grows more insistent.

Then, finally, it comes to me.

Cloudia's best friend supposedly ran off with a traveling minstrel. And didn't Delphine mention the girl was close with Rowenna?

"Unfortunately, Vallista didn't even make it off the

mountain," Rowenna continues soberly. "The minstrel boy was a vile drunk. He beat Val and pushed her body off a cliff during their descent. I happened to find her body, and I saw an opportunity to make something good come from a terrible tragedy."

My mouth bobbles open and closed, and I stare at my sister in disbelief. "Even if you just *happened* to find her, you had no right taking her body. Her family and friends will never know what became of her! They will never have the opportunity to mourn and say goodbye."

"Assuming any of that story is true," Alaric says in a painful whisper.

Rowenna shoots him a lethal glare. "It's the truth, and allowing me to use her body is what Vallista would have wanted. Trust me." She turns to me imploringly, and I toss my hands with exasperation.

"How am I supposed to trust you when you've lied about so many things?"

"I didn't want to lie or keep secrets from you, Indira, but I didn't have a choice. I'm more than happy to answer your questions now, but we should do it *while* we journey back to Tashir instead of wasting time on this freezing mountaintop."

"What about *this*?" I reach over Alaric to snatch the broken length of chain from the pebbles. "How in the name of the kings is there a 'memory' of your death when you're still alive?"

"Listen to you! Swearing in the name of the kings—just like *them*." Rowenna shakes her head with disbelief. "Thank goodness we're leaving before they indoctrinate you further."

"Answer me!" I roar. "Where did that memory come from?"

Rowenna's thick brows shoot up her forehead. "When did you become so snippy and demanding?"

"Oh, I don't know—maybe when you faked your death and tricked me into stabbing the boy I love! Or maybe I've been like this all along, but we never knew it because I wasn't allowed to think or act for myself."

Rowenna waits, stone-faced, until I finish yelling. "No one can *make* you think anything, Indira. You *wanted* me to tell you what to do and think because you've always been too weak and indecisive to trust yourself."

I flinch, and Alaric's fingers curl around mine in a weak squeeze. Comforting me, even as he lies dying—at my hand.

"You love me?" His voice is barely a whisper, but the smile on his face is as bright as the stars overhead.

A sob tears up my throat, and I increase the pressure on his wound, sending a silent prayer up to Earth Mother to preserve his life.

None of it feels like enough.

Ro forges on. "I know all of this must feel like a shock, but I assure you, everything has worked out perfectly. I wanted to involve you from the beginning, but I feared you wouldn't be able to win the Vanzadorians' trust if you knew the truth. You've never been a good liar. Do you remember the time Birdie caught you—"

"*Stop!*" I yell, making Ro jump. "We don't have time for this. Alaric needs a healer. *Now*."

Rowenna folds her arms and holds her ground, tilting her chin in that brash way I've been trying so hard to emulate. Except it looks different now. Less bold and brave, and more vicious and calculating.

"No one is going back down the mountain until you and I are realigned," she says.

"I have no desire to realign with someone I can't trust," I volley back.

"What are you talking about? I've answered your questions. And I'll happily answer more, but let's do it *while* we travel back to Tashir. Cut out the gemstones, and let's be on our way."

I shake my head and position myself protectively over Alaric, whose breaths have grown disconcertingly shallow. "I'm not going *anywhere* until you've explained *everything*."

Rowenna sighs and looks up at the sky. "I can't believe you're being so unreasonable.

"Tell me where the false memory of your death came from!" I shout.

Rowenna blinks at me for several seconds before she finally says, "I created it."

"What do you mean you *created* it? You can't just *create* memories of events that didn't happen."

"Of course you can. People misremember things all the time. Haven't you ever heard someone describe a party in such detail you'd swear you were in attendance? Or maybe you've retold a friend's embarrassing story so many times you forget it didn't actually happen to you? Memories are slippery, persuasible things. Especially if the mind is in a weakened state."

Goose bumps break out across my skin, and I hug my arms around my chest. "What does that even mean? Weakened *how*?"

"How do you think?" Rowenna's dark eyes lock on mine.

Every muscle in my body pulls taut, braced for the word I know she's going to say—the one word I don't want to hear.

"With bagrava, of course."

FORTY-FIVE

IT ALWAYS COMES BACK TO THE SEEDS-FORSAKEN bagrava.

Furious tears trickle down my cheeks, and I wipe them roughly on the back of my wrist, wishing I could go back to before I was a master gardener, before the Marauders became addicted to bagrava, before Earth Mother blessed my people with the miracle in the first place, and stop her from creating the plant altogether. It would have been better for my ancestors to perish on the Tomb Flats than for Earth Mother's gift to be twisted and misused like this.

"How?" I snap. "How, pray tell, do you use a *soil conditioner* to alter people's memories?"

Rowenna lifts one shoulder in an innocent shrug. "The idea came to me during the interminable hours I spent in

Queen Tessa's salon, watching them sip their purple tea and float away from reality. I started to wonder if their hallucinations could be molded. If, perhaps, the bagrava made their minds malleable enough to plant ideas or make suggestions. So I started experimenting and eventually discovered it *is* possible to alter memories if a high concentration of bagrava is injected directly into the bloodstream."

"You've been *injecting* the bagrava?" I ask, aghast. "Into whom? Do you know how dangerous that is?"

Rowenna waves a dismissive hand. "It doesn't cause lasting damage. Just a little sickness that subsides as soon as the injections cease."

"How could you possibly know that? How many people have you experimented on? And why? I still don't understand *why* you felt the need to fake your death!"

"It's the only way I could carry out my plans," Rowenna snaps back. "I didn't come to Vanzador just to wear glittering dresses and prance around fancy salons. I came to dismantle it from the inside out. I tried to ingratiate myself with my new husband and the royal family, but they wouldn't let me in. So I attempted to weasel my way into their government, certain I'd find weaknesses to use against them. And I did. But I couldn't take advantage of Soren's weaknesses *without* compromising the security of Tashir. Eventually, I realized stealing his power and harnessing it myself was the only way forward."

I nod because I knew my sister's silly simpering and

prancing about with the courtiers had to be an act. "Keep going."

Rowenna's eyes narrow with annoyance—unused to taking orders from anyone. Especially me. "I easily uncovered most of Vanzador's secrets—like the memory sacrifices that fuel Soren and Alaric's power and the resulting hospitals full of dying people. I was elated to learn Vanzador was slowly destroying itself, but I still needed a way to maintain the protective mountain range around Tashir *without* Soren or his son. So I started scouring the library for more information about their power and eventually came upon Callahan's journal and the mysterious mention of blood, flesh, and bone. And thanks to our husband's fondness for reliving the past, I discovered they were gemstones. But I couldn't figure out where they were kept. There aren't royal coffers or a vault of any kind on the mountain, and despite being a model wife and acting like a perfectly brainless courtier, Soren and Alaric remained as aloof and impenetrable as the Fortress walls."

"Because we knew what you were all along," Alaric says "A wolf is still a wolf, even cloaked in wool."

"Will you please hurry up and die so I don't have to endure your insufferable company?" Rowenna snarls at him.

"I've suddenly recovered my will to live," Alaric bites back, but his words slur, and the effort makes him wince.

"Good luck with that." Rowenna looks him up and down pointedly.

Alaric does look terrible: sunken, blood-spattered, and paling by the second. If I don't staunch the bleeding and get him to a healer soon, there will be no prayer of saving him.

Rowenna proudly continues her recollection. "When it became clear I was never going to find the gemstone triad on my own, I decided to stage my death—implicating Soren and Alaric, of course—so I could bring in someone more unassuming and earnest. Someone easily overlooked, who could worm into the royal family and Soren's political operations without suspicion."

"Someone like me," I say flatly.

"Don't say it like it's a bad thing!" Rowenna chides. "You're precisely what we needed—someone naïve and idealistic who had something to offer in return. Something Soren wanted so badly, he might let down his guard and lower his defenses to attain it."

I force myself to laugh to keep from crying.

Even Rowenna was using me to get to the bagrava. Its roots are so entangled with mine, I don't know where the plant ends and I begin. I don't know if anyone has ever actually cared for *me* or if I've only ever been a means to an end—a host for this parasite that's slowly killing me.

I shake my head as another realization dawns. "*You* told Soren I was a master gardener! Not Mother or Father."

"It wasn't that big of a deal." Ro waves me off. "I let your secret slip to Elodie—that girl's never been able to keep her mouth shut. I had to ensure Soren would bring you here. I couldn't trust anyone else to follow the breadcrumbs I laid. Only someone who knew me, inside and out, would be perceptive enough to carry out my plans."

Ro grins as if this is all a grand compliment, but I hear the opposite. She needed someone mindless and codependent. Someone she could easily use and manipulate, who would follow her orders without question.

A pawn. A soldier.

Pain spreads through my chest like a blight, devastating and all-consuming. Just when I think it can't get any worse, Alaric casts me the most empathetic look. Like he knows exactly what I'm thinking. How deeply these revelations hurt me.

His kindness is even more unbearable than Rowenna's confession.

"Once you were here," Ro continues, oblivious to my devastation, "I planted clues—like the carvings in our maid's chamber and the zinnia in Callahan's journal. Little things that would prompt you to look for the gemstones and people who might be able to help you locate them, like Elodie Tomasko and Garitt Von Nevus."

The sound of the councilor's name scrapes my ears like iron dragging across rock, waking something primal and ferocious within me. "Garitt Von Nevus was the opposite of helpful! He tried to assault me because of an arrangement he supposedly had with *you*. Please tell me you didn't sell yourself like that—and knowingly endanger me."

Rowenna blows out an exhausted breath. "He isn't *that* bad. Sometimes leaders must pay a small price in exchange for—"

"My body isn't a small price!" I shout even louder. "Just as staging your death isn't a small lie!"

Alaric tries to chime in, but a wet, hacking cough curls him into a ball.

"Shhh. Save your strength," I murmur.

"Sometimes our own comfort must come second to the future of Tashir," Rowenna says.

I gape at her, completely gobsmacked by how much her time in Vanzador changed her. Hardened her.

Has it, though? a tiny voice in the back of my mind asks—a voice I used to attribute to Rowenna. But now that I'm truly listening, I recognize it instantly—so calm and encouraging and so clearly my own, I don't know how I ever thought it belonged to my sister.

Rowenna has always been calculated and controlling, it tells me, *but you failed to see it because she made you believe she was protecting you, looking out for you, like an older sister should.*

"I knew you were too weak to handle the requirements of this job," she says with a derisive snort. "It's exactly why I kept you in the dark—why I sheltered you from the real work. How dare you judge me for doing what needs to be done for Tashir?"

Not long ago, these accusations would have sent me into a spiral of shame and doubt. I would have fallen on my face to apologize and begged Rowenna to tell me what to do and how to feel, but now I boldly meet her stare.

"That's the thing. This *isn't* what needs to be done. We don't have to steal the gemstone triad. In fact, it's a terrible idea, as it will require *our* people to sacrifice memories to fuel the stone's power."

"Only for a short while," Rowenna says, "Just until—"

"I wasn't finished," I say over her. "There's a good chance the stones won't even work in someone else's skin. We need to work together, *with* Vanzador, not against each other. Alaric and I have discovered so many ways we can strengthen both countries. I've been growing goblin's gold to light their mine shafts, and in return, I've been given a percentage of the output. I'm going to use that money to purchase new farming equipment and food stores from the isles across the sea to send to Tashir. Just think what a difference that will make."

"You're daft if you think the Vanzadorians will actually let you have a penny. Why would they suddenly pay for things they've always taken?"

"Because Alaric is different." I fist the lapels of his jacket and silently beg him to open his eyes and voice his agreement. But he's so quiet, so deathly still. "The future will be different with Alaric as king—and with me as his queen," I add softly.

"*You're* the one who's hallucinating if you honestly believe that," Rowenna says with a tired sigh.

"Or maybe I'm finally seeing clearly for the first time in my life because I'm not looking through *your* jaded eyes."

Rowenna scoffs. "How can you say that when you haven't *seen* anything? I've been prowling around the Fortress, setting all of this in motion, and you saw none of it."

"You're lying. You couldn't have been creeping through the Fortress. Someone would have recognized you."

"I had help, of course."

"*Who?*" I demand. "Von Nevus?" I shudder at the thought of him slinking through my chamber, touching my things.

"He volunteered, but I knew you'd never let him close enough."

"Who else would have unfettered access to my rooms? What sort of Vanzadorian would agree to help you destroy their own country?"

"The desperate kind," Rowenna says with a vicious smile. "A person with something—or *someone*—they'd do anything to protect if they were, say, gripped by a sudden strange illness. Do you happen to know anyone like that?"

She bats her eyes and my stomach lurches.

"No," I argue. But all the pieces fit: Cloudia's sudden

illness, brought on by Rowenna's injections. Delphine befriending me, supporting me, when she had no reason to do so. How she's been there, at my side, every step of the way.

"It was so easy to manipulate her," Ro continues. "I followed her home one night and saw how happy she and her sister were—the best of friends, merrily playing house together. A lot like you and me." Rowenna winks playfully.

"It isn't possible," I say weakly. "Delphine is my friend. She despises you."

"You're right about the second part." Rowenna laughs. "Delphine definitely despises me. But she *is* working with me—and has been from the start."

"I don't believe you," I say, but my voice is small and shaking.

"Ask her yourself." Rowenna's gaze darts over my shoulder, and I hear the sound of shifting pebbles, the unsteady intake of breath. But I refuse to turn. Can't bring myself to look. I don't know how I'll survive if Delphine is, in fact, standing there.

"Did you bring everything I asked for?" Rowenna asks.

After a long prickling pause, I hear her familiar voice. One whispered word that rips through me like an arrow.

"Yes."

FORTY-SIX

I don't realize I'm sobbing until Alaric's fingertips graze my cheek, wiping my tears. But even that small movement is too much. His face contorts, and his body.

"Shh," I murmur, trying to hold him steady. "Everything's going to be okay."

But he has to know it's a lie.

"I'm so sorry, Indira," Delphine babbles as she steps up beside me, still wearing my cloak. It's charred at the hem, so is the tail of her golden braid, and several angry pink burns dot her forearms. But she's alive.

Because I saved her.

Because I thought she was my friend.

"I didn't want to betray you—not after meeting you—but I didn't have a choice."

"What do you mean, you didn't have a choice? Of

course you had a choice!" I explode, even though, deep down, I know she didn't. I would have done the same thing in her shoes—whatever it took to protect my sister.

I round on Rowenna. "Why did you target an innocent girl like Cloudia? How did you do it? If you can plant false memories into anyone's mind, why not attack Soren or Alaric directly? Wouldn't it make more sense to take control of Vanzador and their power to move the earth that way?"

"Because Soren and Alaric wouldn't let me get close enough to stick them with a needle. And in order for the hallucinations to linger like a memory, the person must be *kept* in a drug-induced state. It would have been rather suspicious if the rulers of Vanzador suddenly couldn't get out of bed. I needed to come at this from an unexpected angle, and I knew you'd befriend our sniveling maid and feel compelled to help her ailing sister. I also knew you were more likely to believe the worst about your lover"—her upper lip curls as she looks down at Alaric—"if proof of his crime came from a 'credible' source—like a friend's beloved sister. Especially if her 'memories' had proven truthful before."

"Listen to yourself!" I say with disgust. "All these lies and manipulations! This isn't who you are."

"This is *exactly* who I am, who I've *always* been! I'm not the one who's changed, Indira. I'm not the one who wants an alliance with our oppressors over freedom for our people outright. Cloudia will be perfectly fine once I stop the injections."

Delphine staggers back, as if slapped. "You said she'd need an antidote! One you'd only provide if I upheld my end of the bargain."

Rowenna smirks. "I couldn't have you running off with your sister before our work was finished."

"Well, now it is." Delphine dumps a heavy satchel at my sister's feet. "Supplies for your journey back to Tashir. Von Nevus is waiting at the base of the mountain with horses. I pray to the gods of rock and stone I never see you again."

"Von Nevus is in on this too?" I sputter. "You're bringing him back to Tashir?"

Rowenna shrugs. "I told him he could be my king regent in exchange for his assistance."

"You'd let *him* rule alongside you?"

Ro shrugs again. "Anyone will do, because *no one* will be ruling alongside me."

She picks up the satchel, which looks identical to the ones Alaric and I filled with bagrava. That's the real reason Delphine helped us carry them up the mountain, so she could hide Rowenna's provisions in among the others.

I have to be here. That's what she said, and fool that I am, I assumed she meant she *wanted* to be here to support me. Not that she physically had to be present because she was being blackmailed.

"I wanted to tell you so many times." Delphine blinks at me through watery eyes. "I wanted to stand up to Rowenna and refuse to cooperate. But I *couldn't*. I had to think of Cloudia. It's like I told you from the very beginning—there's *nothing* I wouldn't do for my sister."

I don't tell Delphine it's okay or that I forgive her, because I don't. But I do nod once in understanding because I said the same things—came here under the same pretenses.

"You can go," I tell her. "Return to the Fortress and Cloudia. My sister won't bother you anymore."

She studies me, tears streaming down her face, and for a minute, I think she might choose to stay—choose to help me, to atone for her betrayal and prove our friendship wasn't a complete lie. But then Delphine lowers her head and sprints back toward the caves without looking back.

Pain carves through me like a red-hot poker, almost as unbearable as the moment I learned of Rowenna's "death." At least she was ripped away from me unwillingly.

Delphine is *choosing* to abandon me.

She was never with me from the start.

"It's time for us to be off too," Rowenna says, as if everything's resolved.

I shake my head and rise to my feet, standing over Alaric like a towering, immovable oak tree.

"Stand aside, Indira. I've been more than patient. We're leaving this mountain with the blood, flesh, and bone of Callahan, which *I* will cut from Alaric's skin, since you're too weak to stomach it."

"I won't let you kill him."

"That's rich, considering he's mostly dead already, thanks to you," Rowenna retorts.

"Only because you deceived me and framed him! Alaric is innocent in all of this."

"You already know my thoughts on his *innocence*, but fine." Rowenna lets out a long exasperated sigh. "Since you're too tangled up in your feelings to think clearly, I'll concede. *Again*. Because, contrary to what you think, I am a thoughtful, reasonable person. Instead of killing Alaric, we can bring him back to Tashir, throw him in a prison cell, and allow him to live as long as he cooperates and continues feeding his power into the mountain range. While I'd obviously prefer to control the earth myself, this will do for now. It might even be preferable for a short while—we won't have to worry about the logistics of reimplanting the gemstones."

I look down at Alaric's broken body and picture him languishing in one of the dark damp cells beneath the hillock palace. Everything about it is wrong. Most obviously, that it would be impossible to keep him there.

"He'll just move the earth and escape," I point out.

Rowenna sucks an irritated breath through her teeth. "Then we'll let him live free from a cell—give him the same 'comforts' he afforded us in Vanzador. You can't possibly take issue with that."

I try to imagine this scenario—Alaric in Tashir, wandering through the rolling fields, sweating beside me in the planting beds, lying on his back as dragonflies buzz overhead and the sun browns his marble chest. I see us laughing as we chase each other through the tunnels and dancing beneath the golden harvest moon. We could be happy, away from these cold mountains, without the dark legacy of his father looming over us.

Except I know, deep down, it would kill him to abandon his people. And it would quite literally kill them—Vanzador's economy would collapse if he wasn't there to oversee the mining operations.

A stone will never have a place in a planting bed. Just as a flower is never going to thrive on this frigid mountaintop. There's nowhere on this continent a girl born of seeds and a boy forged of stone can exist together. Not without sacrificing our seminal roots—the core of who we are.

"We're not taking Alaric back to Tashir," I say firmly.

I *feel* Rowenna's reaction before she says a word—like grass, standing on end before a lightning storm.

"What do you mean *we're not taking him back? This* is a generous compromise! Did you forget the other option is killing him?"

"I won't let you do that either."

Rowenna blows out a long breath. "Stand aside, Indira, or I'll be forced to remove you."

"What does that even mean?"

Ro's eyes dart sideways, and before I realize what she's doing, she snatches the discarded knife from the ground—still slick with Alaric's blood—and levels it at my chest.

"You wouldn't," I whisper.

"There's nothing I wouldn't do for Tashir. I'm beginning to think you never really knew me at all—that you never truly loved me, as you always claimed to."

Before, this accusation would have gutted me and made me question everything I thought I knew about myself. But now I hold my ground and raise my chin high, because if Rowenna truly loved *me*, she wouldn't make me feel this way. Her love wouldn't be contingent on my obedience. She'd let me put down my own roots and become my own person instead of treating me like an offshoot of herself.

The seconds tick past, and even though discomfort twines through every part of me, I stand tall. Meet her stare. Surprised to find that the longer I sit with these feelings, the more I'm cleansed—like a controlled fire, sweeping through fallow fields. Burning everything down in order for it to grow back stronger.

"You don't want to do this," Rowenna warns, raising the blade.

"You're right. I don't," I admit. "But I won't sentence either nation to death when there's a better way forward. You're just too stubborn to open your eyes and see it."

"And you're too blinded by love to admit Alaric and

his people are feeding off us like spider mites. Tashir is better off without them."

"No. We're *dead* without them!" I cry out. "I think that's what Earth Mother has been trying to teach us—why she blessed each country with power that the other needs. We have always been meant to work together. To unite and thrive or perish alone."

Rowenna closes her eyes and squeezes the bridge of her nose. "Tell me, Indira. What happens when worms infest apples before the harvest?"

The shift is so abrupt, I stammer over the answer, "Th-they rot?"

"And cucumbers, left too long on the vine?" Ro demands.

"Again, they rot. I don't see what any of this has to do with—"

"And what must be done with rot?" Ro's voice is as sharp as the knife in her hand.

"You have to cut it out, before it spoils the entire crop."

"I'm glad you understand," she says with a sad smile.

Then she lunges at me.

FORTY-SEVEN

MY MIND REFUSES TO PROCESS WHAT MY EYES ARE seeing:

The glinting blade. Rowenna's seething expression.

My sister would never hurt me. *She wouldn't!* my heart screams, even as the knife arcs through the moonlight, slashing toward my chest.

I am frozen. Transfixed. Watching from outside my body.

Right before the blade tears through me, Alaric makes a horrific sound, and his feet jerk, kicking my legs out from under me. Saving me the same way I saved him from Soren.

Rowenna's knife whizzes past my face—a blow meant to kill, not injure—and a long, low wail bleeds from my lips. The blade may have missed its mark, but the pain in my chest is just as excruciating. Maybe even more so. If the knife had ripped through me, the physical pain would have overwhelmed the bone-wrenching grief of knowing my sister wanted to kill me. The darkness would have pressed in, blurring the flash of the knife and her hateful expression.

But I'm forced to see it all.

Rowenna curses as her boots slide through the scree, thrown off-balance by the miss. Readjusting her grip on the dagger, she turns to face me, hot breath flaring from her nostrils like the bulls in Tashir before they charge.

This time, I don't need Alaric to kick me into motion. I duck and roll beneath the knife, gripping a stone in each fist. Rocks wouldn't have been my first choice of weapon, but they're better than nothing. And in a strange way, it feels fitting to wield fragments of the mountain as I fight for Alaric and the Vanzadorians. Almost like they're helping me in what little way they can.

"That's the best you can do?" Rowenna asks with a cruel chuckle. "Throwing rocks like a child? Like one of *them*? I'm embarrassed for you, little sister."

I set my jaw and hurl the first stone—not directly at Rowenna, but higher, like the competitors in the stone-throwing courts. Rowenna laughs even louder, thinking I missed, until the stone lands squarely on her foot.

Her eyes flare, and she grits her teeth. "Why are you suddenly being so difficult? You've spent your entire life trailing me like a duckling, happy to be led along, until *now*, when it matters most."

While she's yelling, I pelt her again in the thigh.

"Stop this! We both know you're never going to kill me throwing pebbles."

"I don't *want* to kill you!" I cry. "I want you to come to your senses. You're better than this, Ro."

She screams with frustration and slashes the knife.

A flat slab of shale catches my eye, and I raise it over my head as she brings the knife down. The force shatters the thin rock, and my ears ring as the pieces pelt me. While I try to get my bearings, Rowenna throws her weight into another attack—swinging with blind rage, like the Marauders. It's ferocious and intimidating, but ultimately avoidable, because, like the Marauders, she always takes the obvious shot. Always swings with the most effort.

I, on the other hand, have spent my life fighting smaller, quieter battles in the planting beds—against enemies like locusts and root weevils that required patience and persistence to eradicate.

That's how I fight my sister now. Not by meeting Rowenna in her strength, but by settling into mine. I let her swing, rage, and run herself ragged, while I retreat across the narrow summit like a sure-footed rabbit, lobbing an occasional stone when I can.

"Stop this!" Rowenna shouts again, breathless and stumbling over divots that would never have tripped her up before.

I continue retreating, drawing her away from Alaric and closer to the cliffs—the place where Soren died, where I thought *she* died. The place this journey for vengeance began. It seems fitting it should end here too. The future of two nations teetering on the precipice.

I peer over the edge, and the dizzying height grips my throat. It's terrifying and breathtaking—almost too stunning to be real. Craggy purple peaks jut into a velvet blue sky, embroidered with stars and swirling snow. Beauty so at odds with this moment.

"It's magnificent…" I don't realize I've spoken aloud until Rowenna barks out a derisive laugh as she trudges closer.

"This place is an abomination. Ruined by the Vanzadorians and their power—much like you. You let them fracture your foundation and erect something new and unnatural in its place. This new version of you may *look* brave and impressive, but your core is rotten because you have no loyalty, no roots."

"That isn't true," I argue. "Sometimes we have to adapt and change to survive. Sometimes new branches must be grafted onto old trees to help them thrive and grow in different ways."

Rowenna groans. "I can't listen to this drivel any longer. This is your last chance to walk away from this madness and return with me to Tashir. Do whatever you need to appease your misguided conscience. Purge every memory of your time here if that's what it takes. We never have to speak of this again. Things can be exactly as they were before—*we* can be exactly as we were before—only better," she says with sudden tenderness. "We'll be together, and Tashir will finally be free."

Rowenna's looking at me the way she always used to—overflowing with pride and love—and it's almost enough to make me say yes. It would be so easy to sacrifice my memories and wash my hands of this place and these people. I could regain the sister I knew and seize the future we fought so hard to create. But then I look back at Alaric, still sprawled across the rocks in a pool of blood, and it reminds me of Besnik's broken body on the banquet table and the choice Alaric had to make in that moment. The very same choice I'm faced with now.

Forget and return to the way things were—go back to tending my plants, never thinking about anything or anyone beyond my own little plot. Or I can thrust my shovel into this hard new soil and cultivate a real relationship between Tashir and Vanzador. It won't be easy—I'll undoubtedly get blisters and cramps—but that pain will give both countries the opportunity to grow back taller and stronger and better than before.

"Forgetting the truth doesn't make it go away, Ro," I finally say. "It may temporarily ease our conscience, but in the end, it perpetuates the cycle of hate and oppression. Can't you see that?"

Rowenna shakes her head sadly. "The only thing I see is a traitor."

She fists the dagger and comes at me again, but she's out of strength—weakened from months of living on the frigid streets of Vanzador—and I easily block the attack.

The knife sails from Rowenna's hand and skates across the rocks, spinning precariously close to the edge.

She scrambles after it like a woman possessed. Like she expects me to fight her for it. But I haven't moved. I know better than to go near the edge where Soren fell. Where the rock is practically hollow from overmining.

But Rowenna doesn't know any of this. She never took the time to learn about Vanzador's mines.

"Rowenna, stop!" I shriek. "It isn't safe!" But that just makes her move faster, scrambling farther out onto the ridge, oblivious to the hair-raising sounds of the earth shifting.

As she reaches for the knife, a loud crack splits the air.

Ro skids to a stop, frozen with her hand outstretched. We stare at each other, waiting. Wincing. After several agonizing seconds, Rowenna's shoulders relax. And that's when the ground gives way.

I am acutely aware of every detail: the fractures in the stone racing outward, the dirt jamming beneath her fingernails as she claws at the crumbling rock, her eyes darting to mine the moment she realizes there's nothing to grab. And that's what undoes me. They're not the eyes of the feral, desperate girl who tried to stab me, but the brave girl who shoved me behind her every time the Marauders crashed through our bedroom windows. Eyes that sparkled with wonder the first time I coaxed a bagrava seedling to life. The eyes of the girl in her chain mail wedding dress, daring the world to bring her down.

And I can't let that girl fall.

I dash forward, over the widening cracks, and slide onto my stomach to distribute my weight. Rowenna reaches for me, screaming my name, and I lean out farther, farther, until I'm surrounded by more sky than rock. Just when I'm certain I'm going to follow her over the edge, our fingers brush, then miraculously catch.

The sudden jerk of Rowenna's weight drags me farther over the disintegrating ledge. My arms feel like they're going to wrench from my body, and my fingers are still wet with Alaric's blood.

"Don't let go, Indira! Don't let go!" Rowenna cries.

"I won't," I say through gritted teeth. "But I'm not strong enough to pull you up. You have to help. Find footholds and climb."

Rowenna bites her lip and nods, and with a look of sheer determination on her face, she manages to dig her toe into the rock face and lift herself a fraction.

"Good." I breathe out heavily. "Now, do it again."

As she inches higher, I slowly squirm backward, trying to time the jerking of my body with the forward thrust of hers. Little by little, we retreat until Ro's elbows, then chest, then knees are back on solid ground.

I let out a hysterical laugh and collapse on my stomach, cheek pressed against the frozen rock, every part of me exhausted, aching, and tingling—but alive.

Somehow, we're both alive.

Rowenna is coughing and gagging like I pulled her from water instead of open air, and she refuses to let go of my hands, like she's afraid she might be dragged back over the edge if I let her go.

"You're okay," I murmur soothingly.

"Why did you save me?" she croaks with what's left of her voice. "After everything I just did?"

I give her hand a gentle squeeze until her tear-filled eyes find mine. "I know you didn't mean it. You're my sister. I love you. I know you would have saved me if our roles were reversed."

Ro cocks her head and considers me, and the longer the moment stretches, the tighter she grips, until I cry out in pain.

"No, Indira," she leans in close and whispers, "I would have let you fall."

Before my limp, wrung-out body can react, Ro throws herself forward and turns, using her momentum to whip me around. So our positions are reversed, and the crumbling ledge is at *my* back.

"What are you doing?" I yell.

"What's best for Tashir," Rowenna says.

"*No!*"

The scream is so loud and sharp, it must be coming from me. This is the sound I make when I die. Except my lips are closed, and Rowenna has turned to look back over her shoulder.

The scream rends the air again, followed by a splintering crack—different from the deep groan of the crumbling cliff edge. This is more like the sound Soren's head made when he tripped and fell from this very same cliff.

Rowenna's golden eyes widen, and she almost looks like she's going to laugh. Then she collapses on top of me, and I see the sickening dent in the back of her skull, feel the warm trickle of blood running over my hands, and, finally, notice Lady Elodie Tomasko, standing there in her glittering gown, holding a large, bloodied rock.

I have just enough time to sputter Elodie's name before the momentum of Rowenna's body carries us both over the edge.

FORTY-EIGHT

ELODIE DROPS THE STONE AND STUMBLES FORward, reaching for me the same way I reached to save Rowenna.

I don't know how she found her way up here, or where she found the courage to strike Rowenna, but I do know one thing: She did it for *me*. To save *me*. My most unlikely and truest friend.

Her fingers lock around my wrist, and she gasps as the added weight drags her forward. Her braids fall from their intricate knot, and her skirt tears as she's dragged through the rocks, but she notices none of it.

"I've got you," Elodie promises, but she's wearing silky gloves adorned with pearls, and I already feel them slipping off her delicate fingers. Her face contorts with effort. She struggles and strains forbidding me to fall, but every second the glove slips a little lower until it eventually rips free.

Elodie screams my name as I plummet. I can see the panic in her eyes, her mind frantically searching for another solution, but she's already done far more than expected. More than my own sister did. So instead of screaming with terror, I muster a small smile. So she knows how grateful I am, how much her efforts mean, and how comforting it is to die, knowing I wasn't alone. I had a few true friends on this mountaintop.

"Help Alaric!" I scream into the wind, but I don't know if she heard before her face is replaced by the gray blur of the cliff.

Then it's just me and the sky. And Rowenna, too, I realize—falling with me. Leading the way, even in death.

It's tragic but also, inexplicably, *right* that we should die together. She was there from the very beginning—my oldest friend, pulling me into her arms as I drew my first breath and, now, falling into oblivion with our last.

I wonder if she felt a twinge of remorse in her final moments. If she regretted trying to shove me over the ledge. I don't regret saving her, but I *do* regret living so much of my life in her shadow. I regret that she never got to know this stronger, braver version of me. This girl who has always had so much more to offer our people and country beyond the planting beds. But in my desperation to be exactly like Rowenna, I didn't leave space for my own roots to grow. I loved my sister so much, I forgot to love and nurture myself, and she never tried to correct me. She was more than happy to soak up all of the sunshine for herself.

This should probably infuriate me, but even now I can't bring myself to hate her. Just as I don't fault myself for loving her—for always seeing the best in her, even when it was no longer true. There's beauty in loving someone for their potential, for treating them as if there was never any doubt they'd grow into the most glorious version of themselves.

I can't hate the bagrava for the same reason. And I don't regret sowing and tending it, despite knowing it could be stolen by the Marauders or taken by the Vanzadorians. The plant isn't to blame when wicked people misuse it. Just as I'm not to blame for how Rowenna used me. We can't control how our love is received or what others choose to do with it. We can only sow the best of ourselves into the soil of each relationship and hope our hearts are tended well.

And if not, there's still hope. Just like plants can be propagated and replanted, there's always an opportunity to start over and try again. A way for a piece of us to continue on, even if the original roots have rotted.

That's all I can hope for now—that some piece of me will live on to see the future I attempted to cultivate with Alaric. A world where Tashir and Vanzador will flourish together. I want so badly to see it. To till the ground of the new world we sacrificed so much to create. But even knowing the seed has been planted is enough.

It has to be.

The bottom must be close now. I wish it would come faster. I'm ready to escape this place between worlds and sprint into the Great Fields Beyond—wherever, and whatever, that may be.

I used to try to picture it when I was young, but I could never conjure anything other than light, even brighter than the sun. Now that I'm so close to crossing that threshold, I feel strangely certain the Great Fields Beyond are different for each of us—like millions of individualized planting beds we can cultivate as we see fit, each of us pruning, planting, and tending our own eternity. And in mine, there will always be a sea of purple bagrava.

Surprisingly, I see Alaric there, too, sprawled out on his back, hands clasped behind his head. His bare, pale chest a stark contrast to the deep violet petals.

Even in my fantasies, he refuses to wear a shirt.

My heart judders as I realize this might not be a fantasy. Alaric could be joining me there soon. He could be there already, dead from a wound *I* inflicted. I can only pray he'll eventually forgive me. That he'll be waiting for me with his smoldering smile and beautiful eyes.

Perhaps the afterlife has always been the only place a Tashiri girl and Vanzadorian boy can be together.

The thought brings the tiniest smile to my lips, but

pain obliterates it a second later—bone-crushing, earth-shattering pain that starts in the soles of my feet and spirals up my ankles. It cleaves through my calves, thighs, and hips, exactly how I expected slamming into the ground at the base of the mountain would feel, except I hoped not to feel it. I assumed death would claim me on impact, but I'm in far too much pain to be dead.

My legs are pulsing, my back is hot and tingling, and when I manage to crack my eyes, I decide they must be damaged too, because what I see doesn't make sense. Rowenna and I are sprawled across a smooth slab of stone, rather than shattered across boulders and scrub oak. And while the wind continues to blow, my hair streams down my back instead of up around my face. The sheer cliff wall seems to be moving perplexingly downward. Something that could only happen if *I* was surging upward.

My heart somersaults, and disbelieving laughter spills from my lips, because there's only one way a slab of stone could be moving contrary to the laws of nature. Only one way rock could burst from the mountainside and catch me out of thin air.

"Alaric!" His name is a laugh, a cry, a prayer on my lips. I can't stop saying it as the stone slab reaches the summit and dumps me back into the scree before returning to the earth, just as quickly as it appeared.

I tumble to a stop, and Rowenna's lifeless body lands

beside me. I stare at her blank face and unseeing eyes, and my eyes finally flood with tears. In part because she's really, truly gone this time, but more so because she's *here*. Because Alaric caught her too. He knew it's what I'd want, despite everything.

With a painful grunt, I push up to my knees and squint across the summit, praying I'll find him alive and conscious, maybe even sitting up. But he's precisely where I left him, face down in the red-black puddle of blood. The only change is that one arm is extended, fist clenched. Proof he moved the earth to save me, though I still can't fathom where he found the strength. He was already so close to death.

Elodie is kneeling beside him, flapping her hands and crying hysterically. "You have to wake up! I can't carry you down the mountain, and I can't just leave you to die. Too many people have died today already."

My body screams with pain as I hobble closer, but it's nothing compared to the other feelings exploding in my chest—feelings of love, joy, relief, and regret, but most of all profound gratitude for these two people who risked everything for me. Who sacrificed everything for me.

"Elodie!" The sound is a rasp in my throat, but somehow she hears it and turns.

Her mouth drops open, and now she's crying even harder, tripping over herself as she runs toward me. "Indira! H-how is this possible? How did you survive?"

"Alaric moved the earth and caught me," I say as I fall into her arms.

We sink awkwardly to the ground, both of us crying too hard to speak, holding on to each other like neither quite believes the other is real.

When I finally catch my breath, I pull back and grip Elodie by the shoulders, so I can look into her brave, beautiful face. "Thank you for saving my life."

"Alaric is who really saved you. I was too late."

"Your timing was perfect. You did what I couldn't. You…" I steal a glance back at Rowenna, and an awful, strangled noise escapes my throat.

"I didn't mean to kill her," Elodie admits. "I just saw her driving you toward the edge, and instinct took over. I saw the stones, and it felt like they'd been placed there by fate—the one weapon I was equipped to use. I didn't mean to hit her so hard."

"Thank you." I cut Elodie off with a hug. "I'll never be able to thank you enough. I just don't understand how you're here. How did you know where to find me?"

Elodie wipes snot and tears across the back of her arm without a thought for her gloves or dress. "I followed Delphine." Elodie watches me as she says the name, gauging my reaction. "She was acting so strange—all of you were—but when she excused herself from the queen's gala preparations, I knew something was afoot. She'd been having such a grand time barking orders and overseeing plans. She wouldn't have left—and she certainly wouldn't have delegated authority to *me*—if it wasn't something important. So I excused myself and followed her. I'm a much slower climber, though, so I saw her running back down the mountain as I was coming up. She didn't see me, and I didn't stop her to ask what happened, but she seemed to be in a hurry."

"She was working with my sister," I say flatly. "They were using me to get close to Alaric's power—so Rowenna could cut the gemstones from his wrist and take them back to Tashir."

"Is that why he's so injured?" Elodie looks over her shoulder at him. "Rowenna attacked him?"

I bite my lip and look down. "No, that was me…when I believed my sister's lies."

"I see," Elodie says gently. "But I don't see why Delphine would help your sister. She hated Rowenna."

"She did. But Ro is the reason Delphine's sister has been sick. Ro was using the girl as blackmail to force Delphine's cooperation, so I understand why she initially betrayed me. But I don't understand why she ran away instead of trying to help me once everything was out in the open."

A sniffle escapes me, which feels utterly ridiculous. Of all the people who've betrayed me and things I have to cry about, a maid should hurt the least. But we shared so much. I thought we were friends.

"She said we were *family*," I blubber, "and now she's gone. They're all gone." I gesture back at Rowenna and over to Alaric, each loss more crushing.

Elodie takes my hand. "I'll be your family. So will Alaric."

"Not if he's dead." I peer at him over Elodie's shoulder, lying completely still. I can't even tell if he's breathing, and I can't bring myself to check. If he's gone, it will shatter me, and there are already so few solid pieces left.

"Come on. I'll be right there with you," Elodie says. When I still don't move, she adds, "Whether he's alive or dead, you still want to take care of him, right?"

With a painful cry, I nod and let her lead me to where Alaric lies. I drop heavily to my knees and take his outstretched hand. It's heavy and cold, and he doesn't react, no matter how hard I squeeze.

"Alaric?" I whisper.

He doesn't answer, doesn't move. There's no whoosh of breath when I hold my hand over his lips.

"Forgive me," I whimper. "I should have believed you, should have trusted *you*. I can't believe you saved me and retrieved Rowenna's body, after everything I did."

I curl forward and rest my head against Alaric's bare chest, thinking of our first night together on the Tomb Flats. That girl would be appalled by the traitorous feelings I have now, by this scandalous brush of skin. But I'm not that girl anymore, and the girl I am now wishes I could go back and tell past Indira to spend less time doubting and distrusting, and more time embracing moments like this—burrowed in the heat of his body, listening to the soft beat of his heart against my cheek.

Thump-bump, thump-bump, thump-bump.

My eyes snap open.

I turn my head and place my other ear against his chest to be sure I'm not imagining it. And there it is: the *thump-bump* of a heartbeat. Weak and fluttering but undeniable.

"He's alive!" I say with disbelief.

Elodie lets out a happy shriek, and I shriek too, and for a second, we're both laughing and crying for joy before the grim reality of our next hurdle sobers me.

"How are we supposed to get him down the mountain?" I ask.

Elodie looks down at Alaric, then up at me. "One step at a time."

We leave Rowenna's body on the mountaintop, for the time being, and each lift one of Alaric's arms. Then we begin the slow and excruciating climb down the mountain, pulling his body behind us like a plow.

Our progress is slow. Alaric's long legs catch on branches and boulders, and the weight of his limp body feels like a saw dragging across my back. There's a good chance I'll never stand completely straight again, but it's worth it because he's alive. Alaric is *alive*. And we're almost there.

When the walls of the Fortress appear through the low-hanging clouds, I'm flooded with relief and the oddest sense of rightness at this reversal of roles. I'm carrying Alaric into the Fortress the same way he carried me the day I arrived in Vanzador.

Elodie and I collapse at the base of the city wall as the rising sun paints the outline of the mountains gold. We pound on the gate, shouting for help, crying for a healer, both of us too tired to think about the blood soaking Alaric's clothes and smearing our hands, and how this might look.

In an instant, we're surrounded by a swarm of guards, all of them shouting questions and accusations that I'm too exhausted to follow. The only word that matters, the only word I'm capable of saying, is "Healer!" and I shout it like a madwoman until they finally lift Alaric's limp form and rush him through the gates.

The guards come for Elodie and me next, shouting questions and making threats as they haul us to our feet. Elodie whimpers painfully as they tie her arms behind her back. Her eyes roll with fear as they roughly yank her forward viciously. And I can't let this happen. Can't let her take an ounce of blame for any of it.

"She did nothing!" I shout. "Elodie Tomasko is innocent. She saved King Alaric!"

The guards eye me warily. "Does that mean *you* are to blame? Is this your confession?"

I release a breath and bob my head, despite Elodie's horrified expression, because it's true.

I stabbed the king of Vanzador.

FORTY-NINE

FORTY-NINE

FOLLOW OBEDIENTLY AS THE GUARDS DRAG ME INTO the Fortress and toss me into a prison cell deep below the castle. It's cold, dark, and dripping, the walls hewn from solid stone.

It's the Vanzador I expected to find—the place Rowenna invented in her letters.

Turns out it does exist, after all.

I lie down in the wet rushes and close my eyes, vaguely aware of the guards still shouting at me. One spits in my hair. But I'm too tired to respond. Too tired to explain or defend myself. I just want to sleep. I want to drift into a world of eternal sunlight and endless grass. A place without rocks, bagrava, memories, or Marauders.

A place that exists only in my dreams.

When I wake, hours or days later, it takes a moment to

remember where I am. The freezing wind and cold rock make me think I'm still on the mountaintop—that the viscous puddle surrounding my head must be Alaric's blood. But when I bolt upright, my forehead slams into the low rocky ceiling, and it all comes rushing back: the guards, gates, and shouted accusations.

I'm in prison.

For attempting to murder my husband.

There's a hellish crick in my neck, and my body feels like it was run over by a plow, but I crawl to the front of my cell and press my face into a thin gap between the bars. A grisly-bearded guard sits on a stool outside my cell, whittling what looks to be a bird.

"Where's Alaric?" I ask without preamble. "How long have I been here?"

The guard jumps, and his knife clatters to the floor. He scowls at me as he retrieves it. "*His Majesty's* whereabouts are none of your concern."

My questions keep coming, flowing out of me like a raging river. "Were they able to treat his wounds? Is he stable? Awake?"

"His Majesty's health is *also* none of your concern," the guard says with a sniff.

I slam my palm against the bars. "I'm his wife! Of course it's my concern!"

The guard rolls his eyes. "I'm afraid you lost those privileges, and that title, when you tried to assassinate him."

"I didn't try to assassinate him—" I start to argue. Except that's *exactly* what I did. It doesn't matter that I was manipulated and deceived. Or that I changed my mind and tried to save him in the end. My hand still wielded the knife, drew his blood.

Alaric has every right to despise me. I don't blame him if he never wants to speak to me again. I just need to see him, at least once, to ensure he's alive and well.

"*Please*," I beg hating the smug smile that twists the guard's paunchy face. "Just a brief audience."

The man shakes his head and resumes whittling—and humming now, too, to drown out my pleas.

Eventually, I slump to the ground and wrap my arms around my knees. My head is pounding, and I'm drooping with exhaustion, despite having just woken up. But I won't go back to sleep. I may never sleep again. Every time I close my eyes, I see Alaric's lifeless body and Rowenna's scowling face. The vicious flash of her knife and blood. So much blood.

I don't know how much time passes while I sit in a heap, but the guard changes, and this one is even more implacable than the first. The woman refuses to even look at me and acts as if I haven't spoken, no matter how loudly I scream. Eventually, I lose my voice and take to pacing instead, prowling the length of the bars, trying to catch a glimpse beyond my cell.

There must be other prisoners in this dungeon, but I

can't see other cells, and I never hear voices. Not even the skittering of mice. And the longer I spend in utter silence, the more the stone walls start to feel like a coffin. Like I'm dead already, buried deep beneath the earth, with no final words, no chance to explain. Not that any explanation could ever be good enough, but I thought Alaric would at least give me the opportunity. I thought the feelings between us ran deep enough that he'd want some sort of closure, if nothing else.

But the guards change again and again, and I'm still alone. Still in the dark. I still haven't been fed, and I still can't close my eyes for fear of being accosted by the horrific memories. Minutes feel like days. Hours crawl by like years. And as my eyes grow heavier and my belly grows emptier, my thoughts grow even more erratic.

What if Alaric hasn't come because he's dead—or close to it—confined to his bed and clinging to life? Why else wouldn't he come? Surely, he'd want to condemn me at the very least? Make his hatred known and sentence me to death?

But I remain alone, ensconced in this maddening silence.

When I'm too weak to sit up, they finally toss me some bread crusts and a bowl of murky water. The bare minimum to preserve life. Though part of me wishes they'd just let me die. It would be better than this endless waiting, with nothing to distract me from the parade of regrets, marching across my mind.

I see my parents' devastated faces. Not only did I blame them for betraying my secrets to Soren and accuse them of never loving me, I failed to save Tashir. They've lost two children now, and nothing good has come from it. I imagine them receiving the news of my capture and execution and feel certain neither will survive it.

Delphine torments me next. I can't stop replaying the moment she left me on the mountaintop with nothing but a clipped goodbye, and I vacillate between hating her and worrying about her. I assume she and Cloudia left the Fortress, but where could they possibly go? Cloudia is still so weak, and two lone women crossing the Tomb Flats would be an easy target for Marauders. And maybe that's what Delphine deserves—what I should want. But I find myself praying they met up with a caravan. That they're happy together, somewhere. That at least one pair of sisters made it out of this tragedy alive.

Then comes visions of Elodie, with her tinkling laugh and bright smile. A reminder of my own failures and misjudgments—all the ways I don't deserve her as a friend. I pray she's been found innocent of any crime, that she isn't suffering the same indignities. But I also, selfishly, pray she'll come to my rescue again. That she'll appear from out of nowhere, like she did on the mountaintop, and hurl a stone through the bars of my cage. Sometimes, I swear I hear her trilling voice, so real and close, I drag myself to the front of my cell, convinced I'll find her there.

But of course she isn't.

If Alaric has sentenced me to death, he won't allow her to visit. She probably hasn't even tried. She may have saved me from Rowenna, but that was before she knew *I* was responsible for stabbing Alaric.

Alaric.

His presence haunts me most, begging me to believe him yet still saving me from the burning cave when I refused; offering immediate forgiveness and insisting I take the gemstone triad moments after stabbing him; the feel of his cold, weak hands squeezing comfort into me, and literally using the last of his strength to save me from plummeting to my death.

After what feels like several months, when my body is so heavy with regret I can no longer rise from the floor, and my mind is so filled with ghosts, I can't tell the real world from my nightmares, I hear heavy footfalls and a new voice that makes me sit up so fast, stars burst across my vision. I scramble to the front of my cell, this time praying it's another delusion. Of all the horrors that have haunted me in prison, this is by far the worst.

Which is precisely why it's real.

Councilor Garitt Von Nevus rounds the corner and excuses the guard with a flip of his hand. Then he marches to my prison cell and leaps back when he realizes the grimy, matted creature pressed against the bars is me.

"Gods of the mountain, you look positively feral," he

says, crinkling his nose and peering down at me. "It's only been a week."

"What are you doing here?" I snap, my voice rough from lack of use. "Weren't you supposed to flee to Tashir? Or were you too afraid to go without my sister? Did you finally realize you're nothing without her?"

Von Nevus darts a quick glance over his shoulder. "Quiet."

I laugh—loud and vicious. "You should be imprisoned alongside me for your part in Rowenna's schemes."

"Enough!" Von Nevus slams his fist against the bars. "I hoped a week down here would make you cooperative, but clearly, I was mistaken. Perhaps after another week..."

"Leave me forever. I'd rather rot than help you."

Von Nevus leans down so our faces are level "Where is your sister?"

The question catches me so off guard, I topple onto my backside. "What do you mean?"

"She never came. I waited at the base of the mountain with horses and supplies for our journey to Tashir, but she never came. And you somehow ended up back in the Fortress with the bleeding prince. And she hasn't tried to contact me this entire week. Did she return to Tashir on her own?"

He sounds almost hurt by the prospect, and I'm more than a little tempted to tell him that's *exactly* what Rowenna did. She abandoned him because she never actually cared about him. She was only using him. But I'm too flummoxed by his utter lack of knowledge. Surely, Alaric told his councilors everything that happened on the mountaintop as soon as he awoke?

Unless he still hasn't awoken.

My throat is so tight, I almost can't get the words out. "Is Alaric dead?" I whisper.

Now it's Von Nevus's turn to look flabbergasted. "Of course he isn't dead. Why would you think that?"

"Because he had one foot in the grave when I dragged him back to the Fortress. And I obviously haven't seen or heard from him since." I gesture around my cell.

Von Nevus sets his jaw. "Tell me where Rowenna is; then I'll tell you about Alaric."

I shake my head and rise up on my knees, refusing to cower beneath this vile man. "If you're telling the truth and Alaric's alive, why hasn't *he* told you about Rowenna and what happened on the mountain? How do I know you're not lying about his condition? About everything?"

"I had three hours of meetings with the man before breakfast this morning," Garitt erupts with frustration. "Alaric awoke the morning after you brought him to the gates, not long after the healers administered blood and stitches, and he was discharged the following day. He immediately resumed his responsibilities, except he's even more unrelenting than before—if that's possible."

For the first time in a week, I draw a full breath. He

pulled through. But the longer I sit with this update, the more my relief is overshadowed by confusion and a feeling of prickling unease. Alaric has no reason to stay silent about my guilt. No reason to protect me or my reputation after what I did to him. He clearly *isn't* protecting me, seeing as how I'm imprisoned, so why isn't he shouting the truth for all to hear? And proclaiming Rowenna's demise?

"What *has* Alaric said about that night?" I ask Von Nevus. But he folds his arms across his chest.

"No more answers until you tell me where Rowenna is."

"You really don't know?"

"I wouldn't be down here if I did." He sneers down at me.

"Rowenna's dead—actually dead this time." I spit the words out like a poisonous berry and gaze down at the floor, so I don't have to see Von Nevus's reaction. His pain will shatter me and infuriate me. He has no business mourning my sister, but I don't seem to be capable of doing it, so perhaps I should let him. A week later, and I still don't know how to feel. Can't decide if I miss her or despise her. Revere or revile her.

Von Nevus staggers back, his gloved hand pressed to his lips. "You're lying. She can't be dead."

"I'm not and she is," I say, flat and matter-of-fact. "I'm sure her body's still lying on the mountaintop if you want to retrieve it. I obviously haven't had a chance to do so."

Von Nevus shakes his head with horror. "You really killed your own sister instead of the enemy prince?"

"*I* didn't kill anyone," I fire back. "Rowenna fell over the cliff edge."

Garitt rolls his eyes and tosses his hands. "That lie has already been used."

"Ask Alaric if you don't believe me. He watched it all."

"Alaric doesn't even remember his own father's death or taking the throne, let alone what happened atop the mountain," Von Nevus mutters.

"What do you mean *he doesn't remember*?" I demand, hardly able to hear my own voice over the pounding of my heart.

"Exactly that. King Alaric couldn't tell us why he was on the mountain or who attacked him. He insisted he never saw Elodie Tomasko up there and refused to acknowledge any sort of relationship or attachment to you beyond your perfunctory marriage on the Tomb Flats. That seems to be the last thing he can recall—almost as if the last few months never occurred. Or were erased."

Not erased, I think as I melt bonelessly back to the ground.

Sacrificed.

The dull ache that's lodged in my chest sharpens to a point—every bit as deadly as the knife I plunged into Alaric's back. I wrap my arms around my shaking body and try to blow out long breaths to manage the pain, but it's staggering. Crushing. I feel like I'm the one sprawled out across the scree, bleeding to death

This was the cost of saving my life. *This* was how he found the strength to move the mountain and catch me, despite being all but dead himself. With the Vanzadorians feeding fewer memories into the ground, Alaric must have fueled his power with his own memories. And since there was no time to pick and choose as I was falling, he sacrificed everything that was there, at the ready.

By saving me, he forgot me entirely.

That's why he hasn't come to the dungeon. Not because he's dead or despises me, but because he has no reason to visit a virtual stranger who stabbed him in the back. I'm lucky he didn't sentence me to death immediately. It honestly might have been easier. It couldn't be more painful than knowing it's all gone—every moment, every word, every touch. All of our struggles, plans, and hopes for the future, swallowed up by this insatiable mountain.

I can feel my lower lip trembling, sense the tears teetering on my lash line, and even though I want to scream at the unfairness and rage against the cruel irony, I refuse to fall apart in front of Garitt Von Nevus. He's taken too much from me already.

After a long uncomfortable silence, he finally straightens his robes and turns to go. "If Rowenna is truly gone, you and I have nothing further to discuss." He hesitates before mounting the stairs. "*Unless* you decide you'd rather not rot in this prison. Once again, it seems we have a lot in common—both of us shattered and devastated by losing the people we loved most. We might be able to come together in our grief and work out an arrangement that would be mutually benefi—"

"I'd rather die," I snarl.

The councilor's cheeks burn almost as red as his auburn hair. "That was my final offer. Enjoy the rest of your life in prison—with nothing but memories to keep you company."

He smirks as he saunters off, clearly pleased with his parting blow. But instead of giving out entirely, my failing heart sputters back to life, beating with hope for the first time since my imprisonment.

Alaric may not have his own memories of my time in Vanzador, but I remember enough for us both.

FIFTY

BEGIN SIFTING THROUGH MY MEMORIES, AGONIZING over which moment will resonate most, praying the past will stir within Alaric if I show him the right glimpse of our time together. A moment that proves I meant something to him.

I think of our soft stolen kisses. Of kneeling together in the bagrava beds. Of defending each other from the councilors and courtiers. We've had so many beautiful moments, but none of them feel right. Eventually, I realize it's because none of them are where our story truly began. The foundation of our relationship was never built on each other, but on the very first keepers of our hearts:

Rowenna and Besnik.

Alaric and I never would have come to understand each other and trust each other if not for those two little girls, running hand in hand through the fields. Or without the rambunctious, laughing brothers, sparring on the sofa in their father's council chamber. We never would have opened our hearts to each other if we hadn't experienced such similar earth-shattering love. And suffered such parallel heartbreaking loss. So these are the memories I carefully siphon into pebbles and broken bits of stone from the walls of my prison cell—reminders of the boy and girl we used to be. Moments I couldn't possibly know about unless Alaric *chose* to share them with me.

The rest of our story, I'll reveal in time. If he gives me the chance.

Then the only thing left to do is find a way to see him.

I keep thinking he'll come to question me. He must be craving answers about what really happened on the mountain that night. But more and more days pass, and I eventually give up hope. He has so little regard for me, he doesn't care to know the truth. He'd rather just forge on and pretend none of it ever happened. That I was never here.

Since Alaric isn't coming, and begging the guards is useless, I decide to use the only other tool at my disposal.

My gift from Earth Mother.

My mind goes first to bagrava, of course, but I don't have any seeds or cuttings, and I know Alaric won't be lured by its dark promise anymore. He won't continue taking memories from his people and bandaging the side effects. So I scour the floors, walls, and ceiling instead, searching every corner of my cell for something I can use. For something already present, like the goblin's gold I found in the silver mines.

At last, I find a patch of black mold growing in the perpetually damp straw beneath my leaky window. Living underground in the hillock palace, it was commonplace to find all types of mold peppering the walls and floors. Most were harmless and easily removed. But black mold is far more volatile and invasive, and the side effects of exposure more severe: coughing and wheezing, headaches, rashes, and fever, even memory loss and bleeding from the lungs. All conditions I'm certain the guards assigned to watch me would rather not suffer.

Using one filthy fingernail, I gently scrape the black mold into my palm and bring it to the front of my cell—so the current guard will have a clear view of what I'm doing. Then I tuck my nose into my shirt to save myself from inhaling the worst of the spores, and begin to sing.

At first, it creeps across the floor like a slow-growing vine, but the louder I sing, the higher and faster it spreads, climbing the walls and hungrily twining through the bars.

"Quiet down!" the guard shouts without looking up from his whittling.

"I'll quiet down if you take me to see King Alaric," I shout back.

The guard chuckles. "Prisoners don't get to see the king."

"This isn't' a request. It's a *demand*—one I suggest you fulfill sooner rather than later if you value your health."

The guard finally looks up, and his face twists with horror at the sight of the spreading blackness. "What are you doing? Stop it!" he cries as he leaps to his feet.

I keep singing, faster and louder, urging the noxious mold to overtake the floors and walls beyond my cell. Inching ever closer to the guard. It emits a musty, fetid smell that usually takes months to accumulate, but with the aid of my singing, it's already unbearable. My throat burns and my eyes water. The guard coughs painfully as he stomps over to my cell.

"Enough!" he roars, banging a fist against the bars to scare me. Ironically, he's the one who ends up screaming and frantically brushing at his arm as mold climbs the sleeve of his coat. He peels off the jacket and shucks it into the corner, but it's too late. The mold has already found his skin. Black dots spread across his chest and arms like freckles, slowly covering him in what looks like a thick layer of hair.

"Please!" He claws at his skin, leaving long bloody nail marks.

"You know what I want!" I bellow—or try to. The air is so thick with spores, I'm wheezing almost as much as the guard.

"Fine! *Fine!* I'll take you to him!" he cries, fumbling for the key at his belt.

I drop the original patch of mold, grab the handful of pebbles containing my carefully chosen memories, and allow the guard to chain my wrists and drag me down the hall.

As he shoves me up a flight of stairs, the mold grows sparser, the air clearer. By the time we reach the landing, it's all but gone, contained behind us in what looks like a pulsing black pit. A monstrous entity I find oddly beautiful.

When we reach the doors of the king's council chamber, the guard shoves through without announcing himself. The heavy doors crash against the walls, and at least two dozen blue-robed councilors fall silent and turn to gape at us. Their expressions morph from confusion to hostility when they see me and the guard, who's still frantically muttering and pawing at himself.

"What is the meaning of this? How dare you bring a dangerous prisoner into the king's council chambers?" says a councilor with long white hair and equally white teeth. He takes a bold step toward us, and the other councilors follow his lead, arranging themselves into a human wall.

I crane my neck, trying to see past them, curious to know if Alaric's pleased they're protecting him. If he finally feels he's earned their respect and support. But I can't see through the barricade of bodies.

"You heard Councilor Ignacious!" a brawny guard bellows as he steps away from the wall. He eyes the guard responsible for me with open revulsion. "Be gone, or I'll be forced to remove you."

"I can't go back down there," the guard holding me howls. "She tried to poison me with her noxious plants! I would have perished if I hadn't given in to her demands."

"Then you should have perished!" the higher-ranking guard snaps. "It's your *job* to defend our king or die trying—not to bring a known assassin into his presence!"

"I'm not an assassin," I interject. "All I want is a quick word—"

But none of them acknowledge that I've spoken.

Councilor Ignacious stabs his crooked finger back the way we came. Behind him, the other councilors nod, and several more guards come forward. But I won't go back to that dungeon. I'd rather they kill me here, fighting for the bright and glorious future Alaric and I imagined, rather than withering away in the cold, stony shadows.

"I promise I'll leave after I've spoken with Alaric!" I cry out. "I just need a moment of his time."

"You must be mad to think we'd let you anywhere near His Majesty after the wounds you inflicted!" Von Nevus's voice rises from somewhere in the group, breathy with exaggerated horror.

My nostrils flare, and I blow out a breath, fighting the urge to throw myself at the hypocrite. It's precisely what he wants—what he's banking on, so he can claim I'm unhinged and hysterical, and discredit me, should I ever mention his alliance with Rowenna. So I curl my fingers into fists and say with deadly calm, "If you refuse to give me an audience with the king, I'll use every morsel of plant life in Vanzador to overrun the Fortress and bring it crashing down."

I would never actually do such a thing and endanger so many innocent Vanzadorians, but something in my heaving shoulders and flinty eyes must unnerve the councilors. Or maybe it's the state of the guard who brought me here, still scratching and muttering helplessly. Councilor Ignacious sputters. Even Von Nevus is momentarily at a loss.

In that breath of quiet, an achingly familiar voice rises from behind the line of councilors. "Gods of the Mountain, let her pass so we can be done with this already."

Alaric's words are cold, and his tone borders on venomous, but my stomach still dips at the low, velvety timbre of his voice.

"But Your Majesty!" Von Nevus is the first to recover. "Think of your safety."

"Are you suggesting I'm incapable of defending myself?" Alaric shoves past the councilors, and there he is, bathed in a shaft of sunlight streaming in through the floor-to-ceiling windows. He looks as cold and terrifying as he ever has yet, somehow, even more beautiful than I remembered. Even better than the memories I've obsessively revisited while languishing in my cell.

"*Well?* Here I am." Alaric spreads his arms wide. "What do you have to say, *dearest wife?*" He spits the term of endearment like a curse, and even though I knew to expect this and tried to prepare myself for it, the reality further splits my already broken heart.

I lick my trembling lips and search his face for a trace of softness, for the slightest pulse of recognition. Some indication that seeing me sends shivers through his core the way it does mine. But Alaric continues scowling, wearing the same resentful expression he wore the day we left Tashir in ashes.

A lifetime ago.

I didn't realize how much I was hoping that Von Nevus was lying about Alaric's memory loss, or that Alaric was bluffing in the presence of the council, until this moment. When I'm bludgeoned by the full force of his contempt.

"Hurry up and speak your piece," he barks. "Then run along and tell that relentless Tomasko girl I've seen you, so she finally stops pestering me. If I have to listen to her insist I'm in love with you one more time, there's a good chance an 'accidental' rockslide will bury her."

I hate seeing him like this—so cruel and callous, so like his father—but a smile touches my face at the mention of Elodie. She's been here, fighting for me. Petitioning Alaric on my behalf, despite everything.

I've never had a friend as stalwart and determined as

Elodie Tomasko, and I know I don't deserve her, but I vow to spend the rest of my life earning her friendship—supporting her as she's supported me.

"What could you possibly have to smile about?" Alaric snaps. "What could you have to say that warrants threatening my guards and interrupting me in my council chambers?"

The smile drops off my face, and I look down. "I just wanted to thank you for saving my life."

Alaric snorts and cocks his head, regarding me like a smear of manure on his boots. "I did no such thing."

"You did," I argue before I can stop myself, earning several scandalized looks from the councilors. "When my sister sent me over the cliff's edge—"

Alaric cuts me off. "Your sister has been dead for months. These are clearly the ravings of an addled mind."

Everything in me screams at me to tell him he's wrong. To explain how Rowenna was hiding in plain sight, manipulating us all. But he won't believe a word I say, so I decide to show him a memory instead, featuring someone he does trust.

I bring a pebble to my lips and softly sing, releasing the memory of Alaric and Besnik as boys, sword fighting in this very room, laughing as they jump from sofa to sofa.

The councilors gasp with disbelief, and Alaric goes rigid.

"Stop this at once!" he shouts, batting at the golden

images as if he can clear them like smoke. "Where did you find this? How could you possibly—"

"*You* shared this memory with me," I whisper. "You taught me how to call them forth."

Alaric's lips part, as if ready to dismiss my claims, but he rakes his hands roughly through his hair, because he knows it's the only logical explanation. No one, other than himself and an old woman who's long dead, has this skill.

"Out!" he shouts, surprising everyone when he waves at the councilors and guards rather than me. "Everybody out! I need to have a word alone with *my wife*."

Von Nevus and the others loudly protest. It isn't safe. I can't be trusted. Alaric needs to explain the vision they just saw. But he shoos them all into the hall like a brood of clucking chickens.

Once the doors are closed, he takes several deep breaths, then turns to face me. "How did you do it? You clearly wormed inside my head and stole my memories. I haven't shared that moment with anyone, let alone a…a…"

"Murderous Tashiri princess?" I supply wryly, hoping to elicit a smile, but Alaric's eyebrows draw even lower.

"This isn't a joking matter. The security of my nation is on the line."

"I know. That's why I came." I squat down and lay out the pebbles containing the memories I siphoned to prove my innocence. "I can only imagine the lies your councilors have told you about me, and I know you don't remember what happened on the mountaintop—or anything that came before," I add, voice wobbling. "But *I* do remember. And I can show you the truth, if you'd like to see it. Truths you willingly shared with me. Moments *we* shared before you sacrificed them all to save my life."

Alaric sputters and shakes his head. "How do I know these supposed 'memories' are real and not something you fabricated? And if they're genuine, how do I know I shared them with you, and you didn't steal them out of my head?"

"If your father wasn't able to steal your memory of the day he tried to kill you but killed Besnik instead by ripping the floor out from under him, I assure you that I, a Tashiri planter with no prior knowledge of your memory sacrifices, could never manage it."

Once again, Alaric's eyes widen. "You know about Besnik?" he whispers, shaking his head again. "You couldn't. Not unless—"

"*You* showed me," I finish for him.

We lock eyes, and that gorgeous storm-gray sears through me. Without looking away, I squeeze another pebble in my fist and sing the secret words.

A whoosh of cool air rustles through my tattered clothes, and the golden light of the past surrounds us, transporting us back to the rambunctious, laughing brothers riding the bookcase ladder. Instead of watching the memory, however, I watch Alaric—noticing the exact moment his jaw unclenches and his eyes go glassy.

When I reach for the next stone, Alaric doesn't stop me, so I show him the moment things began to change between us—when we came to each other's defense in the queen's salon. Followed by the two of us in my planting beds, growing bagrava.

There's so much more I want to show him, so much more he *needs* to see, but I don't want to overwhelm him, and even more important, I want it to be his decision. I want Alaric to *want* to see the truth—to want *me* and the future we were fighting for. So I place the rest of my pebbles in a line on the floor to do with as he pleases, and back away with a small bow.

"I'll return to my prison cell now, and I won't make any more trouble if you choose to leave me there, now that you've seen the truth. But if you ever want to see more. If you want to know the full breadth of your bravery—and the beautiful story of *us*," I add shyly, "you know where to find me."

I steal one last glance at his gorgeous, bewildered face, then I turn on my heel and walk myself out of the council chamber—into the mob of furious councilors and guards waiting on the other side of the door.

FIFTY-ONE

Alaric doesn't stop me like I secretly hoped he would. Nor does he oversee my return to the dungeon, which takes the better part of the night and involves dozens of torches and metal scrapers to remove the worst of the black mold. He doesn't even come the following morning, after having all night to mull over the memories I showed him. Or the morning after that. And as the days slowly creep by, I have no choice but to accept the devastating truth.

He isn't coming.

He doesn't believe me.

I told you so, Rowenna tries to whisper from beyond the grave. *You deserve to die here for choosing him over me. For choosing Vanzador over Tashir.*

But I swat her accusations away the way I'd swat a fly from fresh cream.

Whatever becomes of me, I know I made the right decisions for both Tashir and Vanzador. I tried my best to bring us together, like Earth Mother always intended, and even though I may not have succeeded, at least I tried. I can rest knowing I did everything in my power to do right by my people. So instead of continuing to torment myself with my many failings and regrets, I spend my days lying face up on the floor with my eyes closed, dreaming of a different ending. A different world. Where I run through the underground halls of the hillock palace and wander through fields of bagrava as high as my shoulders, but also sit in salons with crystal windows and hike steep trails that extend into the sky. Birdie is there, and Elodie too. As well as Alaric, Lewis, and my mother and father. An amalgamation of people and places that shouldn't fit together but do.

Even the Marauders are there, sitting peacefully in the streets rather than ransacking our fields, with one hand pressed to the ground, the other draped over their eyes. I realized the memory tithes could be the perfect solution—at least for a while. The Vanzadorians may not have enough of themselves left to give the earth, but the Marauders have too much ravenous vitality from years of misusing bagrava. If we could somehow contain them and teach them how to give their hunger to the ground, it could fuel Alaric's power while greatly diminishing his need for power altogether. If the Marauders were no longer a threat to our bagrava, Tashir wouldn't need protective mountains. Alaric's power would only be needed for mining, and much of that can be done the old-fashioned way. My people wouldn't have to starve and break their backs, and the Vanzadorians wouldn't have to sacrifice their memories.

It would be perfect—if anyone was willing to listen to my ideas.

Since they're not, I'm the only one who gets to experience this new and better world. I spend so much time there, the real world starts to drift away, and I happily let it go. I have no reason to miss reality, no reason to look back.

Until the day it starts raining in my new world—pouring like I've never seen. The sudden deluge is so fast and pummeling, it wrenches me back and I lurch up from the prison floor.

I feel like I'm drowning, and I can't see a thing. After spending so long in the blackness of my mind, even the murky light of the dungeon burns. I blink and squint, but I think my eyes have been permanently damaged. It's the only way to explain the two blurry figures standing outside my prison cell, one holding a dripping bucket, the other wearing an ornate golden jacket embroidered with azure gemstones.

"I told you she wasn't dead," the man with the bucket says.

"No thanks to you," the second man scolds.

And now I know this can't be real because it's *his* voice, and there isn't a chance in the world Alaric Alaverdi has come for me. I showed him the truth, and he left me to rot. But then he speaks again, and despite myself, my entire body hums to life at the sound—like the first buds of spring pushing up through the frozen ground.

"Open the door and release her," Alaric commands.

I rub the water and grime from my eyes, fully expecting him to vanish, but Alaric's visage sharpens, revealing a face soft with concern and a hand reaching out to help me up.

"Come on, let's get you out of here. Elodie's waiting in your chambers to clean you up. We need to get you in better shape before your parents arrive."

"I don't understand," I croak, shocked by the sound of my forgotten voice. "Why are you here now? And why would my parents come? Did you bring them to witness my execution?"

"What? *No!*" Alaric shakes his head with horror. "I invited them to visit—to celebrate everything we've accomplished and to discuss new terms for the treaty. They're so proud."

"I don't understand," I say again, gripping my throbbing forehead.

"I finally watched your memories—*our* memories," Alaric corrects. "I'm sorry it took so long. I was confused and frightened. I wanted to investigate each claim on my own—my father's death, the effects of the memory tithes, double-crossing councilors like Von Nevus—I had to sort it all out before..." His words trail off and he looks down at his shoes. If I didn't know any better, I'd think he was blushing.

"Before what?"

I dare to glance up at his mesmerizing eyes and immediately wish I hadn't. He's so stunning and strong—the picture of power and competence, in his crisp jacket with his confident, kingly demeanor—while I'm weak, filthy, and half-feral after all this time in prison. Even if he believes my memories are accurate, it doesn't mean his feelings for me have returned. How could they? How could you possibly love someone who didn't believe in you? Who tried to kill you?

"Before I do *this*." Alaric leans down, silencing the cacophony in my head with his lips.

I gasp into his mouth, which only seems to encourage him. Alaric's hands snake around my waist, pulling me into him. I'm laughing so hard, tears are falling down my face. This can't be real. But then his hands are cupping my cheeks and sliding into my filthy hair, and he gently murmurs, "Thank you, Indira."

"What are you doing?" I try to squirm away. "I'm completely disgusting. I'm going to ruin your jacket. And what are you thanking me for? I stabbed you!"

Alaric shakes his head and presses his forehead against mine, looking into my eyes as he says, "No, you *saved* me. You saved us all from the harrowing future my father and Rowenna were forcing on our kingdoms. You showed me a better way."

I let out a pop of incredulous laughter and try to avert my gaze. "You're giving me far too much credit."

But Alaric tightens his hold, keeping our heads locked together. "Show me your memories from the beginning, then *I'll* decide how much credit you deserve." He wags his dark brows suggestively, and my stomach fills with a kaleidoscope of butterflies.

I'm still not convinced I'm awake. That he's here. That my parents could be coming to Vanzador. It's the end of a story far too happy to be mine.

"You're lying. This isn't real." I frantically search the dungeon for signs of a setup or ambush. "And if it is real, you deserve someone so much better than me."

"Are you suggesting I can't make good decisions?" he challenges, but there's a smile in his eyes, mischief on his lips.

"Are you sure you want to see *everything*?" I finally relent. "I'm afraid you were rather unbearable for a good portion of our relationship."

Alaric laughs and kisses me slowly. "I've never been more sure of anything. I want to remember it all. Every detail."

I realize I do too.

As difficult and heartbreaking as it will be to relive Soren's cruelty and Rowenna's deception, to witness Delphine's betrayal and my own glaring mistakes, I would never purge those memories because they led me here, to this moment. To a stronger version of myself and a love built on understanding instead of obedience. To a boy who's willing to change and fight for something better, who encourages me to grow in new directions instead of cutting me down and keeping me small.

This time, when Alaric offers me his hand—finally free of his gloves, the gemstone triad sparkling against his skin—I take it. And together, we step out of the dungeon and into the light.

ACKNOWLEDGMENTS

The idea for this book came to me during a season of life that was not particularly conducive to writing. I had a toddler, back-to-back newborns, and a newly adopted puppy—what was I thinking?! Needless to say, this story had to wait patiently to be written in the small pockets of time that mom-life allowed. A lot of wonderful people also had to wait patiently as I drafted at a snail's pace, begged for more time, and missed my deadlines by *years*, rather than weeks or months.

Thank you a million times over to my brilliant, understanding editors, Annie Berger and Gabbi Calabrese. Not only did they have the best ideas to take this story and elevate it beyond anything I could have achieved on my own, they offered compassion, encouragement, and reassurance as I learned to juggle human babies and book babies at the same time. I couldn't have asked for a better editorial experience, and I'm so grateful for the opportunity to work with both of you.

To my fairy godmother and agent-of-my-dreams, Katelyn Detweiler. This book would not exist without your genuine enthusiasm for my words, your keen editorial eye, and your never-ending encouragement and pep talks. No matter how slow or frustrated I became, you never doubted me or this book, which made all the difference in those sleep-deprived, covered-in-baby spit, existential-crisis moments. I'm so lucky to call you my agent and my friend.

Thanks as well to the entire team at JGLM, particularly Denise, Sam, and Jill. It's an honor to be part of such a fabulous literary agency.

I'm very grateful to the team at Sourcebooks Fire and all the talented people who had a hand in creating this beautiful book: Erin Fitzsimmons for the gorgeous cover design, Jessica Cruickshank whose illustration captures the details of Indira's story perfectly, and Ash Jon who made my dream of having a book with designed edges come true. The inside of this book is just as beautiful thanks to Tara Jaggers and Renee Kahler. I'm also grateful for production manager Kirsten Clawson and production editor Thea Voutiritsas. A special thanks to copy editor Aimee Alker and proofreader Lynne Hartzer for wading through the mire of my mistakes and catching all of my bad habits and inconsistencies. There would be approximately one thousand more colons and ellipses without you!

Thanks to my family: Sam, Kaia, Amara, and Archie, for living with the stress of having a wife/mom on endless deadline and for lovingly accepting that I have my head in the clouds most of the time. Thanks for cheering me on, picking up the slack around the house, and always urging me to follow my dreams, even when it's hard and inconvenient. You are my reason for everything.

I'm so lucky to have brilliant writer friends like J.C. Davis and Hannah Karena Jones. Your writing inspires me, and your friendship keeps me afloat in this crazy industry.

This book would have taken even longer to write if not for the awesome teachers at the Princeton Lifetime Kids Academy. Thanks for playing with my babies for two hours every day so I could sneak in some words.

Last, but certainly not least, thanks to my fabulous readers. It's such a privilege to dream up characters and stories for a living, and I'm beyond grateful you chose to spend your valuable time with me.

ABOUT THE AUTHOR

Addie Thorley spent her childhood riding horses and scribbling stories. After graduating from the University of Utah with a degree in journalism, she decided "hard news" didn't contain nearly enough magic and kissing, so she flung herself into the land of fiction. She lives in San Diego with her family, and when she's not writing, she can be found walking her wolfdogs or crocheting tiny stuffed animals.

sourcebooks fire

Home of the hottest trends in YA!

Visit us online and
sign up for our newsletter at
FIREreads.com

·······································

Follow
@sourcebooksfire
online